YOUNG BOND ™

BOOK TWO

Blood Fever

A JAMES BOND ADVENTURE

CHARLIE HIGSON

Disney · **HYPERION BOOKS**

New York

Blood Fever copyright © 2006 by Ian Fleming Publications Ltd.
All rights reserved.
Blood Fever is a trademark of Ian Fleming Publications Ltd.
Young Bond is a trademark of Ian Fleming Publications Ltd.

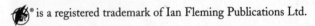 ® is a registered trademark of Ian Fleming Publications Ltd.

Published by Disney • Hyperion Books, an imprint of Disney Book
Group. No part of this book may be reproduced or transmitted in any
form or by any means electronic or mechanical, including photocopying,
recording, or by any information storage and retrieval system, without
written permission from the publisher.

For information address:
Disney • Hyperion Books
114 Fifth Avenue
New York, New York 10011-5690

New Disney • Hyperion paperback edition, 2009
10 9 8 7 6 5 4 3 2
Printed in the United States of America
ISBN 978-1-4231-2261-6
Library of Congress Cataloging-in-Publication Data on file.

Visit www.youngbond.com and
www.hyperionbooksforchildren.com
V475-2873-0 10316

For Jim

* * *

*Thanks to Michael Meredith and
Nick Baker at Eton for all their help.*

Amy Goodenough was the luckiest girl alive. Here she was, in the Mediterranean, on her father's beautiful yacht, when she should have been at school.

It was a glorious day. Apart from a long black smudge of smoke to the south, the sky was a deep, unbroken blue. She tilted her face up to catch the warmth of the sun, breathed in slowly, and smiled. Really, she had no right to be here. A fire had destroyed several of the buildings at her school and it had been forced to close early for the summer. Many of the other girls had been hurriedly packed off to other schools to finish the term, but not Amy. She had easily persuaded her father to let her join him on his annual spring cruise around the Greek islands, on condition that a personal tutor came with them. Since Amy's mother had died of scarlet fever two years ago, her father had been very lonely, and he was glad of his daughter's company.

Amy spent the mornings belowdecks with her tutor, Grace Wainwright, and the rest of the time was hers to enjoy. Grace, a serious and slightly nervous young woman from Leeds, had been strict at first, but the gentle lapping of the water against the hull and the warm scented air of the Greek islands had soon worked their magic on her. With each day the lessons grew shorter, the worry lines on Grace's face softened, and the light shone more brightly in her eyes.

This morning they had finished lessons at eleven o'clock. Grace had sighed and pushed away the book of French grammar they had been struggling over, then stared longingly out through a porthole at a perfect disk of blue sky.

"That's it for today," she had said. "Don't tell your father."

Amy stepped up on to the bulwark and peered into the water. It was rich turquoise and as clear as glass. She could see the anchor chain angling down, surrounded by a school of tiny fish that glinted as they swam in and out of slanting, golden shafts of light.

She flexed her long thin body and prepared to dive in.

"Shouldn't you be studying?" It was her father's voice, but Amy pretended not to hear him, stretched up on to her tiptoes, bent her knees, and sprang lightly off the edge of the yacht. For a moment she was suspended in space, the clear blue waters of the Aegean spread out beneath her like a glittering carpet. Then she arced down and the sea raced up to meet her. It was a perfect dive; her body barely disturbed the surface, and the next thing she knew she was down with the fish in a cloud of silver bubbles. She bobbed to the surface and swam away from the yacht toward the nearby rocks that formed a wall around the little natural harbor they were anchored in. After a while she turned and looked back to see her father standing at the rail waving to her.

"I say! Amy! Should you not be studying?" he called out.

"Grace had a headache, father!" she called back, lying easily. "We're going to carry on later when it's not so hot."

"Very well . . . See that you do."

Her father tried to be severe with her, but in this weather, in these beautiful surroundings, with such a lazy lifestyle, he found it as difficult as Grace to maintain any sense of discipline. Besides, Amy thought, diving down and scattering a shoal of snappers, she had always known how to get round him. It was harder for Mark, her older brother. If there had been a fire at his school, he would have been moved somewhere else instantly and there would have been no question of him coming to Greece.

Their father, Sir Cathal Goodenough, was a sailor through and through. He had joined the navy at sixteen and served under Jellicoe at the Battle of Jutland, before being made an admiral himself in 1917. He had been knighted for his services in the Great War, protecting convoys from submarine attack in the Atlantic. When his wife died he had left the navy, but the sea was in his blood. He hated to be on dry land, and at any opportunity he would be on one of his three yachts: the *Calypso*, which was moored in the West Indies; his racing yacht, the *Circe*, which was kept in Portsmouth; and this one, his most prized vessel, the *Siren*, which overwintered in Nice.

The *Siren* was a three-masted schooner, with ten passenger berths and a crew of eight. Amy looked at her now, sitting serenely at anchor, her gleaming black hull reflected in the water. The yacht was perfectly at home here, and so was Amy. She had learned to swim almost before she could walk and would sometimes stay in the water for hours on end. She had no need of a bathing cap because, to the horror of her father, she had recently cut off all her long curls and styled her hair into a more fashionable bob. She was often mistaken for a boy, but that didn't bother her. She knew who she was.

She reached the rocks and hauled herself out to sit in the sun and warm herself. It was late May, still early enough in the year for there to be the occasional cold current in the sea.

She shook sparkling droplets from her freckled skin and looked over at the shore. A dense wood of dark green cypresses grew right down to the little sandy beach where last night they had set up tables and eaten their supper under the stars. The island, one of the Cyclades that spread out across the sea south of Athens, was tiny and uninhabited and didn't even appear on most maps.

A diving knife in a leather sheath was strapped to Amy's leg. It belonged to Louis, the big French first mate, and he had shown her how to pry shellfish from the rocks to eat. Around her waist was strung a net that she used to hold her catch of mussels and clams. Sitting here on the rock, she felt like a savage, a million miles away from England and her boring school. She was the happiest girl in the world, and this must surely be paradise.

She heard the ship before she saw it, a dull throbbing sound, but thought nothing of it. The Mediterranean had been a crowded maritime highway for centuries. She busied herself searching for shellfish, dimly aware of the engine noise getting nearer, but it was a shock when she saw a tramp steamer chug into view, pumping smelly, black smoke from its short funnel. She watched as it moved alongside the *Siren* and noisily dropped anchor. Amy could see several crewmen hurrying about the deck, their skin tanned dark brown by the sun, their outfits grimy and stained.

Next to the sleek, clean lines of the yacht, the steamer looked squat and ugly. Amy peered at the name on the side, written in peeling red paint—*Charon*.

The wind shifted, smearing the plume of black smoke across the sun and throwing the harbor into shadow. For a moment Amy, who was standing knee-deep in a rock pool, was chilled, and she shivered.

From the deck of the *Siren*, her father watched the arrival of the steamer with some curiosity. Other than the name, he could see no flags or markings of any kind and wondered why it had chosen to put in here, in this obscure and secluded harbor.

The obvious answer was that she was in some kind of trouble.

"Hello there, *Siren*!"

Goodenough squinted across the water and made out the figure of a stocky blond man with a neatly trimmed beard.

"Ahoy," he called back. "Are you all right, sir?"

"Engine trouble, I'm afraid," the man called back.

Goodenough tried to place the accent. It sounded Eastern European, but he couldn't pinpoint it exactly.

"Can I be of any assistance?" he shouted. Any seaman was duty bound to come to the aid of a fellow mariner in trouble at sea. But, even as he shouted the words, he saw that the other ship had already lowered a rowing boat into the water. Without another word, the blond-haired man sprang over the side and landed neatly in the cutter, in a move that was unconventional but highly dramatic.

Six strong sailors pulled at the oars and the boat sped toward the *Siren*.

Goodenough frowned. There was something not quite right about all this. He looked at the crew and saw two Chinese men; two who looked African; a skinny, pale-skinned man with a broken nose; and a nearly naked, hairless and tattooed giant from the South Seas, wearing a woman's straw hat and smoking a fat cigar.

The blond captain stood in the stern of the boat and grinned, his teeth flashing. His arms, which were as thick as his legs and knotted with muscle, were crossed on his broad chest. He wore knee-length boots and a loose, open tunic fastened with a wide belt.

Goodenough saw, with some relief, that at least none of them were armed.

The cutter pulled alongside, and the captain sprang up the ladder as effortlessly as if he were skipping up a flight of steps.

He jumped on to the deck and gave a little bow. Up close his eyes were startling. The irises were so pale as to be almost colorless and were ringed with a gray that seemed to shine like silver.

"Please allow me to introduce myself," he said. "I am Zoltan the Magyar."

"A Hungarian?" said Goodenough, intrigued. "From a country without a coastline?"

"Yes, sir," said Zoltan.

"You Hungarians are not known as sailors," said Goodenough. "It is unusual to find one captaining a ship."

"We are an unusual ship with a crew of many nations. You see that we fly no colors? It is because we are a ship of the world." Zoltan spread out his arms and slowly turned to all points of the compass. "I love the sea," he said. "It reminds me of Az Alföld, the Great Plain of Hungary. A big sky, and miles of nothing in every direction."

The crew of the cutter were all on deck now, and crowding round Goodenough. He looked into their sullen, dull faces, and they looked back at him with an utter lack of interest. He took a step toward the Magyar and offered his hand.

"Welcome aboard," he said. "I am the captain of the *Siren*, Sir—"

"I know who you are," said the Magyar with a grin. "You are Cathal Goodenough." He had trouble pronouncing the "th," and the name came out sounding more like "Cattle."

"It's pronounced Cahill, actually," said Goodenough automatically, and then stopped himself. "But how did you know my—"

"With respect," Zoltan interrupted with quiet authority in his voice, "it is pronounced however I want to pronounce it."

"I beg your pardon," said Goodenough, taken aback. "There is no cause to be uncivil. I have offered my assistance to you—"

"My apologies," the Magyar interrupted again and bowed even lower this time, with a faintly mocking manner. "You are right. There is no need for any unpleasantness. My men will simply take what we have come for and leave."

"I'm sorry, I don't understand," said Goodenough. "Take what?"

Louis, the first mate, and two other crewmen, wearing their crisp white uniforms, were cautiously approaching along the deck.

"This conversation is becoming boring," said Zoltan. "Like a boring English tea party. I went to England once. The food was gray, the sky was gray, and the people were dull." He clapped his hands. "And now that my men are all in position, I can stop this chitchat and get on with my business, Sir Goodenough."

"It's just Goodenough, actually," said the Englishman with some irritation in his voice. "You would say 'Sir Cathal,' but never 'Sir Goodenough'—"

"I will say whatever I want to say," Zoltan snapped. "Now, please don't annoy me. I am attempting to stay calm and polite, like you Englishmen, because when I am angry I do things that I sometimes later regret. Now, please, I am busy. . . ."

So saying, Zoltan the Magyar clapped his hands again and a group of men appeared from behind the deckhouse.

With a shock, Goodenough realized that while he and his crew had been distracted, another rowboat had put out from the tramp steamer and several more sailors had climbed aboard. This new group *were* armed—with knives, cutlasses, and guns that they quickly handed out to their friends. The huge South Sea Islander was passed a whaling harpoon, which he held lightly in one massive, tattooed hand. With his other hand he removed the cigar from his mouth and then spat a flake of tobacco onto the deck.

"What is the meaning of this?" said Goodenough, outraged—but he knew the meaning all too well.

They were pirates, and there was nothing he could do.

For emergency use there were two rifles and an ancient

prewar pistol locked away in his cabin, but to this day they had never left their strongbox.

And now it was too late.

The first mate, Louis, made a move, but Goodenough glared at him, and he stopped. For a captain to have his command taken from him like this was appalling, but it would be madness to try and resist.

It was best just to get it over with.

"This is a private vessel," he explained as calmly as he could. "We have no cargo; we have no hold full of treasure. There is a small safe with some money in it, but not a great amount. . . ."

The burly Magyar ignored Goodenough and snapped some orders in Hungarian. A group of his men hurried belowdecks.

"You have two choices." Zoltan approached Goodenough. "You can tell me the combination of your safe, or I can cut it out of your pretty boat with axes."

Once again Louis stepped forward, and in a quick, expert movement, Zoltan pulled a small pistol from inside his tunic and leveled it at him.

Goodenough recognized the pistol: it was an Italian navy-issue nine-millimeter Beretta. These men were no scruffy, disorganized opportunists: they were serious professionals.

He quickly gave the combination for the safe, and Zoltan shouted another order to his men.

In a moment there were screams from below, and Grace Wainwright was dragged onto the deck. She was followed by the pale-skinned sailor carrying the contents of the safe.

Zoltan looked from Grace to the haul, then shook his head peevishly and rubbed his temple.

There was a deep, guttural grunt, and the tattooed giant tossed something across the deck. Zoltan caught it and his face brightened.

It was a small bronze statuette.

"Thank you, Tree-Trunk," he said.

Tree-Trunk smiled and exhaled a cloud of cigar smoke.

Zoltan held the statuette up to his mouth with two hands and kissed it.

"Leave that!" yelled Goodenough, his anger getting the better of him. "That will be of no value to you. It is a very well-documented piece of art. There is nowhere in the world you could sell it . . . And if you melted it down it would be an absolute tragedy."

Zoltan smiled, turned slowly, and fixed Goodenough with his steel-rimmed gaze.

"I am not a peasant!" he said. "I am no ignorant *gulyás*. I know what I want. I want this bronze, Sir Cattle."

"Cahill, man—it's *Ca-hill*!"

"Be quiet, you damned Englishman."

"You know nothing of its true worth," Goodenough protested.

"I know it is by Donato di Betto Bardi," said Zoltan. "Commonly known as Donatello. Fifteenth century, cast in Florence, a model for the design of a fountain that was never built." He turned the statuette in his hands. "It is a figure from Greek mythology. A Siren. The very Siren that this boat was named after. The Sirens were monsters—half woman, half bird. With their beautiful voices they tricked passing ships onto the rocks and ate their crews." He looked at Goodenough. "Women, Sir Goodenough. You must always be careful of them. They are dangerous."

"That statuette belonged to my wife," Goodenough said quietly.

"This statuette was stolen by Napoleon from the Duke of Florence," said Zoltan. "And it was stolen from Napoleon by one of your wife's family after Waterloo. Now it is my turn to steal it."

Goodenough made a grab for the bronze, and the Magyar flicked a hand at him as casually as if he were swatting away a fly, but it was enough to send Goodenough crashing to the deck. He lay there for a moment, stunned.

Louis cursed and ran at Zoltan, but he stopped suddenly and fell back with a gasp. Tree-Trunk had hurled his harpoon into him with such force that half its length protruded from the Frenchman's back. Louis struggled for a few moments on the deck, then lay still.

"I did not want any bloodshed today," said Zoltan. "But you have forced my hand."

Goodenough hauled himself groggily to his feet and glared at Zoltan. "You are a barbarous pig, sir. A common pirate."

Zoltan passed the statuette to the tattooed giant and grabbed Goodenough by his shirt.

"Do not make me angry," he hissed.

Goodenough looked into his eyes; the pale irises seemed to have darkened.

"Take what you want," Goodenough pleaded. "But can you not leave the Donatello? It means a great deal to me."

Zoltan pushed Goodenough away and took the bronze back from Tree-Trunk.

"No," he said simply.

Despite himself, Goodenough grabbed him.

"You will not take that! I don't care what you do; you can pry it from my dead hands if you wish, but I won't give it up without a fight."

He took hold of the statuette and grappled over it, pressed right up against Zoltan, who was backed against a bulkhead. They struggled for half a minute before a muffled bang suddenly erupted and there was the smell of singed flesh and cloth. Goodenough staggered backward, clutching his stomach.

"You've shot me," he said, and dropped to his knees.

"That is very perceptive of you, Sir Goodenough. I told you not to make me angry."

"I'll see you rot in hell for this."

"I doubt it very much. In a few minutes you will be dead. Good day to you."

So saying, Zoltan the Magyar leaped overboard into the waiting cutter. In a moment he was joined by his oarsmen and they raced back to the steamer. Once there, he climbed over the side and stood on deck, studying the statuette and breathing heavily through his nose. Despite some minor complications, it had been a good morning's work. He ran a finger over the shapely curves of the Siren's body and smiled. In many ways it had been too easy.

As he turned to go below he suddenly felt a searing pain in his left shoulder and he dropped the bronze to the deck. He spun round and saw a short-haired girl of about fourteen wearing a bathing costume, water dripping from her thin body, a mixture of anger and fear showing on her young face.

Zoltan looked down at his tunic. It was stained dark with his own blood. He put his right hand up to where a cold, dull ache drilled into his shoulder. A knife was stuck fast there; jammed into the joint. Half of him felt like weeping and the other half felt like laughing. This girl had spirit. If he had not turned at the last moment, the knife would have stabbed him next to his spine.

His left arm hung uselessly at his side; the pain and loss of blood were making him weak.

"You're going to regret that you didn't kill me," he said quietly.

"One day I'll finish the job," the girl said bitterly.

Zoltan was now swamped by his crew, all yelling and shouting in panic. Three of them took hold of the girl.

"Give me air, and bring me wine," Zoltan snarled. "Bull's Blood!"

Someone handed him a bottle and he took a long gulp, dribbling the dark red wine down his chin. Then he steeled himself and, with a furious cry, wrenched the knife out of his shoulder.

"Sink the boat," he said, flinging the knife into the sea. "Take the women . . . and kill all the men."

The knife sank through the silent water, turning and twisting, the blood washing away. It landed in the sand at the bottom and stood there like a cross on an underwater grave.

CHAPTER 1—THE DANGER SOCIETY

James Bond hated feeling trapped. Wherever he was, he always wanted to know that there was a way out. And preferably more than one way out. Lying here in his tiny room at Eton, packed away under the rafters, he pictured the whole building as it slept beneath him. In his mind he wandered the dark maze of corridors and stairways that made up Codrose's house. There were several doors downstairs, but only one that the boys had access to and that would now be locked for the night. It was no concern of his. He had his own way in and out of the building, his own secret route that nobody else knew about.

For James the most important thing was to be free, to be in charge of his own life. He didn't really fit in at Eton, with its endless rules and age-old traditions, and Eton couldn't hold him.

He lay perfectly still in his narrow, uncomfortable bed and listened for any sounds. Nothing. It was all quiet. He slipped out from under his sheets and went over to his ottoman. From the untidy mess within, he took out a pair of black trousers, a dark-blue rugby shirt, and a pair of plimsolls, listening the whole time. He pulled the clothes on over his hated pajamas. How he wished he didn't have to wear them. Especially on a hot, stuffy night like this, when the air

1

hung heavy and no breeze came in through the open window. But his housemaster, Cecil Codrose, had introduced a rule that all boys in his care should sleep in pajamas and keep them buttoned up to their necks.

Ever since a fire had gutted one of the houses in 1903, killing two boys, the school had employed "night watches," elderly ladies and gentlemen from the town who shuffled along the corridors at night sniffing for smoke. James wasn't bothered about his night watch, a little old lady called Florence. She was easily evaded. But he did worry about Codrose. He was fond of creeping around the house at all times of day and night, trying to catch the boys misbehaving, and James had hit on the plan of sprinkling sugar on the bare wooden floorboards so that it crunched underfoot and gave away anyone trying to sneak up on him.

There was no crunch now. No rustle of movement anywhere in the building. For the time being he was safe.

Once dressed, he removed a short section of skirting board and slid out a loose brick from the wall. Behind it was the hiding place where he kept his valuables. He took out his penknife and flashlight and dropped them into his trouser pocket. Then he put everything back as it was and carefully opened his bedroom door. He kept the hinges and the handle well greased with bacon fat so that it opened without a sound. There was a creak and James paused. But it was only the two-hundred-year-old building settling. He looked left and right down the corridor, which was lit by a dim electric light at either end. Another of Codrose's ideas. The corridor was empty, apart from a big brown moth that sent huge shadows flapping across the dull green walls.

James's room was on the top floor. To the right was a flight of narrow stairs and a wall separating the boys from Codrose's part of the building. At the other end of the corridor was a storage room whose door was secured shut with a massive, rusty padlock. Halfway down was a washroom and on either side of it was a row of identical doors. Behind each door was a sleeping boy. But while they only dreamed of escape, for James it was a reality.

He always left a clear path through the sugar and soundlessly made his way along the corridor to the washroom. The hinges on this door were also well greased.

He slipped inside and closed the door behind him.

He didn't risk turning on the light. He could make his way through here with his eyes closed, but there was enough of a glow from the moon through the windows to show him a row of tin basins, four big baths, and at the far end, the lavatory stalls. He tiptoed over the tiled floor toward the end stall and went in.

He fished his penknife out of his pocket, opened the blade and, crouching down, levered up a floor tile, exposing the floorboards beneath. Soon he had three more tiles up, and he was able to remove a neatly cut square of boards.

It had taken him two sessions to work the tiles loose, slaving away in the dead of night, using tools filched from the School of Mechanics. And it had taken him a further week to cut through the boards underneath with his penknife, as a saw would have made too much noise. Twice he had nearly been found out. On the first occasion, he had heard footsteps outside, but nobody had come in. On the second occasion, though, the door had opened. James just had time to replace the tiles, scoot up the walls of the stall like a monkey, and wedge himself on top of the cistern before the lights were turned on and the familiar sound of Codrose's dry cough had filled the night.

James had heard him walking around, and then he had glanced into the stall. James caught a brief glimpse of his wiry, gray hair and pale skin before he coughed once more and went on his way.

Since then James hadn't been disturbed, and now he was able to use this secret route out of the building whenever he needed to.

Under the floor was a crawl space just large enough to fit his slim body into. He passed the boards down, lowered himself in after them, and replaced the tiles above his head.

He could now risk using the flashlight. He switched it on, illuminating a tiny passage that ran along the entire length of the building between the joists. It was filthy and dusty and laced with blackened cobwebs. He shuffled awkwardly forward on his belly, trying not to make too much noise. Above and below him were sleeping boys, but if they'd ever heard anything they'd kept quiet about it.

James crawled along until he was directly beneath the locked storage room at the end of the corridor. He remembered the night he had first got this far, and how relieved he had been to discover that several of the floorboards were loose and rotten. It had only taken him a few minutes to pry two of them free. Now he simply pushed them out of his way and wriggled up into the room.

He replaced the boards, stood up, knocking the dust off his dark clothes, and sneezed. Nothing had changed in here since his last visit. The room was piled high with forgotten school junk: broken tables and chairs, rotting camp beds, prehistoric sports equipment, and boxes of yellowing books and papers. There was a tiny window in the roof, so encrusted with dirt and dust and birdlime that it barely let in any light at all. James climbed onto a pile of boxes and forced the rusted latch open. Then he folded the window back, grabbed hold of the edge of the frame, and hauled himself up. In a moment he was out on the roof, in the fresh air, with the whole of Eton spread out beneath him.

It was a beautiful, clear, summer's night and the moon was nearly full. James could see over the rooftops down to the river Thames and across to Windsor Castle on the other side. It was close to midnight, but there was still some activity on the streets, the odd car moving about, lights in windows, a barge going upriver toward Maidenhead.

James had planned carefully for this. He had noticed that the storage-room door never seemed to be opened, and, just to make sure, he had fixed a hair across the keyhole in the padlock, sticking it in place with two tiny dabs of grease. A week, two weeks went by, and the hair was undisturbed. A quick check outside had shown him the window and a possible way on to the roof, so then he only needed to work out how to get into the room. Spotting the space beneath the floorboards when a leaking pipe was being repaired in the washroom had solved that problem.

He took a last look around to make sure that the coast was clear, then gingerly crawled up the tiles toward the top of the roof. He used the chimneys to support himself as he went over the crest and slid down the other side onto a flat section of roof, which was set into the top of the building. There was a long, oval glass dome sticking up here and, crouching low so as to avoid making a silhouette against the night sky, James sneaked along until he was looking down into Codrose's study. As often as not, the housemaster would be sitting up here at night, writing in his journals with tiny, spidery lettering, and drinking from a secret bottle of gin.

James pressed himself against the roof and sidled along, peering down through the murky glass. Sure enough, Codrose was there. He was a thin man with a short beard that covered half his face, and the cold, dead eyes of a fish. Many of the housemasters at Eton were well loved by the boys, but not Codrose. He was mean and joyless and served the worst food in the school.

James watched him for a while, scratching away with his pen, and wondered what he found to write about. It gave James a feeling of power to be up here, seeing but not being seen. He soon moved on, however. There were things to do.

When he reached the other end of the roof, he climbed over the ridge and carefully slid down to a wide stone gutter. He walked along the gutter like a tightrope walker, holding his arms out for balance, until he reached the corner. This was the most dangerous part of the route: jumping across a narrow cobbled alleyway to the building on the other side. He looked down to make sure that there was nobody below, before shuffling back along the gutter to give himself a run-up. He took a deep breath, then raced to the end and hurled himself into the air at the last moment. He landed comfortably, kept up his momentum, and continued running across a short flat roof, then leaped across another, smaller gap on the other side. This was James's favorite part of the route, over several easy rooftops, running, jumping, climbing, until he finally arrived at a long, lead-lined gully, which led to the top of the final roof. He darted up it and squeezed between the chimneys, where he was stopped by a boy's voice hissing in the darkness.

"Who is it?"

"James Bond."

"Enter."

The roof of this building was similar to the one at Codrose's, with a flat section set into the top between the chimneys; but this one was smaller and had nothing as grand as Codrose's dome. Apart from a small inspection hatch in the middle, it was featureless. But it made a perfect hideout for a group of adventurous boys who called themselves the Danger Society.

There were many clubs at Eton—the Musical Society, the Film Society, the Natural History Society, and the Archaeological Society, for instance. But the Danger Society was different. It was a secret society of boys who liked to take risks. If the Danger Society was ever discovered, its members would be in deep trouble.

James, who was still only in his first year at Eton, was the youngest member; he had been approached by a friend called Andrew Carlton, who was two years older than him. They had got to know each other in the previous half, as terms were called at Eton. Andrew had realized that James was a boy like himself, easily bored by the routine of school who might like a little spice in his life.

It was easy to join the club. You simply had to make your

way to this rooftop den at night without being seen. It had taken James a while to work out how to do it, but he had persevered, and this was the fifth meeting he had attended.

He soon spotted Andrew, and he did a quick headcount of the others.

"Five," he said. "Who's missing?"

"Gordon Latimer," said Andrew. "He's always late. Probably fast asleep, knowing him."

"And what about Mark Goodenough?" said James. "Isn't he usually the first here?"

"M-Mark's not going to m-make it tonight," said Perry Mandeville, the founder and captain of the club. "He's had some bad news, not bad news like so-and-so's caught a cold or something, proper bad news, he's cut up something rotten, m-most likely won't m-make it again this half."

Perry was a restless, reckless boy who was always urging the others to try ever more dangerous escapades. He could never sit still, and his words tumbled out in such a mad rush that, as his brain fought to catch up with his mouth, it caused him to stammer.

"What's happened?" said James, sitting down with his back against the wall.

"His family has been lost at sea," said Perry dramatically. "In the M-Mediterranean. . . ."

"Don't be so sensational," said Andrew. "Nobody knows exactly what's happened." He sat down next to James and handed him some chocolate. "They were sailing," he went on, "and their boat's gone missing."

"Sounds m-much m-more exciting to say 'lost at sea,'" said Perry, fidgeting. "Sounds like an adventure book, "m-maybe they're shipwrecked on a desert island, or something, or they've been eaten by sharks, they do have sharks in the M-Mediterranean, though not very big ones."

"Yes," said Andrew. "And it sounds rather like you hope they *have* been eaten by sharks."

"That's not fair," said Perry. "M-Mark's my friend."

"Precisely," said Andrew. "And this is real life, not a story. We were all kind to you when you had your break-in."

"What break-in?" said James.

"Happened last half," said Perry, "before you joined the society. Burglars broke into our house in London and stole a load of paintings, luckily m-my folks were away at the time, but one of the servants was pretty badly beaten and m-my m-mother and father are still fairly fragile about the whole thing."

"Exactly," said Andrew. "Well, imagine if they *had* been there at the time, and had got hurt. You wouldn't think that was something to make fun of, would you?"

"Sorry," said Perry. "But you m-must ad-m-mit, it does all sound rather exciting."

Andrew sighed and looked heavenward; but, after all, excitement was what the Danger Society was all about. They met here every week, on a different night, chosen at random out of a hat so that they would have no noticeable routine. They didn't really do very much on these nights; it was the getting there that was the important part. Once they were all assembled they'd just sit and chat and smoke cigarettes and plan other activities. But although the Danger Society members may have looked relaxed, they all knew that if they were caught it would be very serious. That was what made these meetings so thrilling. Despite the fact that it was late and James was tired, he felt alive and buzzing with the excitement of being out here at night.

James had had a confusing time since starting at Eton. At Easter he had become entangled in the insane schemes of Lord Randolph Hellebore, the father of a fellow student. James had nearly been killed and had seen things he never wanted to see again. When he had at last recovered from it all, he was left with the feeling that life sometimes seemed rather flat.

He had tried to return to being just an ordinary school-boy, but what he had experienced set him apart from all his friends, and no matter how hard he tried to forget it all, he couldn't.

Apart from the risk of falling off the roof, this trip tonight could hardly be said to be truly dangerous, but it was better than lying in bed trying to sleep. His lessons tomorrow would suffer, of course. No matter; there was more to life than Latin grammar. If James worked hard later in the week he would probably catch up. Mr. Merriot, his classical tutor, the man who looked after his schooling, often told him off for not working harder, but James was naturally bright and was keeping up with the other boys, so he didn't worry too much.

"Listen," said Perry. "I propose a jaunt in the m-motor, daft to leave it sitting there m-moldering away. What say Andrew and I drive it up to London one night? That'd be something to talk about."

"Sounds risky," said James.

"That's what the society is all about," said Perry. "I don't m-mind a spot of risk."

"I wasn't thinking about you," said James. "I couldn't care less what happened to you, Perry. I was thinking about the car."

One of the reasons James was popular with the Danger Society, despite being its youngest member, was that he owned a car. It had belonged to an uncle, who had taught him to drive in it, and when he'd died he'd left it to James. James had persuaded his guardian to let him bring it to Eton, telling her that it would be kept at the school and used by the boys to learn about mechanics, under the careful supervision of a master, of course.

In reality it was kept hidden away in a garage in a backstreet in Windsor near the barracks. The garage belonged to Perry, and he was always planning ways to use the car—a four and half liter Bamford and Martin roadster—but they had to be very careful. Not only was it against school rules to drive a car, it was also breaking the law.

They were in the middle of arguing about Perry's proposed trip when they heard hurried footsteps and Gordon Latimer flung himself over the top of the roof and rolled down toward them.

"That's the way to make an entrance!" said Andrew, laughing.

"Shhhh!" said Gordon, twisting onto his knees and crouching low. He was desperately short of breath, his clothing ripped and untidy. "They're on to us."

"Who are?" said James, looking around.

"I'm not sure," said Gordon, his voice high and strained. "I was spotted. They were looking for me."

"Who? The police?" asked Andrew.

"Beaks, I think," said Gordon. "I've been all over the place trying to shake them off. There's a big search party heading this way. We've got to get out of here."

Even as Gordon said this, they heard shouts from the street below.

"Split up," said Andrew, and he was off.

In a second all the other boys were up and running in different directions, each taking their own chosen route.

James didn't hesitate. He sprang to his feet, vaulted over the rooftop, and was away, his heart hammering against his ribs.

If he had wanted danger, he had it now.

CHAPTER 2—DOUBLE M

James tried not to think about what would happen if he were caught. He knew he would definitely be beaten, but worse than that, he would probably be expelled from Eton. He didn't mind so much for himself, but he hated the idea of upsetting his guardian, Aunt Charmian.

James's parents had been killed in a climbing accident when he was eleven, and since then he had been brought up by Charmian. He didn't want to do anything that might hurt her.

He realized, of course, that he probably should have thought about that before he got himself into this mess.

He intended to take his usual route, but halfway back he saw that his way was blocked. His pursuers had set a ladder against one of the buildings, and a large, fat man was climbing it.

Risking an unfamiliar path, James turned off to the side, sprinted over the top of a couple of rooftops, then shinned down a drainpipe. He found himself in a maze of low buildings and sheds. It was very dark here, and he was soon lost. He was scurrying around trying to find a way back to more familiar territory when he heard a search party coming his way. He climbed up the side of a timber-framed house and hid himself behind a tall brick chimney stack until they had passed. He thought he recognized the nearby rooftops, so he scuttled along the side of the building and jumped across to the next roof. As he landed, a tile slipped beneath him and crashed to the pavement. He heard pounding feet, and someone yelled something very nearby; the sound echoed around the deserted night streets.

He raced up the roof and over the other side, but his luck was fast running out. Two more tiles came loose, and he found himself sliding uncontrollably down toward a drop into darkness.

There was ivy on the roof, and he grabbed hold of some, but it pulled away and he slithered over the edge, wildly scrabbling for a purchase. Thankfully, the ivy growing up the wall below was dense and overgrown, and he managed to get a grip and stop himself from falling any farther. The two roof tiles continued to the ground, noisily shattering on the paving stones below. Then there was silence.

James hung in the ivy and tried to slow his racing heart.

The Danger Society was fun, but it wasn't worth risking his life for.

He took stock of his situation. He was badly scratched and bruised, but for the moment he was safe.

He looked around. He was about twenty-five feet above a courtyard, nesting in gnarled tendrils as thick as the branches on a tree, but beyond that he had no idea where he was. The place looked uncared-for and run-down, and was so covered with ivy that it didn't look like Eton at all, more like some abandoned jungle temple.

James was just thinking about climbing down, when a

light showed in a ground-floor window, and shortly afterward, a door opened and he heard voices.

The dim light from the window wasn't enough to show him what was going on, but the flare of a match revealed the dark shapes of two men. One of them was smoking a cigarette—James saw an occasional red glow and could smell the burning tobacco.

The men looked around briefly and evidently spotted the broken tiles. James could just make out their pale faces as they looked up. Luckily, they couldn't see him as he was safely nestled in the thick, waxy leaves of the ivy, and his dark clothing helped to keep him hidden.

One of the men must have picked up a piece of tile, because James heard it clatter to the ground as he dropped it. Then the second man, the one who was smoking, laughed.

They stood for a while in the courtyard, talking, their voices low and muffled by the thick growth of ivy on the walls. James strained to hear what they were saying, but, try as he might, he couldn't seem to focus on their words. It was only after a while that he realized that they were speaking a foreign language. He concentrated harder. Was it Spanish?

No.

Maybe Italian . . . ?

No.

But there was definitely something familiar about it.

James was good at languages. He had grown up in Switzerland and spoke fluent French and German. So why was he having so much trouble placing this language?

And then it struck him. The two men were speaking Latin.

The odd word and phrase jumped out at him . . . *tutus est*, it is safe; *navis*, boat; and *sanguis*, blood.

James was amazed. Latin was a dead language. Nobody spoke it nowadays. Maybe it was the only common language these two men shared. That seemed unlikely, but it was a possibility. Or maybe they were two Latin masters practicing their skills and showing off to one another. That seemed a more plausible explanation. Certainly one of them had something of the air of a schoolmaster about him.

Once again the smoker laughed. A harsh, brutal sound. He stubbed out his cigarette, and the two men went back inside. After a minute or two the light was switched off and the courtyard once more fell into darkness and silence. James waited, straining his ears, and eventually heard what he thought was the sound of the front door slamming in the street.

He was now faced with a dilemma: to go back up and risk the rooftops again, or to climb down and try to escape through the building?

Either way posed a risk.

As he was wondering what to do, the decision was taken for him as, with a ripping sound, the ivy began to peel from the wall. Quick as he could, he let himself down and managed to reach the ground without falling.

He could make out more details of the courtyard now. Half of it was paved, and the other half was made up of ancient, tumbled-down masonry. There was a round construction that might have been a well, the remains of some stone pillars, a sunken pit, and a section of wall that had damaged carvings on it. It was all so broken and covered in ivy that it was hard to tell just what had once been here, but James's feeling that he might be in a temple of some sort might not have been that far wrong.

He tried the doors and windows. They were all locked. He was considering whether to try climbing back up, when he spotted another window by his feet, half hidden by ivy. It was open a crack and appeared to lead into a cellar. He crouched down and jiggled it with his knife, and found that it was so decrepit he could quite easily force it up and squeeze through.

He closed the window behind him and switched on his flashlight. He was indeed in a cellar. Propped against one wall were two or three large, dark, oil paintings, and there were a couple of packing crates in the center of the room, which somebody had been using as a makeshift table. In the gloom James could just make out a map of Italy and a pile of books laid out on top of it.

Stenciled on the side of one of the crates were two large red letters—a double *M*—and James noticed that one of the books had the same double-*M* motif on the cover. He picked it up and opened it, but it was full of dense Latin text.

He didn't have time to be reading books. He had to get out of there.

He put the book down, turned to leave, and then jumped back in fright, swallowing the urge to cry out.

There was a pale, ghostly figure standing in the darkness by the door, beckoning to him.

A man, white as death. Staring and unmoving.

It only took James a second to realize, however, that it was just another painting.

He let out his breath. "You really shouldn't do that," he said quietly, hoping to ease his tension. "You scared me half to death."

He rubbed the back of his neck, and when his heart had stopped hammering and his legs shaking, he stepped forward for a closer look.

It was a life-size painting of a man, wearing a Roman toga and standing imperiously with one arm resting on a marble column and the other stretching out toward the viewer.

His close-cropped hair was white, and his chalky skin almost luminous. James felt uneasy looking at him; the eyes were painted in such a way that they appeared to be looking straight back at you.

At the bottom of the ornate frame, four letters were carved into the wood—*UCMM*—but there were no other clues as to who the man might be.

"I'll see you later," said James, and he quickly opened the door.

He found his way blocked by a heavy curtain. He pulled it aside and walked through. If the courtyard outside resembled a temple, this room appeared to be a chapel. There were bare walls and a plain wooden table set up like an altar at one end.

But this was no Christian chapel.

The painting above the table showed a man in Roman armor plunging a sword into a bull's neck and sending a long spray of scarlet blood into the air.

There were two bowls on the table, ordinary cooking bowls, but one contained the head of a cockerel and the other was half full of a thick brown liquid that was congealing around the edges.

James sniffed it and remembered one of the Latin words he had recognized—*sanguis*, blood.

This wasn't right. He was suddenly very scared and knew he had to get out of there quickly. He hurried to the door at the other end of the chapel. It led to a short flight of stairs. He tiptoed up and found himself back at ground level. There was a short corridor here with a shuttered window. He swung the shutters back and peered out. The street looked empty. As soundlessly as possible, he opened the window and swung out onto the ledge, then dropped to the pavement.

He was unsure of exactly where he was, so he went carefully, keeping to the shadows and heading in what he hoped was the general direction of Codrose's. He was beginning to think that he was lost, when he turned a corner and almost bumped into the ladder that the men had put up against the wall. There was still no sign of anyone, but far off, he heard a shout and running feet, and without a second's thought, he scaled the ladder two rungs at a time.

In a minute he was back up on the roof peering down through the dome in Codrose's ceiling, and he realized he'd only just made it in time; the fat man from the search party was there, talking excitedly to Codrose, who stood up, pulled on his jacket, and left the room.

He was evidently going to check up on his boys.

James cursed. It was a race now. He had to get back into his room before Codrose found it empty. He tore across the roof and threw himself in through the skylight. He pulled the floorboards out of his way and dived into the hole. He didn't waste time putting them back behind him. He could return and do that later; for now the important thing was to get back into bed.

He pictured Codrose and the fat man; they would start on the floors below and work their way up, opening all the boys' doors on the way.

How long did that give him?

Not long enough.

He squirmed back along the crawl space, up into the washroom. He checked the corridor. No sign of Codrose yet, thank God. He ducked back into the lavatory and quickly replaced the floorboards and tiles. Then he cautiously returned to the washroom door. This time he could hear voices outside and people moving around. He eased the door back a crack, just wide enough to look one way down the corridor. He saw Codrose with the fat man and the Dame, Miss Winfrith Drinkell.

Miss Drinkell, who helped Codrose to run the house, was a tired-looking, middle-aged lady who always seemed disappointed by something. Probably by having to work with Cecil Codrose.

The three of them were just entering one of the boys' rooms. As soon as they were in, James shot out and managed to duck through his door a moment before he heard the search party emerging from the other room.

James tore off his shirt, kicked it under the bed, and dived under his covers just as he heard a short brisk knock and the click of the door as Codrose came in.

The light snapped on and James stirred, blinking, trying to appear groggy and confused.

"Sir?" he said.

"Have you heard anything tonight, Bond?" asked Codrose, glancing suspiciously around the room. "Any boys up and about?"

"No, sir. I've been asleep, sir."

The fat man waddled into the room and stared at James.

"Do I know you?" he said.

"I don't think so, sir," said James.

"Sorry to disturb you, James," said the Dame. "There's been some trouble tonight."

Codrose sniffed, then turned out the light and slammed the door.

James slumped back on to his pillow, exhausted and relieved.

He'd got away with it, but he wondered if the other members of the Danger Society had been so lucky. And if one of them had been caught, would he keep his mouth shut?

CHAPTER 3—THE FOURTH OF JUNE

"How long ago was this?"

"Last Thursday."

"And you've kept quiet about it all this time?"

"I couldn't risk talking about it. I didn't want to involve anyone else. I had to be sure I was in the clear."

"And are you in the clear?"

James shrugged. It was the fourth of June and he was in his room with his friend, Pritpal Nandra. The morning had started like any other morning—early school, breakfast, and then chapel—but now the boys had returned to their rooms to change because the rest of the day was a holiday.

"I don't know," he said. "Think so. All the others managed to escape, except for Gordon Latimer. His housemaster was waiting for him when he got back, worse luck. He was beaten, but he hasn't squealed. How he avoided being thrown out of school I'll never know."

"I think you will find," said Pritpal, "that his father is distantly related to the king."

Pritpal was one of the two boys James messed with. This meant that they took it in turns to cook their tea together in each other's rooms and generally looked out for one another. Pritpal and Tommy Chong, his other messmate, were the only other people in the house who knew about James's involvement with the Danger Society.

Pritpal was a clever and slightly round Indian boy who loved to hear James's tales of adventure, but would never have dreamed of joining him.

"And where exactly was this mysterious building with the shadowy figures speaking in Latin?" he asked, sitting down in a wicker armchair and rubbing a speck of dust from one of his highly polished shoes.

"I'm not sure," James replied. "I've been back to try and find it a couple of times, but no luck. It was dark that night, and I was being chased, so I couldn't say for certain *exactly* where it was."

Pritpal whistled. "You are one lucky boy, James," he said.

"Am I?" James laughed. "Maybe if I was lucky I wouldn't have been chased in the first place."

James checked his appearance in the little mirror on his mantelpiece. He saw a slim boy with gray-blue eyes and an unruly lock of black hair that, no matter how hard he tried to keep it in place, always fell forward over his forehead. He licked a hand and pushed it back. It would have to do for now.

"Are you ready?" Pritpal was eager to be off. He was studying his pocket watch and impatiently tapping its glass with a fingernail

"Think so," said James, checking himself one last time.

Most boys in their first year at the school wore short "Eton" jackets and clownish shirts with huge stiff "Eton" collars. The cut-off jackets were more commonly known as "bum-freezers"—for obvious reasons—and the shirts were awkward and uncomfortable. However, once a boy was taller than five foot four, he could wear the same uniform as the older boys—a black coat with long tails, a shirt with a more ordinary collar, and a fiddly little white tie.

James had recently been measured by the Dame, and it was discovered that he was now fractionally over the required height. As was the custom, he had saved changing into his new clothes until today—the Fourth of June. It was one of the most important days in the Eton calendar, and the only day of the year when the younger boys were allowed to dress up.

Pritpal, who was only just over five foot, still wore his bum-freezer, but he had put on a smart gray waistcoat and was wearing a shirt collar with folded wingtips called a "stick-up."

The senior prefects at Eton, known as "Pop," were instantly recognizable, with their gaudy waistcoats and tightly rolled umbrellas. All the other boys in the school had to carry their umbrellas unrolled. But not today. On the Fourth of June all boys were allowed rolled umbrellas.

It wasn't raining, so James had no use for an umbrella, and he wasn't going to cart one around just for the privilege of having it rolled. He would buy a flower for his buttonhole, but that would be the extent of his showing off. He had no desire to ape the foppish dress of Pop.

He turned to Pritpal. "How do I look?"

"Very grown up, I'm sure," said Pritpal, getting up from the chair. "Now, come along. Let us go and buy some flowers before they are all gone."

There was one last thing and James would be ready.

He glanced sourly at his freshly cleaned top hat sitting on his bed. How he hated that hat. He longed for the day when he could throw it in the bin and be done with it. But rules were rules.

He picked up the hat, and they left.

Outside, they joined a mob of excited boys who were wandering down through town toward the river. On the Fourth of June the school was open to all, and the streets were already growing busy. Later they would be busier still, packed with parents, brothers and sisters, aunts and uncles, locals, sightseers, old boys, and groups of newspaper photographers eager to get pictures of it all.

Eton was the most famous school in the country, and many of the important men in England had studied here. King Henry VI had founded it nearly five hundred years ago, and since then it had built up countless bizarre traditions that were fascinating and baffling to outsiders. Most of them were bizarre and baffling to James as well, and he wondered if he would ever get the hang of the place.

But he felt carefree and relaxed today. It was a fine sunny morning and he was enjoying the holiday atmosphere. He had been tense ever since that night on the roofs and was at last beginning to unwind.

A pack of boys was clustered around an old woman with a stall selling flowers on Barnes Pool Bridge. James and Pritpal pushed in, and James was just offering his money, when he was grabbed from behind and pulled backward. He spun round angrily and saw a wild-eyed boy whose blotchy face was streaked from crying. At first James didn't recognize him.

"Get off me, you idiot," he snapped, slapping the boy's hands away.

"I need the keys, James," said the boy, his voice strained, and at last James recognized him.

It was Mark Goodenough, the boy from the Danger Society who hadn't made it the other night. The boy whose family was missing.

"Oh, it's you, Mark," said James. "Are you all right?" he added, although he could see quite plainly that he wasn't.

"I need the keys," Mark repeated.

"What keys?" asked James, confused and embarrassed for Mark. "I don't know what you're talking about." People were beginning to look at them.

"For the garage," said Mark. "I need the car."

James put a hand on Mark's arm and led him away from the crowd.

"Mark," he said quietly, "I can't let you take the car. Not today. Not like this."

Mark was older than James and considerably bigger. He tore his arm free and glared at James with such anger in his eyes that James feared he might hit him; but in the end he just swore and stormed off.

"I'll find Perry," he shouted over his shoulder. "He'll let me take it."

James and Perry were the only two members of the society who had keys to the garage.

"What the devil was all that about?" said Pritpal, fitting a flower into his buttonhole. "What car was he talking about?"

"It doesn't matter," said James thoughtfully. "He's upset. Forget it."

James hadn't told anyone outside the society about the

car. He had let Pritpal in on some of his secrets, but not all—even your best friends are liable to blab.

"Do you think he will be all right?" said Pritpal.

James watched Mark disappearing over the bridge, scattering boys in his path. "I don't know," he said, trying not to sound worried. "I hope so."

Two hours hour later, James was strolling with his Aunt Charmian, trying to get a glimpse past a great crush of people at the cricket match being played on Agar's Plough between the school XI and the Eton Ramblers, a team of old Etonians. Nearby, on Upper Club, a band from the Rifle Brigade was playing a lively tune, but it was nearly drowned out by the roar of chatter coming from the circulating crowd, as parents caught up with the latest gossip and boasted about how well their boys were doing at the school.

James caught sight of Andrew Carlton, standing bored and restless as his parents pestered a bishop. Charmian didn't know anyone else here, but she enjoyed the spectacle, observing it all with the detached eye of an outsider, and James enjoyed showing her around.

Charmian was an anthropologist and had traveled the world studying different peoples and cultures. In her time she had lived with Eskimos in Greenland, the Tuareg in the Sahara, the Mindima mud men of Papua New Guinea and the Paduang hill tribes of Burma, whose women stretched their necks with heavy brass rings, but she had seen nothing more exotic than this gathering at Eton.

"I really should know the significance of all this," she said, an amused grin on her face. "But I'm afraid I don't."

"It's to celebrate King George the Third's birthday," James explained.

"Why on earth would anyone want to do that?" said his aunt with a little laugh.

James laughed as well. "He was a great friend of the school, apparently. He was always hanging about the place, chatting to the boys."

"Good for him," said Charmian.

Windsor Castle was just over the other side of the Thames, and ever since Henry VI's day the English monarchs had taken varying degrees of interest in the school. An Eton boy had once saved the life of Queen Victoria when a madman had tried to shoot her outside the railway station. James had seen the current king, George V, on a couple of occasions, and often wondered what the life of a king must be like, behind those high castle walls.

Charmian took James for lunch at a restaurant on the river, and afterward they made their way down to some meadows next to the river known as the Brocas. A large and excited crowd had gathered here, ready for the main highlight of the day, the Procession of Boats.

The sun was sparkling on the water, turning the usually dull and muddy Thames an attractive bright blue speckled with silver shards.

"How are you getting on with your lessons?" Charmian asked, turning her face to catch the sun.

"I don't suppose I'll win many prizes for my work," James said. "I try to be interested in it all, but I do sometimes wonder what the point of studying Latin is."

Charmian laughed. "Well, don't ask me! They didn't

teach me much more at school than how to snag a husband. And I don't think I can have paid enough attention in those particular lessons. Now, good Lord, what's this?"

The first of the boats had appeared from under the railway bridge, being rowed by a crew of boys wearing old-fashioned sailors' outfits from Nelson's time—white trousers, striped shirts, blue jackets, and straw hats decorated with huge bunches of flowers. A tiny cox sat in the back, dressed as a miniature admiral, steering.

As the boats reached the end of the Brocas, the rowers stood up and held their oars upright beside them in the boats, a tricky and wobbly maneuver. James, like many of the boys watching, hoped that someone might fall in, but it didn't happen today.

As the other boats went past, Charmian turned to James.

"I know what I've been meaning to talk to you about," she said. "The holidays."

"Are you still going away?" said James.

"I'm afraid so. It's the chance of a lifetime. An expedition up the Amazon. We'll be meeting tribes who've never seen an outsider. With a way of life unchanged for thousands of years . . ." She paused for a moment and put an arm round James. "I'm sorry to abandon you," she said, "but perhaps we can think of a tame relative to pack you off to."

"I'll be all right," said James.

"I'm sure you will," said Charmian.

James stepped back to get a better view and, in so doing, trod on someone's foot. He turned round to apologize.

It was Mr. Merriot, James's classical tutor.

"Steady on, there, James," he said with a smile. Merriot

was tall, with unruly gray hair and long, gangly arms and legs, like a stick insect. As usual, an unlit pipe jutted out of his face from beneath his big beaky nose.

James introduced his aunt, and Merriot introduced a man at his side.

"This is my colleague, John Cooper-ffrench."

Cooper-ffrench was a stocky, fierce-looking man wearing a Homburg hat and gray suede gloves. He had a wide, bull-ish nose, deep-crimson skin, and a fussy little mustache.

"Mister Cooper-ffrench is president of the Latin Society here at Eton," Merriot explained.

"James was just telling me that he doesn't see the point of studying Latin," said Charmian, and James broke into a nervous sweat.

"Oh, doesn't he now?" Merriot's eyes widened with mock amazement.

James tried not to blush.

"And I'm afraid I'm with him on that," said Charmian.

"Poppycock!" Cooper-ffrench barked, his voice croaky and hard-edged. "I couldn't expect you to fully understand, madam, but I can assure you that Latin is the very root and foundation of our great English language. Without an understanding of Latin, how can a boy ever hope to be truly eloquent? Perhaps it is not so important for women, who need not concern themselves with these matters, but for a man to get on in the world, the study of Latin is absolutely vital. No man can consider himself educated unless he is fluent in the language."

"Oh, please don't get me wrong," said Charmian politely. "I think the study of language is a fine thing. I myself

30

speak five, and I've come across more varieties around the world than I could count, each one fascinating in its own way." She paused for a moment and smiled at the beetroot-faced master. "But, come along, Mister Cooper-ffrench, do you really think that in this day and age the most important thing a boy can learn at school is Latin?"

"I do, madam," Cooper-ffrench snorted, his face growing redder by the minute. "Why, if I had my way, a boy would be taught nothing else."

"Would a knowledge of Latin help James if he were shipwrecked?" said Charmian. "Or if he had to escape from a burning building? Would a knowledge of Latin help him if he were faced with gangsters, or diamond smugglers, or a madman with a bomb?"

"Really, Miss Bond," said Cooper-ffrench, with a patronizing chuckle. "You mustn't let your feminine imagination run away with you. This is Eton. I hardly think this boy, James Bond, is going be living a life of high adventure. Why, I would think a career in banking more likely, or insurance, or perhaps the law, where a knowledge of Latin is essential. I am not just talking about the language, however, but also the civilizing influence of the culture."

"Oh, but Mister Cooper-ffrench," said Charmian sweetly, "the classics are chock-full of stories of gods coming down to earth in disguise and ravishing women. Though, perhaps you think that's all us women are good for?"

"That is a gross misrepresentation of the classics," said Cooper-ffrench.

"The Romans were a thoroughly rotten bunch," said Aunt Charmian. "Their emperors were forever killing each other. In the fifty years between 235 and 285 A.D. they got through twenty of them! So I hardly think these are the people who should be showing us how to behave in a civilized manner."

"Well!" Cooper-ffrench scoffed. "I'm not going to argue with you about this. I think that whoever said that a little learning in a woman is a dangerous thing was absolutely right. Good day to you."

So saying, he gave a little bow and walked off in a huff.

Merriot laughed. "I'm afraid our Mister Cooper-ffrench is somewhat lacking in a sense of humor."

Merriot himself was considerably less pompous about the classics, and was, all in all, rather easygoing and genial. He and Charmian soon fell into a noisy conversation, ignoring the stately procession of passing boats.

James was only half paying attention, feeling drowsy in the late afternoon sun, when Perry Mandeville barged through the crowd, looking worried and out of breath.

"Have you seen M-Mark?" he asked.

"I saw him earlier, yes," said James. "He was in a bad way."

"He hit me," said Perry indignantly. "Quite hard, actually, I think he's m-mad, he was trying to get the keys for the garage off m-me, when I wouldn't help him he punched m-me, a proper punch, m-mind you, and ran off saying he was going to break in."

"How long ago was this?" said James, anxiously glancing over at Merriot and his aunt, who were still deep in conversation.

"About five m-minutes," said Perry. "M-maybe m-more,

I've been looking all over for you, what do you think we should do? It was like confronting a wild m-man, he quite put the wind up m-me."

"We'd better go," said James.

He gabbled a hasty excuse to Charmian and set off at a run with Perry.

"We've go to get to the garage and stop him," he said, elbowing a fat lady in a fur stole out of the way. "The state he's in—if he takes that car, anything might happen."

"It seems they found the remains of his father's boat," said Perry. "Pretty grisly stuff. Floating wreckage and dead bodies. It looks like there was a fire of some sort."

James and Perry were pushing through the aimlessly milling hordes, ignoring the complaints and shouts as they jostled people aside.

"Have they found his family?" said James.

"I don't know," said Perry. "It's all a bit of a m-mess. When M-Mark's housemaster told him the news, he lost his cool."

The narrow roads of Eton had not been built for cars, and on days like this, when everyone turned up in a motor and then proceeded to wander in the roads, the traffic was at a near standstill. So the boys left the pavement and ran in the road, moving faster than the traffic.

"But what does he want the car for?" James shouted, dodging round a big black Daimler.

"To get away from all this, I im-magine," Perry shouted back. "I don't think he could cope with seeing all the other boys with their parents."

They crossed the Thames into Windsor. It was less busy here, though traffic for Eton was still backed up. They were concentrating too hard on running now to be able to talk anymore. They passed the castle, turned into Peascod Street, then left the main road. In a few minutes they were in a scruffy part of town, running down a grimy alley between small factories and warehouses, their footsteps echoing off the high gray walls.

At last they came out into a small courtyard and crossed over to some crumbling mews buildings. In the days when transport had still been pulled by horses these had been stables, but they had long since been converted into garages for motor vehicles.

They immediately saw that Mark had already been here. Been and gone. The doors to the garage were hanging open, the padlock lying broken on the cobbles.

The garage itself was empty.

"We're too late." Perry shook his head and looked at James. "If he has a smash, that's the end of your m-motor."

"Never mind that," said James. "If he has a smash, that's the end of him."

"But what can we do?" said Perry, peering into the empty garage.

"He can't be long gone," said James, sniffing the air. "I can still smell fumes. He must have left only a few minutes ago. He won't risk going through the center of Windsor and back through Eton; it's too crowded and he'd be stopped straight away if a beak saw him. The quickest way out of town from here is Albert Road toward Staines."

"Then there's still a chance," said Perry. "It'll be slow going. You saw how busy the roads are."

"Think we can catch him?" asked James.

"We can try," said Perry. "I know a shortcut. Come on."

Perry led James out of the courtyard and up a narrow flight of steps that led to a dark, twisting alley behind a row of shops. Halfway along, Perry ducked into the back garden of a pub and then vaulted over a wall on the other side. James followed and found himself in a row of allotments. Perry steamed ahead past neat plots of beans and cabbages and out on to a long side street lined with lime trees. They pounded down the pavement and reached the main road just in time to see a car approaching and slowing for the junction.

The black-and-white Bamford and Martin was unmistakable; it was a sleek, open-topped roadster, built for speed. And the boy behind the wheel was unmistakable too, despite his tear-stained face and windswept hair.

"There he is," James yelled, and put on a burst of speed.

"Be careful," Perry shouted after him as James sprinted across the road and threw himself into the path of the oncoming car, which came to a shuddering halt.

Mark sounded the horn and cursed. There was a wild fury in his eyes. His hands were gripping the steering wheel so tightly his knuckles were white.

"Get out of the way, James," he said, his face screwed into an ugly scowl.

"No," said James. "You've got to go back. This is crazy."

"Get out of my way," Mark repeated. "Or I'll run you down."

"You wouldn't do that," said James, but even as he said it, he was not so sure.

"Move," Mark yelled, and he pressed his foot down on the accelerator, gunning the engine.

"I'm not moving," said James, stepping backward warily.

"Don't be stupid, Mark. Let's take the car back."

With that, Mark slipped the engine into gear and the car jerked forward. James just managed to dodge to the side, and as the vehicle passed him, he made a quick decision and threw himself over the door into the passenger seat.

The car screamed down the road. Mark Goodenough was not an experienced driver, and he had it in too low a gear. The engine was complaining; at this rate it would overheat.

"Shift up," said James. "You'll burn her out."

Mark wrenched the gear lever and it churned and grated through the change. The noise of the engine settled down, but the car was far from being under control. Mark was veering all over the road as he fought to contain the powerful machine. There was the blast of a horn as another car sped past them on the other side, only a few inches away.

"Slow down," said James. "You'll get us both killed."

"I don't care," Mark yelled. "I didn't ask you to get in, did I?"

They skidded around a corner, careering across the road into the right-hand lane. If there had been anyone coming the other way they would have had a head-on smash.

"Maybe you've forgotten," said James, trying not to sound either angry or scared, even though he felt both keenly, "but this is my car."

"I told you, I don't care," said Mark. "I don't care about anything anymore."

James looked at him. There were tears streaming down Mark's cheeks, made worse by the wind battering his face. He was blinking and shaking his head to try to clear his eyes, but he obviously couldn't see too well.

"Where are you going?" asked James.

"Away . . . Anywhere . . . I don't care. Maybe when I've got up enough speed I'll drive straight into the first wall I come to and put an end to it all."

"That would be stupid," said James.

"Shut up," shouted Mark. "Just shut up, won't you?"

They were out of Windsor now, driving through farmland. Mercifully, the roads were quieter, but they still passed the occasional alarmed motorist. Mark was driving faster and faster, and even if he didn't stick to his threat of driving into a wall, he was dangerously out of control and could spin off the road at any moment. James hung on to the side of the car for all he was worth.

"All right, Mark," he said at last, "you may want to die, but I don't. Stop the car and let me out."

"No," said Mark.

"Then at least slow down," said James. "I'm scared. You're not thinking straight."

"I don't care," Mark screamed. "I don't care I don't care I don't care. . . ."

"It's your family, isn't it?" said James, and Mark screwed his head around briefly to glare at him.

"What would you know about it?" he shouted, his voice hoarse. "What would you know about anything?"

"My parents were killed when I was eleven," said James bluntly.

Mark looked around again, frowning now, unsure; but he had taken his eyes off the road for just a moment too long, and when he turned back there was a bus heading straight for them. Mark froze and James grabbed the wheel, desperately turning it to the left. They swerved around the bus. James was aware of a blur of hot metal thundering past them, sucking the air away, too close and too loud. He caught a glimpse of startled faces at the windows, then the bus was gone. Mark wrestled the wheel off James, but turned the car back too sharply. The momentum forced the rear end of the car around, and they spun off the road into a field, narrowly avoiding a huge oak tree. The car rotated two or three times, the tires throwing up dirt behind them, and then it stalled and rocked to a halt.

The sudden silence was startling. James let out his breath. He tasted blood in his mouth. He had bitten his tongue. Mark was slumped forward on the steering wheel. His whole body was shaking and he was sobbing uncontrollably and swearing over and over again—the worst words he knew.

"It's all right," said James, putting a hand on his shoulder. "We're alive and the car's in one piece."

Mark lifted his head from the wheel. His face was streaked with snot and saliva. He had hit his head, and a bruise was already rising on his brow. His eyes were red, but the fire had gone out of them and he looked ashamed.

"I'm sorry," he said quietly. "I didn't know about your parents."

"I don't talk about it," said James. "But would you like to, you know, tell me about . . . what's happened?"

"A fisherman from Rhodes . . ." said Mark, looking into the distance and sniffing. "He found wreckage, floating, bits of the boat, burnt . . . and bodies . . . floating . . . my father—"

"Dead?"

"Yes."

"And your sister? Have they found her?"

"Not yet."

"She may be safe, then?"

"It's been ten days," Mark sobbed. "If there was anyone alive, they would have been found by now."

"Not necessarily," said James. "There is still some hope."

Mark looked at James, and James saw that there was no hope left in his eyes.

"I'm sorry," said James, and Mark tried to smile.

"Thank you, James," he said. "I think maybe I just needed someone to talk to. But I can't believe this is happening. . . ."

"I know the feeling," said James quietly. "Now, we'd better get back before someone sees us."

"Yes." Mark sniffed and sat up straighter in his seat. "Do you think the car's all right?"

"Only one way to find out . . . But I think you'd better let me drive. When we get back near town we'll park somewhere out of sight and work out what to do with the car later, when there's not so many people around."

Mark nodded mutely. All the life had gone out of him; he seemed numb and exhausted.

They swapped seats and James drove carefully back toward Windsor.

"I couldn't stand it," said Mark flatly. "Seeing all the other boys strolling through Eton with mama and papa. So happy, so normal. It was bad enough when my mother died, but now this. . . . My father should have been here today. He always came back for the Fourth of June, every year. But not anymore . . . Never again."

"Listen, Mark," said James. "I don't know how I can help, but if there's anything I can do—*anything*—I will. Okay? That's a promise"

"Thank you," said Mark, his voice barely audible over the roar of the engine.

When they reached the outskirts of Windsor, they went even more cautiously, keeping to obscure backstreets. James was just beginning to think that they might have got away with it, when he heard the honk of a horn behind him. He turned around to see a young master, wearing his black robes, following him in a car and angrily gesticulating for him to stop.

"Watch out," James muttered. "It's a beak. This could be trouble."

Cursing under his breath, James pulled over and got out of the car.

This was not turning out to be a good day after all.

The beak was driving a smart green Lagonda sports. He climbed out and slammed the door so hard the car rocked on its springs.

"What on earth do you two boys think you're doing?" he shouted, and James stopped on the pavement.

"This is my aunt's car," he said, trying to sound confident.

"Explain yourself," said the beak.

"It had to be moved, sir," James said, looking the beak straight in the eye. "It was causing an obstruction. I couldn't find my aunt so I moved it for her."

"So just what exactly are you doing all the way over here in Windsor?" There was a dangerous note of scorn in the man's voice.

"It was too crowded in Eton, sir," said James. "I've been driving around trying to find a decent space to park. I got lost . . . She lets me drive it, sir. . . ."

James ran out of steam. He knew that his story sounded feeble, but it was all that he could think of in the time.

He looked at the master. He was younger than most, perhaps thirty, with an athletic build, and despite his anger, he had a kind, open face. He reminded James a little of the American film star Gary Cooper.

"What is your name?" said the beak. He was still fuming, but James could sense that he was calming down a little.

"Bond. James Bond."

"Well, Mister Bond, this won't do, will it?"

"No, sir."

"Leaving aside the fact that you are too young to be driving a car, there is the reputation of the school at stake."

"Yes, sir, I know, sir, it was stupid of me. But the car was blocking a road and—"

"So you say," the teacher interrupted impatiently. "And who is that other boy with you? What is his involvement in all this?"

"His name's Mark Goodenough, sir, he's—"

"Goodenough?" The beak appeared shocked, then his expression softened and he looked unsure of himself. He walked over to the car and saw the condition that Mark was in.

"Are you all right, Mark?" he said.

"Yes, thank you, Mister Haight."

James closed his eyes and let out a long, slow breath. So the two of them knew each other. That might help.

Mr. Haight leaned over the car and put a hand on Mark's shoulder. "I heard about the . . ." he paused, searching for the right word, "accident. I'm very sorry."

"Thank you, sir. But I'm all right, really I am. Bond has been helping me, sir . . . I just . . ." But Mark couldn't go on. He broke down again and crumpled in his seat.

Mr. Haight looked embarrassed. He glanced up and down the street, then made up his mind about something and walked over to James, out of earshot of Mark.

"Listen to me, Bond. I don't know what you two boys are up to, and maybe it's for the best that I don't try to find out, but I do know that Mark has had a nasty upset. So as long as there's no harm done, I'll let you off this time." Haight stopped and nodded back toward the car. "How is he?" he asked gently.

"He's not well, sir," said James. "I didn't think he should be left alone."

"I understand that his grandfather's on his way down from the family estate in Yorkshire. In the meantime I'll keep an eye on him. I'll take him to the sanatorium, and stay there with him until his family arrives. Leave the car here, Bond, and we'll say no more about it."

"Yes, sir, thank you, sir."

"And Bond . . ." Mr. Haight looked searchingly into James's eyes. "You've a reckless look about you. . . . Be careful." So saying, Mr. Haight offered him a grim, tight-lipped smile, turned on his heel, and strode off to fetch Mark.

CHAPTER 5—THE TOMBS OF THE GIANTS

*"G*ood evening," said Mr. Haight. "I'm delighted to see such an excellent turnout. But first, I hope you won't be disappointed when I tell you that although tonight's lecture is entitled 'In Search of Sardinian Bandits,' it's not really about bandits at all."

There were a few groans and catcalls from the assembled boys.

James was sitting with Pritpal and Perry in Upper School, one of the oldest of the school buildings. The bench they were on was hard and cold. James hoped that Haight's talk was going to be entertaining, because it would be a long and very uncomfortable evening otherwise.

It was Perry who had persuaded him to come. When James had found him back at the garage and told him what had happened, he'd gushed excitedly about what a great sport Haight was and how popular he was with the boys.

"'Love-Haight' we call him," Perry had said with a laugh. "I'm up to him for history. He's excellent on the Romans, knows his stuff, and knows how to put it over, m-more's the point, but he's interested in all sorts of stuff—art, architecture, m-music—his lessons are great fun. I'll tell you what, I wish he would actually teach art, I love art, something of a buff. I was very fond of our collection at home, before someone

44

pinched it. He's giving a talk this weekend to the Archaeological Society, you should come along, bound to be interesting."

James had resisted at first, but it was a Sunday evening and he had nothing else to do. Pritpal had tagged along, even though he had a lot of work to finish before the morning. So now here they were in Upper School with a horde of other boys. This was only Mr. Haight's first year at the school, but it was obvious that he had already attracted a large and devoted following.

"To be fair, though," Haight went on, "how many of you would have come tonight if I'd called my talk 'In Search of the Ancient Nuraghic Monuments of Sardinia'?" Again there were more catcalls. "Exactly," said Haight. "But fear not, bandits will feature. Bandits are an important part of Sardinian history. What I mostly want to tell you about, though, are the extraordinary prehistoric monuments that litter the island. Yes. Prepare to be amazed as I show you ruined castles and towers built a thousand years before the birth of Christ, and Le Tombe dei Giganti—the Tombs of the Giants! But, before all that . . . Who here knows anything about Sardinia?" He looked around at the eager but blank faces. "Anyone . . .? No? Nothing. I knew it!" Haight clapped his hands together. "We all know about Corsica, birthplace of Napoleon and home to fierce bandits. And Sicily, the 'football' of Italy, with its volcano and Roman ruins . . . and, yes, its fierce bandits. But what of Sardinia? Sitting there below Corsica, halfway between Europe and Africa, how can it be so unknown to the rest of the world? Because it is a fascinating place, with a fascinating history and . . ." he paused, looking round at his audience, "the fiercest bandits in Europe, the Barbati. . . ."

James listened as Haight told a bloody history of invasions and warfare, and of how the Sardinians were forced inland, up into the mountains, where they lived a remote life of banditry and feuding. And he talked of the mysterious ancient civilization that had existed on the island thousands of years ago and left behind extraordinary stone monuments, known as Nuraghi.

James wasn't very good at sitting still, and as Haight talked, he looked around the room. It had been the custom for boys to carve their names here when they left the school, and every inch was covered in writing. The wood paneling on the walls, the benches, the upright desks, even the block at one end that the Head Master used to flog boys on had been scratched and chiseled over the centuries. There were hundreds and hundreds of names, with more recent additions overlaying the older carvings.

James had spotted the names of two prime ministers, Pitt and Walpole, the poet Shelley, and on one panel, at least twenty-eight members of the Gosling family.

Sitting along one wall beneath a row of marble busts were some beaks. They were sticking together, nodding their heads and smoking. James cast a casual glance over them and recognized the beetroot face of John Cooper-ffrench, the classics master who Charmian had teased on the Fourth of June. He was wearing a faded tweed jacket and a striped tie, and sat with his arms folded across his chest.

James marveled at how it was that once you'd met someone you'd never seen before you suddenly saw them everywhere.

When the lecture ended Pritpal dashed off to finish his

work, and Haight came over to where James and Perry were chatting.

"Have you heard?" he said, clapping Perry on the shoulder. "There's been another burglary."

"M-more art stolen?" said Perry. "Where from this time?"

"Tatsmere House. Belongs to the family of a dry-bob I coach, Nicholas Cresswel. I don't think you know him. He told me on the way here this evening. Quite a haul, I'm afraid. Two Gainsboroughs, a Titian, and a Canova."

"Do you think it m-might be one gang doing it all, sir?" asked Perry. "A gang of m-murderous art thieves."

"That might very well be the case," said Haight. "Though, luckily, so far they haven't murdered anyone, of course. You must tell all your friends to be on the lookout. None of these great houses that your families own are terribly secure. You must be *en garde!*" So saying, Haight struck a dramatic pose with an imaginary sword and managed to crash into Cooper-ffrench, who was hurrying out of the room.

As the two men collided, Cooper-ffrench was nearly knocked off his feet. Haight gabbled an apology and Cooper-ffrench tutted irritably and mumbled something about clumsiness.

James glimpsed a flash of silver and looked down to see a thin bracelet on the floor.

"What's this?" he said, picking it up. He turned it in his hand. With a start of surprise he saw the letters *MM* inscribed on it.

"Someone's dropped a bracelet," said Haight, looking around.

"Maybe Mister Cooper-ffrench," said James. But Cooper-ffrench had gone.

"I'll look after it," said Haight, taking it off James. "See if anyone claims it—"

"The double *M*, sir," James blurted out.

"What?"

"On the bracelet there are two *M*'s. I've seen them before."

Haight studied the bracelet, frowning. "Oh, yes," he said. "I see what you mean."

But James stopped himself from saying anything more. He could hardly tell Haight about the chase over the rooftops and breaking into the house, so he decided to change the subject.

"How's Mark Goodenough, sir?" he said. "Have you heard anything?"

"He's with his grandfather. He's bearing up, I think," replied Haight. "But I don't know if he'll return this half. He's taken it all rather badly, and who can blame him." For a moment Haight's face clouded and he appeared lost in thought, then he snapped out of it and smiled at James.

"I thought I recognized you," he said. "The racing driver, James Bond."

"That's right, sir," said James.

"So tell me, young James Bond," said Haight, "are you interested in Sardinia?"

"I think a relative of mine has a house there," said James. "But until tonight I didn't really know very much about the place."

"Exactly my point." Haight beamed at him. "Nobody

does. But I intend to open a few boys' minds. I'm taking an expedition there at the end of the summer, to look at some of the monuments. Perhaps you'd like to join us? Visit the Tombs of the Giants."

"Perhaps," said James. "I'm not sure yet what my plans are for the holidays. . . ."

"Well, if you fancy it, just add your name to the list in School Yard. Are you still coming, Perry?"

"Think so, sir, if I can get the old m-man to stump up, he's feeling frightfully poor since the burglary." Perry turned to James. "They didn't just take paintings, but also a lot of jewelery and silver and the like, but I reckon I'll go to the M-Med and take a look at these *Neurotic* m-monuments. What do you say, James? Why don't you come?"

Before James could reply, he felt a tug at his sleeve and turned to see a small milk-faced boy.

"I think you'd better come," he said. "Your friend Pritpal's in trouble."

James followed him out of the building and found an unruly gang of boys running off down the High Street, singing and chanting. He gave chase, and as he got closer he could make out the words of their chant.

"Throw Nandra in the river! Throw Nandra in the river!"

He managed to get the attention of one of the stragglers, a skinny lad with spots all over his face.

"What are you doing?" James asked.

"We're going to throw Nandra in the river," shouted the boy.

"Why?" said James.

"I don't know," said the boy. "It just seemed like a good idea."

The mob bundled off the road and made its way down to Fellows Eyot by the Thames, where it stopped. James fought his way to the front and saw the frightened face of Pritpal. He was cornered by the river's edge, clutching his hat and trembling.

Three of the largest boys advanced on him. "Come along, little rabbit," said one of them. "You're going in the pot!"

"Stop it!" James yelled, and they turned around laughing.

James stepped out of the crowd. "What do you think you're doing?" he said, looking from one boy to another.

He recognized the ringleader, a large boy with floppy hair. He would have been quite handsome if his ears and nose hadn't stuck out so much, and he wore an expression of arrogant superiority that only the truly stupid can pull off. He was well known in the school. His name was Tony Fitzpaine and he was the Duke of something, or the Earl of somewhere.

"We're going to throw Nandra in the river," he drawled, as if it was the most obvious thing in the world.

"What's he done?"

"He's not one of us," scoffed Fitzpaine. "He's an invader and we're going to throw him back into the sea, just like Haight's Sardinian bandits."

"Wash him in the Thames!" someone shouted.

James stepped forward and put himself between the boys and his friend. "Leave him alone," he said. "He's better than the lot of you."

"Ha!" snorted Fitzpaine. "Do you know who I am, you dirty little pleb?"

"Yes," said James. "And you could be the King of England, for all I care. Pritpal is my friend and you're *not* going to throw him in the river."

"If you don't get out of my way," bawled Fitzpaine, "I'm going to throw *you* in the river." He looked to his friends and brayed with laughter like a donkey.

"No, you're not," said James flatly, and Fitzpaine frowned at him.

The two of them stood there staring at each other. Fitzpaine was not used to anyone standing up to him. His father was an important, powerful man, so, within Eton, Fitzpaine was also important and powerful. For a moment he seemed confused, then the arrogant look returned. In his mind there was a certain order in the world, and this order was being threatened. He didn't know James, which meant that James wasn't important. And you could do whatever you liked to unimportant people. Fitzpaine pulled his lips back from his large teeth and forced his mouth into a superior smile.

"Well, you asked for it," he said, and pushed James hard backward in the direction of the river's edge. But James had been expecting something and stood his ground. Then, before the older boy knew what was happening, James punched him hard in the mouth.

Fitzpaine rocked on his feet, stunned, trying to focus his eyes, his knees shaking and his legs wobbly.

There was a shocked silence from the other boys.

James calmly walked around Fitzpaine and gave him a shove. He toppled over into the Thames and floundered about in the reeds at the river's edge, spluttering in amazement. Two of his friends went to haul him out.

James confronted the rest of the mob. Now what? They'd probably lynch him.

However, someone laughed.

"Good show!" said someone else, and before James knew what was happening, he was hoisted up onto the boys' shoulders and carried off in triumph amid much laughing and singing.

"What are you doing?" asked James.

"Oh," said one of the boys carrying him, "we didn't much care who went into the river, just so long as it was someone. Nobody likes Fitzpaine."

Pritpal was hoisted aloft as well, and the two of them were paraded down the High Street like champions, before being dumped in a back alley. The other boys hurried away, their laughter echoing off the walls.

Pritpal tried to thank James, but James shrugged it off.

"I'd have done it for anyone," he said. "People like Fitzpaine think they can do whatever they want, just because of who their father is."

"My father's a maharaja," said Pritpal, "but I don't go around beheading people."

"Well, maybe you should," said James. "Then people might show you a little more respect."

"You are lucky, James," said Pritpal. "People keep clear of you. You can look after yourself, but if you go around hitting people you're going to get into trouble one day."

"I know," said James. "I shouldn't have done it. But you must admit he did look funny sitting there in the river."

Pritpal laughed. "Come along. We'd better get back," he said, anxiously checking his watch. "We'll miss lockup."

"Wait a minute," said James, who was standing staring at something.

"What is it?"

"It's the building."

"Building?" said Pritpal. "What building? There are lots of buildings here."

"From the other night," said James. "Where the two men were speaking Latin."

"Are you sure?" said Pritpal.

"I'm positive. Seeing it here, like this, at night, I recognize it."

"Well, there is no time to investigate now," said Pritpal. "We must get back."

"You go," said James. "I'm going to take a quick look."

"All right," said Pritpal, trotting off. "But please hurry!"

James walked closer. From the outside there was nothing special about the place. Its windows were shuttered and it looked deserted. There was no clue as to whether anyone lived here. It looked like a perfectly ordinary Eton house. Except James knew that in the cellar was a chapel dedicated to some strange god.

He approached one of the windows and pressed his nose up against it to try and see past the crack between two partially opened shutters, and he was surprised to find that there was someone inside. A dim light was burning, but all he could make out in the gloom were the shoulder of a tweed suit, a white shirtfront, and a black-and-red striped tie. He thought he vaguely recognized the clothes, and then the man moved and James got a glimpse of a red face and a mustache.

Cooper-ffrench. It could only be him.

James was straining for a better look when he suddenly heard the front door opening.

He ducked down and turned away and pretended to be a tying a shoelace, but he was aware of someone's eyes boring into the back of his neck, and he stood up. There was a man standing on the doorstep in his shirtsleeves. He had lank red hair and two long scars running from the edges of his mouth to his ears. He appeared to be smiling, but he looked at James with such a blank expression in his eyes that the effect was menacing and hostile. He put a cigarette to his mouth and inhaled a lungful of smoke, which he let out slowly, his gaze all the while fixed on James. James saw that the hand that held the cigarette was tattooed. There was a crude red letter *M* on the back of it. And there was an identical tattoo on his other hand.

James remembered the stenciled letters on the packing crates that he had seen the other night. *MM*. He wanted to know more, but now wasn't the time to ask questions. He smiled politely and sauntered off down the street as nonchalantly as he could, aware of the man's stare following him to the end of the road.

"Oh, but that sounds like an excellent idea!"

It was three weeks later, and James was on long leave. He was free from Friday morning to Monday night. A lot of the other boys were up at Lord's for the annual Eton versus Harrow cricket match, but James had taken the opportunity to get away from anything to do with school—in particular the stifling uniform and the top hat. He had gone home to his aunt's cottage in Kent, where he could happily spend the weekend sunning himself in the countryside wearing his comfortable old shirt and trousers.

He and Charmian were eating a picnic lunch outside in the shade of an old apple tree, and James had mentioned that he might be interested in joining Haight's expedition to Sardinia.

"You could spend the start of the hols here with me before I leave for Brazil," said Charmian, cutting a slice of pork pie. "Then ship out with Mister Haight. How long is the trip?"

"Three weeks, I think," said James. "Though I'm not sure I want to spend all that time tramping round ancient ruins."

"Well, stay with the school party for as long as you can bear it, and then peel off to your cousin Victor's in Capo d'Orso. I'm sure Mister Haight wouldn't mind. You could stay with Victor until the end of the holidays." She handed James a plate of food. "There," she said. "We have it. A plan. It'll do you the world of good to get away from dreary old England."

"I suppose so," said James. "I can't say I'm that interested in Nuraghic monuments, but Mister Haight's good fun, and one of my friends will be going. Are you sure that Victor will have me, though?"

"You've stayed with him before, haven't you?"

"Yes," said James. "But that was years ago. At his old house in Italy."

James couldn't remember much about his cousin, who

was a lot older than he was, so that James thought of him as more of an uncle.

"Well," said Charmian, "from what I hear, he's getting more and more eccentric in his old age. But I'll write to him and see what he has to say."

"Okay." James smiled and took a sip of water. "Aunt Charmian," he said after a short pause, "you know a bit about tattoos, don't you?"

"Tattoos? Yes. A little. Why?"

"It's only that I saw a man in Eton with some, and I was curious about them. Do you know what a tattoo of the letter *M* would mean? Two *M*'s. One on each hand."

"Not off the top of my head," Charmian replied. "Could be the initials of almost anything. Or the number two thousand."

"Two thousand?" said James. "What do you mean?"

"*M* is the Roman numeral for a thousand. Two *M*s—two thousand."

"But why would you have it tattooed on your hands?"

"Oh, people get tattoos for many different reasons," said Charmian. "But it most commonly means you belong to a tribe, or gang. The custom goes right back to ancient Egyptian times."

"What sort of people get tattoos?" James asked.

"In England? Well, they were first brought here in the eighteenth century by men who'd sailed to the South Seas with Captain Cook. They copied the idea from the natives out there. They started quite a craze. Did you know that King George has a tattoo?"

"Really?" said James, who couldn't quite picture it.

"Yes," said Charmian. "He and his brother both have dragons on their arms. It's all down to their father, the old king. He had the Jerusalem cross tattooed on to his arm in the Holy Land when he was Prince of Wales. Well, after that, everyone in smart society had to have a tattoo. You weren't anybody unless you had one. King Edward had several more done and then got his sons tattooed in Japan by the celebrated master Hori Chiyo. But it all ended in 1891."

"Why? What happened?" said James.

"A man named Samuel O'Riley went and invented a mechanical tattooing device, and suddenly everybody could afford one. Overnight, tattoos changed from being the decoration of an aristocrat to the mark of a lowlife. But in many other cultures around the world they still use tattooing and ritual body-scarring as a sign of manhood."

"What would it mean if you had a scar from the corners of your mouth to your ears?" said James, indicating the lines on his own face. "Would that be a ritual thing, too?"

"No," said Charmian. "That would mean you were an informer. A criminal who'd given information to the police and been found out by his gang. It's an underworld punishment. Rather gruesome. You swipe a long knife crossways into a man's mouth and slice through both his cheeks."

She demonstrated with a sweep of her hand and a ghoulish look on her face. "He's marked for life, you understand?" she said. "It's clear for all to see that he has betrayed his own kind. Criminals are a charming bunch. Talking of criminals, there was another article in *The Times* this morning about your friend Mark Goodenough's family."

"Any news?" James asked.

"It didn't say much more than what you'd already told me. They're almost certain it was pirates. They've found the bodies of all the men, but still not the girl and her tutor. The fear is that they might have been taken for the white slave trade."

"I didn't think there were still pirates in the world," said James. "When I think of pirates I think of the Spanish Main, Captain Kidd, Blackbeard, and Long John Silver. . . ."

"Oh, as long as men have taken to the sea in boats there have been pirates," said Charmian. "And there always will be. We have a romantic notion of them, James, but in reality they are simple criminals, no different from any other burglar or thief, except that they're usually more ruthless and murderous. You will just have to hope, James, that you never come face-to-face with one outside of a picture book. . . ."

CHAPTER 6—THE SAILOR WHO FEARED THE SEA

The *Charon* was lifted by the heaving water, and then slammed down into a trough between two waves. The sea thumped against her hull and she shuddered like a dog shaking itself. On the bridge, Tree-Trunk looked out through the thick glass of the window, a cigar clenched between his teeth. The huge, tattooed Samoan was wearing a yellow oilskin and had a woman's fur hat jammed on top of his head.

This was the worst storm he'd seen in the Mediterranean for many years. The waves were fifteen to twenty feet high, and rain thrashed relentlessly down on to the surface of the water, tearing at it and throwing salt spray into the wind. All the color had been drained from the day; sea and sky were the same ugly slate gray. It was four in the afternoon but it was almost as dark as night. The temperature had dropped to winter levels.

All in all, it was a filthy day.

Another wave reared up and the vessel turned into it, sending a wall of water crashing over her bows.

To an ordinary man the churning sea would have seemed to be a formless mass, but the Samoan could read shapes in it. He had learned to paddle a canoe when he was four years old and had signed on to the crew of a whaling ship when he was eleven. Salt water was in his veins. He understood the sea and could predict its furious movements. An even bigger wave took the ship now, and he braced himself as the *Charon* lurched beneath his feet, seeming to hang in midair for a moment before thudding down against a solid mass of water. Tree-Trunk made a small adjustment to the controls and shifted his cigar to the opposite corner of his mouth, all the while staring dead ahead. The gusting wind now changed direction, and rain whipped against the windows with a noise like rattling pebbles.

Tree-Trunk scratched his armpit and yawned. She could take it. The *Charon* was built to withstand anything the elements could hurl at her. She was small and tough and easily shouldered the storm, chugging resolutely through the boiling water. But they were making slow progress. Tree-Trunk had been standing here battling the storm for several hours, and it looked like he might be here for several more. As fast as they moved forward, they were battered back, and they would be using up a lot of fuel.

The noise of the wind was deafening as it howled all about the ship, drumming against her sides as if it were trying to get in. But beneath the cacophony the Samoan could hear the ship's engine steadily throbbing down below. And that was a very reassuring sound. From the outside, the *Charon* looked like a clapped-out old tramp steamer. But it was a deception. She was fitted with a fast and powerful steam turbine engine and could reach a top speed of thirty-five knots. The turbine had enough muscle to drive a vessel twice this size. The *Charon* may have looked fat and slow and solid, but she could outrun almost any other ship in the deep ocean.

There were footsteps on the iron stairs behind him, and Tree-Trunk glanced around to see Davey Day, the first mate, arriving in the wheelhouse looking pale and cold.

Davey peered out at the boiling sea and sniffed. "This is bad," he said.

"Stinking weather," said Tree-Trunk, and he spat onto the floor.

"How long now, d'you reckon?" asked Davey, shivering.

Tree-Trunk glanced briefly at the compass, bobbing and twisting in the binnacle. "It not good," he said. "We're into the weather all the way."

"Will we make Tunis before morning?" said Davey.

"No. And if it gets worse we'll have to put into Malta. Wait till it blows itself out," replied Tree-Trunk.

"Do you want to tell the boss, or shall I?" said Davey.

"I go," said Tree-Trunk. "You take the wheel."

Davey reluctantly took over, and Tree-Trunk clattered down the stairs belowdecks. He was almost too tall and too wide for the corridor, and bowled along it, bouncing off the sides and muttering dark curses under his breath.

When he reached the captain's door he knocked and barged in without waiting for a reply. Zoltan the Magyar was sitting at his table with the girl. His short blond hair was greasy, and his strange silvery gray eyes were filmed with moisture as if he might be about to burst into tears. He was sick. It was clear. Blood was seeping from his injured shoulder into his shirt.

Zoltan listened as Tree-Trunk explained their situation, but he didn't seem concerned.

"We press on," he said. "We've weathered worse than this."

Tree-Trunk nodded and left without saying anything.

Zoltan poured himself some thick red wine, steadying the cup with his feeble left hand.

His cabin was small and dark, lit by a wildly swinging oil lamp whose guttering flame was turned low. Down here the sound of the engine was very loud. It was like being inside a great beast, next to its beating heart.

Across the table from Zoltan sat Amy Goodenough. She was pale and unwashed, her dark eyes glinting feverishly in the half-light.

"Are you sure you won't join me?" said Zoltan, putting the bottle down in a rack. Amy said nothing; she merely shook her head with a tiny, almost imperceptible movement. She didn't want to accept anything from the man who had killed her father.

"When you are in the belly of a storm, the only thing to do is drink," said Zoltan, raising his glass. "Bull's Blood," he said. "You know why it is called this?"

Amy glared sullenly at him but didn't speak.

"I am going to tell you anyway," said Zoltan. "Times like this are made for stories." The ship keeled over and the two of them were thrown sideways. Zoltan automatically tried to brace himself with his bad arm, and gasped with the pain. "There was a great fight hundreds of years ago," he said, straightening up and raising his cup. "Between the Hungarians and the Turks. The Hungarians were weak and beaten, but their commander gave them wine and they were filled with the spirit of battle. The Turks run away, thinking the Hungarians must have drunk the blood of bulls to give them such strength." Zoltan laughed and winced, clutching his arm. Amy's knife had gone in between the collarbone and the shoulder blade, right into the joint, severing the tendons. A doctor in Istanbul had tried to repair the wound, but it had recently opened up again and now seemed to have become infected.

A girl had done this. A fourteen-year-old girl. She had a look of defiance about her that he admired, despite what she had done to him.

He laughed and clumsily lit a cigarette. "You think I'm an ogre, don't you, Amy?"

Still Amy said nothing.

"You know perhaps where your word 'ogre' comes from?"

Amy shook her head.

"From the word 'Magyar.'" He laughed again and took a gulp of wine. "We Hungarians are descended from the tribes that swept into Europe from the east. First the Huns and later the Magyars. We built castles everywhere. And we scared the living daylights out of everyone. We were ogres. In the fairy tales we grew huge, with giant teeth. We ate children! But the ogres were men like me. Magyars. So, yes, maybe I am an ogre. But I am still a man."

"Ha!" was all that Amy had to say. She was wearing a baggy shirt and trousers that had belonged to the smallest member of Zoltan's crew, and she hadn't changed them in weeks. They smelled sour and fit badly, but she was too exhausted to care. Ever since the attack on the *Siren* she felt like she had been walking through a dream.

Smuggling was Zoltan's main concern, rather than piracy, and for the past few weeks they had been crisscrossing the Mediterranean; first to Turkey, then to Cyprus and

Beirut, then Alexandria in Egypt, then back to Turkey. In each port Zoltan had unloaded some of his spoils and traded them for other goods: opium, hashish, wine, brandy, guns. But he had never unloaded Amy. Whenever they put in to a new port she was locked in a secret compartment in the hold with her tutor, Grace. The compartment was used for contraband and wasn't designed for the comfort of living people. There was no light and no portholes.

They had tried not to despair. Huddled together in the stifling heat, they fought to keep each other's spirits up, but each time they were sent below, Grace grew more miserable and scared.

Alexandria had been the worst. Amy had always dreamed of visiting Egypt, of seeing the pyramids and the Sphinx and the Temple of Karnak, but she had never dreamed that when she got there she would spend the time locked in darkness in a smuggler's hold. The heat had been extraordinary, and there was no sense of time or space down in the bottom of the ship. No sound even penetrated the walls of their hellish cell. The most awful part of it was not knowing what was going to happen to her. She had terrible black thoughts, but said nothing to Grace, who seemed close to giving up.

From Turkey they had crossed the Aegean to Athens, then steamed on to the ancient walled town of Otranto in the heel of Italy. And it was here that Zoltan had finally let Amy go ashore.

"Your teacher will stay on board," he had explained. "So that if you do anything foolish you know she will be punished."

"Not in the hold," Amy had pleaded. "You can't keep her in the hold again."

"All right. As long as she stays belowdecks."

Zoltan had led Amy up through the winding medieval streets of the city to see the cathedral. The whole of its floor was covered in an extraordinary mosaic showing the tree of life surrounded by strange animals and mythical creatures, but Zoltan wanted to show her something else. There was a small chapel off to one side, the walls of which were decorated with hundreds of yellow skulls and human bones.

"They are martyrs," he explained. "The city was attacked by corsairs—Muslim pirates. The eight hundred survivors were offered their lives if they converted to Islam. They refused and were beheaded. There are many things worth dying for, but God is not one of them."

"Why have you brought me here?" said Amy. She felt light-headed. The cathedral smelled of incense and burning candles, and there was a gloomy, oppressive atmosphere.

"I thought you would find it interesting," said Zoltan.

"It's horrible," Amy said angrily. "Why did you think I would like this? You are horrible. What do you want with me?"

"You are valuable, Amy," said Zoltan. "You will be useful to me."

"So I'm just like all the things you smuggle on your ship, am I?" said Amy. "An object to be bought and sold?"

"I have contacted your family to arrange a ransom," said Zoltan.

Amy didn't know what to say. She didn't know if she should be pleased by the news, with its hope of returning home, or upset that she was to be bartered.

"My grandfather won't pay," she said. "He will come after you. He will hunt you down and kill you."

"He would never find me," said Zoltan. "He wouldn't know where to start. The trail is very complicated. It will take time, but I will get my money. The first thing he will ask for is proof that I have you. What do you think I should send to him? A finger? An ear? The tip of your nose?"

"You're disgusting," said Amy, and Zoltan laughed.

"I was teasing you, Amy," he said. "I would not harm you. I like you. I want to talk with you. I am bored with the company of men. You are a civilized person. Talk to me."

And ever since then, at any available opportunity, Zoltan had brought Amy to his cabin, like today, and sat across his table from her, drinking wine and talking.

"I believe you were sent, Amy," he said. "You are my fate. Do you think maybe I am dying? Do you think you killed me after all, with your knife?"

"I hope so," Amy said, and Zoltan smiled.

"I am not scared of dying," he said. "I am not scared of anything—except the sea."

"The sea?" Amy said. Despite herself she was intrigued.

"Yes. When I think of you, Amy, I think of you coming out of the water like a mermaid. Like a sea sprite, sent to claim me. You are a spirit of the water, and I have always known that the sea would be my death."

"But you're a sailor," said Amy. "How can you be afraid of the sea?"

"A sailor should fear the sea," said Zoltan. "He should respect it."

"I love the sea," said Amy. "I love to swim in it."

"I can't swim," said Zoltan.

"You can't swim?"

"Oh . . . Many sailors can't swim. It is considered bad luck. Tempting to fate."

"But that's so dangerous," said Amy.

"The trick is not to fall in," said Zoltan, and for the first time in a long while, Amy smiled.

"I will never swim," Zoltan went on. "I fight the sea. I have mastered the sea. I sail my boat upon it, and I will not put myself into its mouth. The sea is for the fish, for crabs and lobsters and squid. I never even saw the sea until I was sixteen. I had left my farm to join the army of the Austro-Hungarian Empire. The whole world was at war. I was sent to the Italian front, but I soon realized that it was stupid. Our young men fought the young Italian men, and for what? To try to win back some land that the Italians said was theirs and we said was ours. It was nothing to do with me. I had no stomach for it. I ran away and made my way down through Albania into Greece, where I fell in with criminals, smugglers, pirates, murderers and deserters. In the chaos of war there are many opportunities for a clever man. I soon had my own ship, after the captain fell overboard and sadly drowned."

"Fell, or was pushed?" said Amy.

"He was old and weak," said Zoltan. "I simply put him out of his misery like a sick dog. And one day, if I get too old and weak, I am sure that one of my crew would do the same to me. That is why I keep on, Amy. That is why I will not take to my bed and let your wound have the better of me. My men must not see me sick." He stopped and poured himself more wine. "I am hoping, though," he said after a while, "that I will not grow old on this boat. Soon I will be rich enough to leave this life behind me and buy land and a fine house and settle down."

"You think my grandfather will pay that much for me?" Amy scoffed.

"It is not only you," said Zoltan. "It is everything I have in my hold below. Don't you worry, it is all planned. Once we get to Sardinia everything will be different."

The tower had stood there for three thousand years. Built from massive blocks of black stone, some over six feet long. How the ancients had got them here and piled them on top of each other, James couldn't imagine. There was something of the mystery of Stonehenge about the place.

"It is known as the Sant'Antine Nuraghe," said Peter Love-Haight, with a dramatic sweep of his hand. "We don't know a great deal about the Nuraghic people who built these towers, or for that matter, why they built them. The most obvious answer is that they were castles of some sort, built for defense against the many invaders who used to plague this island. But they may have had a religious significance. There are over seven thousand of them here in Sardinia, and this is one of the largest and most impressive. The main tower used to be three stories high, some seventy feet, but a local mayor removed the top layer to build a fountain in the nineteenth century."

They were in the Valle dei Nuraghi—the Valley of the Nuraghis—a wide, volcanic plain, baking under the burning sun. It was studded with the cones of long-dead volcanoes, and as James looked more closely, he realized that there were several more of these mysterious ruined towers dotted about the valley like broken teeth.

They had left Dover five days ago, crossed the Channel by ferry, then traveled by train down to Genoa in northern Italy, where they had boarded a steamer for Sardinia.

A bus had been waiting for them in the port of Terranova, manned by a burly, dark-skinned Sardinian called Quintino, who was to be their driver and guide.

The had driven westward across the island to Torralba, through countryside that was wild and open, with not a building in sight. Its only inhabitants were flocks of sheep and goats being looked after by craggy shepherds in sleeveless sheepskin jackets.

They had settled down for the night in a local school, sleeping on army-issue camp beds under dusty mosquito nets. This morning they had driven out to the Neolithic site, which was looked after by a gnomelike man wearing the traditional local costume of loose-sleeved white shirt, black waistcoat, full white trousers bound tightly below the knees with black gaiters, and a wide belt with a sort of short black skirt, or apron hanging below it. On his head he wore a black stocking cap. He had folded the long flap, which would normally have dangled down his back, forward over his forehead so that it shielded his eyes from the fierce sun.

The site was dominated by the huge central tower, but clustered around it, and encircled by a low drystone wall, were the ruins of what looked like a whole village of small houses and huts, mostly circular in design.

Haight explained that the boys would be helping to excavate a roped-off patch of land outside the wall, digging in the dirt with small trowels and sifting it with sieves. A makeshift canvas awning had been erected among the thistles and corn stalks, and underneath it were two long tables. Haight showed them the various artifacts that had been unearthed so far—fragments of pottery and a small bronze figurine.

"These bits and pieces have been buried under the ground for centuries," he said, delicately turning a piece of broken pot in his hands. "I don't expect we'll dig up anything that will shake the world, but I wanted to give you boys a taste of what archaeology is all about."

A serious young man from the local museum was supervising, sweating heavily in a dark suit. He seemed nervous and slightly miserable, obviously worried that the clumsy boys would damage something.

As James bent down for a closer look at one of the objects, somebody gave him a shove from behind, and he sprawled across the table, knocking over the figurine.

The museum curator tutted, and James spun around angrily.

Just as he had expected, he saw the grinning face of Tony Fitzpaine.

Fitzpaine was the arrogant, aristocratic youth James had knocked into the river after Haight's lecture to the Archaeological Society. Finding out that Fitzpaine was on the trip had been something of a shock to James, and ever since confronting him on the Channel ferry, Fitzpaine had gone out of his way to get up James's nose.

James let it go, and chose to ignore him. It was too hot to risk getting worked up about anything.

Haight told the boys to be more careful and organized them into three work parties.

For a couple of hours James helped out, kneeling in the

dirt alongside Perry Mandeville, and as he worked his mind was free to think.

Last night, as he'd been unpacking his suitcase, he'd found a letter. Charmian had stuffed it into his pocket when he was leaving her cottage, and in his excitement he had forgotten all about it.

He'd sat down on his camp bed, slit the envelope open, and taken out an untidily folded sheet of notepaper. He'd recognized the handwriting immediately: thin and slanting and spidery, it was from Mr. Merriot, his classical tutor at Eton.

Dear James,

Forgive me for writing to you in the holidays, old chap. I'm sure the last thing you want to be thinking about right now is school, but I thought you might be interested in this. You asked me in private business the other day if the Roman numerals MM held any significance. At the time I could think of nothing, but last night I was having dinner with my colleague Mr. Cooper-ffrench. I don't think he's forgotten about meeting your formidable aunt, by the way!

Our conversation turned to Roman history, as it so often does with Cooper-ffrench, and he mentioned a secret Italian society known as the Millenaria.

If you'll permit me a short history lesson, I'll fill you in on some of the background. While we teach a great deal about the ancient Romans, there's very little room left in your poor aching noodles for more recent Italian history. But, to be brief, a hundred years ago there was no country called Italy, as such. That is to say, the area we now know as Italy was made up of various rival city-states, many of them governed by foreign rulers. Then, in the first half of the nineteenth century, a nationalist movement sprang up. The idea was to unite the land into one country and boot out all the foreigners.

Well, the Italians have always been fond of secret societies and spies and skulduggery, so rather than simply form an army, the nationalists created a great number of underground groups instead, whose aim was to spread the word about unification and generally stir things up. Most of it came to nothing until, with the help of a great general called Garibaldi, a movement called the Risorgimento eventually succeeded in uniting the whole country in the 1870s. They created what we now know as Italy, under one king—Victor Emmanuel of Sardinia (where you're off to, I believe).

But, for some Italians, that wasn't enough. Why stop there? they argued. Rome had once ruled the entire known world. Could it not do so again? The unification of Italy was only the beginning; the ultimate aim should be the rebuilding of the entire Roman Empire.

So another secret society was formed—the Millenaria—and they set about plotting and planning and scheming and spying.

Come along, you old duffer, get on with it, I hear you cry! What has this to do with the two M's? Well, the secret symbol of the Millenaria was a double M, standing for two thousand years. I have tried to drum some knowledge of Latin and Roman history into you, so perhaps you may recall that Julius Caesar was born in 100 bc. And he was the greatest of all Romans and father of the Roman Empire, and therefore a suitable figurehead for a cult dedicated to reminding the world of the glories of ancient Rome. MM. Two thousand years.

Well, two thousand years after Caesar's birth, 1900, was the year the Millenaria launched their campaign. Over the next few years there were some skirmishes, much shouting and waving of hands, but not a lot really happened. The one notable incident was when one of their number stole the Mona Lisa from the Louvre and tried to return it to Italian hands. Then war broke out and Italy was caught up in the monstrous events of 1914. After the war the Millenaria were all but forgotten, and Signor Mussolini and his fascists took control. Some say that remnants of the Millenaria helped him gain power; certainly some of his ideas and style were borrowed from them. However, if they did help him, Mussolini soon got rid of them. He would have had no desire to share his power with anyone else.

And now Mussolini has declared himself a sort of Roman emperor and has designs on the rest of the world!

I think your aunt was right, James. The ancient Romans are not a great role model. They had an unhealthy lust for power and glory and bloodshed.

I hope this may be of some interest to you. As I say, please forgive the history lesson, but I thought it might answer your question. . . .

* * *

James had smiled when he'd first read the letter last night. It was kind of Mr. Merriot to write to him, but there was little chance that an obscure Italian secret society that had died out years ago could have anything to do with the nondescript house with the ivy-clad courtyard and the scarred man with an *M* tattooed on either hand.

But on the back of the letter was a hastily scribbled addition:

> *P.S.: You might like to know that the Millenaria*
> *spoke Latin in all their secret meetings and proposed it*
> *as a new world language, hence Mr. Cooper-ffrench's*
> *interest in them. As you know, he would have us all*
> *speaking Latin!*

Now, sweltering under the sun that hammered down out of a clear blue sky, James was turning over in his mind the few parts of the puzzle that he had, seeing if they would fit together. He felt like an archaeologist trying to piece together some random bits of broken pottery.

There were the two shadowy figures speaking Latin in the courtyard. The crates with the stenciled letters. The weird chapel with the bowl of blood and the cockerel's head. The dropped bracelet. The scarred man talking to Mr. Cooper-ffrench behind the shutters.

The pieces didn't fit together. James couldn't make anything resembling a pot out of them. Why would a secret Italian society have a base in Eton? It didn't make any sense.

As the day wore on and the sun climbed higher in the

sky, James began to feel dizzy and overheated. There was no shade where they were digging, and the dirt clung to the sweat on his body. He had unearthed nothing more interesting all morning than some sharp basalt rocks and an ants' nest. He eventually stood up, removed the straw hat he had been given, shook a spray of sweat from his hair, and chucked his trowel to the ground.

"What's up?" said Perry. "Not enjoying being a road digger?"

"This isn't quite what I was expecting," said James. His mouth was full of sticky saliva, and he realized he hadn't had anything to drink since breakfast.

He sat down and suddenly the sun was blotted out by a boy.

James squinted up at the familiar silhouette of Tony Fitzpaine.

"Don't think I've forgotten about you," said Fitzpaine sneeringly. "I'm just waiting for the right moment. I must say I'm very glad you came on this trip, Bond. Away from Eton and the beaks, you've nowhere to hide. You'd better watch your back, pleb."

"Go away, Fitzpaine," said James. "I'm not interested."

"Don't think you can speak to me like that," said Fitzpaine, and James laughed.

"How do you want me to speak to you, Your Majesty?" he said.

"Your name is going to be mud at Eton," spluttered the older boy.

"Is it really?" said James. "Well, I shall have to live with that. But, as you say, we're not at Eton now, Fitzpaine." James stood up and confronted the other boy. "We're not even in England. Your name means nothing here. We're just two boys in the middle of a very hot island in the Mediterranean . . . So maybe it's *you* who should be watching his back."

"Are you threatening me?" said Fitzpaine.

"Yes," said James. "I think I probably am."

James smiled at Fitzpaine and strode off to look for something to drink.

He found a big canteen under the canvas awning with some warm water in the bottom of it. He tipped some into his mouth and swilled it around before swallowing.

"Hot enough for you?" Haight strolled into the shade from out of the harsh sunlight carrying his shoulder bag.

"I had to get out of the sun," said James.

"We'll pack up for the day soon," said Haight, wiping his face with a handkerchief. "A couple of hours of this is about all anyone can take."

He put his bag down on the table. It went everywhere with him and contained everything needed on the trip: all the official documents, the first-aid kit, charts and plans of the different Nuraghic sites, and several rolled-up canvases for sketching on. Since leaving England he hadn't let the bag out of his sight. He removed a map from it and unfolded it on the table.

"This is wild country," he said. "Bandit country."

"Really?" said James, looking at the map.

"Yes," said Haight. "See these villages here?" He showed James two or three villages on the map, and then pointed down the valley. James made out the shapes of distant stone buildings clinging to the sides of the surrounding mountains.

"Those places are very difficult to get to and almost impossible to attack," said Haight. "The people up there have never really been tamed. Italy was united during the last century, but the heart of Sardinia is a country unto itself."

"I was reading a bit about that last night, actually," said James, recalling Merriot's letter. "I wonder, sir have you ever heard of a secret Italian society called the Millenaria?"

"Secret society, eh?" said Haight. "Can't say that I have. Why?"

"It's just . . . Do you remember that bracelet, sir?"

"What bracelet?" said Haight, frowning.

"You remember, it was after your talk. I found it on the floor. You were going to ask Mister Cooper-ffrench if it belonged to him."

"My word, you've got a good memory. I must confess I'd forgotten all about it." Haight searched in his bag and took out another map. "I did get round to showing it to Cooper-ffrench," he went on, "and he said it was nothing to do with him. I put it in a drawer somewhere in my rooms. It's probably still sitting there. I don't think it's valuable, James. I wouldn't worry too much about it."

"No . . . It's just the symbol on it," said James. "The double *M*."

"That's right. I remember," said Haight. "I thought it might be someone's initials. But I racked my brains to think of an *MM*. I came to the conclusion that it must have been lying there on the floor for some time before you spotted it. But you've lost me, I'm afraid. What's this got to do with this secret society of yours?"

"The double *M*, sir; that's the sign of the Millenaria."

Haight laughed. "You'll be telling me next that you think they've a hideout in Eton and they're plotting to kidnap the new Head Master and set up Mussolini in his place!"

James laughed too, now. The whole idea did seem faintly ridiculous.

"I wouldn't have thought anything of it," he said. "Except, one day in Eton I saw a man with an *M* tattooed on each hand."

"*M* for mother, probably," said Haight. "What did he look like? Was he a strange masked figure with an assassin's dagger?"

"No . . . . But he was quite distinctive. He had scars on both his cheeks."

"Well, well," said Haight, rolling up his maps. "I never knew Eton was such an exciting place."

James picked up the canteen and put it to his lips, but only a tiny trickle of water came out, and he put it down thirstier than before.

"Here, have some of mine." Haight put his maps back in his bag and rummaged about for a moment before producing a water bottle.

"You've got everything in there, haven't you?" said James.

"It certainly feels that way when I have to lug it about the place," said Haight.

James took a drink. The water was salty and bitter.

"Don't be put off by the taste," said Haight, smiling. "I always use water-purifying tablets. You can't be too careful out here." He took the bottle from James and replaced the stopper. "Now then, if you've had enough of digging, why don't you take yourself off and explore the tower? It'll be nice and cool in there."

"Thank you, sir," said James. "I'd like that."

"It was bashed about a bit by the Carthaginians in the fifth century B.C.," said Haight, "but I think it would have taken their whole army to knock it down. Quite extraordinary. You know, they didn't use any cement or mortar to stick the stones together. They were simply cut to shape and placed one on top of the other. The builders must have known exactly what they were doing, though, because it's still here after all this time. Have a good look inside. And the view from the top is magnificent. I'll see you when you get back down to terra firma."

James strolled back out into the sunlight and made his way across the site. As he neared the tower he saw that it was surrounded by a raised terrace supported by three lower towers in a triangular shape.

He found the entrance in the massive outer wall and went inside to a courtyard with a ruined well in its center. There were doors leading off from here into the various towers. He chose one at random and passed through a circular room into the darkness on the other side. He was momentarily blind as his eyes adjusted, but eventually saw that he was in a long corridor of gigantic stones whose sloping sides met at the roof. He shuffled forward. The place was confusing and utterly unlike anywhere he had ever visited before. It seemed to have walls within walls. He groped his way around in the cool darkness until he found himself in a windowless domed chamber, some twenty feet wide by twenty feet tall. This must be the heart of the monument, the base of the main tower. There was a square of dazzling white light in the doorway, but very little of it penetrated this deep. He could see, though, that the black volcanic rocks were tinged with red, almost like rust, and he imagined for a moment that the tower was built of iron rather than stone. It was eerily quiet and he had the weird feeling that he had traveled back in time to somewhere truly prehistoric. He felt unnerved, as if these ancient stones held the ghosts of the long-dead people who had lived here. The outside world, the modern world, seemed a long way away. A wave of sickness struck him and the room started to spin. He thought he heard voices, but it could just have been the blood roaring in his ears. He closed his eyes and rested his forehead against a wall to cool it.

He had a sudden horrible image of blood congealing in a bowl and snapped his eyes open. The room was full of people. They were wearing primitive robes and had dark watchful faces. Some carried glinting knives. He shrank away from them, and as he felt the stones press into his back he realized that it was an illusion and he was merely seeing shapes in the black walls of the chamber. He felt desperately tired and light-headed, and wanted more than anything else to get back out into the fresh air, but he couldn't face stepping into that square of harsh white light. The very thought gave him a headache.

There were four other exits leading to a corridor that ran around the outside of the chamber and a staircase that spiraled up to the next floor. He climbed it and found three smaller rooms. Then he carried on up to what was now the top of the tower and stepped, blinking, into the light.

A vulture hung in the air overhead, the feathers in its wingtips like long black fingers against the sky. James watched as it wheeled and glided away toward the dusty blue hills at the horizon.

He took a deep breath, but it didn't help. The air burned his lungs and he still felt woozy.

He heard footsteps and walked to the edge to look down. Fifty feet below was the courtyard with the well, and James had the weird sensation that he was staring into a bottomless black hole. He felt out of control, as if the floor might crumble beneath his feet, and he had a terrible urge to throw himself off. He fought it and swayed giddily, spots dancing before his eyes. His vision blurred and swam, and there was a singing in his ears.

He thought he might faint and for a moment didn't know where he was.

The feeling slowly passed, and as his vision slid back into focus, he realized he was looking down at someone. They were staring back at him with red, angry, bloodshot eyes, a look of intense disgust on their features.

James thought he must be imagining it. It was another illusion.

The face belonged to Cooper-ffrench; the purple complexion and mean little mustache were unmistakable. But it couldn't be . . .

It wasn't possible that he was here.

James felt hypnotized by the man, as if he were willing him to jump. He felt like he was going to vomit, and he staggered forward until he was right at the edge of the tower. The singing in his ears rose in pitch, up and up and up. . . .

He closed his eyes and sensed a movement behind him, something rushing toward him.

Cooper-ffrench called out his name, and the sound seemed to pop and spin off into space with a noise like a firework.

James tipped forward.

And he was falling, down, down, down into that black abyss. . . .

CHAPTER 8—ESCAPE

James woke to find the sun in his eyes and Peter Haight wiping his face with a damp handkerchief, a concerned look on his face.

"Are you all right, old chap?" he said, when he saw that James was conscious.

"I think so," James croaked. His mouth and throat felt painfully dry, as if all the liquid had been drained out of him. He propped himself up on his elbows. "I'm sorry," he said. "I don't know what happened."

He looked around. He was still at the top of the tower, lying on the stone floor.

"It's lucky I grabbed hold of you," said Haight grimly. "You should be careful, standing so near to the edge; these old ruins aren't at all safe."

"I know. I felt unwell for a moment," said James. "I still don't feel quite right, sir."

Haight put his hand to James's forehead.

"You feel pretty hot, old chap."

James was just about to ask Haight for a drink, when the beak splashed the remaining contents of his water bottle onto his face. "That should feel better," he said, helping James to his feet. "Now, let's get you down, eh?"

James was very wobbly and Haight had to stop him from

84

falling over again. James shook his head and let Haight support him as they descended the winding staircase. Halfway down they met Cooper-ffrench coming up. He was sweating even more than he had been before and looked flustered.

"Is he all right?" he said.

"Nothing damaged," said Haight, "but I want to get him down and into the shade. Touch of sunstroke I imagine."

Cooper-ffrench followed them outside and across the site to the canvas awning. A small group of curious boys clustered round asking questions, but Haight shooed them away. James sat down. He was horribly tired and his stomach felt light and fluttery. He thought that at any moment he might be sick.

"You shouldn't have been up there by yourself," said Cooper-ffrench.

James remembered Cooper-ffrench's angry look from the courtyard. "Why did you shout?" he said. "You called out my name."

Cooper-ffrench glanced nervously at Peter Haight. "I was trying to warn you," he said. "You looked . . . you looked like you might fall."

"Yes," said James. "I felt giddy for a moment."

"The main thing is that you're all right, old man," said Haight. "I wouldn't want to lose one of my charges."

"The main thing is that it doesn't happen again," said Cooper-ffrench bruskly.

"Leave him be, John," Haight snapped. "The boy's had quite a scare."

"Yes, well . . ." Cooper-ffrench muttered and walked off, mopping the back of his neck with a grubby cloth.

That evening, back at Torralba, James was getting ready for bed in the school hall when Haight approached him with a cup of strong tea.

"Feeling more yourself now, lad?"

"Yes, thank you, sir," said James. "Much better."

"Care for a cuppa?"

"No, thank you, sir, I don't drink tea."

"Can I get you anything else?"

"No, I'm really all right, sir. It's passed. I don't know what came over me. I think it was seeing Mister Cooper-ffrench like that; it gave me quite a shock."

"He does have that effect," said Haight, and they both laughed. "Gave me quite a shock, too, as matter of fact. I didn't know he'd arrived yet."

"But what's he doing here?" asked James.

"Apparently Eton regulations state that you must have at least two staff members along on these jaunts. I had no idea. I'm still fairly new to the school, so I'm not quite on top of all the rules."

"I know what you mean," said James.

"Just before we were due to leave, he announced that he was going to come with us," said Haight. "But he could only get a later ticket. I can't say I'm totally upset that he's here. I thought I was going to have sole charge of you lot. It's always useful to have another pair of hands to help out. His main interest is in the Roman history, of which there's quite a lot on the island. The Sardinians speak a version of Italian that's much closer to its Roman origins than what's spoken in the rest of Italy. *Domus* for house, for instance, instead of the Italian *casa*."

James wondered whether to say anything more to Haight about the Millenaria, or would it just make him look foolish? He didn't have much to go on, and even if Mr. Cooper-ffrench *was* somehow connected to the secret society, did it really matter?

Haight hadn't been particularly interested before, so James decided that from now on he'd keep his mouth shut. He knew one thing for certain, however: coming on this trip had been a mistake. Here he was, miles from Eton, and he was still surrounded by masters and boys.

He had to get away.

He borrowed some notepaper from Perry and dashed off a letter to his cousin Victor, asking if he could come to stay with him sooner than they had arranged.

Four days later, when they arrived in the small town of Abbasanta to visit the Losa Nuraghe, yet another ruined stone tower, there was a reply waiting for James at their guest house. He ripped the envelope open and read the letter anxiously, but he needn't have worried: it was the response he had been hoping for.

That night Haight took all the boys out to a restaurant for a treat. There was a raucous, holiday atmosphere. Haight was drinking the strong local wine, and he had even persuaded the stuffy Cooper-ffrench to take a glass.

"I can't believe you're jumping ship, you m-mountebank." Perry was sitting next to James, stuffing long coils of pasta into his mouth and talking at the same time.

"It's Cooper-ffrench," said James. "Ever since the other day in Sant'Antine he's attached himself to me like an over-protective dog. I'm sick of the sight of him: his fat, red face, his bristling little mustache—"

"The huge black stains under his armpits," added Perry.

"Exactly," said James.

He couldn't get out of his mind the image of the man staring up at him from the courtyard at Sant'Antine, with that murderous look on his face. He still had the feeling that somehow Cooper-ffrench had been trying to will him toward the edge of the tower. Was it because James had seen him with the tattooed man in Eton?

No. James had never spoken to him about that.

But he had spoken to Mr. Merriot, and Mr. Merriot had discussed the Millenaria with Cooper-ffrench. And it must have been shortly after that when Cooper-ffrench announced that he wanted to come on the trip to Sardinia.

Well, whatever the reason for him being here, James was very soon going to be getting away from him.

"You can't leave m-me with the dread Fitzpaine," Perry complained. "He gets worse every day. The chap's a m-monster!"

"Just ignore him," said James. "I've learned not to be pushed around by boys who think they're something more than they really are."

"It's all right for you," said Perry. "You can look after yourself." He stopped eating for a moment and raised his head from his plate. "What does old Love-Haight think about you jumping ship?" he said.

"I haven't told him yet," said James. "I've been waiting for the right moment."

"No time like the present," said Perry, and before James

could stop him, he bellowed down the length of the table, "I say, James Bond's had enough! He's leaving us in the lurch."

Cooper-ffrench's ears pricked up. "What's that?" he said.

"I'm still feeling a little odd, sir," James lied. "I'm leaving the trip early. I have a cousin in the north of the island. I shall be staying with him for the rest of the holidays."

"This is not acceptable," said Cooper-ffrench, who looked slightly panicked.

"But it was always understood that I wouldn't be staying on for the whole three weeks," said James.

Before Cooper-ffrench could respond to this, Haight interrupted. "That was the arrangement," he said.

"I knew nothing about it," protested Cooper-ffrench.

"It was decided before you joined us," said Haight. "I spoke to James's aunt before we left." Haight turned to James. "But you're leaving much sooner than I thought," he said. "You'll miss out on a lot." He looked a little disappointed.

"Tell me about this cousin," said Cooper-ffrench. "Is he respectable?"

"He's an engineer," said James, "or at least he used to be. He's retired now, I think. He's a lot older than me. He paints."

"Really?" said Haight. "Is he well known?"

"I don't think so. He just paints for fun."

"We are rather straying from the point here," said Cooper-ffrench.

"Oh, come on, John," said Haight, and he laughed. "I'm just trying to find out a little about Bond's cousin."

"His whole house is stuffed with paintings, apparently,"

said James. "And a famous Italian artist lives there with him, Polly something—"

"Not Poliponi?" said Haight.

"Yes," said James. "Have you heard of him?"

"I'll say. Interesting chap." Haight smiled. "You are full of surprises, Bond. Imagine your cousin knowing one of the most famous artists in the world."

"I've seen some of this Poliponi man's work," said Cooper-ffrench. "And, quite frankly, it's disgusting. But if that was the arrangement, I shan't interfere. I still don't like the idea of James just flitting off like this when he was supposed to be on an educational trip, however."

"Well, he could always write us an essay all about it!" said Haight, and he laughed.

"That's an excellent idea," said Cooper-ffrench.

"It was supposed to be a joke, actually," said Haight quietly.

"Bond," said Cooper-ffrench, ignoring the other master, "I will need all your cousin's details: his full name and address, and so on and so forth. You will write me a letter as soon as you get there, letting us know that you have safely arrived. Then you will send us a thousand-word essay telling us all about that part of the island, your cousin's villa, and so on. You can send it to us in Cagliari. Then we'll know that you won't have been idle."

James and Haight exchanged looks, and Haight raised his eyebrows before quickly disguising his expression as Cooper-ffrench looked up at him.

James smiled, glad that he had an ally.

He sat back in his chair and crossed his legs, pulling his

right ankle up onto his left thigh, the position he always adopted when he felt at his most relaxed. He was getting away from all this. And he could stop worrying about Cooper-ffrench and his possible connections to the Millenaria. From now on the summer would be his to enjoy.

James's cousin Victor lived in the far north of Sardinia, where the Straits of Bonifacio separated the island from Corsica. The nearest town was Palau, and the journey there by train and bus took the best part of a day.

James arrived in Palau with a splitting headache, hot and tired, and in need of a wash. There was dust everywhere: on his clothes, under his clothes, in his mouth and ears. Even his eyes felt gritty.

Palau seemed to consist of little more than a miserable, dusty street of single-storied houses washed a grubby pink. There was a dilapidated, dirty inn, where a group of local men were eating octopus, and nearby two other old men slept on stone benches. It felt like the end of the world.

James waited in the shade of a tree for over an hour, and it felt as if time was standing still. A lizard darted out from under a stone and ran over his shoe. The men in the inn stared at him. The two old peasants snored on their benches. Flies buzzed. The sun shone.

James put his head in his hands and let out a long, slow breath, feeling it burning down the front of his shirt.

He waited for a few minutes longer, then took his suitcase and walked to the edge of town. He looked up the road. He could see nothing. He wiped sweat from his face. His throat was dry. His clothes stuck to him and he was sore where they had been rubbing. The heated air felt solid, pressing down on him.

Gradually he became aware of a sound, a far-off engine noise, as of a motor car approaching. He didn't dare raise his hopes and imagine that it might be Victor. He stood, squinting into the fierce sunlight, and at last saw, coming down the hillside, the black shape of a car.

He smiled. It must be Victor. The car looked big and expensive. But as it grew nearer his heart sank. It was being driven by a boy, a local boy by the look of him, with olive skin and thick black hair. He appeared to be about sixteen and was wearing sunglasses that completely hid his eyes.

This couldn't be Victor, who was at least fifty, with fair hair.

The car was a Hispano-Suiza Cabriolet, long and powerful, with wide running boards. It was a deep maroon color but was so covered in dust it looked almost white. This was a rich man's car and seemed totally out of place in this squalid, flyblown little town. When it drew level with James it stopped, and the boy sat staring at him with a sullen, bored look.

James looked back, holding his stare, unblinking, and after a while the boy turned his head and spat into the road. Then he said something in a thick Italian accent.

"I beg your pardon?" said James, and the boy repeated what he had said. James suddenly realized that he was saying his name.

"James Bond? Yes," said James. "Has Victor sent you? Victor Delacroix?"

The boy nodded and jerked his head back, indicating

that James should put his luggage in the tiny backseat. James tossed it in.

"You're late," he said. "I've been waiting here for over an hour."

The boy just shrugged and threw the passenger door open without looking round.

James climbed in, and with a crunch of gears, the boy turned the car around and set off back up the road.

"Well, better late than never, I suppose," said James, trying to break the ice, but the boy didn't reply. "I'm sorry," said James irritably. "Maybe you don't speak English."

"Little," the boy grunted.

"And do you have a name? A name . . . ? What—is—your—name?"

"Mauro."

"Well, Mauro, I'm pleased to meet you . . . I suppose."

Mauro muttered something but kept his eyes fixed on the road ahead, driving with one hand on the wheel. His other hand draped nonchalantly over the side of the car.

They left town and veered off the road onto a rutted dirt track that followed the cliffs around the coast to the east. It was wild scenery here, with outcrops of twisted, honey-colored granite that had been carved by the winds into dramatic shapes. James kept a lookout for the landmark that gave this area its name. After ten minutes of uncomfortable jostling and shaking, he spotted, high up on top of a promontory, a wind-eroded rock that must surely be it.

"Is that Bear Rock?" he shouted over the noise of the engine, but Mauro said nothing. "*Orso*," said James. "Bear."

"*Sì*," said Mauro without looking up. James peered at the

rock and, with a little imagination, he found that it did indeed resemble a huge bear on all fours peering out to sea.

This, then, was Capo d'Orso, the Cape of the Bear.

Mauro steered the Hispano-Suiza off the dirt track onto an even more primitive trail, which wound its way over rocks and stones between the scrubby vegetation down the side of the hill toward the sea. The car swayed wildly from side to side and James was bounced out of his seat. He began to wonder whether they would make it at all, but Mauro must have driven this way many times before and didn't seem at all fazed, although James noticed that he now had both hands on the wheel.

When they at last arrived, James felt like they had been driving for hours. He was stiff and bruised and caked with dust, and the back of his neck felt burned.

Mauro parked the car under the shade of some umbrella pines, switched off the engine, and got out. Then he grabbed James's suitcase and strode off without saying anything. James shook his head and followed him down a flight of winding steps cut into the rock. As they came around a corner, they arrived at a large open doorway set into a short white wall. James could see little more of the building, which nestled, hidden, among the rocks. He could see enough, though, to tell him that it didn't follow the lines of an ordinary house and appeared almost to have grown out of the landscape.

Through the door was a long snaking corridor, which twisted and turned as it led deeper into the villa.

They came out into an unexpectedly large room with an

undulating curved roof and a wide sweep of floor-to-ceiling windows that led out onto a terrace.

The room was neither square nor circular; like the rest of the building it was organic in design, with odd little hidden corners and holes cut into the walls of all shapes and sizes, some leading to the outside, others to rooms within the villa itself.

If the room was unusual, what was in it was extraordinary. It was filled with paintings and statues and odd, incongruous objects. The paintings were unsettling and nightmarish. One gigantic canvas took up almost all of one wall—it showed an octopus floating in the air, crushing various objects in its tentacles: naked women, an animal that looked like a hairless cow, and a car that seemed some-how fleshy and alive. Then there was a bronze statue that consisted of nothing more than the lower half of a man, wearing trousers, and standing next to it was a stuffed giraffe whose neck went up through a hole in the ceiling. Another painting showed a woman with no face stabbing a crucifix into a human-sized beetle. The largest fish tank James had ever seen held a variety of exotic fish swimming in and out of a pile of animal skulls.

James suddenly realized that he had lost sight of Mauro, who had gone off with his suitcase down one of the several corridors that radiated from the room. He tried one, but it opened into a small inner courtyard, where a seminaked young man with a shaved head was posing in front of a mir-ror. James wasn't sure whether he might not be real at first, and wondered whether it might not be another of the strange art objects that filled the place. But then the man moved. He picked up an iron bar with weights on either end. He looked at James without saying anything as he lifted the bar above his head, his sharply defined muscles bulging.

"Sorry," James mumbled and backed out. Not knowing which way to go and feeling slightly unnerved, he wandered outside onto the terrace.

The view from here was stunning. Past the polished granite rocks, dotted with prickly pear, he could see the sparkling turquoise ocean and a group of nearby islands.

"Hello."

James heard a soft voice and turned around. Standing there was a man wearing a long, loose Moroccan robe and curly, pointed gold slippers. He was small and slight, his skin tanned a deep nut brown, and he had a curly mustache and pointed beard. His oily hair had been teased into what looked like two horns on either side of his head so that he resembled some sort of devil.

This was not cousin Victor.

CHAPTER 9—LA CASA POLIPO

The man was staring at James intently with gleaming, brown eyes.

"James Bond . . . ?" he said in a thick Italian accent.

"Yes," said James, and the man advanced on him and fixed him with his gaze, looking deep into his eyes.

"James Bond. Such an English name. Such a boring name. A dull, blunt name. Like a stone. But you," he said, "you hide behind your name. You are not boring. You are interesting." He paused, then said quickly, "Imagine a number, James Bond."

"I'm sorry, what do you mean?"

"Close your eyes and think of nothing else," said the little man. "Only a number. Not higher than ten. Do not tell me what it is. Hold it in your mind, deep in your mind. This is your special number. Do you have it?"

"Yes," said James.

"I know it," said the man, widening his eyes.

"Okay," said James. "What is it?"

"It is seven."

James smiled. "That's right. How did you guess?"

"I did not guess . . . I know you. Seven is your number; it will be a very important number for you in your life. Seven is the luckiest of numbers. There are seven deadly sins. Seven wonders of the world. Seven archangels—"

"Seven dwarfs," said James.

"What?"

"In the fairy tale. 'Snow White and the Seven Dwarfs.' Or the number seven bus. In Kent, where I live."

"Ah . . ." the man thought for a while, studying James with an unnervingly steady gaze. Finally he spoke. "You fascinate me, James Bond. You have the mark of death upon you."

"I beg your pardon."

"I can see it. Seven is also the number of Death. I see you and I see the number seven and the figure of Death. Death will walk by your side through your life."

"If you say so." James smiled politely and wondered how he could get away from this strange little man.

"I do say so," the man murmured. "But there is more . . . Death is following you. Somebody is trying to kill you; he wants you dead. I see a tower. I see—"

"Stop that, Poliponi!"

There was a shout from the house and James turned to see his cousin Victor coming out. He also was dressed in a Moroccan robe, which looked incongruous, matched, as it was, with a battered old straw hat perched on his head. He was smoking a long yellow cigarette, and was almost as tanned as the satanic artist. He had grown his hair long, and it was tied behind his neck, where it hung down in a loose mane, the blond locks streaked with gray.

"James, welcome!" he cried, and gave him a startling hug. "Forgive me. I am so sorry that I was not able to meet you myself at Palau." Victor spoke English impeccably, with only a slight Swiss accent. "I trust Mauro looked after you well."

"Yes," said James. "He was a little late, but it didn't matter."

"We have had some problems with the car. It was not designed for these rough conditions. I really ought to get something different, or go back to using a donkey!" He smiled. "Is your room all right?"

"I don't know," said James. "I lost Mauro. He seemed in a bad mood."

"Mauro is always in a bad mood," said Victor. "It is just his way. He is a bandit. From the Barbagia."

Before James could ask Victor what he meant, his cousin led him to a long wooden table under a shady vine. "Come," he said. "Have a drink."

Victor poured two glasses from a jug of iced fruit cocktail. "You mustn't worry about Poliponi," he said, passing a glass to James. "He likes to be mysterious, but it is all just an act. He has a reputation to maintain. The great surrealist. Painter of dreams. Reader of your inner fantasies. He has probably already done his number trick on you, I imagine?"

"Yes," said James.

"Seven," said Victor.

James grinned. "How did you know?"

"He always says seven. Most people, if you ask them to think of a number between one and ten, they think of seven. If they say another number he bamboozles them with some mumbo jumbo."

The two of them laughed, and James took a long sip of the cool drink. He couldn't quite believe he was here.

"He designed this house for me," said Victor. "La Casa

Polipo. And those are his paintings on the walls. He is probably a genius, but I would never tell him that. It would go to his already swollen head. So. We have arranged a feast in honor of your arrival for later, but first—do you want to go to your room and wash and rest, or down to the beach for a swim?"

"A swim, definitely," said James. "I've been looking at the sea all day, unable to dive in, and it's been driving me mad."

Just then, Mauro appeared, wearing swimming shorts and carrying a towel. Victor rattled off some Italian at him, and James saw the boy raise his eyes heavenward.

"Good," said Victor. "Mauro will show you to your room. You can get your costume, and then he will take you to the beach."

James would rather have gone alone. This moody Italian boy evidently didn't like him, but he was not going to let anything spoil his holiday.

Twenty miles away to the south, the harbor at Terranova, the main port of Sardinia, was busy. The stink of fish hung in the air, as fishing boats unloaded their catches. Men ran in all direction with trolleys, shouting. Great cones of salt stood everywhere, ready to be exported. Sardinia supplied most of the salt used in Italy, which was harvested from the salt marshes that dotted the island.

Zoltan the Magyar stood on the quayside, supervising, as several large, wooden crates were winched out of the hold of his ship, the *Charon*. He was wearing a wide-brimmed hat, and his bad arm was hanging in a sling, which was stained yellow and brown where blood and pus were leaking from his wounded shoulder. He swatted irritably at the flies that clustered around him, and coughed. The infection was in his throat and moving down to his lungs now. It felt as if acid flowed through his veins, and the itchy, crawling heat burned behind his eardrum.

Lying in bed at night, unable to sleep, he wanted to tear the side of his face open and pull the infected tubes from inside his head.

He didn't want to be standing out here where there was no shade, but his cargo was too precious to leave to anyone else.

He cursed as something bit his neck, and he finally lost all patience with the swarming flies, yelling and flailing his good arm like a wild man. Two crewmen up on deck stopped what they were doing and stared at him.

Was he signaling to them?

"What are you doing, you lazy idiots?" Zoltan screamed. "Get on with your work. I do not want to be out here a moment longer than I need to!"

There was a shout, and through the shimmering, heated air, Zoltan saw a figure approaching along the quayside. He instantly recognized the man's red hair and scarred face; it was Smiler.

He walked over, and the two men shook hands.

"You should wear a hat in this heat," said Zoltan. "Your white Scottish skin will burn."

"I know," said Smiler, and he wiped sweat off his forehead with a hand tattooed with a large red *M*. "But I'm not a big one for wearing hats."

Because of the long upturned scars on either side of his

mouth that had earned Smiler his nickname, Zoltan was never sure whether the man was really smiling or not. But he had known him long enough to realize that he probably wasn't.

"You're late," said Smiler.

"We hit a storm," said Zoltan. "It delayed us getting into Tunis. Is all well?"

"Couldn't be better," said Smiler, taking out a rough Turkish cigarette and lighting it. Zoltan grabbed hold of his hand and studied the tattoo.

"That is new," he said.

"Aye," said Smiler.

"You should be more careful," said Zoltan. "The Millenaria are not loved by everyone."

"Ach," said Smiler. "With this face, nobody bothers me."

"So, where are the trucks?" asked Zoltan. "I do not want to keep everything sitting here on the quayside for too long."

Smiler looked away and sucked his teeth. "Ah, well," he said. "The trucks . . . There's been a small problem with the trucks."

"What sort of problem?" said Zoltan. "Are they here?"

"Not yet."

Zoltan swore. "You said things couldn't be better. Well, I think they could, Smiler."

"It's hard to get the parts out here," said Smiler. "But the trucks are on their way, don't you worry. In the meantime, I've arranged a warehouse for you to put this lot in."

"How long will it be?"

"A few days."

"A few days? It is not good enough," said Zoltan.

"It's Sardinia," said Smiler with a shrug.

As he said this, a rope slipped on the cradle holding one of the crates, and a warning shout went up from a crewman as the net swung out crazily over the water.

Zoltan swore loudly and colorfully, calling his men every name he could think of, and thankfully they got the crate under control and lowered it gently to the quay.

Smiler watched. Was he amused? It was hard to tell.

Victor's table was set with the weirdest meal James had ever seen.

There was the figure of a naked woman sculpted out of food—her body made of cheese, her skin ham, her hair salad leaves, and her lips cherries. There was a bowl of pasta dyed dark blue with cuttlefish ink, a loaf of bread baked in the shape of a motor car, two stuffed cats for decoration, and a live lizard that crawled slowly over the table. There were bright red lobsters and spiny crabs with long spindly legs. There was a tray of tiny fish with their heads and tails still attached, and scooped-out sea urchins containing little orange stars. There were edible flowers, vegetables carved into the shape of flowers, the fruits of a prickly pear cactus, a bowl of green jelly with toy soldiers suspended in it, and in the middle of it all, on a gleaming silver platter, an octopus with purple tentacles.

"Welcome, James," said Victor as they sat down. "This is a surrealist feast created by the great Poliponi."

"It is food as art, and art as food," said the artist, teasing the pointed horns of his black hair. "You cannot eat a Rembrandt," he said, "or a Picasso. You cannot fill your stomach with a Michelangelo statue! But tonight you will devour a genuine Poliponi."

He broke off a piece of bread and popped it in his mouth. "Now," he said, "in the true spirit of surrealism, we will start with the dessert and finish with the soup."

He took a scoop of jelly and slopped it onto James's plate.

"Please don't think me stupid," said James, fishing a soldier out with his spoon. "But what exactly is 'surrealism'?"

"It is the greatest artistic movement of the century," said Poliponi. "From now, realism is dead. Why would I want to paint a picture of a vase of flowers, or a sunset? If you want a picture of the real world, then take a photograph. My art goes beyond reality. I paint the world of dreams, of fear, of desire. Everything that goes on inside your brain. The purpose of my art is to free the conscious mind and express the subconscious. To show you that the world we live in is ABSURD!"

The food may have looked absurd, but it all tasted good. Victor showed James how to crack open the lobster to get at the juicy flesh inside its claws and tail. And, once he'd overcome his squeamishness, he found the tiny fish were crispy and full of flavor. He discovered that the orange stars inside the sea-urchin shells were their eggs. He scooped them out with a spoon and tried them. They were gritty and tasted of the sea, but not unpleasant. The only thing he wasn't sure of was the octopus. Poliponi put three pieces of tentacle on to his plate, saying he must eat them.

"It is *polipo*," he said lovingly. "The food of the gods!"

"*Polipo*?" said James.

"Yes," said Victor. "Didn't you know? *Polipo* is Italian for octopus. Signor Poliponi named himself after the creature."

"The octopus is the most pure example of a surrealistic animal," said Poliponi. "What could be less human and more absurd than an octopus?"

James put a piece of tentacle into his mouth and chewed . . . and chewed. It was the chewiest, rubberiest thing he had ever tried to eat, but he persevered.

"So this house," he said, after washing the last pieces of flesh down with a glass of water, "La Casa Polipo, is 'The House of the Octopus'?"

"But of course," said Poliponi. "The greatest house in the world."

"You have not seen it properly," said Victor. "To fully appreciate it, you need to see it from above. In the morning we will climb up to the rock and I will show you. Now, you must take a glass of wine, James."

"No, thank you," said James. "I don't think I'd better."

"Nonsense. You should learn how to drink. So that you know how not to get drunk. There are few sights more pathetic in the world than a man who is drunk. You must know your limits. You must know when to start and when to stop. I shall give you the smallest measure of wine, and you can add some water. Come. This is a Cannonau, a local wine, from near Oliena."

He poured James a glass of deep red wine, and James drank some.

Mauro and the cook, Isabella, a loud, jolly woman, cleared away the plates. Victor kept a permanent staff of three, who all lived in the villa. As well as Mauro and Isabella there was Horst, the muscled young man James had seen lifting weights in the inner courtyard. He looked after the gardens and did odd jobs about the place, but seemed to spend most of his time exercising and studying himself in the mirror.

Mauro's sullen manner hadn't changed. As he took James's plate he gave him a dirty look as if to say, "What do you think you're doing here?"

Victor said something to Mauro in Italian, and the boy slouched across the room and put a jazz record on the windup gramophone.

"How I wish I could play a musical instrument," said Victor, conducting the music with his wine glass. "It is my one great regret. I love music, but my life has been spent working with steel and concrete. We have had many musical people stay with us here at Casa Polipo. In the spring the great Cole Porter was over from America, and last summer your own Noël Coward stayed for a weekend. He played us many songs on the piano. Such a witty man. I think I was not born to be an engineer, James, but it is always too late when we realize that we are only given one life."

"You only live once," said Poliponi. "But you can live a thousand times in your dreams."

James awoke in the morning in his small, bright room, still wearing his clothes and covered in mosquito bites. He knew he wasn't supposed to scratch them, but he couldn't stop himself. He tore at his skin with his fingernails, but after a brief feeling of satisfaction the itching returned worse than ever. He hurriedly found his bottle of quinine tablets in his wash bag and swallowed one. He had forgotten to take it the night before, and while it wouldn't stop the mosquitoes from biting, it should at least help to keep malaria at bay.

He had gone to bed very late, exhausted after the day's traveling and staying up late for the feast. He had slumped onto his iron-framed bed without undressing, and had forgotten to unfurl the mosquito net hanging above it.

He would not be this careless again; there were ugly raised red lumps all down his arms and round his ankles, and he had even been bitten on his ears and in his hair.

He searched his room, in the vain hope that he might find one of his six-legged tormentors still here. He eventually found one—a big, fat brute sitting on the wall near the door, too bloated and lazy to fly away. He took his shoe and hit it as hard as he could. The insect left a wide smear of blood on the plain white wall.

James noticed a painting next to the smear, not one of Poliponi's grotesque works but a simple watercolor of a local view with the signature "Delacroix." It must have been painted by Victor, but hanging nearby were two scenes of Venice that looked old and valuable.

"They are Canalettos," said a voice, and James turned to see Victor in the doorway. "Beautiful, aren't they?" he said. "I did some work for a prince whose palazzo was sinking into the lagoon. I managed to shore it up and save the building. He could not afford to pay me, so he gave me those instead. Now, come, we need to make a start before the day is too hot."

After a quick breakfast, still feeling miserably itchy, James started out on the climb to Bear Rock with his cousin. The path wound steeply up between huge boulders through the familiar low scrubby Mediterranean maquis of juniper, myrtle, and rosemary. Lizards sunned themselves on the rocks and scurried away as the two figures approached.

It took them forty minutes to reach the summit, from where there was a magnificent view of the whole of this part of the island.

The rock itself was huge, and towered above them like some bizarre ancient monument. James was fascinated by the way the wind had scooped and scraped it into caves and arches. Indeed, the wind up here was terrific, and James felt as if he might be blown away.

"It is the mistral," shouted Victor. "The north wind. It is always blowing here. The sailing is some of the best in the Mediterranean. Do you like the wind, James? I love the wind. It is so clean and pure. You sense the power of nature when the wind blows; it reminds us how small we are."

James nodded, not sure what to say. He had never really thought about it, and if he was to be really truthful, he felt slightly scared. He hadn't experienced wind this strong before; it seemed to have an almost physical presence, as if it were some giant, invisible beast tugging at him and buffeting him.

He felt suddenly very unsafe. The height unnerved him. He had never been afraid of heights before his experience at the Nuraghic tower, but now he was trembling and nauseous. He fought to control his emotions. This was not like him.

He staggered back across the polished stone ledge on which they were standing into the shelter of the rocks. Victor joined him; it was quieter here, and, away from the edge, James's vertigo receded.

"Are you all right?" said Victor.

"I think so," said James. "I just need a moment."

He took a long deep breath and told himself not to be so stupid. He could cope with this.

He forced himself back out onto the ledge and looked down.

He didn't want to jump. He knew that if he was careful there was no danger.

His heart rate dropped.

He swallowed.

Something had happened to him back at the tower. Something he didn't understand. It had knocked him for six, and now he had to control his fears.

"Better?" said Victor, walking over.

"Yes," said James. "I'm fine."

Victor pointed down to where the land met the sea.

"What do you think?" he said, and James saw the villa properly for the first time. It was built in the shape of a great white octopus. The large central living room was the body, and the various corridors leading off it made up the eight tentacles.

"I like it," said James. "I think all houses should look like that."

"Poliponi wanted me to paint it red," said Victor with a chuckle. "We fought over it like two dogs, but in the end I won. It was my money, after all, that was paying for it. White is better, it keeps the heat away. It can get very hot here. What your English schoolteacher is doing organizing a field trip to the Nuraghic monuments at this time of year, I do not know. He will lose half his students to heatstroke. Why did he not come in the spring or autumn, when most sensible people visit the island?"

"I have no idea," said James.

"So," said Victor as they started back down, "should I ask Mauro to take you sailing this afternoon?"

"I'm not sure he likes me," said James.

"Oh, that is just his way," said Victor. "He is very protective of me, and suspicious of outsiders—even if they are family. And, of course, at heart he is a bandit."

"Why do you say that?"

"He is from the Supramonte Mountains," said Victor. "The Barbagia region."

"Oh, yes," said James. "I've heard about the villages hidden away up in the hills, to avoid attacks from the sea."

"That is right," said Victor. "You have seen how beautiful the island is, and its coastline is the most beautiful part, but it is largely uninhabited, and the people are not great seamen, because the true Sardinians live inland. They are fierce, tough people up there. There are still whole villages of bandits, and they are always fighting. Mauro's father was killed in a feud with another family."

"Really?" said James.

"Yes," said Victor. "When Mauro was old enough, he left home to find work so that he could send money home to his mother and sister. I have tamed him a little. I have tried to educate him and teach him to read and write, but he will always be a bandit at heart. I hope you two can become friends, because it is not a good idea to become his enemy. Horst is meant to protect me and the villa. He is a big young man covered all over with muscles, but I would rather have Mauro by my side in a fight."

When they arrived at the villa they found Horst exercising on the lawn in a pair of swimming trunks, his body glistening with oil. He struck several dramatic poses, his flesh bulging unnervingly, before retrieving a towel from where it was draped over a statue that James hadn't noticed before.

It was ancient and worn, but it unmistakably showed a man plunging a sword into the neck of a bull, exactly like in the painting he had seen in the chapel in Eton.

"What's that statue?" he asked.

"It is Roman," Victor explained. "It was dug up when we were building the villa. It seems there might have been a Roman villa here at one time, though we could find no other evidence."

"Who is the man?" said James, gently running his hand over the yellow stone.

"Not a man, a god. Mithras."

"Mithras? Was he a Roman god?" asked James.

"In the last days of the republic, the Romans were threatened by pirates," said Victor. "They would capture ships and ransom the rich men and women on board. They followed the example of the Romans and became organized, joining together into an underground movement that spread terror through the whole of the Mediterranean. They had kings and they called their men soldiers, but they operated in secret, and like any secret society they had their secret rituals. They worshipped Mithras, originally a Persian god. And to join the cult you would have to endure the pit of pain and drink the blood of bulls."

"What happened to them?" said James.

"In the end their empire was destroyed," said Victor, "but not their god. He slowly became a Roman god; the chief Roman god before Christianity took hold. He is a great favorite of Poliponi, especially since we found the statute here. He saw it as a sign. Come, I will show you something."

Victor led James indoors and down one of the tentacle corridors to a small round room with a window in the ceiling. Hanging on the wall was one of Poliponi's paintings in an oval frame. It showed a man dressed similarly to the carving of Mithras. He was bursting from a giant egg holding a sword and a flaming torch. Around the frame were the twelve signs of the zodiac.

"This is the birth of Mithras," said Victor. "He is emerging from the cosmic egg. After that, he had many adventures before slaying the primeval bull and releasing its life force for mankind. Where his blood hit the ground all good things sprung up—plants and herbs, vines and animals. He is also associated with the stars and astrology. He appeals greatly to Poliponi, who has a love of magic and mystery and is a great follower of the zodiac."

"Does anyone still worship Mithras?" said James.

"Oh, wherever there are secret societies they will have their little rituals," said Victor.

"I wonder," said James. "Have you ever heard of the Millenaria?"

Victor gave James a harsh look, and for the first time, James saw his calm exterior ruffled.

"Listen to me, James," he said. "Do not talk about things you do not understand. I came to Sardinia to retire, to sit in

113

the sun and paint. I want nothing more to do with the world of men, their petty wars and their vain struggles for power."

"I'm sorry," said James.

"No, it is me who must apologize," said Victor, his expression softening. "I did not mean to get angry, but there are rumors that the Millenaria are here on the island, and I do not want to think about such things. Life should be for pleasure, not for war. Now, come inside; I have something to show you."

"They are the very latest thing. I ordered them in Cannes from the man who invented them. An American airman called Guy Gilpatric."

"What are they?" said James.

Victor passed to James what looked like a pair of flying goggles. "They are for seeing underwater," he said. "They work surprisingly well."

James studied the goggles. They had glass lenses sealed all around with rubber.

"Keep them," said Victor, as James tried to give them back to him. "They are yours. And here, this is a tube for breathing, so that you can hold your face under the water. It is called a schnorkel. And to complete the ensemble, I have these . . ." he produced two outsize shoes that looked like a frog's flippers. "Swimming fins," he said. "To go on your feet, so that you can be a shark and speed through the water. Try them on and see if they fit."

"Do they work?" asked James, squeezing the fins onto his bare feet.

"But of course," said Victor. "I saw them being used in Cannes. They were invented by a Frenchman, Louis de Corlieu. I am fascinated by anything new and modern. You must try them out. Go down to the beach and say hello to the fishes."

James had by now put on the fins and the goggles and slipped the schnorkel into his mouth. Victor laughed at the sight of him, and a sharp cry caused James to turn. Poliponi was standing in the doorway with a hand to his mouth.

"But I must paint you like this," he said. "You are not human. You are a frog man? It is exquisite. Exquisite!"

Twenty minutes later, James was standing knee-deep in the clean, crystal-clear waters of the Mediterranean. He had already put on the fins and a clip to stop anything from going up his nose, and now he clamped his teeth around the hard rubber of the schnorkel's mouthpiece and slipped the goggles over his eyes. He felt strangely claustrophobic and panicky. The goggles narrowed his vision, and he had to concentrate on his breathing for a while so as not to hyperventilate. When he felt more relaxed he waded out a little farther and tentatively dipped his face beneath the surface. The underwater picture snapped into focus and he gasped with surprise. It was like suddenly peering through a window into another world. One moment he had been in a bright world of harsh sunlight and vivid colors, and the next he was in a quiet, liquid world of shifting shapes and murky yellows and greens. From above he had been able to make out nothing of this world under the water, the picture had been fractured and blurred; but now he was in it, and he could clearly see a shoal of tiny silverfish nosing around his feet.

He laid his body flat and kicked lazily with his fins. They

sped him through the water without making a splash and he marveled at the new sights.

He glided over a bare stretch of sand and into a forest of sea grass. A shoal of striped sea bream, with black bands around their tails, broke in two as he approached and scattered briefly before regrouping. Then he spotted some larger fish, brown meagres, and a great pipefish, long and thin, like a piece of drifting seaweed. He swam deeper until he was past the sea grass. Below him now was an alien landscape of fan mussels, Neptune grass, and slimy black sea slugs, which gouged long trails as they dragged themselves through the sand. He headed toward a large rock that stood like a mountain, its top rising above the water. Starfish and sea urchins clung to its side, and sea anemones, their delicate pink fronds waving in the water. A spiny spider crab, with long gangly legs, poked about looking for scraps.

James peered into a crack and saw two great gloomy eyes peering back at him. He smiled and moved on, and as he swam out past the rock, the seabed suddenly fell away. His breath caught in his throat when he found himself suspended in endless deep blue sea, surrounded by teeming shoals of fish: red mullet, pilchards, and beautiful little wrasse with yellow-striped bodies and pale blue heads.

James hung there watching the fish until he decided to go deeper and see if there was anything bigger out there. He swam on, feeling tiny in this great blue void. He soon lost all sense of time and space, and it was only when he heard the dull throb of an engine that he was brought back to reality.

He assumed it must be a fishing boat and realized that he might be in some danger out here on the open sea. He briefly put his head up to look around, but could see nothing. He was amazed at how far he had swum, though: the shore looked miles away. He ought to head back. He felt suddenly cold and tired, and as he bobbed there in the water regaining his strength, the engine sound grew steadily louder and louder. Something was coming straight for him. But the goggles had steamed up and he was almost blind.

Where was it? Where was the boat?

He thrashed in the water, spinning left and right, but could see nothing. The noise rose to a deafening scream, and from out of nowhere a huge shadow swallowed him up. In his panic he dived down and looked up just in time to see what appeared to be the hull of a boat ploughing into the water above him, only inches away. It caused an almighty splash and an explosion of swirling bubbles. He felt a great boom and a thud, and his body was hit by a shock wave. He tumbled through the depths, not knowing which way was up or down, tangled in a confusion of churning water. He swallowed a bellyful of sea and wildly groped for the surface. Then at last the water stilled, and he found his way up into fresh air and sunlight.

He floated there, treading water, choking and spluttering, wondering just what the hell had happened.

He tore the goggles off his face and was amazed to see a big white Sikorsky seaplane cruising through the waves and executing a long, lazy turn. What he had thought was the hull of a boat was one of its two big floats, which were suspended in a complicated forest of struts below the wings. It coasted along under the power of its four propellers and finally came to a halt, its belly resting on the swell.

A double door at the front opened up, and James saw a man in military uniform preparing a small dinghy.

James swam over for a closer look, but the dinghy was launched before he got there, and he followed it on the long tiring slog toward the shore. It was too far away for him to see clearly who its occupants were, but he could just make out the figures of a man and a woman sitting in the stern.

Below La Casa Polipo was a small natural harbor. The dinghy put in here; the crew tied up, and the passengers made their way up the steps toward the villa.

James was intrigued. Who was grand enough to arrive at Victor's in a seaplane with their own military escort?

He swam round to the beach, fetched his towel, and followed the party up to the villa.

Victor met James on the terrace; he looked amused and slightly flustered.

"We have visitors," he said to James, who was standing dripping on to the tiled floor, wrapped in his towel.

"I know," said James. "I saw them arrive in their seaplane. They nearly drowned me. Who are they?"

"His Excellency Count Ugo Carnifex," said Victor, with a faint mocking tone. "And his sister, the Contessa Jana Carnifex."

"He sounds grand," said James. "Who is he?"

"A local man. Big in the mining industry. He has a palazzo up in the mountains."

"And what's he doing here?"

"It seems he is just paying us a social call. I was looking for Mauro to serve some drinks. Have you seen him anywhere?"

"I'm afraid not," said James.

"Never mind," said Victor. "Come in and meet the man. I think you'll find him interesting."

James went indoors, and it took a moment for his eyes to adjust. The first thing he saw was a pair of uniformed guards. They were standing awkwardly next to the stuffed giraffe and had the look of locals, with dark faces, sleepy eyes, and drooping black mustaches. James didn't recognize their uniforms. They weren't police. He wondered if they might be part of the Sardinian army. The uniforms were certainly very extravagant. The trousers and tunics were a deep purple color, with scarlet and gold trimmings. Their caps, which they wore jammed forward on their heads, had flat peaks that shaded their eyes.

Both men were armed with pistols that hung in black holsters on their hips above tall, highly polished boots.

One of the guards spotted James and looked him up and down before turning away with profound disinterest.

"How do you like their uniforms?" said a voice from the darkness at the back of the room. "I designed them myself."

A very tall man was walking toward James. As he stepped into the light, James was hit by a shock of recognition.

It was the ghostly, white-skinned man from the painting he had seen in the cellar of the house in Eton. He even held his arm out in the same beckoning way.

James tried not to show anything in his face as he shook the offered hand.

"Count Ugo," said Victor, "I would like to introduce my cousin from England, James Bond."

"Carnifex is pleased to meet you, James," said Ugo, flashing a silver tooth that caused him to lisp slightly.

He was wearing a pristine version of the white Sardinian peasant's outfit, but there the similarity to a peasant ended. His fingers were festooned with silver rings; he had silver chains around his neck, and small silver earrings. His skin, unlike that of his two guards, was a pure milky white; so pale that James could see the blue veins beneath it. And his close-cropped hair was as white as everything else about him.

"Bring the boy to me. . . ." came another voice from the gloom, and James was startled to see a woman sitting in an upright armchair, for all the world as if it were a throne.

Ugo went over and kissed her hand, then turned back to James.

"James, I would like to introduce my sister, the Contessa Jana Carnifex."

"Charmed to meet you," the woman drawled, her voice slinky and purring like a cat.

Where her brother was pale, Jana was dark. Where Ugo's skin was luminous and glowing, Jana's was dry and dead. Whereas Ugo looked like he had spent a lifetime trying to keep out of the sun, Jana looked like she had never spent a moment in the shade. Her brown, creased face was plastered with thick, orange pancake makeup. She wore bright coral lipstick, and the heavy eyelids of her kohl-rimmed eyes were painted blue. She had an elaborate hairstyle, piled high on her head and entwined with silver chains. The hair was so black and glossy and perfectly sculpted that James felt sure it must be a wig.

Jana was dressed in swathes of gold and pink satin, and

was laden down with the most jewelery that James had ever seen on one person. Huge pendant earrings dangled from the stretched lobes of her ears like miniature chandeliers. Amber, gold, and diamond rings glittered on her clawlike fingers; round her scraggy neck were gold necklaces and strings of pearls, and she had a gigantic silver brooch studded with jade. There were even diamonds set into her toenails, which protruded from her golden sandals.

"Come, boy," Jana purred and crooked a finger at him, its painted nail long and curling. "Kiss my hand."

James reluctantly stepped forward. As he approached, he could smell the perfume which hung around her like an evil cloud, choking him when he bent to take hold of her hand. She looked at him hungrily and ran the purple tip of her tongue over her pink lips, moistening them.

"You have a pretty face," she said, staring deep into his eyes.

James didn't know what to say. He felt uncomfortable and embarrassed in just his swimming shorts, but he couldn't get away. Jana held him fast in her talons, smiling at him possessively.

"You will break many girls' hearts," she said, "though you have a cruel mouth."

As she said this she ran her dry fingers over his lips, and he drew back from her.

"I think I'd better go and put some clothes on," James mumbled and backed out of the room, Jana's throaty laugh following him down the corridor.

When he came back a few minutes later, wearing thin South Sea Island cotton trousers and a short-sleeved shirt,

Mauro was serving drinks, with his familiar, sullen expression.

Ugo was deep in conversation with Victor.

"But you must come, Signor Delacroix," he was saying, "my palazzo is a marvel. As an engineer you will appreciate all that I have achieved."

"You seem to know all about me, Count," said Victor.

"I make sure that I am always very well informed," said the Count, grinning and displaying his silver tooth. "But it is not just my palazzo. I have built a magnificent dam and an aqueduct, the likes of which has not been seen since Roman times."

"That is quite an achievement," said Victor.

"Yes," lisped the Count. "It is. The dam supplies all my needs. All my water and electricity. I am reliant on no one."

"And the aqueduct?" said Victor.

"To bring me water, of course," said Ugo. "I will explain. My dam is built between two mountains, across a wide gorge. My palazzo is built into the side of one mountain, my machinery into the other. Water comes down from the dam through the turbines and then across the gorge on the aqueduct to my palazzo."

"And why could you not just bring the water straight down from the dam on your side? In pipes," said Victor, frowning quizzically.

"Where would be the glory in that?" scoffed Ugo. "My aqueduct is a monument you can see for miles. You have the mind of an engineer, Signor Delacroix. I am an engineer as well, but I am also a soldier, a poet, and a dreamer. I have a vision, Victor."

"That is clear," said Victor, and James detected a mocking hint in his tone that luckily Count Ugo didn't register.

"Ah, James," said Victor, noticing James for the first time. "Count Ugo has graciously invited us all to his palazzo for a grand carnival."

"The building work has only just been completed," said Ugo, "after many years. You will be among my first visitors. This carnival will announce to the world that Count Ugo Carnifex has arrived—"

Ugo suddenly stopped and put a hand to his mouth, staring at something on the floor.

"Are you all right, Count?" said Victor anxiously.

Ugo shook his head quickly, and James looked down. On the marble floor was a small, damp, sandy footprint that he had left behind when he first came in.

"I am sorry," said Ugo, "but I cannot stand mess or dirt of any kind. This island is filthy. The people are filthy. Up in the mountains I can get away from them. I can at least try to keep my own house clean. Dirt is a sin."

Victor quickly signaled to Mauro, who reluctantly knelt down and wiped the offending sand away with a cloth. Ugo watched him with an expression of extreme distaste.

"Would you care to stay for dinner?" said Victor, trying to lighten the mood. "It is late and you have a long journey back."

"That is most kind of you," said Ugo. "My sister and I would be delighted, Signor Delacroix."

James was sick of the sound of Ugo's voice. The man couldn't stop talking, and he had only one subject—himself. All through dinner he had bored everyone with his views on philosophy and religion and politics, and how the local people were lazy and untrustworthy.

Now he had got on to the subject of money, or to be more precise, his own great wealth.

"Silver," he was saying, as Victor nodded politely. "It was silver that paid for everything. Inside the mountain, beneath my palazzo, is my silver mine. I had other mines on the island before—lead and zinc and coal—but they were not profitable. I sold them all and went to the Gennargentu. I had a hunch." He tapped his nose. "I can smell silver. Everyone said that I was mad. But I didn't listen. I tunneled into the mountain with explosives. No silver. I tunneled deeper. Still no silver . . . but then one day—silver! I proved them wrong."

He laughed, then stopped to wipe his lips on a pristine white napkin, which he instantly dropped to the floor as if it were some disgusting dead animal.

There were five people around the table. Victor and Poliponi; Ugo and Jana, who barely touched her food; and James.

James missed the relaxed informality of his previous meals at the villa. Victor had pulled out all the stops tonight, and the table was covered with gleaming silverware, fine porcelain, and a crisp white linen tablecloth.

"I tore the heart out of the mountain," Ugo went on. "And I used the stone I removed to build my palazzo." He turned and said something quickly to Poliponi in Italian. The artist smiled and looked impressed.

"I was just saying to Signor Poliponi how much art I have

in my palazzo," said Ugo. "I love art. I am a very cultured man. I love art and architecture and music. I want to live among beautiful things. The Emperor Napoleon stole art from all around Europe, including much Italian art, the greatest art the world has ever seen. Like him, I am filling my home with art."

"Napoleon was a great man," said Poliponi. "A strong leader. He understood that fame is the most important thing. To be immortal."

"Just so," said Ugo. "The human body is frail, and when it finally gives up, it becomes the same decaying matter as everything else. In death we are all soup. We soon become forgotten unless we can do something tremendously good, or tremendously bad. It does not matter which. But you must do it always with style."

"Exactly so," said Poliponi. "If you kill a few men you are simply a common murderer, but if you kill millions you are a great general, remembered for all eternity, like Attila the Hun or Julius Caesar."

"How true!" said Ugo. "The very word 'Caesar' has come to mean a glorious ruler. The Russian word 'Czar,' the German word 'Kaiser,' they all come from 'Caesar.' The Romans built the greatest empire this world has ever seen. They brought civilization to Europe. Their achievements were extraordinary, far in advance of anyone else at the time. They put the rest of the world to shame. Well, I hope to remind the world of all this. My dam is just the beginning."

Ugo had become so excited that he was waving his hands around, and he jogged Mauro's arm just as he was attempting to serve him some food. Red sauce spilled over his white suit.

Ugo leaped up from the table, madly wiping at the stain and screaming a torrent of Sardinian at Mauro in a horrible, high-pitched voice. Finally he stormed out of the room, onto the terrace, still yelling and followed by his anxious guards.

"It appears that dinner is over," said Jana, putting down her knife and fork. "We must go home now. Thank you for your hospitality."

She stood up to leave, and Victor jumped to his feet.

"Surely he can be placated, madam?" he said. "It is not so bad."

"A serving girl once stained his clothes with wine," said Jana, "and Ugo had her thrown from his dam."

She laughed mirthlessly and followed her brother out into the night.

"What a man!" exclaimed Poliponi, when they had gone. "He is like a crazy god!"

"Oh, do be quiet," said Victor. "He is a bore. I do not think we will be going to his carnival."

"But I insist," said Poliponi. "We must go. I want very much to see his palazzo and the dam, and the aqueduct."

"I would like to see the mountains," said James. "After all I've heard about them."

"I'm sure you would," said Victor. "But we shall not be going. There are rumors about Ugo Carnifex."

"What rumors?" said James.

"I don't want to go into it," said Victor. "We are not going."

"You are an old woman, Victor," said Poliponi. "Frightened of ghosts and shadows." The artist poured himself a glass of wine. "Ugo is just a man who loves secrecy. He does not welcome many visitors; we should be honored. I adore carnivals, James," he added. "Such fun. There will be music and dancing and wrestling. I love wrestling. It is so manly."

"Carnifex is a crook," said Victor. "And we are *not* going."

"Oh, many men in that part of the island are crooks; it is bandit country," said Poliponi. "But Carnifex is different. He is a strong man, a modern-day Augustus. He could make this country great again, like Mussolini is trying to do."

"Mussolini is a clown," said Victor. "They are all clowns. Why can't they just leave us alone and stop trying to change the world?"

"The world needs changing," said Poliponi. "It is boring. I insist that we go, Victor, or I will sulk."

Victor stood up. "I will think about it," he said, and went outside.

"Don't worry," said Poliponi with a sly grin and a wink. "We *are* going, James."

In the distance, James heard the roar of the Sikorsky engines and saw its lights as it climbed into the night sky.

CHAPTER 12—LET DOWN YOUR HAIR, RAPUNZEL

Amy sat at her window and looked out at the now familiar view. Slowly the sun was setting and the light was fading, but she could still see, far below, the dry valley, dotted with yellow stubble fields, and on the other side, the craggy gray mountain rising up to the darkening sky, its lower slopes carpeted with trees that from this distance looked like tiny green pom-poms.

Under different circumstances she might have found the view beautiful, even romantic, but now she just found it bleak and desolate and lonely.

She was a prisoner in this room.

There was a thick iron bar in the middle of her window, but even if it hadn't been there she wouldn't have dared to climb out. There was a drop outside the window of several hundred feet.

As prisons went she supposed that this room was at least comfortable; it was certainly better than the hold of the *Charon*. It was nicely furnished with a dressing table and chair, a comfortable bed, and a rug on the floor.

But she was still a prisoner.

By the time they had arrived in Sardinia, Amy had grown used to the routine of life on board the *Charon*. Since coming ashore, however, things had changed, and changed for the worse.

When was that? She tried to think. Could it really have been only just over a week ago? So much had happened.

She and Grace had spent the first few days in a dingy hotel in the backstreets of Terranova, sweltering in the damp heat, while Zoltan waited for his transport to arrive. They hadn't been allowed to leave the room, and one of Zoltan's men kept watch outside the door twenty-four hours a day.

At first they passed the time by playing cards, practicing their French, and fighting off the mosquitoes, but Grace had slowly become more and more depressed until she just sat in the corner all day, hugging her knees and sobbing. In the end, Amy had had enough of it and let fly at Grace, telling her that they had to be strong and look after each other. Feeling sorry for themselves wasn't going to help.

That seemed to snap Grace out of it. She dried her tears, washed her face, and got busy around the small room, tidying and cleaning and trying to create some sense of normality. Then one evening Zoltan had come to the room and told them they were leaving in the morning.

"Where are you taking us?" Amy sneered. "To market? To be sold?"

"No," said Zoltan.

"I told you my grandfather would never pay you the ransom," said Amy.

"He will pay," said Zoltan. "But it will take a little more time."

"What about me?" wailed Grace. "My family's not rich. They can't pay for me."

"Be quiet, Grace," said Amy softly. "You'll be all right. We won't be sold like cattle."

"I have brought you something to wear," said Zoltan, dropping some packages on to the bed. "In the morning I want you to be clean and dressed. There is everything you will need here, including . . ." He stopped and blushed slightly. "Other clothes. To go underneath."

"I don't want them," said Amy. "I don't want anything from you."

"You get rid of those filthy clothes you are wearing and put this on," said Zoltan, angrily tearing open one of the packages and pulling out a frilly yellow dress. "But first you will wash. There is soap here. Use it. You smell."

"I won't wear that dress," said Amy. "It's ugly."

"It is all I could find here in Terranova."

"I don't care. I'm not wearing it."

Zoltan grabbed Amy and thrust her in front of the mirror. "Look at yourself," he said. "You have been wearing these same clothes for weeks."

Amy looked, but hardly recognized the person she saw reflected in the mirror. Her face was pale and grimy, her hair had grown into an untidy tangle, and her borrowed clothes were now gray and ragged.

"We are going to the house of a wealthy man who has a hatred of dirt," said Zoltan. "I am going to sell him some of my treasures, and I do not want to do anything that might make him angry."

"And am I one of your treasures?" said Amy.

"Yes," said Zoltan. "My greatest treasure. But I am not going to sell you to him. I will keep the best for myself."

In the end, Amy was too tired to fight, and the next day, wearing the ill-fitting yellow dress, she was loaded with Grace into the back of a canvas-sided military truck. The truck was part of a small convoy made up of two other trucks and an open car that moved slowly out of Terranova southward down the coast road. They traveled at a snail's pace and had to make frequent stops as one or other of the vehicles broke down.

Zoltan rode alongside on a big white horse, his Samoan lieutenant at his side on an even bigger horse. Zoltan had his bad arm in a sling and seemed frustrated by the slow progress they were making. He frequently lost his temper and shouted at members of his team. As well as the crewmen from the ship, some local men had joined them: fierce-looking bandits wearing long black stocking caps. Amy had noticed them watching her and Grace, and asking questions, no doubt curious as to who they were.

The truck was full of packing crates and, as much as for something to do as anything else, Amy tried to open one of them, working away at the nails with a cutlery knife she had stolen from the hotel.

After a couple of hours she managed to loosen the lid enough to pry it back and look inside.

She found a row of oil paintings and a marble bust that looked like it might be Roman.

She was just showing the contents to Grace when they felt the truck rock on its springs and she looked round to see one of the local men climbing over the tailgate.

He was clutching a bottle of wine and appeared to be drunk.

"*Buon giorno!*" he said and offered them a wobbly bow.

He smiled at Grace. "*Come si chiama?*" he said, and Grace shrugged.

"What does he want?" she said, turning to Amy.

"I don't know," Amy replied. "I think perhaps he wants to know your name."

"I am Grace Wainwright, from England," said Grace. "And I do not wish to be here."

The man laughed and mimicked her thin, frightened voice, and then he patted his chest. "*Mi chiamo Salvatore*," he said and offered her some of his wine, nearly falling over as the truck lurched around a bend.

"No, thank you," said Grace, pushing the bottle away. Again Salvatore laughed and copied her.

"Please," said Grace. "Please, go away."

The truck suddenly braked, and they were all thrown forward. Salvatore fell in a heap on the floor, laughing like a madman. Grace tried to hide behind the packing cases.

The Sardinian got shakily to his feet, spilling wine down himself. He wiped his mouth and held out his arms as if to welcome her into them. Amy had had enough. She quickly stepped forward and gave Salvatore a shove. He tipped over the tailgate, falling into the road with a startled shout.

The following truck had to brake sharply and veer to the side of the road to avoid running over him.

There were angry shouts and the driver jumped down in a cloud of dust, gesticulating wildly.

The whole convoy came to a halt, and Zoltan galloped over on his white horse.

Salvatore lay very still in the road, spread-eagled on his back. One of his friends went to him and slapped him, trying to revive him. Then he poured water over his face from a canteen, and Salvatore spluttered and groggily raised his head before he snapped back into life and stood up, yelling a stream of insults at Amy, who was looking out of the back of the truck.

"Shut up!" said Zoltan, and there was silence. "Now, will somebody please tell me what is going on here?"

Again, a stream of excited Sardinian poured out of Salvatore, and one of his friends translated.

"He say the girl push him from the truck. He say he is going to kill her."

"He is going to do nothing," Zoltan snapped. "I am in charge here." He turned angrily to Amy. "Is this true? What this man is saying?"

"Perfectly true," said Amy calmly. "That man is drunk." She picked up the bottle and tossed it into the dirt. Salvatore looked disappointed as the dark wine spilled out into the road.

Zoltan closed his eyes and fought to control his emotions. For a moment he looked very weary, then he wiped his face, opened his eyes, and walked his horse over to Salvatore, so that he was towering over him. When he finally spoke, he spoke quietly. "I gave orders that nobody was to interfere with my prisoners."

Salvatore tried to interrupt, and Zoltan yelled at him. "You should not have disobeyed my orders!"

"You not my boss," said Salvatore, with a note of scorn in his voice.

"As long as you are traveling with us," said Zoltan, "you will respect my authority. *Rispetto*. You understand? If you go near the women again, I will have you thrashed."

Salvatore raised his chin defiantly, made an obscene gesture, and muttered a curse. One of his friends laughed, and

Zoltan suddenly kicked Salvatore in the face, knocking him to the ground.

Zoltan swung down out of his saddle, and by the time Salvatore had scrambled to his feet, the Magyar was standing next to him.

"Do you understand?" he said.

Salvatore swore and took a swing at Zoltan. The Magyar easily dodged it and hit Salvatore hard with the back of his hand. For the third time Salvatore ended up lying in the road. His face was battered and streaked with blood, but Zoltan stood calm and relaxed. He pulled the Sardinian to his feet and looked at him.

"Do you understand now?" he asked.

There was still a dim glow of defiance in Salvatore's eyes. He feebly raised a fist and Zoltan hit him again. The blow was so powerful it whipped Salvatore's head back and he spun away into the arms of one of his friends.

"Stand him back up," said Zoltan.

"Stop it," Amy screamed from the back of the truck. "Stop it. Can't you see he's had enough?"

Zoltan turned to face her, and at that moment Salvatore's friend pulled a knife from his belt.

Zoltan saw Amy react and turned back again, reaching inside his tunic. By the time he was facing the Sardinian his Beretta was in his hand and leveled at the man's head.

"Go ahead," he said. "Try me. I will shoot you three times between the eyes before your body hits the ground."

The fight went out of the Sardinian and he dropped his knife.

Zoltan looked at Salvatore. He was barely conscious.

"Get that sack of horse manure in one of the vehicles and let's get moving," said Zoltan, and he glanced at Amy before jumping onto his horse and riding back to the front of the convoy.

The rest of the journey passed without incident. Amy sat in the back of the truck staring out as the road unwound behind them, too numb to know what to think anymore.

They left the coast behind and climbed up into the heart of the island, passing through the town of Nuoro, before veering southward toward the Gennargentu Mountains.

As darkness fell they arrived at their destination: a large, man-made cavern at the foot of a mountain. It was lit by harsh, yellow lights, and the smell of oil hung in the air. There were more trucks parked here and various large pieces of rusting machinery.

Zoltan's crew unloaded the crates onto what looked like miniature train wagons, and Amy saw a narrow track disappearing down a tunnel cut into the rock wall.

Once the cargo was safely loaded, Zoltan helped Amy and Grace on board before climbing in beside them with Tree-Trunk and a couple of his men.

"It is a mining car," Zoltan explained. "To bring the ore out of the mountain."

There was a jolt and the car moved forward into darkness.

The tunnel snaked up through the inside of the mountain, lit here and there by flickering lamps. At regular intervals they passed other tunnels going off into the shadows on either side, and everywhere were piles of seemingly abandoned tools and equipment.

After what felt like ages, the car finally emerged into a large vault lit by powerful arc lights. This appeared to be the center of activities in the mine. Men in purple uniforms were waiting to unload the packing crates, and they quickly began moving them into various side chambers that were already half filled with similar boxes.

Supervising the activity was a very tall man dressed all in white, his skin as pale as his clothing. He stopped a group of men who were struggling with a particularly heavy case, and they put it down. He said something to them and they began to open the lid.

Zoltan climbed out of the car.

"Ugo," he called out. "Are you not pleased with me?"

"*Salve, amice,*" said Ugo, and he smiled, flashing a silver tooth. "I am very impressed. You have excelled yourself, Zoltan."

So saying, the tall man reached into the open crate and took out a gun. It was like a short rifle with a round drum attached to the bottom. Amy recognized it from American gangster films. It was a Thompson submachine gun—a tommy gun.

"You have done well, Magyar," Ugo said, fondling the weapon. "You have brought me some beautiful things." He gave a little bow. "You are too generous."

Zoltan laughed. "You know very well that these are not gifts," he said. "I hope you have the money for me."

"But of course," said Ugo. "I would not let you down. You are, after all, my oldest friend."

"That's because all of your other friends are dead," said Zoltan.

Ugo grinned. "As soon as I have checked everything," he said, "you shall be paid. But you are staying for the carnival, I hope? It will be your first opportunity to meet my other colleagues."

"I am staying," said Zoltan.

"Good." Ugo handed the gun to one of his men, who gave him a cloth. "But I think you have not been straight with me, Zoltan," he said, wiping his hands on the cloth and dropping it to the floor. "You have not given me all your treasure."

"I have," said Zoltan. "There is nothing more. I have given you all that we agreed."

"No." Ugo smiled and stepped toward Amy and Grace. He raised a hand as if to touch Amy's hair, then recoiled with a slight look of distaste.

"Your hair is not clean," he hissed.

"She is not for sale," Zoltan said wearily.

"Why?" said Ugo. "I will give you a good price. Her family may never pay you."

"She is not part of our bargain."

"I do not care," said Ugo. "I want her."

"What for?" Zoltan moved forward angrily and put himself between Amy and Ugo.

"You beat one of my men," said Ugo. "You did not have the right. He is useless to me now. In the hospital. You owe me something for him. I am told that you are fond of the girl."

"You cannot take her," said Zoltan, putting his face close to Ugo's. "She is mine."

Ugo backed away from him. "Keep away from me," he

said, staring in horror at the Hungarian's bloodstained tunic. "You are disgusting. You pollute the air. You come here like that, with these filthy girls, trying to tell me what I can and cannot do. I am the capo, Zoltan. You are in my world now."

Ugo gave a signal, and two of his guards took hold of Amy's arms. Another trained a machine gun on Zoltan.

"If anything happens to me, my men will kill you," said Zoltan.

"I will hold the girl for as long as I think necessary," said Ugo. "To make sure you behave yourself in my home. Then we shall see. Maybe I will let you have her back. Maybe I will ransom her myself. Or maybe I will keep her here as a servant."

The two guards dragged Amy up some steps toward a big iron door.

"Why do you do this, Ugo?" said Zoltan.

"Because I can, Zoltan. What is power if I cannot use it?"

Amy watched from the steps as Grace suddenly grabbed hold of Ugo. "Please," she said. "This is nothing to do with me. Won't you let me go?"

Ugo lifted his hands in the air, afraid to touch Grace.

"Take your hands off me!" he screamed, and a guard pulled Grace away.

"I beg you," said Grace. "I'm not worth anything to you. I'm not from a rich family. Can't you just let me go? Please. . . ."

"She is right," said Zoltan. "She is not part of this."

"*Sì*," said Ugo. "She is right. She is worth nothing to me. I do not want her. She is free.

"Thank you," said Grace. "Thank you, sir."

139

Grace looked up toward Amy and gave a small smile of encouragement, but Amy watched in horror as Ugo walked behind her and took the machine gun back from the guard.

His long, thin, white finger curled around the trigger.

Amy tried to cry out and warn Grace, but she was pulled up the steps, and as the metal door slammed shut behind her, she heard the brief muffled rasp of the gun on the other side.

She could still hear that terrible sound. When she closed her eyes at night it haunted her in the blackness. And she heard it now, as she looked out across the valley from her prison.

She clamped her hands to her ears until the sound went away. When she removed them the noise of gunfire was replaced by the distant clonk of cowbells and the warbling of a dove, somewhere up on the roof; the same irritating sound, over and over. . . .

There was a rattle of keys and the door opened.

Amy smiled. It was Stefano, the boy from the kitchens who brought her food. Stefano's visits were the only parts of the day she looked forward to.

He placed a tray on her dressing table, unloaded a plate of boiled meat and vegetables, and collected her dirty dishes from lunchtime.

As usual she had hardly touched her food, and as usual Stefano tutted.

"You must eat, Amy," he said quietly. "You will get sick."

"I don't care," she said.

Stefano glanced back at the door to make sure it was shut and spoke to her in a low voice.

"I have brought you some chocolate," he said. "From

Ugo's own supply. Don't let the guard see you eating it." He quickly handed her a small lump of something hard wrapped in waxed paper.

"Thank you," said Amy, feeling pathetically grateful, and she squeezed Stefano's hand. The boy brought her all sorts of pilfered treats, but she was most grateful for the human contact and simply having someone to talk to.

Stefano had learned to speak English working in the kitchens of an English family living in Cagliari.

"You make me feel sad, Amy," he said. "I do not like it. You should not be here."

"Is there nothing you can do?" said Amy.

"No," he said. "If Ugo knew I was even talking to you he would have me whipped. If I helped you escape he would hang me. I am as much a prisoner here as you," he added. "Now I must go. I will see you in the morning."

As Stefano went out with his tray, Count Ugo came in.

He had not visited Amy since locking her in this room, and Amy couldn't say that she was pleased to see him.

"I am sorry if I am disturbing your meal," he said as Amy hurriedly hid the chocolate. "But I will not be long." He sat down on Amy's high-backed chair and stared at her for a while.

"What do you want?" she said.

"I just want to make sure that you are well looked after and have everything you need," he said. "I am not a monster, you know. I am a civilized man."

"Tell that to Grace," said Amy.

"You are a strong young woman," said Ugo. "I like that. The women of ancient Rome were strong. They had to be to breed strong children. The wives of the emperors were the strongest of them all."

"I understand a fair number of them poisoned their husbands," said Amy.

"Weak men deserve to perish," said Ugo, standing and walking slowly toward her.

Amy was repulsed by him. By the whiteness. By the silver tooth that caused him to lisp. By the blue veins beneath his translucent skin.

"I have been finding out about your family," he said as she backed away from him. "The Goodenoughs are good English stock. Aristocracy."

Ugo looked her up and down. "I need a wife who is an aristocrat."

Amy put a hand to her thigh. Through her dress she could feel the knife she had stolen from the hotel where it was tucked into the top of her stocking. She had been sharpening it on the stone window ledge, and she wondered if she should pull it out and try to stab the Count. He looked powerful, though, and if she got it wrong, he would surely kill her.

"But my men tell me you still refuse to bathe," said Ugo, turning away. "That is a pity. You must keep clean. And your hair, you must wash it. They tell me that when Zoltan first captured you, you had short hair, like a boy. That is wrong. I am glad you are growing it. Long hair suits you better. Maybe you could grow it as long as Rapunzel and let it down through your window. Who knows, maybe a handsome prince will climb it and rescue you?"

So saying, Ugo laughed and left the room.

Amy sat on her bed.

There was no handsome prince. There would be nobody riding to her rescue. She was lost and alone.

She knew what she was going to do with the knife.

She had made up her mind.

She would use it on herself.

She slipped it out of her stocking top and felt the sharpness of the blade.

Then she grabbed hold of a bunch of hair and started to saw away at it, ignoring the pain as it tugged against her scalp.

CHAPTER 13—BLACK SPINES FILLED WITH POISON

James was standing on a narrow ledge, peering down at the sea thirty feet beneath him. His toes gripped the edge of the rock, curling over it. He swallowed hard. The drop was a lot farther than it had looked. Had he made a big mistake?

A large steamer out in the Straits of Bonifacio sounded its horn as if daring him to jump, and James exhaled noisily.

The sun felt fierce on his back. Its dazzling light was reflecting off the water and the pale rocks so that he had to squint. He could see the two boys watching him expressionlessly, lounging on the sand, not wanting to give anything away, acting casual, as if what James was about to do was something they saw every day.

But was he about to do it? Was the water even deep enough? How far under would he go if he dived from up here? Whatever happened, he would have to wait for a swell of some sort; but still, if he got it wrong, he would drive himself headfirst into the seabed. At best he'd break his neck, at worst kill himself. Maybe he should back down and dive from the lower rock that the boys had been using.

No. He couldn't do that. He would lose face. They would laugh at him and he would never be accepted. He knew he was showing off, coming up this high when he could have simply dived from the lower point, but part of him needed the thrill of danger.

This was the Danger Society all over again.

It was also his chance to conquer the fear of heights that had taken hold of him at Sant'Antine. If he could pull this off, he would prove to himself that he wasn't scared, that the incident at the tower had been a one-off, that he didn't suffer from vertigo.

He would show Mauro that he was not some soft English sap.

Since his arrival, Mauro had become, if anything, even more rude and standoffish. His duties as Victor's houseboy appeared to leave him a lot of free time, and he came and went as he pleased. James had been largely keeping out of his way, but on one or two occasions they had both been on the beach at the same time and had sat as far apart as they could, both pretending that the other wasn't there. And since Victor had left the day before, Mauro had got even worse.

Just as he had predicted, Poliponi had persuaded Victor that they should attend Count Ugo's carnival in the mountains. The artist had pleaded and sulked and teased Victor until he had given in. He had steadfastly refused to take James with them, though.

"If your Aunt Charmian found out that you had been mixing with people like Ugo Carnifex," he had said, "she would never forgive me."

This had caused Poliponi to scold Victor again. "We need more people like Ugo Carnifex," he said. "Europe is falling apart. You cannot hide from the world forever, Victor. I know you Swiss are proud of your neutrality. You will not join in our wars, but you still must live in our world."

"I came to Sardinia to escape," said Victor. "To live in peace by the sea."

"One small carnival in the mountains is hardly the end of the world!"

The original plan had been for Mauro to drive them there, but Ugo had sent his seaplane for them, and Poliponi had gone off like an overexcited child.

Now Mauro was acting as if he owned the place, and James was dammed if he was going to take any more from him.

This afternoon he had thought that he would have the beach to himself, but a small sailing boat with a triangular lateen rig had arrived, skippered by a friend of Mauro's called Luigi. Mauro had come down from the villa to meet the boy, and they'd sat about smoking cigarettes and chatting. Every now and then one of them would look over at James and say something, and the other would laugh.

James had tried to appear uninterested as they'd splashed about in the turquoise water for a while, but then they'd started diving from the steps that climbed up the side of the little natural harbor. They'd started from fairly low down, but had grown bolder with each attempt, until they'd used a ledge some fifteen feet up.

James had watched them until he could stand it no longer. He wasn't going to sit here for the rest of his holiday being ignored by this snooty Italian boy. He'd walked over to join in, but as soon as they'd seen him coming, the two boys had stopped what they were doing and lain down on the rocks to dry themselves.

To hell with them.

James had swum over to the steps, being very careful where he put his feet, as the whole area was carpeted with black sea urchins so you could barely see the stone beneath. If you put a foot wrong you'd be stabbed by a thousand black spines filled with poison.

He had reached the ledge the other boys had been using and instantly decided that he would try a little higher. And now he had climbed as high as he could get, and here he was, stupidly risking death to impress these boys.

The steamer had passed through the straits, and James watched its wake rippling toward the shore.

It was now or never. The waves created by the ship might just be enough to give him the depth of water he needed to avoid breaking his neck.

He watched as the first swell surged in and broke against the rocks, raising the water level by a good few inches.

Okay. There was no time to think; the wake would pass on in a matter of moments, and he would have missed his chance. He'd still have to time his jump exactly, though; if he hit the water between waves it would be disastrous.

He sucked in his breath, tensed, and threw himself out over the water.

Everything happened so quickly, he barely had time to think. There was a brief, breathtaking sensation of falling, the air rushing noisily in his ears, and then the sea slammed into him like a solid object, battering the top of his head. He pulled up as sharply as he could, but still got a face full of weeds and his chest scraped the bottom. Then he was bobbing up in a net of silver bubbles, alive and unhurt.

He swam casually back to the shore and got to his feet. The water was just deep enough here to hide his trembling legs and wobbly knees. He knew he mustn't show anything, but he felt utterly exhilarated; the thrill had been intense.

Mauro stared at him for a moment, then laughed and jumped up. "*Sei pazzo*," he said, shaking his head.

Luigi looked up at the rock and whistled. "*Quella era una cosa pazzesca da fare*," he said.

"*Pazzo*," Mauro repeated and tapped his finger on the side of his head. "Crazy."

James shrugged. He was sure that from now on he and Mauro would be friends. Which was a relief, as he knew that he would be too scared to ever try a stunt like that again.

He waded toward the two boys, grinning happily, but suddenly yelled and fell sideways in the water. It felt as if a nail had been driven into his foot.

Mauro and Luigi hurried over, picked James up and dragged him ashore. They looked at his foot. Several broken black spines were sticking out of his heel.

He'd trodden on a sea urchin.

There was a terrible burning sensation as the poison, still pumping from its broken spines, soaked into his flesh.

The two Sardinian boys shouted excitedly and crowded around him. Luigi put out a hand to prod at the spines, but Mauro pushed him away angrily and the two of them argued. Finally Mauro indicated to his friend to stay back and looked at James.

"Okay?" he said.

"Not okay," said James, and he bit his lip. The pain was awful. His whole foot was throbbing and the poison was already spreading from his heel up into his ankle.

Mauro studied his foot carefully, before delicately plucking the spines out one by one. But they were so brittle that the barbed ends stayed stuck in, and, as they were disturbed, the poison sacs at their tips discharged more of their agonizing cargo.

James winced and tried not to make any sound, but it was difficult. At last Mauro was done. He looked at James, his face concerned.

"Come," he said, and helped James up.

James put his arms round the boys' shoulders, and they struggled with him up the steps to the villa. Once there, Mauro left James on the terrace and busied himself in the kitchen before returning with two bowls and a sponge. He carefully washed James's foot with vinegar from one bowl before plunging it into the other, which was full of very hot water. The pain slowly dimmed to a dull ache and a pulsing sensation, and James was relived that the worst of it was over.

Mauro studied James's heel. It was still studded with the broken ends of the spines.

"Okay?" said Mauro.

"Okay," said James.

Mauro once again talked to Luigi, who looked skeptical, and soon another argument flared up, but once again Mauro won.

"Is okay," he said, then he picked up a large smooth stone. "Okay," he repeated, which made James think that it really wasn't okay at all.

Mauro knocked the stone against his chest and nodded. "I know," he said. "Is okay."

"I don't have any idea what you're going to do, Mauro," said James, aware that the boy wouldn't understand half of what he said. "But so far so good. Just get on and do it."

Without another word, Mauro gripped James's foot and started pounding his heel with the stone. James howled and tried to struggle free.

"Is okay," Mauro repeated as he carried on working away with the stone; and he was right, the pain was lessening still further.

Horst appeared and came over to see what was going on. He was stripped to the waist and had a towel round his neck. Up close his bulging muscles looked ugly and unnatural. He chatted briefly with Mauro and Luigi in Italian.

"He is doing the right thing," he said to James after a while. "Smashing the spines with a rock breaks down the poison and crushes the tips to dust so that your body can easily deal with them. If the spines are left in they can be the devil." He bent down to take a closer look. "You are lucky he didn't let Luigi try and do it his way," he said, straightening up.

"What did he want to do?" said James.

"He wanted to urinate on your foot," said Horst and he laughed loudly before slapping James on the back and wandering off.

James didn't know what to think about Horst. When he had written to Mr. Cooper-ffrench, describing life at the villa, he had put in a lot about him and his ridiculous body-building. He had tried to make it as funny as possible in the hope that Cooper-ffrench might read it out to the other boys. He wasn't completely sure that Cooper-ffrench had a sense of humor, however.

That night James ate supper at the big wooden table in the kitchen with Mauro, Horst, and Isabella, the cook. Mauro enjoyed telling Isabella about James's crazy dive and the incident with the sea urchin. Isabella tutted and clucked and kept firing off bursts of Italian at James, who couldn't understand any of it; but between them they managed to patch together some sort of conversation.

There was a happy atmosphere, with much laughter, and James realized how much more relaxed he was now that Mauro was on his side. This was his favorite type of meal, with good, simple food, fresh bread, and friendly chatter. How much more enjoyable it was than the ghastly formal affair he'd sat through with Count Ugo and his weird sister.

Isabella had just gotten up to go to the stove and serve second helpings when James heard a sound from next door.

"What was that?" he said.

"What?" said Horst.

"I thought I heard voices," said James.

"Maybe Victor is back already," said Horst, but as he stood up to go and investigate, four armed men burst into the kitchen and the atmosphere suddenly changed.

Everything happened very quickly, too quickly for James to be scared. There was a chaotic, noisy blur of hurtling bodies, crashing furniture, and yelling voices.

Horst screamed and ran around the kitchen like a headless chicken, shouting about bandits in a strangulated high-pitched whine.

Isabella was braver. She threw a saucepan of boiling tomato sauce over one of the men, who yelled and tore at his clothing. But two of his friends grabbed her before she could do any more damage.

James picked up a chair and battered one of the men off Isabella, and out of the corner of his eye saw Horst fleeing out of the back door. Mauro, meanwhile, had picked up a big kitchen knife and was attempting to fend off the fourth attacker. He cut him badly across the forearm but two more men appeared. One of them hit Mauro with a wooden club, knocking him to the floor. James ran to his side and swung his chair at the man with all his strength, smashing it across his back and scattering splintered wood around the kitchen.

He helped Mauro up and they tried to make a run for it out of the back door, but the next thing James knew someone had pushed a gun in his face. He caught a brief glimpse of a masked face and a red tattoo of the letter *M* on the back of the man's hand. James jerked his head out of the way, then there was a terrific bang and a blinding white light in his eyes, and after that, blackness and silence.

The whole thing had taken less than thirty seconds.

James awoke in the middle of the night, lying on the kitchen floor amid a wreckage of broken plates and furniture, with a terrible ringing in his ears.

He ran his fingers over his face. His first thought was relief that he hadn't been shot. There was a huge, painful lump on the back of his head, however. When he fell he must have struck the floor and knocked himself out. The men had probably left him for dead. He struggled to his feet and saw Mauro. It looked like he hadn't been so lucky. He was lying beneath the table in a pool of sticky red stuff.

"No," James gasped, and went over to him. Mauro's face was streaked with red gore. Fighting back tears, James wiped the hateful stuff away with his hand.

He smelled tomatoes. He licked his hand. It tasted sweet. It wasn't blood at all; it was Isabella's tomato sauce. He laughed and went to the sink to fetch some cold water. When he got there he saw his reflection in the window. He too was covered in dried sauce. But as he cleaned himself he realized with a shock that the stuff that was dripping down out of his hairline actually was blood.

There was no time to worry about that now. He had to revive Mauro and try to find out what had happened. He splashed some water over him, and as he cleaned his face he saw an ugly purple bruise across his forehead where he must have been struck with the club.

At last Mauro's eyes opened, but as soon as he was conscious he was violently sick. James left him in the kitchen to clean himself up and went to see what damage had been done and try to find some clues as to what the men might have been after.

He soon found out.

The whole villa had been stripped bare. All the paintings were gone. Everything. All of Poliponi's work, all of Victor's work, and all the other art that he had collected over the years. The only thing they'd left behind was the stuffed giraffe.

James knew how devastated Victor would be.

There was no sign of Horst anywhere, but he discovered Isabella in one of the bedrooms, bound and gagged, but still alive.

Mauro, who by now was feeling more human, helped him to untie Isabella, and in their halting, broken way, they planned what to do next.

First of all they carried out a more thorough search of the villa and grounds, and once they were sure that it was safe, they took the Hispano-Suiza out of the garage and drove Isabella to her sister's in Palau.

"Tell her to alert the police," said James. "*Polizia*."

"*Sì, sì*," said Mauro, and he had a hurried conversation with the frightened cook.

There were few telephones on the island, so the only way to let Victor know what had happened was to go to Ugo's palazzo and tell him in person. James realized how devoted Mauro was to his master. He was fully prepared, even now, after the terrifying attack and being knocked unconscious, to drive all night to give him the bad news. Anyone else might have been temtped just to go away and hide, like Horst appeared to have done.

But James wasn't about to let him go alone, and soon they were loading the car to drive down toward the Gennargentu Mountains. Luckily, Mauro knew the way; he had grown up in the mountains. The Barbagia was his home. He showed James the route on an old army map, drawing it on with a thick red crayon, and they set off.

They made good progress to start with, taking the inland route through Gallura and Logudoro as the roads were marginally better than along the east coast. After a couple of hours James saw that they were crossing the Valle dei Nuraghi and he recognized the squat, black shape of the Sant'Antine tower off to their left. After that the road got steadily worse as they climbed into the mountains, until it had deteriorated into a twisting, muddy track, pitted and rocky. Their progress became frustratingly slow, and they had no idea what was going to be around each bend.

By now their faces were caked with dust and grime. James's eyes stung from peering intently at the circle of light thrown ahead by the headlamps. He knew it must be worse for Mauro, who couldn't stop concentrating for even a moment in case they hit a rock or veered off into the bushes. James looked over at him. He was flagging. He had had no proper sleep and had taken nasty blow to the head. His eyes were drooping and he was fighting to keep them open. James knew he had to talk to him to keep him awake.

"Okay?" he asked.

"*Sì*," said Mauro. "You fight good, James. You okay. I sorry I bad to you. Friends now."

"Friends," said James.

"*Le montagne sono belle*," said Mauro.

"The mountains?" said James.

"*Sì*," said Mauro. "*Bene*. Good. You like. My home."

"Tell me about your home," said James, and Mauro told him his story.

He had never wanted to leave his village, but life was hard and the people were poor. He would have liked to stay there and grow old among his own people, but his sister could look after the animals and make cheese with his mother, and there was no real work for him. So, like so many other boys before him, he had gone off to find a job that would pay him enough money to send some home each month.

He had worked at first in the salt marshes around

Cagliari, but it had been hard and the pay small, and in the end he had found easier work in a bar in Sassari, which is where he had met Victor.

Victor had recently built his villa and needed staff.

Mauro liked working for Victor. He was kind and life was easy. Sometimes when he traveled, to Switzerland or Italy or France, he took Mauro with him; at other times he left him behind, and he was free to do whatever he wanted.

"I swim," said Mauro, yawning. "I go in boat. I eat good."

As they crested a ridge, Mauro had to brake suddenly to avoid running into three wizened old men in black cloaks with pointed black cowls riding wiry little ponies. The car stalled and stopped in the middle of the road. Slowly the men rode around them and carried on. They were in no hurry. Life here had gone on, unchanged, for centuries. James thought he could have seen men dressed like these, riding their ponies down these roads, five hundred years ago, maybe even a thousand.

He looked around at Mauro. His head had flopped forward onto the wheel and he was sleeping.

"Come along," said James, shaking him. "Move over. I can drive."

Mauro tried to protest, but he was too tired, and by the time James had manhandled him into the passenger seat, he was fast asleep again.

James took the wheel and looked over the controls. The Hispano-Suiza wasn't too different from his roadster back in Eton, and after a bumpy start, he was driving with some confidence.

The sun was coming up, which would make things

easier, but they still had a fair way to go. Never mind. James felt alive, all his senses alert. The Hispano-Suiza had a big, powerful engine, but he was in control of it. He was filled with a wild, reckless spirit.

He knew that he would never forget this night.

CHAPTER 14—THE LAST THING THAT GOES THROUGH THE MIND OF A DYING MAN

People had been streaming into the small town of Sant' Ugo all morning, mostly poor peasants and shepherds, but also a scattering of richer families and a few sightseers and tourists.

The town had originally been little more than a collection of shepherds' huts, but Count Ugo had enlarged it to accommodate his workers. It was now an ugly, dull collection of hastily built, and in some cases only half-completed, concrete buildings painted a lurid salmon pink and laid out on a formal grid design with wide streets. The only thing of any interest was a sports stadium at the edge of town, toward which the crowds were flocking.

James nosed the big Hispano-Suiza down the packed main road, trying not to run anyone over. He was reminded of the Fourth of June back at Eton. Overexcited people, many of whom seemed to be already drunk, spilled off the pavements and wandered into the streets without a care.

It was hot and noisy and confusing, especially to James, who had been driving on deserted country roads all night. He wondered how he and Mauro must look—two grimy boys driving a big, dusty Hispano-Suiza—but nobody seemed to pay them much attention. Occasionally a group of rowdy young men would surround the car, singing and shouting and banging on the bonnet, but as far as anyone was concerned, they were just two more revelers come to enjoy the party.

James felt utterly worn out; his neck was stiff, his eyes ached, and his mouth was full of gritty dust. The sun was burning in a clear blue sky, and it looked like it was going to be another scorching day.

"This is no good," he said to Mauro. "We should leave the car and carry on on foot. We walk? *Sì?*"

"*Sì*," agreed Mauro, who looked slightly numb and shell-shocked.

They pulled off the main road, dumped the car in a side street, and got out.

Sant' Ugo was built in an arid, rocky valley beneath two mountains; they had not been able to see much on the drive in, but somewhere up there was Ugo's palazzo and Victor Delacroix.

The two weary boys shouldered their way through the milling carnival-goers until they reached the far side of town, and as they cleared the buildings, James got his first proper view of the twin mountains.

The scene was just as Ugo had described it: far up above was the dam, spanning the gap between the two peaks, and directly beneath it was the aqueduct, crossing the valley on impossibly tall arches. To the right of the aqueduct, stuck on to the side of one of the mountains, was what looked like a model. Surely it was too strange and perfect to be real.

It was a gleaming, white, fantasy Roman town, complete with temples, villas, colonnades, and what looked like a small amphitheater.

It had been built on several levels, one on top of the other, so that a terrace in front of one building was the roof of the building below, and seemed almost to hang in space, far above the valley. He couldn't help smiling. It was like a toy. He felt as if he could simply reach up with his hand and put a tiny model Roman soldier on it.

Mauro pointed and James saw a steep funicular railway track leading up the side of the mountain. They headed toward it, leaving a trail of dust behind them.

At the foot of the railway was a scene of frenetic activity. A team of boys was unloading baskets of food from a railway car that was parked in a shed. They bustled around, throwing the baskets to each other, shouting and arguing and laughing, while a bored-looking guard made a halfhearted attempt to oversee the chaos, struggling to stay awake and yawning heavily.

James hurried over to the guard, knocking dirt off his clothing. He started to try and explain what he wanted in his halting Italian, but the guard simply stared at him with the same bored expression and yawned into his face. Mauro joined in, but it was obvious they were getting nowhere. The guard didn't want to know.

James's head was throbbing, and he thought that if he didn't get out of the sun soon, it would explode. He was just wondering what to do when one of the boys came over from the railway car.

"Mauro!" he cried.

"Stefano! *Che cosa fai qui?*"

Mauro grinned from ear to ear, and the two of them gabbled excitedly to each other, interspersed with much Italian hugging and slapping.

It turned out that Stefano was from Mauro's village, and he worked here in Ugo's kitchens. He seemed to know the guard and eventually managed to get through to him that his friends had an important message to deliver to Victor Delacroix up at the palazzo.

The guard shuffled into his hut and came out after a while with a sheaf of densely typewritten papers. He leafed through them, turning from one page to the next agonizingly slowly, but at last a vague glimmer of light came into his eyes.

"Victor Delacroix?" he said, and James nodded.

"*Bene.*"

He nonchalantly waved James and Mauro onto the railway car and explained the situation to another guard who sat inside, sheltering from the sun.

As he climbed aboard, James studied the carriage. It was attached to a thick steel cable and sat on a sloping, wedge-shaped base so that it would remain level as it made its way up the dizzyingly steep angle of the track.

The guard pulled some levers and James heard a swooshing, gurgling sound from below. He looked out to see that a tank of water underneath the carriage had been emptied into a concrete channel. He assumed that the train must operate on some sort of counterweight system.

With a jerk, they moved forward and began to climb up the mountainside.

James sat down next to Mauro. He wondered if this ornate railway had once been part of Ugo's mining operation. It certainly didn't look like a mining carriage now, though: the seats were padded velvet and the walls were covered in carved wood and gold leaf.

Halfway up they passed a second car coming down, packed with more baskets and palazzo workers, then they crossed over a bridge that spanned a deep black chasm in the ground. On the other side of the bridge they passed into a tunnel that had been cut into a great jutting outcrop of rock, and as they emerged back out into sunlight, they came to the first of the palazzo buildings. James looked up at high, sheer walls dotted with small windows, and got the occasional glimpse inside as they climbed past them. The higher they got the finer the buildings became, and James saw lookout towers, large statues, and raised walkways. Finally, nearly ten minutes after setting off, they came to rest at the top of the palazzo, where a wide, handsome piazza had been built.

James looked up. The great, gray mountain continued above the palazzo, and near its peak was the dam that arced across the valley to the mountain on the other side.

The piazza appeared to be at the heart of Ugo's complex. One side of it was open and overlooked the valley and the aqueduct, which joined the palazzo just below here, the water in its canal sparkling in the sunlight. Tall, elegant facades stood to the right and left of the piazza, and at the back, a row of wide marble steps led up to the most imposing building of all, which had a massive portico held up by tall pillars and a statue of Julius Caesar standing on its roof.

This must surely be Ugo's private residence.

The whole place was eerily deserted and looked unnaturally clean after the dirt and dilapidation of the rest of this poverty-stricken island. It felt unreal, like an elaborate stage set. It was all too neat and white. James had to shield his sore eyes from the glare.

The guard led the two boys across the piazza past an extravagantly carved fountain of Neptune on the backs of four dolphins that spouted water from their mouths.

As they got nearer the main building James saw that it was built into the mountainside. The rooms at the rear must have been carved out of the rock. The guard took them up the steps and into a huge, gloomy marble hall, whose walls were hung with oil paintings.

"*Aspettate qui*," said the guard, and he wandered off, leaving James and Mauro alone.

"The Count must be very rich," said James, looking around. "Much money," he added, rubbing his fingertips together.

Mauro gave a dismissive gesture. "He is Barbati."

"From the mountains?" said James.

"*Sì*. He is same as me." said Mauro. "From my village. He is not count. *È un contadino*."

"*Contadino?*" said James. "What is a *contadino?*"

"*Pastore*," said Mauro, then he made a bleating noise.

"He's a shepherd, you mean?" said James and Mauro mimed two horns. "A goatherd?"

"*Sì*."

James laughed, and they sat down on a stone bench. James rested his aching head in his hands, and in a moment he was asleep, but as his head nodded forward it jerked him awake.

He mustn't doze off here.

He got up and went to look at a painting to try to keep himself awake.

It showed a grisly religious scene. In the background various unarmed men were being slaughtered, and in the foreground was a kneeling saint with a neat halo, his eyes upturned to heaven, a small smile on his lips. A barbarian with an equally calm expression was in the process of driving a sword through the saint's head.

"He looks almost happy, doesn't he? The fool," said a voice, and James became aware of a sour-sweet, sickly smell of decay. He turned to see a man with his arm in a sling, his shoulder heavily bandaged. He seemed slightly feverish and had extraordinary gray eyes with irises so pale they looked almost white.

"Look at him," said the man, pointing to the saint. "Do you think he wants to die?"

James didn't know what to say, so he said nothing.

"He wants to go to heaven and see his God," the man went on, his voice heavily accented. "I fear he will be disappointed. This painting is a lie. I have seen men die, good men, strong men, brave men. And at the end it is always the same. Terror. Do you know what every man thinks of the last thing before he dies? Even the toughest man?"

"No," said James. "God maybe."

"God?" said the man, and he laughed. "No, he thinks of his mother. He cries out for her. 'Mama . . .' It is a pitiful thing to hear. I was in many battles in the war. The worst thing was knowing that I would be the same as everyone else. I knew that one day I would be sitting in the mud with my guts spilled out into my lap, trying to stuff them back inside me, crying like a baby and calling for my mother." He sniffed and turned to James. "The best you can hope for is a clean death and a quick one," he said. "One day you might have to fight in a war. One day you might have to kill a man. And you will have to have a hard heart. To look someone in the eye and see his fear, to know that this was some mother's child, that is a difficult thing."

The man fell silent for a while, lost in thought, and James still didn't know what to say. Finally he snapped out of it and offered his good hand to James.

"I am Zoltan the Magyar, by the way," he said. "And who are you?"

"Bond, James Bond."

"Ah. Victor Delacroix's young cousin?"

"Yes. Do you know him then?"

"There was talk about you at dinner last night," said Zoltan. "Ugo was expecting you to arrive with Victor."

"I . . . I couldn't come before."

"But now you are here?"

"I have some news for Victor, some bad news. I need to find him. A guard's gone to look I think, but—"

"Ugo's guards are useless," said Zoltan. "I will find your cousin for you. Trust me."

Zoltan smiled and walked away.

James took one last look at the painting before going to sit down again. Mauro was lying on the bench, snoring, and James envied him.

He sat there, fighting off sleep, until he heard a clatter of footsteps and saw Count Ugo arriving with the guard. He spotted Mauro, and a look of cold fury came on to his ghost-like face.

"What is this dirty peasant doing in here?" he said.

"He's with me," said James.

"You should not bring your servant in here," said Ugo. "He is filthy. Look at him."

"He's not my servant, he's my friend," said James, and he shook Mauro, telling him to wake up.

As Mauro got groggily to his feet, Ugo spoke to him viciously in Sardinian.

Mauro looked half asleep and confused, not sure where he was or what was going on. He'd been through a lot and his face was still horribly bruised from the fight.

"*Pastore*," he muttered to James and sniggered.

Ugo snapped at him, yelling now. Mauro replied, equally angrily, and James saw the Count's eyes go wide and his nostrils flare.

He slapped Mauro hard across the face. Then, before James could do anything, the boy snorted and spat once at Ugo's feet, leaving a sticky gob of saliva on the tiled floor.

Ugo shrank back and put a hand to his mouth, gagging. "Look what he has done!" he screamed at James. "How dare he spit on my floor! He is a disgusting peasant. I will beat him for this."

"No," said James. "You shouldn't have slapped him. He's not your servant. He's with me."

"I am going to hurt that boy so badly."

"No," said James again. "You will do nothing to him."

Ugo glared at James, and for the first time James saw color in his chalk-white face. His cheeks and neck were flushed red.

"How dare you give me orders," he said quietly.

Thank God, Zoltan came back at that moment.

"Come now, Ugo," he said casually. "It is not so bad." He pulled out a handkerchief and quickly wiped up the mess. "There," he said. "It is gone."

But Ugo hadn't finished with James.

"This is your fault, boy," he said coldly. "You should have more control of your servants."

Before James could speak, Zoltan put his good arm across his shoulders. "Really, Ugo," he said. "He is just a boy. And he is looking for his cousin. Come along, James, I think I know where he is."

Zoltan said this all in a rush, and ended by sweeping James and Mauro out of the building.

"Keep walking and don't look back," he said. "I think the more distance we put between ourselves and Count Ugo, the better."

"Thanks for helping me," said James.

"My pleasure." Zoltan smiled at him. "But I think you should get your friend well away from here. Ugo is a dangerous man when he is angry."

"I have to find Victor," said James. "Do you really know where he is?"

"I believe he is at the dam," said Zoltan. "Come, I will take you."

A second funicular railway led from the piazza up to the

dam. They found Poliponi waiting there for a car to arrive. He was so wrapped up in his own bizarre world, he didn't seem in the least surprised to see the two boys there.

"Is it not magnificent?" he said, before James could say anything. "This palazzo! It is the most pure expression of surrealism I have ever seen. I am in love with it. I want to live here forever! La Casa Polipo seems dull next to it. Count Ugo is a god!"

"There's been a robbery," James blurted out, and Poliponi stopped, his mouth hanging open.

"What? Here? What are you saying?"

"No. At the villa. Bandits. They've taken everything . . . All your pictures. Everything . . ."

"My pictures?" Poliponi's skin turned gray, and all the life went out of him. "But surely you are joking. . . ."

"No."

Mauro took over and explained in Italian what had happened. The artist became very anxious and agitated, not quite believing what he was hearing.

Soon the railway car rolled into view, stopped, and emptied water from its tank into a sluice. Poliponi had to be helped on, and he collapsed onto one of the padded benches, too devastated to say anything more.

As they began to move, James looked up at the dam towering above them, cutting right across the sky.

"It is quite a setup Ugo has here, isn't it?" said Zoltan.

"I suppose so," said James.

"But is it a palazzo or a fortress, I wonder? Everything must come up the mountain or go down it on the railway. There is no other way. Apart from through the mines, which are guarded by Ugo's men. Oh, and there is his beloved Sikorsky, of course."

"I was wondering about that," said James. "How do you land a seaplane halfway up a mountain?"

Zoltan didn't answer, for in the process of trying to sit down, he had knocked his bad arm against the side of the carriage and now he cursed loudly.

James had been longing to ask him about his injury and, although it was perhaps not polite, he couldn't stop himself.

"How did you hurt your arm?" he said.

"I got into a fight with a mermaid," said Zoltan.

"I didn't know mermaids were so dangerous," said James.

"Oh, they are," said Zoltan. "People think of them as pretty little girls with fishes' tails from fairy stories, but they are vicious creatures, James. They have sharp teeth. Keep away from mermaids."

"I will." James said no more. If Zoltan didn't want to talk about the wound, he wasn't going to press him.

The carriage trundled into shadow and stopped inside a wooden winch house. As James got out he saw that the cable attached to the front of the car wound round a giant drum and then snaked off down a second track.

"This way," said Zoltan, and James followed him out of the winch house into the sunlight.

Behind the dam, completely hidden from the outside world by high cliffs, was a wide lake. A smart motor launch was moored here next to the Sikorsky, which sat in the water like a giant, ungainly, white bird. So that answered James's question.

"There is your cousin," said Zoltan, pointing, and James

spotted Victor at the far end of the dam, studying the cliffs with a pair of field glasses.

James set off toward him, but felt nervous all of a sudden. He hated being the bearer of bad news.

How was Victor going to take it?

CHAPTER 15—SU COMPOIDORI

"Everything? They have taken everything? I cannot believe it. I thought I was safe there."

"I'm sorry," said James.

"No, James," said Victor. "You could not have done more. You were very brave. I didn't want to bring you here to the mountains, in case of trouble, and look what happened. . . ."

"What will you do?" James asked.

"If it was local men," said Victor, "if they were just bandits, then they will probably try and sell the paintings back to me. That is their way. The paintings will be of no value to them. It just goes to show you, James, you cannot hide from the world."

As they walked slowly back to the winch house James glanced over the edge of the dam. There was only a very low wall here, and it was an awfully long way down. He tested himself, walking right next to the wall to see if the height unnerved him. He was relieved to find that the drop didn't scare him. He didn't feel dizzy and he had no desire to throw himself off. The dive from the rocks seemed to have cured him of his vertigo.

When they reached the railway carriage, Victor spent a few minutes talking to Mauro and Poliponi. James and Zoltan stood outside, by the artificial lake, watching the light play on the water. James was mesmerized by the dancing golden sparkles and went into a trance, half asleep on his feet.

"You look like you could do with a bed," said Zoltan.

"It was a long night," said James.

The peace was disturbed by a splash. One of Ugo's bored guards was throwing stones into the water. James watched the ripples spread out across the surface and disappear where a long overhanging shelf of rock shaded the right-hand side of the lake.

The sound of horns and drumming drifted up from the valley.

"The carnival will be starting soon," said Zoltan. "Will you stay?"

"I don't know," said James. "It's up to Victor."

"I will have to go back immediately," said Victor, on the way down in the carriage. "I am so sorry, James. This has ruined your holiday. I don't know what to do. I don't know if you should come back with us. It might still be dangerous. But what else can you do?" He looked out of the window and slammed his hand on the glass. "I should never have come here."

He sat down heavily on one of the benches, his head slumped in his hands.

James decided to try and change the subject to take Victor's mind off his troubles.

"What were you doing up at the dam?" he asked. "I saw you looking at something through your field glasses."

"I was inspecting the rocks," said Victor, raising his head and wiping his face. "Ugo is crazy. He should never have built a dam there. Any engineer would have told him so. It is not safe."

"Not safe?" asked Zoltan. "I don't like the sound of that. Will we be drowned in our beds?"

"I hope not," said Victor, trying to smile. "But the rock ledge along the northern side of the lake does not look stable. Ugo has drilled deep into the mountain; he will have weakened something that was already weak. These mountains are mostly limestone, which is very soft. He was lucky that one of his explosions didn't loosen anything. It would not take much to undermine that rock ledge. The water in the lake may already be doing it."

"Ugo always did have big ideas," said Zoltan. "But he will listen to no one."

At the piazza Zoltan said good-bye, and Victor and Poliponi went off to collect their belongings from the palazzo. James and Mauro transferred to the other funicular railway, and when the adults returned a few minutes later, they all made their way down to the valley.

Sant' Ugo was even more crowded than before, and it was a struggle moving through the packed streets. When they reached the main square, James was surprised to see Peter Love-Haight and a group of Eton boys, including Perry Mandeville.

"Look!" he said excitedly to Victor. "It's my friends from Eton."

James called over to them and shoved his way through the milling throng.

"What are you doing here?" he yelled, delighted to see some familiar faces.

"Mister Cooper-ffrench heard about the carnival and it seemed too good an opportunity to miss," said Haight. "We're all staying in a campsite just outside town with a lot of Sardinian schoolboys." Haight stopped and frowned at James. "How are you?" he said. "Are you all right? You look done in."

James introduced Victor and Poliponi to Haight and told him what had happened.

"This is awful," said Haight, shaking his head. "Quite appalling. You must be particularly upset, Signor Poliponi."

"My paintings are my children," said Poliponi, who had never married and had no real children.

"What will you do?" said Haight.

"I am driving straight back," said Victor. "But I don't know what to do with James. There will not be a very happy atmosphere at Casa Polipo."

"Why doesn't he stay with us?" said Perry, who had been listening intently. "We'll look after him."

Victor turned to Peter Haight now, with a questioning look on his face.

"It's certainly an option," said Haight. "We're off tomorrow to look at some caves near Dorgali. They've got the largest stalagmite in Europe."

Victor turned back to James. "It makes sense for you to stay with your school party," he said. "Until I am sure it is safe and the villa is back in order. Then I will send a telegram and you can spend the last few days of your holiday with us in Capo d'Orso."

"All right," said James. "And please—don't worry about me. I'll be fine."

"Do you have anything with you?"

"I brought my bag with me. Just in case."

"Always prepared, eh, James?" Victor smiled.

"We'll look after him for you, Monsieur Delacroix," said Haight, "and make sure we send him back to you in one piece."

"Thank you, Peter," said Victor. "But I sometimes think that James can look after himself. Now, where is Mauro?"

They found him lying on a bench, fast asleep.

"The poor boy," said Victor. "He is exhausted. He cannot travel like this. His village is not far from here. He should go there and rest for a few days with his family. He has had quite a shock." Victor put a hand on James's shoulder. "James, we will go quickly before he wakes. Otherwise I know he will insist on driving me. Tell him that I said he must go home. Will you do that for me?"

"Of course."

James took Victor to the Hispano-Suiza and fetched his bag, but just as they were about to drive off, Poliponi became agitated and tried to get out of the car, muttering something about saying good-bye to Count Ugo.

"Forget about him," said Victor, pulling the artist back in. "He is a fool."

"How can you say that?" said Poliponi angrily. "When you have seen with your own eyes all that he has achieved."

"It is because I have seen it that I *can* say it," Victor snapped. "I have seen his palazzo and I have seen his insane dam. Everything here is fake. Nothing is what it seems. His fine buildings, they are not stone. Their fronts are plaster. One heavy rainstorm and they will crumble. Everything about this place is a lie."

"You are just jealous," said Poliponi.

"Of what?" Victor scoffed. "Ugo wants to show off. But he has nothing to show off about. I have seen many silver mines in my time, Poliponi. I understand rocks. There is no silver here. There never was. He is an actor playing at being an emperor. Come, we are going. Good-bye, James."

When Mauro woke, he was furious that he had been left behind and went into an epic sulk, but he was eventually cheered up by the thought of going home to his mother and sister.

"Go quickly," said James. "*Rapido*. You don't want to risk bumping into Ugo again."

"Ugo!" said Mauro contemptuously, and he spat onto the ground again.

"Exactly," said James. "Go." He spotted one of Ugo's guards watching them, his eyes shaded by his cap. "And Mauro, please, no more spitting!"

Mauro smiled. "James," he said, hugging him, "you are good friend. My sister, she would like you. I see you soon."

He waved and strolled off across the square. James watched until he was swallowed up by the milling crush of people.

Presently, Mr. Cooper-ffrench appeared, even more red-faced and sweaty than usual. He was amazed to see James, and even more amazed when he told him his story.

"I knew you should not have gone off on your own," he said. "I should have kept my eye on you. Now, we'd best get inside or we shall miss everything."

James picked up his battered old suitcase. "Don't let me

forget this," he said to Perry. "I'm bound to leave it somewhere if I'm not careful."

As they shuffled through the turnstiles, James got his first glimpse inside the stadium. He could hardly believe his eyes, although he should really have expected it. Count Ugo had built himself a miniature replica of the Colosseum in Rome. There was a wide, sand-covered ring in the center surrounded by a high wall, above which were steep banks of bench seats, and all around the top, silhouetted against the deep blue sky, were statues of Roman heroes.

"Do you suppose there's going to be a chariot race?" James said to Perry. "Or gladiators?"

Perry snorted with laughter. "Yes," he said. "Or m-maybe even a display of Christians being thrown to the lions!"

The locals were ranging themselves noisily on the benches, and girls with trays were wandering among them, handing out fruit and bread and drinks.

All eyes were on Count Ugo, who sat under a canopy on a raised platform with his sister, Jana. He was dressed in flowing white robes and looked every inch the Roman emperor. Jana was wearing even more jewelry than before, topped off with a gold tiara. They were flanked by several armed guards in their purple uniforms and two trumpeters in the garb of Roman legionnaries.

The trumpeters sounded a ragged fanfare, and Ugo rose to deliver an epic speech in Sardinian.

As he was ranting on, James took time to study the occupants of the exclusive guest of honor seats, a motley collection of about twenty men sitting next to Ugo. They didn't appear to be locals. They looked out of place here, in their flashy suits and sunglasses. They had an air of arrogance and self-importance about them, as if they were used to giving orders and being obeyed. They didn't look like politicians, aristocrats, or military men, though. There was something dangerous and secretive about them, something that said keep away. They looked as bored by the speech as James was, and sat there fanning themselves and not speaking to each other.

As James watched, Zoltan the Magyar took his place with them. He seemed perfectly at home among these men.

When Ugo finally finished, there was a burst of applause from the audience and some cheering, then the gates opened and a brass band marched in, playing a dreary tune. Ugo conducted the music with a serious look on his face.

After the band finished playing, there were more cheers from the crowd as a procession of locals in traditional attire marched in and circled the stadium with pipes bleating, trumpets blaring, drums banging, people singing, and flowers raining down onto their heads.

The procession seemed to go on forever, and James kept nodding off as the locals tramped round and round the ring. Eventually, some men in wooden masks and weird hairy goat costumes festooned with cowbells ran into the ring. They danced all over the place and acted out some sort of ritual that James found baffling but the crowd seemed to enjoy. There was a cheerful, rowdy atmosphere, but it was obvious that everyone was waiting for the main event.

James tried to stay awake by chatting to Perry, and told him everything that happened since he had left him in Abbasanta.

"Well, you've certainly had a more exciting time of it than we have," Perry babbled breathlessly. "It's been so dull since you left. Dull, dull, dull. Just ruins and m-more ruins, didn't know there were so m-many ruins in the world, beginning to think the whole world's one big ruin. Cagliari not m-much better, dismal place, and we've been staying in the worst hotel, I m-mean the worst, I'm sure the place has rats. I've been having the m-most awful time trying to sleep. Luckily, good old Love-Haight has some m-medicine. Ghastly stuff, bitter as anything, like drinking seawater."

"Well, I think I would have preferred a quiet time, actually," said James. "Rather than being attacked by bandits and nearly killed. I would have been more than happy if my only problem had been not being able to sleep."

"Tommy-rot!" said Perry. "I know you, James. You like a spot of danger. It adds pepper to your soup. Im-m-agine you getting the chance to drive a Hispano-Suiza, you lucky dog. And you got to see the palazzo as well. Us m-mere m-mortals can only gaze up at it and wonder. What's it like up there? I've heard he's got a lot of paintings and statues and suchlike."

James told Perry about the funicular railway, and Mauro spitting on Ugo's floor, and meeting Zoltan, and the strange conversation about the painting. James had thought the point of his story was Zoltan and his crazy talk of dying, but for some reason Perry seemed more interested in the painting.

"A saint, you say? With a sword stuck through his head?"

"Yes," said James. "You look shocked, Perry. Don't tell me you're squeamish. It's only a picture."

"Do you know who the saint was?" said Perry.

"No idea," said James. "I'm not big on saints. Why are you so interested?"

"Did he look sort of happy?" said Perry.

"Yes," said James, remembering what Zoltan had said about the picture. "Very happy."

"Was he wearing green and gold robes?"

"Think so."

"And the m-man killing him, he had on a sort of fur hat, you say?"

"Yes," said James. "With a big spike coming out of the top."

"It's Saint Boniface," said Perry.

"How do you know that?" said James.

"Because that sounds exactly like one of the paintings that was stolen from our house."

"Come off it," said James. "How could it be?"

"I know it sounds m-mad," said Perry. "But it's not a painting you'd easily forget."

Before James could say anything else, the goat dancers left and the ring was filled with drummers who made such a racket it was impossible to hold a conversation.

Once again the gates opened, and in galloped a horseman with a silver sword, riding a horse decorated with flowers.

There were cries of "*Su Compoidori!*" from the crowd.

The rider was a strange and slightly disturbing sight. He was wearing a baggy white shirt edged with puff and lace, a tight leather belt and waistcoat, and an elaborate mantilla— a Spanish bridal veil—on top of which sat a black top hat.

But strangest of all was his face, which was covered by a mask of a woman's face, expressionless and doll-like. He looked neither male nor female, like the living statue of some bizarre ancient god.

He rode around the stadium, acknowledging the cheers of the crowd and performing various stunts on the horse—standing in his saddle, lying flat, sitting backward. And all the while, the drummers kept up an incessant rolling beat that echoed off the walls and began to have a hypnotic, brain-rattling effect, so that James couldn't help but be caught up in the excitement.

When the horseman was ready, he rode to the center of the ring and stopped. He saluted Count Ugo with his sword, and then waved for the gates to be opened again. Two more horsemen entered, in similar attire, but with simpler white masks and stocking caps instead of the top hat. Their caps matched their waistcoats, one in black, the other red.

Still the drums rolled and thundered, and James was beginning to feel light-headed, almost drunk.

A rope was slung across the center of the ring with a small silver star hanging down from it. The two new horsemen now took it in turns to charge full tilt at the star and try to catch it on the points of their outstretched swords.

There was a storm of screams and cheers when they were successful, and groans of dismay when they failed.

There seemed to be a certain amount of betting going on among the spectators, and for the first time, James saw Ugo's special guests become animated. He could see a lot of passionate arguments taking place and money being thrown around.

James was won over by the noise and excitement, all his tiredness forgotten, and while he had no money to gamble with, he decided to cheer for the red horseman, who won by six stars to five.

When the competition finished, it was lunchtime, and everyone trooped into the town square, where several suckling pigs had been spit-roasted over fires, and stalls were serving food.

The streets were filled with the din of drums and the incessant rasp of trumpets, and the locals milled around, chatting and laughing. Everyone seemed more interested in drinking than eating. There was wine everywhere, and people were getting drunker and drunker.

James was starving, however, and he realized he had had nothing to eat since last night. He found Mauro's friend, Stefano, at one of the stalls and snapped up some of the flat crispy *carasau* bread that he had grown so fond of since he had been here, then helped himself to some roast pork.

Nearby, a group of locals was dancing in a big circle, holding hands, accompanied by guitars and accordions, and next to them was a noisy mob of men clustered around, watching something and yelling at the top of their voices.

James and Perry went over to have a look and found that it was a competition of Sardinian wrestling.

The display seemed to have been put on for the benefit of Ugo, who sat on a platform with his hard-faced guests, watching from beneath a parasol. Zoltan was standing behind Ugo, shouting encouragement.

The other Eton boys were here, too, clustered around

the edge of the platform, yelling as loudly as anyone else.

The rules looked simple enough. Men in loose shepherds' outfits grabbed hold of each other and tried to throw their opponent to the ground. As far as James could make out, the loser was the man who bit the dust two times out of three.

There was more betting on the wrestling, and Zoltan and Ugo seemed to have a major wager on between them. It all came down to the last bout. The two wrestlers paraded round the square whipping up the crowd's excitement, and Zoltan and Ugo chose their favorites.

Just before the bout began, however, James saw Ugo whisper something to a guard, who darted over and had a quiet word with one of the wrestlers. The wrestler looked toward Ugo and nodded.

The man lost the bout and Ugo collected his money from a disappointed Zoltan.

"I'm not exactly an expert on Sardinian wrestling," said Perry, "but I'd say he deliberately lost that m-match."

"It certainly looked that way," said James.

Just then Ugo spotted James and called him over.

"I must apologize for my anger at the palazzo, James," he said. "I was feeling a little tense. This is an important day for me, and perhaps I was rather too quick to lose my temper. Where is your servant now?"

"He's left," said James. "Gone home."

"You must tell him when you see him that I bear him no ill," said Ugo. "I was merely being . . ." he paused while he thought of the right word, "playful." He looked around and smiled. "These must be the other boys from Eton," he said. "When I heard they were on the island I knew I must invite them. Eton is a good school. A school for aristocrats."

"Hello, pleased to m-meet you. Perry M-Mandeville," said Perry, shaking Ugo's hand before he knew what was happening. "Jolly good show you've put on. We were just saying how m-much we enjoyed the wrestling."

"Ah," said Ugo. "The mountain men love to wrestle. *'Prima bevono, poi stringono!'*"

The boys looked blank, and Zoltan translated for them.

"'First they drink, then they fight,'" he said.

"You British boys are famous for your games," said Ugo. "You must put on a display. We have shown you our Sardinian sports. Now you will show us your sports. Do you wrestle?"

"Wrestling is not thought one of the more noble sports in England," said Zoltan. "But boxing is much enjoyed, I believe."

"Do you boys box at school?" said Ugo.

"M-most of us," said Perry.

"Splendid! Then it is decided," said Ugo. "We shall have a competition of English boxing! I will choose my champion and, Zoltan, you will choose yours."

"I choose James Bond," said Zoltan. "He is not the biggest, or the oldest, but he looks the fiercest."

The other boys cheered and jostled James, who stood there reluctantly, not wanting to be made a spectacle of.

Ugo was smiling. "I have chosen my champion," he said and pointed to someone in the crowd. "You, boy, there, step forward."

James looked around and groaned as Tony Fitzpaine walked out and joined him, baring his big teeth in an arrogant smile.

"This time you won't take me by surprise, Bond," he said. "I'll be ready for you. It'll be a fair fight, and you will lose."

CHAPTER 16—GLADIATORS

James and Fitzpaine were taken to a private area behind the stadium to get ready. A guard showed them into a spotless, marble-floored room with paintings of sportsmen on the walls and a big sunken pool in the middle. A waiting attendant gave them towels and shorts, and James started to get changed.

After a few minutes Zoltan came in with Ugo. They were both carrying boxing gloves, and each one went to his champion.

"Do you think you can do it?" said Zoltan, slipping a glove on to James's hand. "Do you think you can beat the big fellow?"

James swallowed hard. He had wanted to get his fight with Fitzpaine out in the open, to put an end to it, but not quite this far out in the open.

He looked across at him on the other side of the room.

"I'll try," he said.

James had done a bit of boxing at Eton and was pretty good. He was light and fast on his feet, with a determination never to give up. He had a strong clean punch and could take a battering. But this was different. He would be boxing out in the stadium, in front of all those people, in the fierce heat, against a boy who hated him. On top of all that, he had been knocked unconscious the night before and had had very little sleep.

These were not the perfect conditions for going into a boxing match.

"He is taller than you," said Zoltan, "but he has shorter arms. So I think maybe you have the longer reach. Use it. He is heavier and maybe stronger, so you must be faster. Be a dancer, not a fighter. Keep moving. Keep out of his way until you see your chance."

James watched as Ugo's guard laced on Fitzpaine's gloves. The boy grimaced and spoke sharply to him, but Ugo leaned over and whispered something in Fitzpaine's ear. The boy's eyes widened for a moment before he nodded his head and smiled.

What was Ugo up to now? James remembered how the Count had paid the wrestler to lose the match earlier. How was he going to cheat his way to victory this time?

Ugo and Fitzpaine briefly glanced over at James, as if they both knew something he didn't.

Well, whatever it was, there was nothing he could do about it now.

"Look at him," said Zoltan quietly. "The great Count Ugo Carnifex. I will tell you a secret, James: Ugo is no more a count than I am."

"I know," said James. "He's a goatherd, from the mountains."

Zoltan chuckled. "You seem to know a lot," he said, and grimaced. He was not finding it easy to lace the gloves with his bad arm, and he had to call the attendant over to help.

"Maybe you also know why Ugo has such a hatred of dirt?" Zoltan went on.

"No," said James.

"Then I will tell you," said Zoltan. "He grew up here in the Barbagia, and his family was as poor as everyone else. So when war broke out, it was a chance for him to escape. He joined the famous Brigata Sassari and went off to fight. For two years he fought against the army of the Austro-Hungarian Empire in the mountains along Italy's northeast border.

"At the battle of Triangular Woods he was wounded in the head, and his younger brother, Guido, who had fought alongside him for the whole campaign, carried him to safety on his shoulders under heavy fire.

"The wound was not serious, but the shock of it caused Ugo's hair to turn white.

"In the confusion of the battle they found themselves cut off from the brigade behind enemy lines. There were four of them, and Ugo was not the only one who was wounded. Another man, Colombo, had caught a bullet in the thigh and was weak from loss of blood, so the men could not travel fast. Lost and scared and confused, they found refuge in a deserted building.

"But it was no ordinary building. It was an abandoned palazzo whose owners had fled and taken everything with them, so that the rooms were bare and empty. The place was still magnificent, however, and Ugo had never seen anything like it. The four Sardinians wandered from room to room, amazed. There were so many rooms, they soon lost count. How could anyone need so many rooms?

"And then they heard the sound of trucks and they knew they must hide. They searched the palazzo and at last found a small trapdoor that led down into a septic tank, where the waste from all the toilets was collected.

"They climbed down and stood up to their waists in stinking filth.

"All that night they stayed there, listening to the voices in the palazzo above and shaking with fear, waiting for the soldiers to leave.

"It was hot and dark and choking down there. The stench of human excrement was foul, and when the enemy soldiers used the toilets above, more filth rained down on them.

"The four trapped Sardinians dared not speak or make any sound, in case they were discovered.

"It was worst for Colombo. His wound was bleeding steadily into the wet sludge. But he was a brave man and made no sound at all.

"It was the longest night of Ugo's life. His eyes were stinging, and he felt as if the filth was seeping into him, into his nose, his throat, the pores of his skin. He tried to keep his hands above the surface, holding them in the air, like this." Zoltan mimed the action, a look of terrible disgust on his face, enjoying the story. "But he was too tired, the effort was too great, and over and over again his eyes fell shut and he was woken as his hands dropped into the thick slime."

Zoltan laughed and pretended to wipe his hands on his tunic.

"What happened in the end?" said James.

"The soldiers went away, and they could at last come

out. But not Colombo. At some point in the night he had quietly slipped beneath the stinking layer of scum and drowned.

"The other three must have been a ghastly sight, covered from head to toe in green and yellow muck."

"That's disgusting," said James.

"Quite so," said Zoltan, glancing at Ugo. "They stripped off their clothes and found a shower that was working. Ugo stayed there for ages, scrubbing his body until it was raw and bleeding. Even now, all these years later, he bathes at least four times a day."

"What a horrible story," said James, who suddenly felt dirty himself.

"But it's not the end," said Zoltan, "because as they were standing there, naked, two enemy soldiers came in. It was hard to tell who was more surprised, and there was madness as the Sardinians rushed to grab their guns." Zoltan sighed. "Scared men do not shoot straight," he said. "There was a quick burst of panicked firing, after which two more men lay dead. One of the enemy and one of the Sardinians.

"It was a stalemate. Ugo was without a weapon. His brother Guido and the enemy soldier standing there, pointing their guns at each other." Zoltan stopped and inspected James's gloves. "You are ready," he said.

"Wait," James protested. "You can't stop there. What happened?"

"I will tell you the rest of the story another day," said Zoltan. "You have a boy to fight."

"No, tell me," said James, but just then the room was filled with the reek of perfume and Countess Jana came in, her high heels clicking on the polished floor. She looked the two boys up and down and licked her lips.

"What strong boys you are," she said. "I hope your pretty faces don't get too badly broken." She slipped a silver ring off her finger.

"This ring to the winner," she said.

The roar of the crowds as James marched out into the sunlight was deafening. He had wondered before if Ugo was going to stage a gladiatorial combat, but he had had no idea that he would be one of the gladiators.

He walked over to where a chair had been set out for him. The sand felt hot beneath his bare feet. Zoltan gave him a long drink of water and poured some more over his head to cool him down.

One of Ugo's guards, who was acting as referee, shouted a few words to the spectators, then rang the bell for the start of the bout.

The two boys came out into the center of the ring, circling each other warily. Fitzpaine was big, but clumsy, and plodded around in an ungainly fashion. James took Zoltan's advice and kept on his toes

There were shouts from the crowd. James looked up to see Ugo smiling imperiously, his chin resting in one hand. He turned to the Contessa, who was watching with hooded eyes, and shouted a few words into her ear.

She looked at James and clamped a long, painted fingernail between her teeth.

Fitzpaine lumbered toward James, who dodged backward, not letting the boy get near him.

"Stand still, you bunny rabbit," said Fitzpaine, and he charged at James like a bull, fists flailing the air. James ducked the blows and skipped sideways, but still Fitzpaine came on, his punches inaccurate and leaving him wide open. James nipped in and gave him a quick jab to the side of his undefended belly, and Fitzpaine swore, launching a wild punch at James's head. The glove glanced off the side of James's face. It should have been fairly harmless, but James felt his whole head jar, and he tasted blood in his mouth

Hell.

Fitzpaine's punch was harder than it looked.

James danced backward, shaking his head to try and clear it, and he saw Fitzpaine smiling in triumph. That gave James fresh energy, and he darted forward with a straight left that Fitzpaine managed to block with his raised gloves. It wasn't an elegant defense, but it worked, and to James it was like hitting a brick wall. His hand stung badly, even within the protection of the glove.

That had nothing to do with Fitzpaine's punch.

The boy had merely held his hands up. Why had it hurt so much?

As James was momentarily distracted and confused, Fitzpaine managed to step in and throw a good punch. James saw it coming a fraction of a second too late. He was just able to twist his body and jerk his head clear, and the punch, which otherwise would have landed squarely on his chin, caught him in the side of the neck.

Again it was like a sledgehammer hitting him. He grunted and dropped for a moment to his knees, stunned. Fitzpaine saw his chance and blundered forward, but James rocked on to his heels and threw himself upward and back-ward away from the punch.

How had he done it? How had Fitzpaine landed such a killer blow?

James remembered the whispered conversation with Ugo—Fitzpaine looking into his gloves.

There was something in them, weights of some sort. Sand, or maybe even metal.

Ugo obviously didn't like to leave anything to chance.

Damn him.

This changed everything. James would have a hell of a job not being knocked cold. He scurried away from Fitzpaine and threw a questioning look to Zoltan, who seemed concerned.

By moving constantly and keeping clear of Fitzpaine, James managed to scrape through the rest of the round, but the bell seemed a long time coming.

He went over to Zoltan and slumped on to the chair.

"What is the matter?" said the Hungarian.

"He's got weights in his gloves," said James. "It's like being hit by a motor car."

"I thought so," said Zoltan, and he fired off a colorful string of insults at Ugo. "But don't worry. You are doing the right thing, James. You have to keep out of his way. Don't let his punches find their mark. Those gloves of his will be heavy, and with each swing they will get heavier. It will get harder and harder for him to keep them up, and as he grows tired his blows will have less strength behind them. If ever you see an opening, go in quickly, hit him and retreat before he has a chance to come back at you. You might just wear him down."

"I don't know," said James. "I just don't know if I can do it."

He was already exhausted. The constant tension and need to keep moving had drained him, but most tiring of all was being repeatedly hit. Well, he would have to concentrate on taking that pounding on the gloves and not the face or body.

The referee rang the bell for the second round, and James took a last swig of water before walking cautiously to the center of the arena, not taking his eyes off Fitzpaine for a moment. It was a burning hot day and the circular stadium walls trapped the heated air. It scalded James's lungs and caused sweat to stream down from his head to his feet. Sand stuck to his damp legs.

But one thought cheered him.

It was just as bad for Fitzpaine.

James could see the strain on his face. If he had thought this was going to be an easy win, he was having to think again now.

Fitzpaine obviously wanted it over quickly. He grunted and charged at James. James blocked his assault, keeping his gloves up and turning his body to take the punches on his upper arms. He backed away and looked down: he was already heavily bruised.

He bided his time. He didn't want to waste any energy. He threw the occasional light jab at Fitzpaine to soften him and keep him scared, but never powerfully enough to give him any idea of how hard he could really punch.

In came Fitzpaine again, but slower this time, his feet dragging.

He lashed out with a punch so wild that James easily

dropped into a crouch and avoided it. The momentum of Fitzpaine's swing kept his heavy glove moving, however, so that he was completely off balance and his defense wide open.

James saw his chance; he forced himself up from his crouch, using the full power of his legs, and drove his fist hard into Fitzpaine's chin. It connected perfectly and whipped the boy's head back.

Then the crowd was cheering madly and Fitzpaine was staggering backward, arms groping for balance. He took three increasingly out of control steps before he stumbled and sat down heavily.

He wasn't knocked out, though. He stood up, spitting blood from his mouth, and shook his head.

He was tough, then, and had no glass jaw. James felt a glimmer of respect for him.

Before anything else could happen, the referee rang the bell. James was sure the round hadn't run its full length, but he was grateful for the rest.

He went over to Zoltan, who gave him more water.

"That was a good punch," Zoltan said admiringly. "I thought he would go down for sure. But you have him now. That will have hurt. It will be hard for him to go on, but you must still keep out of the way of his gloves, or he will finish you."

"You don't have to tell me that," said James as he found Perry in the crowd. He had a wide smile on his face. He offered James a thumbs-up, and that gave him new strength.

The bell clanged and he walked over feeling fresh and ready.

Fitzpaine was really showing the strain now. He was covered in sweat and breathing noisily through his mouth.

"Come on," said James. "Let's get this over with."

Fitzpaine once again started the first attack, raining blows onto James, who managed to keep back far enough for them to land fairly harmlessly. Then he weaved around for a while, tiring Fitzpaine and frustrating him. James knew that when the older boy was angered he made mistakes.

And now Fitzpaine made one: he let both his arms flop down in a gesture of frustration. James powered back with a counterattack, jabbing Fitzpaine with stinging blows to his ribs in a quick combination of left, right, left, and he completed the assault with a right hook that took the boy in the cheek and sent a spray of spit into the air. But Fitzpaine was quick to retaliate, too quick for James, and he managed to land a lucky blow to James's gut.

James gasped as the air was pumped out of his lungs, and he felt like he was going to be sick. For a moment his vision darkened and black spots swam in front of his eyes. He was fighting for breath, his head spinning, and had to stop himself from panicking.

He stepped outside his body for a moment and ordered it to function properly, forcing it to do what it clearly didn't want to do.

Somehow his legs carried him away from Fitzpaine before he could hit him again, but it was a near thing; one more good punch from Fitzpaine would have ended it.

James took a deep breath and skipped backward as Fitzpaine came on. Then he moved sideways and around as Fitzpaine's big heavy gloves swept harmlessly through the air.

The swings were feeble now and dropping low. Fitzpaine could barely lift his gloves to James's head height.

But don't get overconfident again, James.

Bide your time. Don't rush it. Wait for the right moment.

There!

Another missed punch had caused Fitzpaine to tip forward and lose his footing. His guard was down. He was distracted. James's hands were both already coiled back and ready to strike, and now he let them go, hammering his right arm forward like a piston with all his weight behind it. It smashed into Fitzpaine's face and the boy's head flopped back like a rag doll. His knees buckled, he went into a low crouch, and before he could do anything else to recover, James let fly with his left hand, coming down hard on Fitzpaine's temple. The second blow flattened him, swatting him down into the sand, where he lay still.

It was over.

James let his arms fall to his side, and stood over his opponent, feeling empty, barely aware of the cheering and calling from the stands.

Zoltan and the referee ran forward and rolled Fitzpaine onto his back. He was still conscious, but bleeding heavily from his nose. He was fighting to focus his eyes, and James hoped that he was going to be all right.

Zoltan slapped him a few times and splashed water into his face. At last he groaned and sat up. The referee quickly unfastened his gloves and rubbed Fitzpaine's wrists.

James glanced up at Ugo. There was a look of contempt in the Count's eyes. This was not meant to happen.

James stooped down and picked up one of Fitzpaine's

discarded gloves. It felt heavy in his hand. He pulled back his arm, and with the last of his strength, he threw it up into the stadium, where it landed with a thud at Ugo's feet.

Jana's weather-beaten face twisted into a smile, and she tossed something down to James.

He caught it.

It was the silver ring.

As the crowd cheered, Ugo stood up and disappeared into the shadows at the back of his platform.

Fitzpaine was standing, supported by Zoltan. He looked at James and tried to smile.

"Well done," he said. "That was a good fight. And . . ." His eyes dropped for a moment, ashamed. "I'm sorry."

"I'm sorry for the last punch," said James. "I knew the right had finished you. It was cruel to follow with the left. . . . But I suppose I just wanted to make sure."

"It's always best to make sure," said Fitzpaine, and he held out his hand.

James shook it.

"No hard feelings, eh?" Again Fitzpaine attempted a smile, though it looked horrible and twisted on his swollen face.

"No hard feelings," said James.

He just hoped that Count Ugo Carnifex would feel the same way.

Somehow he doubted it.

CHAPTER 17—BLOOD BROTHERS

Mauro had been walking all afternoon, but he didn't mind. He was walking away from the nightmare at La Casa Polipo; he was leaving Count Ugo behind him; but best of all he was going home. He hadn't been back since Easter, and he was looking forward to seeing his mother and little sister.

He enjoyed life at Capo d'Orso. He liked working for Victor and he liked relaxing on the beach in his spare time, but he still didn't think of Casa Polipo as his home. He never would. The village was home, and Victor and Poliponi would never replace his family.

The people of the Barbagia were tough and fiercely loyal to their families. Arguments here were usually settled with the gun. There were feuds going back generations, the original reasons for the fights long forgotten. Mauro's own father had been killed in just such a feud when Mauro was only three years old and his mother was pregnant with his little sister. She had bravely approached the other family and begged them to end the feud, as she didn't want to risk losing her only son. The other family, also sick of bloodshed, had thankfully agreed.

But the feud had not been entirely forgotten, and Mauro's sister had been christened Vendetta. Vendetta Maria Grazia Benetutti.

She was thirteen years old, now; small and dark, with the eyes of a cat and the temper of a wild animal. She was growing up fast, and Mauro missed her.

He was nearly home. He had left the Gennargentu Mountains and was in the Supramonte to the north. These mountains were stark and dramatic, with great, sheer walls of jagged gray rock thrusting up above the tree line as if they had been pushed through from below. The peaks were bare and gaunt, tinged here and there with burned orange.

Mauro knew this land well. He had grown up here, playing among the rocks and trees. He breathed in the scent of wild thyme and rosemary.

He crested a ridge and startled a big mouflon, a mountain sheep, with the curled horns of a ram. It leaped away across the rocks, scattering stones in its wake.

From here Mauro got the first sight of his village. Past a small wooded valley, the ground rose sharply and he could clearly see a little cluster of white buildings, clinging to the side of the far mountain.

He was soon hiking through the woods, singing a song to himself, a silly thing that he used to sing with his mother when he was little. He heard the noise of a large animal in the trees, but thought nothing of it. It was another mouflon, probably, or perhaps a boar rooting for acorns.

It was certainly nothing dangerous. There were no wolves or bears on the island.

As he pressed on, however, he became aware that the animal was following him. No wild animal would do that; they were all too nervous of humans.

He carried on walking, and gradually the animal got

nearer. He could clearly make out the sound of heavy feet stepping on the ground and twigs snapping.

It was too large to be a person. What was it?

Mauro stopped, standing in the center of the track.

"*Chini sesi?*" he called out. Who's there? But there was no answer. "*Faidi biri!*" Show yourself.

The footsteps had stopped. There was only the sound of the woods now, the wind teasing the leaves in the upper branches of the holm oaks, a tiny brook rattling over a stony bed, a bird twittering, bees humming in a nearby strawberry tree.

Mauro peered into the woods to one side, where he thought the sound had been coming from, but could see nothing.

Maybe he'd imagined it.

He turned to carry on, and as he did so, a horse and rider emerged from the trees ahead of him.

Mauro frowned and had a sudden urge to laugh.

The rider had on the outfit of *Su Compoidori* from the festival. With full bridal veil, black hat, and the mask of a woman's painted face.

What on earth was he doing here? He looked completely out of place.

"*Ita oli de mei?*" Mauro called out. What do you want?

The rider said nothing. The mask showed nothing. It just watched him with its steady, unfeeling gaze.

The rider now drew a sword and pointed it briefly skyward before leveling it at Mauro.

Surely he was not going to charge him as if he were a silver star.

It was unreal. This carnival figure here, in the woods, in the middle of nowhere.

The rider spurred the horse and it jumped forward, galloping down the track toward Mauro, the thin blade of the sword unwavering.

He *was* going to charge him.

Mauro shouted, then turned and fled into the trees.

But the rider had picked his spot well. There was space between the trees here for a horse to pass with ease, and the ground was level and firm.

Mauro dashed between the oaks, zigzagging wildly, but the horse was too fast for him. He could hear its hoof beats growing louder behind him.

He cursed.

This was crazy.

He looked back briefly and saw that the rider was almost upon him. He threw himself to the ground and the blade scraped across his shoulder, tearing his shirt.

He scrambled to his feet and bolted back the way he had come. He had to try and head toward the village. His only hope was that somebody nearby could help him.

He called out for help. "*Agiudai! Agiudaimi po presceri!*" but his voice was swallowed up by the trees.

The rider had turned his horse and was now fast approaching again, the mask still showing the same placid expression.

The path widened into a clearing, and as Mauro emerged into the dazzling sunlight, he disturbed a swarm of scarlet butterflies that flew up around him in a swirling mass.

He swore. It was too open here. The horse would be able

to gallop unimpeded. He looked quickly around; there was thick vegetation on one side, dense brambles laden with blackberries and a low holly tree. That would stop the horse.

But could he get there before the horse?

He had to try. He had no choice.

He sped up, sprinting faster than he ever thought possible, the stony ground a blur beneath his feet.

The brambles were getting nearer, nearer; he could see the blackberries glistening. He was going to make it, yes, just a few meters more. . . .

Anyone watching from the village would have seen a cloud of red butterflies spiraling upward into the sky, and if they had been listening they might just have heard a faint cry.

"Mamai—"

It was eight o'clock at night and the festivities in Sant' Ugo were still in full swing. James and Perry had become separated from the other boys and were watching a group of men who were singing on a small stage beneath the walls of the stadium.

The afternoon had been crazy. There were fireworks in the streets. Music and noise everywhere. Some local men had even organized a horse race in the main square.

Things had quieted down now, and James was enjoying the lulling sound of the singers. He drifted in and out of sleep while the unaccompanied voices of the men haunted his dreams. There were four singers, all wearing the local black and white costume with stocking caps, and the music was unlike anything he had ever heard before. The sound was inhuman, like the drones of bagpipes. There was something ancient and primitive about it, and James kept imagining that he was back in the tower at Sant'Antine.

England and its gray skies seemed a million miles away.

The two boys were sitting at a table with a group of drunken shepherds; James slumped forward, his head resting on his forearms. The shepherds were passing a bottle of wine around, drinking straight from the neck and not bothering with glasses.

As one of them plonked the bottle on to the table, James woke and glanced at it. The wine was called Mithras and the label had a picture of the god killing the bull. He was just about to pick it up and have a closer look, when somebody grabbed it.

James sucked in his breath.

The hand holding the bottle had a tattoo on the back of it.

A tattoo of the letter *M*.

He looked up.

Standing by the table, draining the bottle, was the man with the scarred cheeks who James had seen talking to Cooper-ffrench in Eton.

And those eyes.

Were they the same eyes he had seen above the black mask in Victor's kitchen last night?

James turned away quickly, hoping that the man hadn't seen him, and kept his face down.

The man tossed the empty bottle to one side and it smashed against a wall. The shepherds cheered. The man laughed and walked on.

"Wait here," said James, getting up from the table.

"Where are you going?" said Perry.

"I'll be back in a minute," said James.

Before Perry could ask any more questions, James hurried off after the rapidly disappearing figure of the scarred man. The presence of the crowds made it easier for James to follow him. If it had been just the two of them, alone on the night streets, the man would have instantly known that there was someone on his tail. As it was, he had no idea. James kept back far enough so that if the man turned round unexpectedly he wouldn't notice him.

He felt groggy and worn out. It was an effort just to put one foot in front of the other. He was aware of every cut on his bruised and battered body, but the thrill of the chase was on him, and he was rapidly coming alive.

The man walked through the town until he arrived at the funicular railway. The bored and sleepy guard from the morning had been replaced by a group of distinctly more serious-looking men, who made it very clear that nobody was going up to the palazzo without their say-so.

James hung back in a doorway and watched as the scarred man stopped to talk to the guards, who evidently knew him. One of them gave him a cigarette and lit it for him. As they were talking, two more men approached. They looked like they must be some of Ugo's special guests from the stadium, wearing dark suits and acting tough. They showed invitations to the guards and wandered over toward the railway car.

James had to find out who the scarred man was and what he was up to. He made a snap decision. Somehow he was going to follow him up to the palazzo.

The car was stopped inside a wooden shed, which was partially open along one side to let the passengers on and off. If he could get inside the shed he might be able to get onto the roof of the car without being seen.

He spotted a concrete gully coming out through an opening in the end of the shed and running off down a slope into a drain. He remembered from before how a water tank beneath the car was emptied when it stopped. The drain was only protected by a wire fence. It might be a way in.

Moving in a low crouch, and keeping the shed between himself and the guards, James approached the fence. As soon as he was there, he dropped to the ground and was just thin enough to squeeze under it on his belly, then he crawled quickly along the ground and rolled into the gully.

He waited a moment to find out if he had been seen.

Nothing.

He wormed his way along the gully toward the shed. In a moment he was through the opening in the bottom of the shed and inside.

There was the railway car, with water dripping from underneath it. He wriggled forward a few more feet.

Suddenly, he heard a metallic thunk and a rushing sound.

The tank was being emptied.

As a wall of water hit him and washed him back down the gully, he spotted an iron bar above his head and managed to grab on to it. He hung on for dear life as the swirling deluge of water buffeted him and pulled at him, trying to tear him loose.

The water had woken him up, but he had to summon every reserve of strength and determination not to let go.

As fast as it had come, the torrent stopped and he hauled himself out onto the floor of the shed, soaked and half drowned.

But he couldn't rest.

If the tank had been emptied it meant that the car would soon be moving off.

He stood up. All his pain forgotten. He could see the men in the car, chatting and smoking, but it was too dark for them to see him. Moving fast, he climbed a pile of packing crates in the corner and managed to reach up to one of the cross beams that supported the roof. He pulled himself up, and using a second beam as a walkway, he scurried along it until he was directly over the car.

There were shouts from below.

"Come on, Smiler, hurry up."

"We're leaving. Get on board!"

James saw the scarred man approach the car and toss his cigarette to one side before getting on.

Smiler. So that was his name. Well, it made sense.

The car jolted forward, and as quickly and as delicately as possible, James dropped down onto its roof. He got on to his hands and knees, then lay flat, moments before the car cleared the low archway at the front of the shed.

James held his breath, praying that he would not be visible to the guards.

Slowly, agonizingly slowly, they crept forward.

There was no shout. No warning shot. No sudden braking.

At last they began to pick up speed and were soon trundling briskly up the mountain through the darkness.

James stayed where he was, dripping onto the painted wood of the carriage. Slowly he let his breath out.

What the hell was he doing?

He had a reckless side to his nature, and one day it was going to get him into big trouble.

After a while they passed the second car coming down, and then crossed the bridge into the tunnel. It was pitch-dark in here, and James was worried that a low outcrop of rock would smash into him. Thankfully, he emerged from the tunnel unscathed, and heard distant voices, the clink of glasses, music, and laughter. He looked up. The white walls of the palazzo were glowing in the moonlight, and here and there a light showed in one of the lower windows.

They were nearing their destination.

He'd got this far. Would his luck hold out any longer?

He pressed himself as flat as he could as they slowed down and came to a halt at the brightly lit piazza. He waited for the passengers to get off, and watched Smiler make his way across the square to an archway on one side. When James was sure it was safe, he slid down the outside of the car onto the tracks. He rubbed his hair with his fingers, drying it as best he could, and wrung out the front of his sodden shirt.

There were two guards on duty, but having checked the credentials of the men arriving on the railway, they had returned to their card game inside their sentry post.

As soon as he dared, James darted out from behind the car and into the deserted piazza. He ran along the side, keeping close to the buildings, heading toward the archway.

There was a short alleyway on the other side and some winding steps leading down to a lower level.

The steps came out into a courtyard. It was lit by candles and blazing torches, and there was an ornamental pond in the middle of it. There were tables set out with drinks and food, and small groups of men in suits were drinking and chatting.

There were two or three local girls with them, looking self-conscious in expensive dresses and wearing too much makeup. They were laughing too loudly and had a slightly nervous air about them.

James spotted Smiler. He had stopped to talk to someone, but he was soon on the move again. The men finished their drinks and began following him in ones and twos. James realized that if he was going to keep up with Smiler, he would have to show himself.

He picked up a tray of empty glasses from one of the tables and walked briskly across the courtyard, hoping that if anyone spotted him they would mistake him for one of Ugo's servants.

He was just congratulating himself for getting away with it, when a bull-necked man with a broken nose stopped him.

"*Je te connais*," he said, and James shook his head.

"*Oui. Je te connais*," the man repeated. He put James's tray aside, grabbed James by the shoulders, and peered at him, breathing alcohol fumes into his face. Then he laughed. "*Tu es le garçon du stade*," he said and threw a mock punch at James. "*Beau combat. Tu l'as massacré!*"

He laughed again and shook James's hand.

James mumbled something and shuffled off in the direction Smiler had taken.

He thought he'd lost him, but down another alleyway

and more steps, and there he was, striding across a terrace toward what looked like a semicircular temple half carved out of the rock.

Ugo's guests seemed to be congregating here. They were coming from all directions.

James watched as a group of men went up the steps in front of the temple, between the pillars and into the brightly lit interior.

His mind was alive with questions.

What was Smiler doing here in Ugo's palazzo? Was he the man in the mask who had led the attack on Victor's house? And what was his connection to Cooper-ffrench? Then there was the painting of St Boniface. Had it really been stolen from Perry's family? And the painting of Ugo, in the cellar at Eton. Why had it been there?

There were too many coincidences for them to be just coincidences. There was a common thread in all this, something to tie it all together, but James couldn't grasp it. It was too thin and wispy.

There was only one way to find out.

He had to see what was going on inside the temple.

James studied the building. The walls were blank and windowless, but it had a domed roof supported by statues standing on a ledge. Light spilt out from behind the statues. Maybe there were windows there.

The last of the stragglers had gone inside, and there was nobody around.

James crossed the terrace toward the temple.

There was a big equestrian statue of Count Ugo standing in the corner, and he used it like a ladder, quickly scaling the horse and rider. Finally, by standing on Ugo's head, James was just high enough to be able to jump across to the ledge.

He landed well, startling some doves, which flew off with a noisy clatter. He crept along the ledge until he found a gap where he could squeeze through between two statues of semi-naked women. There was a narrow space behind here, thick with birdlime and stinking of ammonia.

He shuffled forward in a squatting position until he came to a small square opening covered by a metal grille that looked down on the interior of the temple.

He could see a mosaic floor covered in signs of the zodiac, and a large circular marble table.

About thirty men were sat around the table. James recognized the bull-necked Frenchman who had accosted him, the two men from the railway, and there was Zoltan, looking yellow and feverish, his tunic spotted with blood from his shoulder.

Standing apart from them was Smiler. From a distance his scar looked even more like a painted-on smile, so that, with his red hair and pale skin, he looked like some horrible clown.

Ugo was standing next to him, a goblet raised in his hand.

"*Salve amice,*" he said solemnly. "*Iterum tibi occurrere mihi placet.*"

"Spare us," said Zoltan. "You sound ridiculous, Ugo. You can play the Roman emperor all you like, but you cannot expect us to join in."

"I forgot," said Ugo patronizingly. "You cannot speak Latin. You always were the more stupid one, Zoltan."

"I can speak several languages, Ugo," said Zoltan. "Useful

ones. Latin is a dead language for dead people. Your secret cult, your speaking in tongues, it is not serious. If you wish to have real power you must learn that it is about more than dressing some peasants in fancy uniforms and speaking Latin and pretending to be Julius Caesar."

"Real power, Zoltan?" said Ugo. "What do you know of real power?"

He went to a guard and took a gun from him. James recognized it. It was a Thompson submachine gun.

"This is real power," said Ugo, fondling the weapon.

"And you would not have it without me," said Zoltan. "Don't forget that. You would have nothing without me."

"I will admit," said Ugo, returning the gun to his guard, "that you have been helpful to me over the years, Zoltan. But you are not the only one. All these men have been helpful to me. The Pasulo brothers from Sicily, Count Armando from Lisbon, Herr Gröman and Doctor Morell from Germany, Henri Boucher from France . . . I look around the table here and I see familiar faces from Spain, from Turkey, from Armenia, from Greece. What language should I speak, Zoltan?"

"I know your dream," said Zoltan. "To have an international language of crime. But we do not understand Latin and we do not care to learn. What is wrong with English?"

There was mumbled agreement from around the table.

"Very well," said Ugo, though he didn't sound too happy about it. "Now, before we start, we must drink a toast."

Smiler went round the table filling up goblets with a thick red liquid. The men peered at it and sniffed suspiciously.

Ugo raised his drink.

"It is the blood of a bull," he said, and there were a few sounds of disgust from the men. "We will drink it and it will unite us, under the protection of Mithras. We will become a brotherhood so powerful that nobody will be able to stand against us."

"Is this black magic really necessary?" said someone.

"It shows that we are not ordinary men," said Ugo. "This blood represents the blood of the ordinary people. The people of Europe. We will grow strong on their blood. Now, show me that you are men and drink . . . to the Millenaria!"

Ugo gulped down the contents of his goblet and then turned it upside down to show that it was empty. Reluctantly the other men copied him. There were groans, and one or two of them choked and spluttered.

"The trick is to drink it quickly," lisped Ugo, with a wet smile. "Otherwise it congeals in your throat. . . ."

UCMM. The letters painted on the frame of the portrait of Ugo in Eton.

Ugo Carnifex and the symbol for the Millenaria.

It had been so obvious. Why hadn't he seen it before?

The men around the table put down their goblets and there was a low murmur of conversation. Ugo had to raise his voice to be heard above them.

"I already have a network of spies, criminals, revolutionaries; people who can spread lies and terror, but with you men here I can create something truly extraordinary. All I require is that you put in a certain sum of money each, to show your commitment and to create a war chest on which we can build our empire."

"It is certainly an interesting idea," said a man with a heavy German accent. "But I hardly think you have the manpower to take on a real army and fight a war."

"I do not need to fight a war," said Ugo. "I will let others do that for me. After all, how did the ancient Romans defeat you Germans?"

"What has that to do with anything?"

"How did Caesar conquer Gaul?" Ugo went on, ignoring the German. "I will tell you. He made sure that the different tribes were so busy fighting each other, they would not be able to fight him. Well, nothing has changed in Europe in the last two thousand years. The tribes have simply got bigger. The English hate the Germans, the Germans hate the Russians, the Russians hate the Italians, the Italians hate the French, and the French hate everyone."

There was scattered laughter around the table.

"And where did all this hatred and rivalry lead?" said Ugo. "To the Great War. To millions of young men blown to pieces in the mud." He walked slowly around the table, looking into the face of each man. "During that time the opportunities for criminal activity were immense," he said. "Many men like us got rich while the authorities were looking the other way, busy fighting the war. Our first aim will always be to push Europe into another war, to turn one country against another. For where there is chaos we can prosper—"

"If what you say is true," interrupted a Turkish man at the far end of the table, "then what makes you think that you can unite us all? We are from many different countries, after all."

"No," said Ugo. "We are all the same. We are criminals. We do not care about borders and boundaries and nationalities. We are already united in crime. We will work together, from within, undermining society, overthrowing governments, even, if we so desire. We can become the most powerful force in Europe, a secret underground empire of criminals."

As James watched Ugo pacing the room, he caught sight of something he hadn't seen before. A statue of Mithras, but not just any statue. It was the one from the garden at Casa Polipo. As he was wondering how it got there, a terrible realization slowly dawned on him.

He was in a very perilous position.

He had blindly stumbled up here, and now, not twenty feet away from him, was the most dangerous collection of individuals in Europe.

He had seen enough. He had to get away, and get away fast, while Ugo and the men were still inside the temple.

If he was caught . . .

Well, that didn't bear thinking about.

He turned around and groped his way back out between the statues onto the ledge, where he paused for a moment to breathe in some fresh air. He stood up, ran along to the end, and jumped across to the equestrian statue, just managing to catch hold of Ugo's outstretched arm. Then he scrambled down and set off back toward the steps at a run.

If he could just get back to the funicular railway, he could maybe walk down the tracks to the valley. With luck he might even be able to hitch a ride on the roof again.

With luck . . .

You idiot, James.

You've been a complete bloody fool.

Don't think about that now, just keep moving.

He entered one of the dark alleyways, his heart pounding.

Suddenly his head was yanked back and he grunted as someone pulled him into a doorway from behind, their hand across his mouth.

He lashed out with an elbow and the grip was released. He spun around, fists raised, ready to fight for his life.

It was a boy. And James recognized him. It was Mauro's friend Stefano. The village boy who worked in Ugo's kitchens. He put a finger to his lips and pulled James farther into the shadows of the doorway, a panicked look in his eyes.

Two of Ugo's guards marched past, their black boots clicking on the cobbled ground.

"Thank you," James whispered when they'd gone past. "*Grazie*."

"I see you before. I follow you," said Stefano. "You come with me now."

"Okay," said James, grateful for the help.

Just when he had been at his most desperate, this unexpected savior had come to his rescue. He was flooded with relief.

Stefano led him through a gate and down a long, twisting, unlit passageway. At the end of it was a neglected courtyard with a large, half-dead shrub growing in it. Hidden in the darkness behind the shrub was a small hole in the wall.

"Come," said Stefano, and he disappeared into the hole. James went through after him and found himself on the roof of a building on the level below.

"Where are we going?" James asked, but the Sardinian boy moved off along the roof without saying anything and jumped onto the next building. James had no choice but to follow.

Stefano led James from one roof to another until they were at the edge of the palazzo, directly above the railway track, then he scrambled down a waste pipe and beckoned James to do the same.

Stefano had obviously done this before.

Once they were both safely on the track, Stefano looked both ways to make sure no train was coming and put his ear to the rails to make doubly sure.

"Is okay," he said, and smiled, though there was enough moonlight for James to see that he looked very strained.

Keeping close to the rocks on their left, they began to clamber down the railway. It was tough going. The track ran at an angle of almost forty-five degrees and was not designed to be walked on.

After several long minutes they came to the tunnel that went through the great jutting outcrop of rock. James was just about to enter it when Stefano took hold of his sleeve.

"No," he said. "This way."

"You're the boss," said James, and watched as Stefano climbed around the rock away from the track and the tunnel.

Once more James followed him, but to his surprise, found that Stefano was climbing up rather than down.

"Wait," he called after him as loud as he dare. "Where are we going?"

"I show you," said Stefano.

James decided not to look down as he scaled the rock. The climbing was easy and the moon bright enough to show him the handholds and footholds, but he was still very aware that the bottom of the mountain was many hundreds of feet below.

Higher up, the rock face leveled out, and they came to some wooden scaffolding that had been built against the outer wall of the palazzo. Stefano didn't wait; he pulled himself up the scaffolding like a monkey, with James hot on his heels.

At the top of the scaffolding they stepped off onto a rough concrete roof. They were in an unfinished part of the palazzo that stood on top of the outcrop of rock. Builders' tools lay everywhere among untidy sacks of lime and sand, mattocks, sledgehammers, pickaxes, and trowels.

Now what?

This didn't look to James like a way out.

Stefano took him to the opposite edge of the roof, and they looked over.

There was a wall below them with two windows in it, one above the other, and past them was a long, giddy drop down into darkness.

"I don't understand," said James. "What do you want me to do? Why have you brought me here?"

"You listen," said Stefano.

"I'm listening," said James.

"Something is happen," said Stefano. "Something bad."

"What?" said James, trying to imagine where this was leading.

"I work here," said Stefano. "Ugo pays me. I say nothing about what I know. I need money. But today I hear men talking. They think we don't listen because we are only servants, but we know everything."

"I still don't understand," said James. "What's happened?"

"Mauro is dead," said Stefano simply.

"What?" Stefano's words hit James like a physical blow. He was stunned. "How did it happen?"

"One of Ugo's men," said Stefano miserably. "Ugo could not forgive Mauro for spitting on his floor. But

219

also because of what Mauro say to Ugo."

"What do you mean?" said James. "Are you telling me that Ugo *had* him killed?"

"*Sì.* They kill him. Mauro told me you are his friend. You must avenge his death. I cannot. I not strong. I am afraid. But you are strong. You fight the boy today. Mauro tell me you are brave. I see you come up here to the palazzo—"

"This is stupid," James interrupted, his mind spinning. "I can't fight Ugo."

"No. You cannot fight him. But you can hurt him. There is a girl." As he spoke, Stefano grabbed a length of discarded rope and tied one end around a half-built stone column.

"What do you mean?" said James. "What girl?"

"The man called Zoltan bring her here," Stefano said, and he began to tie the other end of the rope around James's waist. "Ugo has her. English girl."

He took James back to the edge of the roof. "You go down," he said. "You go to second window. Here you will find the girl. I wait."

"This doesn't make any sense," said James. "Who is this girl?"

"She is prisoner," said Stefano. "You talk to her. You tell someone."

"Please," said James. "This is crazy—"

"Go quickly," said Stefano. "Is not safe here. Go."

James was confused and alarmed, but Stefano was so insistent that he knew he had to do what he asked. After all, Stefano was his only hope of getting away from here.

He threw a loop of rope over the edge, pulled it taut, then lay on his belly and lowered himself over the side backward until he was able to get his feet against the wall and walk down it. His fingers were bruised and sore from the fight, and the rope burned as it slipped through them, but he tried to ignore the pain.

He came to the first window. It was dark and the shutters were closed. He stood on the ledge and rested, looking up. He had come about twelve feet; the next window was roughly the same distance again.

It struck him that getting down was relatively easy. Climbing back up again was going to be much harder work.

Best not to think about that.

He carried on, playing out the rope slowly, and feeling his way down the wall with his feet.

In a minute he had arrived at the second window.

He settled onto the ledge, undid the knot at his waist, shortened the rope, and retied it so that there was no slack above him.

The room wasn't lit, but the shutters were open. He couldn't climb in, though, because there was a single vertical bar in the narrow opening. He peered past it. It was too dark to see anything, but he sensed a movement.

"Hello?" he said, feeling very foolish. "Hello? Is there anybody there?"

Nothing. The sound of crickets chirruping on the hillside.

"Hello . . . ?"

Still nothing.

He was about to give up and go, when he heard a rustle.

"Hello?" he repeated, and after a while a voice answered him, quiet and unsure.

"Hello?" It was an English voice. A female voice. "Where are you?"

"I'm at the window," said James, and in a moment, he saw the face of a girl looming out of the darkness.

She had short, untidy hair cut raggedly into uneven clumps; pale, freckled skin; and big eyes that were shining in the dark. She looked at James as if she couldn't believe he were actually there, and put her hand out through the gap next to the bar. James held it for a moment.

"You're real," she said.

"I think so," said James.

"I thought I was dreaming," said the girl. "Who are you?"

"The name's Bond, James Bond. Who are you?"

"I'm Amy Goodenough."

James was so surprised, he nearly fell off his perch.

"Mark's sister?" he said.

"You know who I am?" she said, laughing with relief.

"Yes," said James. "But what the hell are you doing here?"

Amy quickly told him everything, from her capture at sea to being brought to the mountains.

"Zoltan obviously knew about the statuette," said James. "He knew where to find the *Siren* and what to expect."

"I know," said Amy. "He told me. He stole the piece for the Count."

"But how did Ugo know?" said James.

"He has people working for him everywhere," said Amy. "Even in England."

223

"Even at Eton," said James.

"Exactly," said Amy. "There's a man, posing as a master at your school. He tells Ugo everything he needs to know."

"Cooper-ffrench," said James. "I know him. He's here." Now it was James's turn to talk, as he explained as quickly as he could, everything he knew.

"It's hopeless," said Amy, when he'd finished.

"No," said James, and he squeezed her hand. "I'll get you out of here."

"Now?" There was a look of pitiful hope on her face, and James had to look away.

"Maybe," he said. "There are some tools up top. Maybe I can break this bar, or something. And there's a boy who works here; he can help us."

"Stefano?" said Amy.

"Yes," said James. "So don't give up."

Two big tears squeezed out of Amy's eyes and rolled down her cheeks.

"I don't believe this is happening," she said. "I prayed that someone would come."

"Hang on," James said, standing up. "I'll be back."

The first thing was to get on to the roof again.

He called up to Stefano as loudly as he dared, but there was no answering shout. He obviously couldn't hear him. James shook the rope. Nothing.

He sighed and spat on his hands. He had stripped off some of the skin climbing down, but he just had to forget about that and climb up as best he could.

He gripped the rope tightly, braced his legs against the wall, and slowly walked up, hoisting himself hand over hand as he went. Twice his feet slipped and he crashed painfully against the wall, but he made it to the safety of the first window without falling off and rested on the ledge once again.

"Stefano," he called out. "Where are you?"

Still nothing.

He wondered if he might be able to get inside the building here and find an easier way up. He fiddled with the shutters, slipping his penknife between them to lift the latch, and eventually managed to rattle it loose. He folded them back and crawled inside, still tied to the rope.

The room was bare and empty, and the door was locked from the other side. He couldn't risk the noise it would make trying to force it open, so he reluctantly climbed back outside and set off once more up the wall.

His sheer angry determination eventually got him to the top, but when he got to the roof he discovered that Stefano had gone.

Damn it.

That scuppered things.

He was on his own now.

He sat down, and as he was untying the rope, he heard someone climbing the scaffolding. He quickly pulled the rope loose and went to look.

It wasn't Stefano. It was two of Ugo's guards.

For a moment he felt like giving up. He was so tired. So much had happened lately, he didn't know if he could stand anymore.

Nonsense.

It's not just you now, there's Amy as well.

Get a move on, you lazy idiot. Get away from there.

He ran across the roof and leaped over to the next building.

As he landed, he kept on running, all his tiredness forgotten.

He laughed. This was exactly the same situation he'd been in that night with the Danger Society back at Eton.

Only this time he risked more than a beating. This time he was running for his life.

He sprinted to the edge of a flat roof and jumped down onto a wall. He had no idea where he was; he just had to get away from those two men.

Keeping his arms out for balance, he ran along the top of the wall.

To his left was a dark courtyard with some chicken coops in it. To his right was a dizzying drop down to the valley floor hundreds of feet below.

Don't look down. . . .

At the end of the wall there was a small tree growing. He climbed up through the branches and was able to get on to the next roof. This one was also flat, but it had a low wall around it and a covered area for seating. Steps led from here up toward a raised walkway. Keeping his body bent double, he hurried up the steps on tiptoe, but froze when he reached the top.

The two guards were dashing along the walkway toward him.

Damn . . .

He turned and fled, racing as fast as he could, and he soon came to another flight of steps, this time leading downward. He took them in one giant leap without thinking and, as he hit the bottom, he rolled over, then sprang back onto his feet, and carried on running. He heard an angry shout behind him and the sound of a body falling heavily. Evidently one of the guards had tried the same trick and not pulled it off. James thought with some satisfaction that the man was going to have a pair of very badly grazed knees.

But they were still after him. And he had lost all sense of direction.

This was no good. He had to get back on to the roofs, where the heavier and less agile guards would be at a disadvantage and he might be able to get his bearings. He saw his chance and vaulted over the edge of the walkway onto a building below. He hared across the roof, pumping his arms, taking as long strides as he could. Then he was in a gully between two buildings, then out onto a narrow flat section, then he jumped and was in the air. He landed with a sickening rib-cracking jolt on the edge of the next roof, facedown, the lower half of his body hanging over the edge.

He struggled to his hands and knees and took a deep breath. His lungs hurt like hell. Come to that, his whole body hurt like hell. He wasn't sure he could go on.

Just ignore it.

There's nothing broken.

There'll just be a few more bruises to count in the morning.

He got to his feet and shook his head, but when he looked back he saw the black shapes of his pursuers, hard behind him.

He ran on.

Behind him he heard a yell and a thud, followed by a short scream.

He glanced back.

There was only one guard after him now.

The other one had mistimed the jump.

Up ahead he saw a wide gap between this building and the next one. He had no idea how wide it was and didn't have time to find out; he would just have to risk it.

He put on more speed, powering his body forward, urging his legs to work harder than they had ever done before.

He reached the edge of the roof, and there was a moment of sheer terror as he realized the gap was much wider than he'd thought. Much, much wider than anything he'd ever attempted at Eton. He'd somehow doubled back on himself and had got to the big crevasse between the folds of rock. There were buildings on the other side, but they were an awfully long way away.

It was too late to stop, though. He was going too fast. Instead, he sped up and launched himself across the void.

He was briefly aware of a deep black fissure beneath him as he flew toward the roof on the far side.

No . . .

He wasn't going to make it. It was far too wide. It was impossible. He was dropping down below the rim of the roof. Falling into that bottomless crevasse. He flung out his arms, wildly groping in the air for something to hold on to to stop his descent. And then there was a crunch. He'd hit something.

He clung on with all his strength and wept with relief.

The guard wisely didn't attempt the jump.

James was dangling from an iron support that stuck out

from the wall and held a big unlit lamp at the end. Beneath the lamp was an open window.

Well. If he'd planned this it couldn't have gone better. Except that he was now a sitting target if the remaining guard decided to fire at him.

He let himself down, swung through the window, and dropped into the room.

There was a shrill shriek and a babble of frightened Sardinian voices.

He was in a bedroom with four narrow beds. Probably servants' quarters.

"Sorry," he said, shuffling over to the door. "Don't mind me. Go back to sleep."

He wrenched the door open and bolted down the corridor on the other side. Other doors opened as he went past, and sleepy-eyed Sardinian women stuck their heads out. Soon there was a babble of voices behind him.

He ran through the building and found a spiral staircase. He started up it. It seemed to go on forever, but at last he came to the top, pushed open a door, and came out on to a small terrace.

He stopped for a moment and leaned against a wall. His legs felt like lead, and his heart was pounding so hard his whole body was shaking.

The palazzo was like a labyrinth. How could he ever hope to get away?

For a few minutes he wandered aimlessly, listening to distant shouts and whistles as the guard gave the alarm. From somewhere high up in the mountain, a searchlight was switched on and it began to rake the grounds.

It nearly found James as he was scurrying across an open courtyard, but he ducked behind a fountain and watched it slide over the nearby buildings.

And then it picked out a statue on the level above.

A man on a horse with an outstretched arm.

It was the equestrian statue of Ugo.

James headed toward it. At least from there he would be able to work out where he was.

He was soon by the temple, which was dark and deserted.

There were the steps leading up to the alleyway. Would he be able to find the doorway and remember Stefano's route to the railway tracks?

It was worth trying.

Wearily, he trudged up the steps and then froze.

Someone was coming, and there was nowhere for him to hide.

"Bond?"

He recognized that voice.

It was Peter Love-Haight.

"Sir . . ." James sank down on to the steps as Haight stepped into the light.

"James?" he said. "You look awful. Whatever has happened to you?"

"I'm all right, I think." James winced. He didn't feel right at all.

"What on earth is going on?" said Haight. "What are you doing up here? We've been terribly worried about you. Somebody said they'd seen you come up this way. We've got people searching everywhere for you. . . ." He stopped, a worried look on his handsome features. "Are you sure you're all right?"

"There's a girl, sir," said James, not knowing where to start, his brain too tired to think clearly.

"What girl?"

"Amy Goodenough, sir. Mark's sister. She's alive. She's here. Locked in a room. Count Ugo has her prisoner."

"Amy Goodenough is here?"

"Yes. We have to help her. It's not safe here."

"You sound delirious, James," said Haight kindly, helping James to his feet. "Come with me. We'll go back down."

Haight led him along the alleyway.

"Count Ugo, sir," said James. "He's not really a count. He's a bandit, the biggest bandit on the island. He hopes one day to be the biggest bandit in the world. He's the head of a secret organization called the Millenaria. . . ."

"Now I know you're delirious," said Haight.

"You have to believe me," said James. "I know it sounds crazy."

"I don't know what to think, James. I just want to get you down to the valley and safely into bed."

"No," James stopped walking. "Mister Cooper-ffrench, sir."

"Cooper-ffrench?" said Haight, raising his eyebrows. "What about him?"

"He works for Ugo," said James.

Haight laughed. "What on earth are you talking about. He's a humble Latin master."

"I saw him in Eton, sir," said James. "In a building full of Millenaria stuff. And Ugo's man, Smiler, with a scar on his face, he was there. And that's why Cooper-ffrench came out to Sardinia, sir, to meet up with Ugo. That's why we're all here."

Haight's face showed growing concern.

"This is a very serious claim, James," he said.

"I know," said James.

"But, whether it's true or not, you really shouldn't be here. We'll go down to the town and you can tell me all about it on the way."

"Thank you, sir," said James.

Haight led James through the palazzo. As they walked, James told him all he could, in a rush of confused sentences. He told him all about that first night with the Danger Society, and Merriot's letter, the cult of Mithras, Perry's stolen painting, and he was just starting to tell him about Cooper-ffrench's behavior on the expedition when they arrived at a large, wooden door.

James hadn't really been paying attention to their route as he babbled on to Haight, and now he stopped to see where they were.

"I don't think this is right, sir," he said. "We've come the wrong way."

Haight sighed. "You know your way around here better than I do."

"I'm lost now, though," said James.

"We'll try through here," said Haight. "I'm sure it's the way I came."

Haight opened the door and led James down a wide corridor lined with statues toward another door.

"But how did you find out about Amy?" he said. "Who told you she was here?"

Before he could reply, James stumbled as his frayed shirt tail caught on a statue, and as he pulled it free, a grubby flap tore off and fell to the floor.

Haight tutted and bent down.

"Best not leave that there," he said, and grinned at James. "You know how Ugo hates mess."

As Haight picked it up, James saw a flash of silver at his wrist as something slipped down on to his hand. Haight quickly pushed it back up his sleeve, but not before James had a chance to see that it was a silver bracelet. The same silver bracelet that he'd found on the floor after Haight and Cooper-ffrench collided in the Archaeological Society meeting.

James had a sudden eerie feeling of vertigo. As if the whole world had turned upside down and nothing was as he had thought it was.

He felt like he had done when he'd first looked underwater with Victor's goggles and had been instantly snapped into a different place with a different way of seeing things.

He had been utterly wrong about everything, and now he clearly saw the truth.

What an idiot he'd been.

Ugo's associate wasn't Cooper-ffrench. Of course it wasn't.

It was Haight.

CHAPTER 20—THE PENNY DROPS

"James, you haven't answered my question," said Haight, with a hint of irritation in his voice. "Who told you about Amy?"

James was trying to suppress a rising tide of panic.

It had been staring him right in the face from the start. So close and obvious that he hadn't seen it.

It was Haight's bracelet that had dropped to the floor that evening, not Cooper-ffrench's.

"James?" Haight was looking at him with a questioning expression on his face. Like when a teacher asks you something and you haven't been listening.

After all, Haight was a teacher.

"I'm sorry, sir," James said. "What did you say?"

"I asked you how you knew about Amy."

"Oh . . ." James didn't want to betray Stefano, but he had no other story prepared and his mind was blank. "Er, well, I was trying to find my way out of the palazzo and I sort of stumbled across her."

Haight gave him such a withering look that he knew that the game was up.

They both knew the truth, and they both knew that the other person knew. The question was—how much longer where they going to play this game?

"I think we've come the wrong way, sir," said James, backing toward the door they had come through.

"James—"

James turned and ran. But when he pulled the door open he found his way blocked by two of Ugo's men. When he turned back around he saw that Haight hadn't even moved.

"This way," he said quietly, and James knew that he had no choice but to follow him.

The door at the other end of the corridor opened into a large library. There were shelves of leather-bound books and many paintings and statues.

Ugo sat at a vast mahogany desk, with Smiler at his side. Two uniformed officers stood guard.

"Here he is," said Haight, and he shoved James into the center of the room.

Ugo was pretending to read some papers. For a long while he didn't look up. James could see the muscles moving under his pale skin as he ground his teeth.

James took the opportunity to properly look around the room. He spotted a small bronze figure standing on an antique side table that exactly fitted the description of Amy's stolen siren. On a stand right next to it was what looked like one of the Canalettos from his room at Casa Polipo.

And then he saw, behind Ugo, the unfinished painting of a boy standing on a desolate beach. He looked half reptilian with webbed feet and goggle eyes. He was holding the number seven in one hand and a sea urchin in the other. There was something dreamlike and disturbing about the picture, as if the boy were dead, a ghost.

And James recognized the boy. It was himself, wearing

the swimming mask and flippers. Poliponi must have painted it, just as he had said he would.

Ugo finally looked up and spoke. "Do you like it?" he said, noticing James staring at the picture.

James shrugged.

"I had it brought here from Signor Delacroix's house while you were all supposed to be out of the way," said Ugo. "These Canalettos are exquisite." He nodded toward the two scenes of Venice, then looked back at Poliponi's picture. "But this thing I do not like. I do not care for modern art. It is degenerate, decadent, the product of a sick mind. Art must be pure."

So saying, he took a letter knife from his desk and slashed the canvas three times across the center, destroying it.

James felt furious, as if Ugo had slashed his own body.

The Count walked over to him. "You have put us to a lot of trouble, James Bond," he lisped, his silver tooth glinting.

"My pleasure," said James. He didn't care anymore. He felt numb.

"Be quiet, Bond," said Haight, and he slapped him around the back of the head. "You will show a little more respect."

James was suddenly roused from his slump and filled with a burning fury. He thought of Victor, and Mauro, and Amy. "Respect?" he said. "For him?"

"You're only making matters worse for yourself," said Haight. "I always thought you were quite a sensible boy."

"He's a murderer and a thief," said James.

"You do not know the first thing about me," said Ugo.

"I know that you're not really a count," said James. "That you're just a goatherd from the Barbagia."

"Bond!" shouted Haight. "Any more of this backchat and you are going to be in serious trouble. Count Ugo is a very great man."

James gave a little snort of laughter. Ugo was staring at him angrily, chewing his lower lip like a petulant child.

"I may have been born in these mountains," he said, "but I changed myself. I made myself better than these local scum." He thumped his chest. "One day the whole world will know of my glory."

"Oh, yes, that's right," said James. "You're going to build an empire, with the help of schoolmasters, criminals, and shepherds in fancy dress, marching around in purple toy-soldier outfits."

Haight's face was pale with fury. "This is not acceptable behavior, James," he said.

"I'll write it out a hundred times, shall I, sir?" said James. "'I shall not be rude to murderers.'"

"I warn you, Bond," said Haight. "Any more of your insolence and you'll regret it."

"This is worse than school," said James, and Haight slapped him hard in the face. James started to bleed from a wound he'd got falling face first onto the roof. He put a hand up to stop the flow.

"I used to quite like you, Mister Haight," he said.

"Look here," said Haight, softening his voice. "There's no need for all this unpleasantness. We don't have to punish you. If you'll just tell us who helped you tonight, we can forget all about this. What do you say, hmm?"

"Nobody helped me," said James, and Smiler rasped something in Latin.

James obviously wasn't meant to understand any of it, but he recognized one word—*occide*, meaning kill.

Haight replied, also in Latin, and the two of them argued for a while.

James shivered. These were the two voices he'd heard in Eton that night as he hung in the ivy. Smiler and Haight. Smiler with his harsh, fluent delivery and Haight with his stiff English pronunciation.

It was Ugo who brought the argument to a halt, deliberately speaking English so that James would understand. "You cannot kill him yet, Smiler," he said. "We must first find out who helped him and how he knew where the girl was."

"I've already told you," said James wearily. "Nobody helped me."

"James Bond," said Ugo, "I am a reasonable man. But I do not like things to be . . . messy."

James pictured Mauro carefully picking urchin spines out of his foot, and his temper flared up again.

"You can give orders to kill people," he said angrily, "but maybe you've forgotten what a person's blood looks like."

He flicked his hand toward Ugo's desk. Blood spattered across it and up the front of Ugo's white suit.

"Human blood," said James. "Not bull's blood. That's what this is all about. People dying."

Ugo stood there for a moment trembling, paralyzed with disgust, then he tore off his stained jacket and looked at Haight. Haight blushed and looked at the floor.

"Peter," said Ugo, rubbing madly at a spot of blood on his shirt, "this is your fault. You should have been more careful."

"I'm sorry, Count," said Haight.

"Sorry is not good enough," said Ugo. "Make sure there are no more mistakes, or it will not be good for you."

"There will be no more mistakes," said Haight. "You can trust me."

"Trust you?" said Ugo. "Don't be ridiculous. I can trust no one. I am a criminal, and everyone who works for me is a criminal. How can I possibly trust anyone? Do not talk to me about trust. In my world power is built on fear. If there is a problem, I fix it with a gun or with a knife. I hope you are not going to be a problem for me, Peter. And I hope you know how to solve your own problems."

So saying, he rattled off a string of instructions to his guards, and they dragged James out of the room.

Mr. Cooper-ffrench was tired and jittery and not a little bit worried. It was gone midnight, and he was in the funicular railway car traveling up the side of the cliff toward the dam. Peter Haight was still not back from looking for James Bond, and he had had to leave the boys down at the camp in the care of their Italian guide, Quintino.

The sleepy Sardinian guard watched him impassively as he nervously fiddled with his mustache and looked out of the window. He could see very little except the rim of the dam cutting across the night sky. He checked his watch for the twentieth time since he'd been woken up and given the message that had thrown him into such a panic.

At last the car arrived and came to a bumpy halt against the buffers. The guard opened the door, and Cooper-ffrench stepped out. Two more guards looked him over, but seemed uninterested in what he was doing here, and retreated into the winch house to play cards and smoke cigarettes.

He looked out across the black waters of the lake and saw the bulky shape of the flying boat sitting at the jetty.

The air was much cooler and fresher up here than down in the valley, which was a relief. His heavy suit itched terribly, and he could do little to stop himself sweating all the time. Also, there were no mosquitoes at this altitude. He hated the damned things and they made his life a misery.

He walked along the perimeter of the dam, hearing nothing but his shoes clicking on the concrete, the sound bouncing back off the surrounding cliffs.

He saw someone ahead, standing in the shadows between two spotlights. He squinted but couldn't make out who it was.

"Hello?" he called out tentatively, and the figure stepped forward into the light.

It was Peter Haight.

"Peter?" said Cooper-ffrench. "Have you found him? Is he here?"

Haight shook his head. "I'm afraid not, but what on earth are you doing here, old man?"

Cooper-ffrench cleared his throat. "One of Ugo's chaps came down from the palazzo; he said Bond had been seen up here and that I should hurry."

"That's pretty well the message I was given as well," said Haight. "But sad to report, there's no sign of him."

"This is very worrying," said Cooper-ffrench.

"What do you think we should do?" said Haight, lighting a cigarette. "Should we wait?"

"I don't know," said Cooper-ffrench guardedly. He didn't

trust Haight. He never had. "Have you had a good look around?"

"Yes," said Haight. "Although it's too dark to see properly. But listen, old chap, there's something I need to talk to you about."

"Oh, yes?" said Cooper-ffrench.

"Yes." Haight blew out a lungful of smoke, and then took out a small flask from his breast pocket. "Would you like some brandy? Might keep us awake."

"Not for me, thank you," said Cooper-ffrench. "It's a little late and I'm a martyr to indigestion. So, what did you want to say?"

Haight took a sip of brandy. "I've been finding out a bit about our host, the great Count Ugo Carnifex," he said. "And I think he might be up to no good."

"How do you mean?" said Cooper-ffrench.

"Do you know anything about an organization called the Millenaria?" said Haight.

Cooper-ffrench hesitated. "I've heard of them," he said at last.

"Well, from what I can gather, this is their headquarters, and Carnifex is in charge," said Haight. "The place is crawling with crooks."

For a while Cooper-ffrench said nothing. Maybe he'd been wrong about Haight, but he still didn't trust him.

"How do you know this?" he asked.

"Been talking to some of the locals," said Haight.

"You knew none of this before?"

"How could I have known?" said Haight with a frown.

"Well, it's only that . . ." Cooper-ffrench decided to

show his hand. "I have seen one of these chaps before."

"What do you mean?" said Haight, wide-eyed and attentive.

"As you know, I am a keen amateur archaeologist," said Cooper-ffrench.

"Yes."

"Well, for some time I have been trying to locate a shrine to the Roman god Mithras somewhere in Eton. It's mentioned in various historical records, but has been lost for centuries. I believe it was built on the site of an earlier Celtic shrine to the goddess Tamesis, after whom the river Thames is named."

"I don't follow you, John," said Haight. "Where's this leading?"

"I'll get to the point in a minute," said Cooper-ffrench. "You see, I have always thought that if I could find this shrine it would be an important discovery. My research led me to a building in Eton that appeared to be unoccupied. I visited it on a number of occasions but failed to gain entry. Then one afternoon I found the door open and went in, to find a rather alarming man there. A Scotsman whose cheeks were badly scarred and who has the letter *M* tattooed on each hand. *M* for Millenaria."

"Good God!" exclaimed Haight. "I've seen him here in the palazzo. You saw that man in Eton?"

"The very same," said Cooper-ffrench. "It's strange, is it not?"

"But why have you never said anything to me before?" said Haight.

Cooper-ffrench blushed and coughed. "I must confess I

had my suspicions about you, Peter," he said. "I thought perhaps you might be involved in some way."

"Me?" Haight looked incredulous and then laughed. "Involved with criminals and secret Italian societies? How on earth did you come to that conclusion?"

"Well, it seems ridiculous now," Cooper-ffrench muttered. "And I must say, it's a load off my mind talking to you. Perhaps I will have a small nip of brandy."

Haight passed him the flask, and Cooper-ffrench took a quick drink. The two of them walked to the parapet and looked down at the palazzo and the aqueduct below.

"Have you told anyone else of your suspicions?" Haight asked casually.

"No." Cooper-ffrench shook his head vigorously. "I mean, what if my fears proved to be unfounded? I didn't want to cause a fuss and risk a scandal at the school. But I knew you visited Sardinia regularly, and I knew the Millenaria had their base here, so I thought I'd better come along and keep an eye on you."

Haight looked at Cooper-ffrench. So that was why he kept turning up like a bad penny. The poor fool. He had no idea what he had stumbled into.

He put his arm around Cooper-ffrench's shoulders.

"First thing tomorrow we take the boys and leave this place," he said.

"Yes," said Cooper-ffrench. "There is evil here. We ought to say something to the authorities."

"Indeed we must," said Haight.

"And what about young James Bond?" said Cooper-ffrench. "Where the devil is he?"

"Don't you worry about a thing," said Haight. "Let me sort everything out." So saying, he put a hand between Cooper-ffrench's shoulder blades and gave him a short, quick shove.

Cooper-ffrench had only time to shout "Haight!" before he was over the wall and falling.

Haight watched him to the bottom. It seemed to take an awfully long time.

"The penny drops," he said, and tossed the flask of brandy after him.

James had been put into an empty tool room deep in one of the mining tunnels beneath the palazzo. The steel door was locked shut and the light had been switched off from outside. The room was pitch dark and smelled of damp.

He had no idea what time it was. It might be the middle of the night, or the sun might be blazing in the sky.

He had slept a little, a deep, sluggish sleep filled with confusing dreams; and when he'd woken he was painfully stiff and felt as if his whole body had been trampled on by elephants. On top of the bruising his face and hands had received in the boxing match, there were the other injuries he had got from being chased across the rooftops, not to mention the lump on his head from when he'd been attacked at Victor's.

He knew that it was pointless trying to escape. All he could focus on was thinking of a story, something he could say to keep Mauro's friend Stefano out of danger. He felt partially responsible for Mauro's death; he couldn't bear it if Stefano suffered a similar fate because of him.

His one hope of getting away was Cooper-ffrench. Surely the master would sound the alarm and come looking for him.

245

He couldn't believe he had been so stupid as to trust Peter Haight.

It all seemed so obvious now.

It was Haight who had organized this trip to Sardinia, at the hottest time of the year, so that under the guise of attending Ugo's carnival he could deliver the stolen paintings. James remembered the rolled canvases in Haight's bag, the bag that never left his side. He had the perfect cover to smuggle stolen art out of the country—a harmless schoolteacher on a trip with his pupils.

Haight had quizzed the boys about their families' art collections. He knew the exact location of all the pieces. He knew when the families would be away from home. He knew about the Goodenoughs' yacht and the statuette of the siren it contained. His concern for Mark had nothing to do with feeling sorry for him: he just felt guilty about what had happened. All the other thefts had been quick and simple and no one had been hurt. This one had gone wrong and people had died.

The light was switched on from outside. James jumped, startled, and despite the fact that the bulb only cast a feeble orange glow, he blinked and shielded his eyes from its glare.

He heard the grinding of a key turning in the lock, and the door creaked open.

Count Ugo came in with Smiler.

Smiler wiped some dust from the top of a packing crate and sat down.

Ugo took one look at the unclean conditions, turned up his nose, and decided to stand.

"James Bond," he said, "in my time I have had to deal with soldiers, bandits, pirates, and murderers of all kinds. A mere schoolboy is not going to cause me any difficulties. Now, I wish for you only to answer me some questions, and then we can close this matter."

"And let me go?" said James. "After all, I am a mere schoolboy."

"Why not?" said Ugo. "As I say, you do not worry me. You may have some childish fantasy of alerting the police and sending in the army to rescue this girl. But it must remain a fantasy. I have great power on this island. All men are greedy. It doesn't take a great deal to bribe a policeman; I give them money, they leave me alone. The army are just the same. We are all Sardinians first and Italians second. They have more loyalty to me than to Mussolini. I offer these people hope. This is a poor country, but I will make it rich."

"By stealing paintings?" said James.

Ugo laughed. "When the Emperor Napoleon conquered Europe, he took all of its riches for himself. He emptied the museums and art galleries and put their contents on show in Paris for the glory of his empire. Well, that is what I am doing also. My followers are everywhere. In all the places that were once part of the Roman Empire. In Spain, in France, in North Africa, the Middle East, Germany, and, of course, in Britain. And from all these places they bring me treasure. Most of it, I ransom back to its owners, but the Italian art I keep. An emperor must behave like an emperor and he must look like an emperor. He must be surrounded by the finest things. I will become a new Caesar, a new Napoleon. One day I will show my full majesty to the world. For now, though, I work underground, tunneling beneath the surface of society."

"Like a rat," said James. "In a sewer."

"We have wasted time," said Ugo. "I am very busy. How did you find out about Amy Goodenough? Who took you to her? Who helped you?"

"No one," said James.

"You may think that someone will be coming to set you free," said Ugo softly. "But that is not the case. Signor Delacroix has gone home and Signor Cooper-ffrench has had an unfortunate accident. It appears that the spirit of the carnival took hold of him. He became drunk last night and fell off my dam. Very sad. Now, tell me who helped you."

James felt a cold, sick sensation in his stomach.

"Nobody helped me," he said. He had to stick to that line at all costs. He had to buy as much time as possible for Stefano to get away, or he would go the same way as Cooper-ffrench.

Ugo smiled and ran a hand through the bristly stubble of his white hair. "I will get this information," he said. "I have a way. I am going to take you hunting. Do you like hunting?"

James shrugged.

"Never mind," said the Count. "It doesn't matter. Because in this hunt you are not going to be the hunter, you are going to be the prey." He smiled. "But it will not be a very fair hunt, I'm afraid."

"That doesn't surprise me," said James. "I know how you like to cheat."

"I am going to tie you to the ground," said Ugo. "As bait. But what animal is going to hunt you down? Hmm? Do you know?"

"No," said James sullenly.

"It is the deadliest animal in the world," said Ugo. "Do you know what that is? Are you thinking of maybe a tiger? No. Not the tiger. A few men are killed each year by tigers, but not that many; the same with lions. What about crocodiles? Again, no: only a handful of victims. Maybe snakes? It is true that there are some truly deadly snakes in the world, but not in Sardinia. A spider, perhaps? No. The creatures that are going to attack you are the worst of all. They kill millions of people every year."

Ugo went to the door and his guard opened it. "Think about it, James, think about what this creature might be, and maybe later you will feel more like talking. In some ways, though, I hope that you do not tell me straight away," he said. "Because I am going to enjoy seeing you suffer. My life here is sometimes boring. A little sadism before supper will give me an appetite. Come, Smiler."

The two men left and James was once more alone.

He put his hand in his pocket and felt something. He pulled it out. It was the silver ring that Jana had given him. He looked at it, turning it in his battered fingers.

There was something not quite right about it, but before he could work out what it was, the light was switched off and he sat there in the dark, fondling the ring and brooding.

Some time later—it could have been an hour, it could have been two hours, James had no way of knowing—he had another visitor.

It was Zoltan the Magyar, who had brought him some food.

"James!" he said, tossing him some bread and a hunk of

cold pork. "Always getting into trouble. What are we going to do with you?"

James said nothing and ate the food greedily while Zoltan watched with some amusement. "Ugo does not know I am here," he said. "So we shall keep this as our little secret."

"What do you want with me?" said James. "And don't bother lying. I know who you are."

"I could help you, James," said Zoltan.

"I don't want your help."

"You are strong," said Zoltan. "But Ugo will break you. Why not let me help?"

"Why would you want to?" said James. "What's in it for you?"

"I want Amy back," said Zoltan. "You know where she is. In a way, we both want the same thing."

"No, we don't," said James. "I want to free her, and you want to sell her."

"That is not all I want," said Zoltan.

"She told me," said James. "She told me you're trying to ransom her. What more could you want with her?"

"That is a good question," said Zoltan. "One that I have been asking myself from the start. In a way I feel there is a strange bond between us. Maybe because she nearly killed me. Our fates are joined. I don't think now that I do want to sell her. I want to keep her with me."

"What for?"

"I wish I knew the answer to that," said Zoltan. "She is too young and I am too old to think about marriage, and besides she hates me. I killed her father. That is not a good way to win a girl's heart."

"No," said James. "I don't know much about these things, but I would have thought some flowers or chocolates would have gone down better."

Zoltan laughed, then spoke quietly. "I don't want her to be hurt, James."

"So, if you got her back, what would you do with her?" said James.

"I don't know," said Zoltan. "She was my prize. But everything good I have ever had, Ugo has taken. He talks of being a new Roman emperor. He is not. He is just a thief. A gangster."

"Like you," said James.

"At least I know that is what I am," said Zoltan. "And do not pretend to be something more."

"An honest thief?" said James. "I didn't know there was such a thing."

Zoltan smiled at him. "I never finished telling you about Ugo, did I?" he said. "What happened to him in the war."

"No," said James. "You left him standing naked in a shower, facing a German soldier."

"Not a German," said Zoltan. "A Hungarian."

"Of course," said James. "I wondered how you knew so much about that day. It was you, wasn't it?"

"Yes," said Zoltan. "It was me. That was how I met Ugo." Zoltan sat down and wiped his face. He was dripping with sweat and his pale eyes were yellow and feverish. He took a long deep breath and James heard it rattling in his chest.

"So what happened?"

"Before anyone could shoot," said Zoltan, "I saw an extraordinary thing. Some bullets from our fight had smashed a hole in the floor. And through this hole I saw the glint of gold.

"Hidden beneath those showers were all the treasures from the palazzo. The owners had stored all their valuables there when war broke out. In our excitement we forgot that we were enemies. We climbed down and gazed at a fortune. Ugo's brother Guido was a religious man and said we should not touch it. Ten minutes later Guido was dead. With Ugo's knife planted in his back. Carnifex had killed his own brother, the man who had saved his life. And why? For gold. All for gold.

"Ugo and I worked hard. We dragged the treasure from the cellar and buried it in the woods. Then we swore an oath never to tell anyone about it and arranged to return when the war was over. I had had enough of fighting, though. I made my way down through Albania into Greece, where I started my glorious career as a pirate and a smuggler."

"And was the treasure still there when you came back?" asked James.

Zoltan laughed. "What do you think?" he said. "Ugo is now a rich man, and I just have my boat and the clothes I am wearing."

"He beat you to it," said James.

"Yes. He sold most of it. Those pieces that were easy to dispose of, the silver and the gold. Other pieces he graciously gave to me to sell for him. I knew many men around the Mediterranean who asked no questions. I split the profits with Ugo, always on the promise that there would be bigger, more valuable items the next time.

"But, while I stayed a smuggler, living from one day to

the next, spending my money as soon as I had it, Ugo was more clever. He wanted a palazzo like the one we had looted. He kept his money and went into mining."

James saw a glimmer of hope pierce the gloom of his depression. Perhaps there still was someone who could help him. Someone unlikely, but a potential ally nevertheless.

This wounded Hungarian pirate.

"You're not interested in his plans, are you?" said James. "For the Millenaria?"

"No," said Zoltan. "I just want to get my money and go."

"Ugo hasn't paid you yet?" said James.

"No. I brought him exactly what he asked for, but he is slow to pay."

James could see the bitterness and hatred behind Zoltan's eyes. There must be some way he could use him against Ugo, but he had to be sure.

"He'll never pay you," he said, and Zoltan looked shocked.

"What?"

"He'll betray you again," said James. "Why would you trust him?"

Zoltan stared at James. "You are very wise for a young boy."

"Am I wise, or are you stupid?" said James.

For a moment Zoltan looked like he was going to strangle him, but then his features softened and he started to laugh. "I have killed men for speaking to me like that," he said. "You are lucky that I like you."

James took something from his pocket and handed it to Zoltan.

"What is this?" said the pirate. "A ring?"

"What do you think it's worth?" said James.

"Nothing," said Zoltan, tossing it back. "It is tin."

"Not silver?" said James.

"No," said Zoltan.

"I didn't think so," said James.

"Where did you get it?" asked Zoltan.

"The lovely Countess Jana gave it to me," said James. "Ugo behaves like a rich man, but he's flat broke. All his money has gone on building this place. He's a fake, like this ring. Victor told me that there never was any silver in these mines. He's been selling stolen art to get what little money he has. He'll never pay you, because he can't afford to. That's why he needs those other men to join him, because they're wealthy."

Zoltan was about to say something in reply, when they were interrupted by a jangle of keys at the door, and presently Smiler came in with a scruffy young guard. He looked at Zoltan, and this time James could tell that he definitely wasn't smiling.

"What are you doing here?" said the Scotsman.

"That is none of your business," said Zoltan, standing up.

"I said, what are you doing here?" Smiler repeated, a note of menace in his voice.

Zoltan turned to James. "Smiler used to work for me, you know, James," he said. "He was one of my crew. But when he met Ugo, his greedy little heart told him to jump ship and move up in the world."

"You're a loser," said Smiler. "I just decided to back the winning horse."

"As always," said Zoltan, and he rested his good hand on James's shoulder. "You see that scar of his?" he went on. "His old gang in Glasgow did that to him when they found out he had been selling them one by one to the police. But do you know the funny thing? Smiler is a good Catholic. Before he turned to crime, Smiler trained to be a priest. What happened, Smiler? Why don't you tell the boy?"

"It was the Jesuits," said Smiler affably, happy to talk about himself. "They were rather too fond of whipping us boys. One day I'd had enough. I took the cane off Father McCann and smashed his skull in with it. Then I walked out of there and joined up with a local gang. That was much more to my liking."

"Until you betrayed them," said Zoltan.

"I've never had any loyalty to anyone but myself," said Smiler.

"Of course," said Zoltan. "You had already betrayed your God. Betraying a few mere men was nothing."

So saying, Zoltan walked out, and James heard his footsteps fading into the distance.

Smiler said something to the guard and, before James knew what was happening, he was being dragged out of the cell.

Smiler marched him down through the mine, the young guard kicking him occasionally to make him keep up. After a few minutes they came to a sentry post built into a wall. Two more guards were sitting in there, keeping watch over an exit to the outside world. One of them glanced up and nodded to Smiler, who shoved the gate open and booted James through it.

James stumbled out into the heat of the day, blinking in the harsh sunlight. There was a racket of insects, and he felt suddenly light-headed and confused, but a kick in the backside brought him quickly back to his senses.

They were some way below the palazzo. Above them were the steep sides of the ravine and the tall arches of the aqueduct. They walked across an open rocky area and joined a track that wound down through the scrubby maquis. James considered trying to break away and make a run for it. But where would he go? All his energy had been used up. He looked down at himself and was shocked to see how filthy he was. His torn clothing was crusted with dried blood, and where his skin showed through the rips, it was a livid patchwork of cuts and bruises.

Flies buzzed everywhere through the still, hot air and the two men slapped them away and grumbled to each other. Farther along the path they stopped to drink water from a shared canteen, and after a little deliberation, Smiler gave James some. He drank thankfully and then poured some water onto his hands and washed his face. It was hardly a hot shower and brushup, but for now it would have to do.

At Eton a maid brought round water for him to wash with every morning, and when his clothes were dirty he'd simply leave them out for her to pick up. He'd collect them a few days later, neatly folded and pressed, from a wooden shelf at the bottom of the stairs called the slab. He'd always taken the system for granted, but never again.

After a while they came to the river where the runoff from the dam flowed down into the valley. A smaller muddy trickle fed into it, and they followed this stream into a soggy, steep-sided gorge thick with tangled vegetation. They had to pick their way carefully through the soft ground, which became even mushier the deeper they went.

The men's mood got worse as they pressed into the heart of the bog, and they obviously had no more desire to be here than James.

There was the sound of splashing and running water. James assumed it must be a waterfall, but as they rounded a corner, he saw a waste pipe sticking out of the rock face and dirty brown water pouring out of it. The water fell into a pool and then meandered off haphazardly into a series of stagnant ponds and puddles.

They were in a sort of natural basin where a grove of cork oaks stood. James could see where their bark had been stripped in the past, but they were dying now, drowned by the water from Ugo's waste pipe. Other, unidentifiable, stunted plants with blackish leaves stuck out of the dark swamp. It was hard to tell which were living and which were dead. There was the general reek of rotting cabbage from a stinking gas that hung in the still air and caught in the back of James's throat.

In the center of the basin was a sort of island with a few sick-looking juniper bushes and a dead tree on it. Ugo was waiting for them here with Jana and Peter Haight.

A girl was holding a large sunshade over the Count, who was sitting in a folding chair. A second girl kept him cool with a fan. He was wearing knee-length, highly polished black boots with his white outfit, and held a handkerchief over his mouth and nose to keep out the worst of the foul air.

"Ah, James," he said. "How good of you to join us."

One of his handmaidens shooed a persistent fly away with a whisk.

All around was the whine of mosquitoes, and James caught one feeding on his arm. He swatted it, and with some satisfaction, he saw a red blotch where it had been squashed to pulp on his skin.

"They *are* a nuisance, aren't they?" lisped Ugo, his silver tooth winking from the shadows under the sunshade. "We have done our best to get rid of them, but they are a tough enemy and they never give up. Now, James, before we start, would you like to tell us who helped you last night; then we can take you back to the palazzo, give you some clean clothes, a warm bath, and a hot meal."

Right then it was the nicest offer James had ever had, but he said nothing and simply stared at Ugo.

"No?" said Ugo. "That is good. Otherwise it would have deprived us of our sport."

"It doesn't sound much like sport to me," said James. "Tying me down to be eaten by something."

"It is a blood sport," said Ugo, and Jana laughed.

"Do you know what it is yet?" she drawled. "The deadliest animal in the world?"

James swatted a mosquito on his wrist. "Yes," he said. "I know." He held up his bloody palm.

"Exactly," said Ugo. "The mosquito. She kills millions of people every year. She has been the ruin of this island. The people cannot progress because they are sick with malaria. You see them everywhere with dull eyes and yellow skin. And they are the lucky ones; at least they are still alive. Oh, the government is busy draining the marshes where the mosquitoes breed, but as you can see, we still have a long way to go."

Ugo waved his hand at the insects that were beginning to swarm all around them. James already felt itchy and uncomfortable.

"Perhaps I am being a little unfair on the mosquito," said Ugo, "because the insect itself is fairly harmless. It is what it carried in its gut that kills you. A parasite called plasmodium, which is passed on in the saliva of an infected bug each time it takes a new blood meal. The parasites then multiply in your liver before returning to the blood and breaking down the red cells. There comes terrible fever, shivering, pain in your joints; your head aches like it will explode. Slowly your

259

organs are destroyed, the blood vessels in your brain clog up. If you are not treated, you die."

James felt scared. He hadn't had any quinine for two days, and there would be no insect repellent left on his skin. He looked at Peter Love-Haight, who looked quickly away and down at the ground.

"Did you know," said Ugo chattily, "that it is only the female mosquito that bites you? What do they say? The female is deadlier than the male? Look! Already they come. They detect the carbon dioxide that you breathe out. So if you want to be safe, James, I suggest that you hold your breath until morning." Ugo laughed through his nose. "I will come back then, and we will see if perhaps you are willing to talk."

He barked an order, and Smiler hustled James forward so that he was right in front of the Count. Smiler held on to his arms, keeping him still.

Jana stepped toward him and tore off the remains of his shirt.

"Such a shame that your pretty skin will soon be a ruin," she said, and took a bottle of amber liquid from a bag. "They say that mosquitoes like the smell of perfume. They have such good taste, but then, so do you. . . . At least you will taste good to a bug."

She sprayed James all over with the sickly, heavy perfume. He coughed and screwed up his eyes to stop them stinging.

"Mosquitoes are more hungry at dawn and at dusk," said Ugo when she had finished. "Though there are still plenty around now. It is this place. They love it here. And as they start to bite, just remember that it will get worse . . . and worse, and worse . . . I have known men go mad here as they are covered in a living carpet of mosquitoes, each sticking their long filthy snout under the skin."

Ugo grabbed James's chin and lifted it, staring deep into his eyes.

"Do you still not want to talk?" he said.

James looked down at his body; already two mosquitoes were sitting on his chest, feeding. For now they did nothing more than tickle, but he knew that the itching would come in a while. And after that? Did these two carry the deadly parasite inside them? There was no way of telling.

"All right," he said desperately. "All right. I'll tell you."

"Good boy," said Haight. "I knew you'd see sense. Who was it?"

"It was Zoltan," said James.

Ugo was silent for a long time, watching James, thinking about this, his nasty, suspicious mind turning over. "That makes no sense," he said at last.

"Doesn't it?" said James. "He hates you. You've double-crossed and cheated him all his life. You haven't paid him. You took Amy from him. He'd rather she was free than you had her."

"I do not believe you," said Ugo, but James knew that he had planted a seed. After all, it was Ugo who had given James the idea. Turn the tribes against each other. Make them fight among themselves, then stand back and reap the rewards.

"You don't have to believe me," said James. "But it was Zoltan. Who else knew that she was even here?"

"No," said Ugo. "You are lying. . . ."

But then Smiler went over to Ugo and said something quietly in his ear. Maybe he was telling Ugo that he had found Zoltan in James's cell. Ugo sucked his teeth with a sour look.

"No matter," he said to James. "Even if you were telling the truth, it would make no difference. I have an answer; we can go now."

"You can't leave me here," said James.

"Yes, I can. I can do whatever I like," said Ugo. "I will come back tomorrow. I would love to stay and watch, but it will be a long process, and I do not like the flies. In the morning you will be delirious, you will be softened up; I can get the whole truth out of you then."

As Ugo, Jana, and Haight walked away, Smiler forced James to the ground.

"It was Zoltan!" James yelled. "I gave you what you wanted, now let me go."

"No," said Ugo. "*Arrive'derci*, James. Have a good night."

Set into the earth was a rough concrete square with a rusted iron ring at each corner. Smiler and the guard laid James on it and began to tie his wrists and ankles tightly with leather thongs.

The young guard had a knobbly Adam's apple and a handsome, vain face. He was trying to show off to Smiler how tough he was. He chuckled as they tied James down, and when they had finished, he kicked him in the side. Smiler swore at him and the guard sloped off to sit on a rotten stump, smoke cigarettes, and sulk.

Smiler took one last look at James, then followed Ugo and the others out of the swamp.

James shook his head as a mosquito landed on his face. It walked over his lips and he tried to blow it away with his nostrils. Another insect was crawling round his left wrist, and he felt a third one in his ear. He twisted his head and scraped it against the concrete, and the mosquito flew off briefly into the air with a zipping sound, before landing casually on his chest and rubbing its proboscis between its long front legs.

This was hopeless. He couldn't hope to shake off each individual insect; already he could see that four more had joined the one on his wrist. He wiggled his fingers but it had no effect; they were going to have their meal and nothing was going to stop them.

James could picture more of them, hundreds of them, homing in on him from all around this ghastly swamp. Zigzagging toward him, black and ugly; thin now, but soon to be bloated with his blood.

He felt utterly alone and didn't know where he was going to get the strength from to make it through the long, dark night ahead.

CHAPTER 23—DEADLIER THAN THE MALE

James was in a world of pain. The itching was terrible. He wanted to scratch his whole body, but all he could do was strain and writhe uselessly on his back as the mosquitoes drank his blood. They were all over him, and every second more arrived. They were teeming over his chest, his ankles, his arms, his neck, their spindly legs tickling his skin. They were in a cloud around his head, filling the night with a ceaseless, whining drone. They were flying into his ears, the noise so loud it felt like they were drilling through to his brain.

How he hated the creatures. It was as if God had done all he could to make them repulsive; they looked vile, they had vile habits, and they sounded vile. There was nothing appealing about a mosquito.

The first ones to arrive had been tiny, but as evening had drawn in, larger ones had arrived, great fat brown things that flew lazily through the air and stuck their feeders into him right up to their ugly faces.

What he would give to have a hand free for just one minute. To swat the devils where they sat on him. To have the satisfaction of seeing them crushed and broken. But no. He couldn't move. He could only lie here and feel them suck out his blood.

Slowly the light had faded from the swamp until it was almost as black as his cell had been, and somehow it was worse in the dark, just hearing the insects and feeling them crawling all over him, biting and biting.

At first he had been aware of each fresh itch as it developed, spreading down his arms and up his legs, but now the bites all blurred into one another so that every bit of his skin was burning as his system fought against the germs they injected into him.

He was horribly aware of his blood flowing around his body, taking their poison with it. It only needed one of them to be carrying the malaria parasite and he would be sick for the rest of his life.

He prayed that somehow relief would come, but sleep was impossible; his body hurt too much. If only he could fall unconscious; anything to escape this torture.

The young guard had a bottle and James had been vaguely aware of him getting drunk, splashing repellent over himself and cursing the insects. Twice he had come over and mocked James in a thick dialect and prodded him with his foot. The second time he had blown a lungful of smoke into James's face and laughed. James didn't mind. The smoke kept the insects away for a few precious moments, but the guard hadn't been back since, and for a while James had seen no sign of him or the glow of his cigarette.

He spat a mosquito from his mouth and growled in the back of his throat, shaking his head wildly from side to side, but they wouldn't stop; nothing could stop the insects. They were not afraid like other creatures. They were single-minded and utterly ruthless. If you waved them away they were back a moment later. All you could do was wait till they landed, then flatten them; but with your hands tied to the ground, that was impossible.

There were tears of frustration in James's eyes. It felt like this night would never end.

And then he saw a flashlight beam, zigzagging through the darkness. There was a brief, low exchange of words, and somebody came to stand over him.

It was Peter Haight, swathed in netting like a bee-keeper. "James Bond," he said in an affected, sarcastic, shool-masterly voice. "Could do better . . . James is a bright boy with a lively and enquiring mind, but shows a rebellious spir-it that needs to be squashed. Good at games, though he is perhaps not a team player. His attitude toward masters shows particular room for improvement. James has a tendency to answer back and needs to learn that he must do as he is told without question."

"Very good," rasped James. "It's always amusing when a master tries to be funny."

"Come on," said Haight, squatting down. "We used to be friends."

James forced a laugh, but his throat was so dry that it came out like the croak of some diseased frog. "Why are you doing this?" he said. "Ugo Carnifex is an idiot."

"Why does anyone do anything?" said Haight. "For money, for power, for his place in the world."

"No," said James hoarsely. "Some people do things out of friendship, or kindness, or because they think it's the right thing to do."

"There will always be fools on this planet," scoffed

Haight. "How do you think it was for me, James? A poor teacher, spending his every day with the wealthiest, most privileged boys in the country? The spoiled offspring of aristocrats and admirals, of politicians and royalty? How I hated them. Their arrogance, their smug belief that they belonged at the top of the tree.

"And then one day, traveling in Sardinia, I heard about Ugo and I sought him out. He and I both shared a passion for the emperors of ancient Rome. We discussed all that they achieved and how they achieved it. He opened my eyes. He showed me that it didn't have to be like this. I could achieve something for myself. If I gave him what he wanted, I could be a wealthy man. So I did what he asked. First of all I gave him information. I was in a perfect position to spy on the ruling elite of Britain, through their sons. And the next step was logical: to take what they had and give it to Ugo in return for a reward."

"The only slight problem," said James, "is that you have to kill everyone who gets in your way."

"Look here, old chap," said Haight, squatting down to be nearer to James. "Why don't you tell me the truth? Ugo will be eternally grateful to me, and I can make sure you are unharmed. I'm your only friend here, James."

"Some friend," said James. "You tried to kill me, didn't you? That first day at the tower. You planned the whole thing. You invited me to Sardinia so that you could find out what I knew and, if necessary, arrange an accident, away from the school, in the middle of nowhere."

"I was in a very precarious position at Eton," said Haight. "With the death of Sir Cathal Goodenough, everything changed. It was no longer a game. I couldn't risk being found out. And when I talked to you, I realized that you already knew more than I had feared."

"So you gave me drugged water," said James, "with some kind of sleeping draft in it. That's what caused the bitter, salty taste, not a water-purifying tablet. You drugged me, and told me to climb the tower. . . ."

"It should have been straightforward," said Haight. "A boy with heatstroke tragically slips to his death."

"But you hadn't counted on Mister Cooper-ffrench turning up, had you?" said James. "He saw you and tried to warn me. So instead of pushing me off, you grabbed me and pretended you'd stopped me from falling. He saved my life. But you would have tried again, wouldn't you? If you hadn't found out about Victor and his paintings. Your greed got the better of you."

"You know," said Haight, "a lively and enquiring mind is not something to be encouraged in a boy. You shouldn't ask too many questions."

"What'll you do, *sir*?" said James. "Put me in detention?"

Haight placed a foot on James's throat. "All I have to do," he said, "is press my foot down and you'd be dead within two minutes. I could do it. I could do it as easily as stepping on an insect."

He took his foot away and James coughed painfully. He peered up at Haight. "You weren't always like this," he said. "I saw you with Mark Goodenough that day. You felt sorry for him. You wanted to help him. How could you change so quickly?"

"I had to," said Haight fiercely. "I had to be more like my

heroes. The ancient Romans were utterly ruthless. They cared nothing for their enemies. When they defeated Carthage they killed every man, woman and child, and all their animals, even the dogs, and then they ploughed the city into the ground and sowed it with salt so that nothing would ever grow there again. The only things that mattered to them were power and glory."

"It must be pretty glorious," said James, "murdering schoolteachers and torturing children. I'm sure you'll be in all the history books."

"We'll see, James," said Haight coldly. "We'll see how cocky you are in the morning."

"Just go away," said James, and then added with as much poison as he could, "*sir....*"

Haight grunted and straightened up. Then he said goodnight to the guard, and James heard him splashing away past the dying oak trees.

James's anger had distracted him momentarily from the agony, but now that Haight had gone, the itching and burning returned worse than before. He pulled against the straps, grinding his teeth, and the pain of the leather cutting into his wrists felt almost like a relief.

He was covered in the hateful insects; they sought out any tender parts to feed on: his eyelids, around his nostrils, in his armpits....

"Go away!" he screamed. "Get off! Leave me alone. Please, leave me alone...."

But it was pointless.

The mosquitoes kept coming.

Slowly he started to slip in and out of consciousness. He

kept imagining he was somewhere else, as his brain sought to give him some release.

He was lying on the beach at Capo d'Orso with Mauro. It was a golden afternoon. The sun shone in the azure sky, but it was hot—too hot—it was burning down on him, and his skin was peeling and blistering. . . .

He shook his head and forced his mind back to reality.

But he wasn't back in reality; he was in his bed at Aunt Charmian's cottage in Pett Bottom, cozy and safe. She was bringing him a cup of coffee in the morning, to wake him up, but she spilled it and it fell onto the bedclothes, seeping through and scalding him.

No.

Not that.

There was no escape; every route he tried to take led straight back here, to this reeking swamp and these blood-sucking monsters.

He gave in. He let go.

Let them come.

Let them do their worst.

There was nothing he could do.

He opened his eyes, looked up at the patch of slightly paler darkness above him that must be the sky, and accepted the pain. If this was how he was going to die, then so be it. He wasn't going to waste his last moments fighting it.

There were two Bonds now. One had a body that was crawling with mosquitoes, itching and sore and bleeding; the other was just a spirit and it floated above the body, observing it, separate from the pain, detached. Slowly his consciousness dimmed, like the flame turned down on a lamp.

At last he must have fallen asleep, because when he awoke, something was different. The patch of sky had gone. He was aware of someone leaning over him. The guard, probably, come to gloat.

James swore, but then he realized that it couldn't be the guard. The figure was too small, its movements too quick and furtive. Maybe it was a wild animal of some sort. He strained his eyes and tried to clear his foggy brain, and as his vision focused, he was amazed to see a girl's face.

She had dark skin and black, glinting eyes framed by a tangle of thick hair. He was about to say something, when she put a finger to his lips and scowled at him with the fierce, intent look of an animal.

He kept quiet.

She held a jackknife in her brown hand. It had a five-inch blade shaped like a long narrow leaf that tapered to a vicious point. Mauro had shown him a knife like this before: it was a *resolza*, a shepherd's knife, and it was deadly.

Quickly and expertly, she cut the thongs and helped James up. It was agony, but he managed not to cry out. He was stiff all over, and his skin hurt dreadfully when he moved.

She again signaled for him to be quiet, then beckoned him to follow her. She was small and wiry and moved like a cat, looking around her all the time, her whole body tensed and alert. She hurried away across the island and into the water on sure, bare feet, making no sound.

James suddenly froze. He had seen the shadowy bulk of the young guard waiting for them in the swamp, sitting utterly still. He wanted to call to the girl, but she hurried straight past the man, ignoring him completely, and James now realized why he wasn't moving.

The guard was sitting in the water, slumped against a slimy rock, his head tipped backward, his eyes staring and white-rimmed, his mouth open in a silent scream of terror.

Below his chin was what looked like a second mouth cut into his throat.

The girl had sliced clean across it with her knife.

James retched and shrank back, horrified.

He looked around for the girl and could just see her on the far side of the bog disappearing into the gully, crouched low and hurrying forward.

James stumbled after her and caught up. She looked around at him and smiled, showing two rows of gleaming white teeth that flashed in the dark.

Then she was off again, with James close behind her, not caring about the branches that lashed at his bare chest and face. Any sensation was better than the feeling of the mosquitoes on him.

The girl led him out of the marshy area, down to the river and across it, using slippery stepping-stones. On the other side they climbed a narrow stone track that cut into the mountainside. James struggled to keep up. He could barely see three feet in front of him, and if he didn't keep right behind the girl, he didn't know where to safely tread; but she was dressed all in black and was very hard to see.

James was sweating uncontrollably and shivering at the same time. His vision was swimming and filming over. He wanted to tell the girl to stop or at least slow down, but he was scared of what might happen if they did.

Finally he stumbled and fell forward, and found himself unable to get up again.

"Please," he called out. "Wait . . ."

He heard the girl stop and come back. She squatted down and inspected him, kissed him once briefly, then ran off.

James lay there panting, his head pressed against a cool rock. Maybe this was just a dream, another fantasy of escape. Maybe the strange, deadly girl hadn't really existed.

He rested there for some time, stones cutting into him, too weak to move, and then he heard male voices.

Was it Ugo's guards? What was going on? He felt so feeble and helpless.

He forced himself up, ready to hide if necessary, but he saw the girl again, and she flashed her vivid, bright smile at him.

She was with two tough, weather-beaten men wearing hairy shepherd's jerkins who looked at James with unblinking coal-black eyes. One was short and thickset with bandy legs, and the other was tall with a barrel chest and a huge drooping mustache.

"Please . . ." said James, and he tipped forward in a faint.

The barrel-chested man caught him and lifted him as easily as if he were a baby lamb. Then he slung him over his shoulders and set off at a steady trot.

James was dimly aware of being jogged and bounced through the mountains. The jerkin that his face was buried in smelled strongly of sheep, but he didn't mind; he felt safe for the first time in two days.

The journey seemed to take an awfully long time. They climbed ridges where the wind blew cold; they scrambled down steep slopes and clattered through narrow passes. At some point they padded through a dense wood. Then, as day broke, James opened his eyes to see that they were moving along a path that clung to the side of a mountain with a heart-stopping drop beneath them and a view out over a wide valley.

They came into a village that seemed part of the mountain itself, built of crumbling, square stone buildings all huddled together and perched on the cliffside like Ugo's palazzo.

Old women in scarlet dresses and head scarves came to their doors as they passed. They looked at James with impassive, leathery faces. In a tiny square, two old men with watery, malarial eyes and white beards were sitting on some steps smoking.

James could see straight away that the people who lived here were very poor. They all looked worn down and craggy, like the granite rocks they lived on. There was tiredness in their faces, as if everything was an effort. He knew how hard it must be to try and scratch a living from this barren soil.

The shepherds stopped and exchanged a few words with the locals. James was given water and bread, then the big man picked him up again and they left the village, climbing higher up the mountain.

James dozed for a while, and some time later he found himself in a dark place, being gently lowered on to a soft bed of animal skins. The last thing he remembered before he slipped into oblivion was the girl's brown, animal face watching over him.

CHAPTER 24—THE DANCE OF BLOOD

James awoke to an agony of itching. For a moment he didn't know where he was; all he knew was that he was in pain. There wasn't a bit of him that didn't hurt; his whole body crawled with irritation. He knew he couldn't move. He could feel the tight leather straps at his wrists and ankles cutting into him. He remembered the dream he had had about being carried through the night, and then he realized that he was scratching himself. His hand was somehow free. He could feel his chest studded with angry red lumps. He clawed at it with his broken fingernails before someone grabbed his arm and stopped him. He opened his eyes and saw a girl leaning over him, her black hair falling into her face, her eyes serious and intense.

"No," she said, and shook her head.

So it wasn't a dream. Slowly the details of last night began to come back to him. The arrival of the girl, the young guard with his throat opened up, trying to follow the girl through the swamp, falling over and being carried by the shepherd, first to the village and finally to this place.

He propped himself up and looked around.

He was lying on a bed of straw and animal skins inside a massive cave with a domed roof. At the back were a row of ancient, worn steps that led up to a vertical crack in the rock and a bright slash of sunlight. Four swallows flew through the crack, dodging and swooping, but always keeping in formation. James watched as they darted up through a jagged, round opening in the roof. The light from the opening fell on the remains of a Nuraghic village that filled the cave. James could make out the low stone walls of some fifty or sixty huts, and thought that this must once have been a fairly substantial settlement.

A group of Sardinian men had made camp. They had lit a fire below the hole in the ceiling to keep the insects away, and were sitting around it, chatting in low voices. They wore the traditional black and white peasants' outfits with shaggy sheepskin waistcoats and black stocking caps.

Each man had a rifle at his side.

James twisted his head and looked the other way. Here, the cave wall was partly open to the outside world, and through the low, wide gap, he could see thick vegetation baking and shimmering in the heat of the day.

He felt something cold on his skin and turned to look at the girl. She was sitting on a low wooden stool with a bowl in her lap, smearing a thick greenish-gray paste onto him. She began to gently rub it in with her strong, bony fingers.

James lay back and tried to keep still. It was very difficult. He badly wanted to scratch himself, but whenever he moved his hand, she slapped it away and gave him a nasty look.

The girl had her own small fire on which aromatic twigs and leaves were burning and sending off scented smoke. A little kettle hung over it on a tripod. The girl stopped what she was doing and peered into it. She then pounded up some wormwood leaves, bark, and berries on a flat stone and scraped them in. She stirred the mixture for a while before pouring some into a tin cup and passing it to James to drink.

It smelled foul, but he didn't want to annoy the girl, so he took a sip. It was disgusting—bitter and gritty. He fought back the urge to vomit and caught the girl's eye. She evidently expected him to drink the whole lot. He forced down another couple of sips before handing her back the cup and shaking his head.

She looked cross and went back to applying the paste to his bites with intense concentration. The paste felt cool and soothing, but it did little to stop the horrible itching.

After a while the girl grew impatient with his fidgeting and left.

James took the opportunity to scratch himself all over, even though he knew that he shouldn't.

His arms were the worst affected, and he raked them till they bled.

The girl suddenly returned and yelled at him. She was with the big barrel-chested man who had carried James last night. He stroked his long black mustache, smiled at James, and then lashed his arms to his sides with thin ropes so that he couldn't move his hands. The man gave him a friendly, apologetic look and wandered back over to the fire.

Even though James knew it was for the best, he felt humiliated and helpless.

He struggled up into a seated position, and the girl fed him a cup of water like a baby. He drank some and dribbled the rest down his front.

She laughed and suddenly looked years younger. She

became a cheerful, happy child, not the grim-faced assassin who had rescued him last night.

A couple of minutes later there was a shout from across the cave as Stefano came down the steps. James was so relieved to see a familiar face, he almost wept.

"What's going on?" he said, as Stefano hurried over. "Who are these people?"

"The girl is Mauro's sister, Vendetta," said Stefano. "She is crazy, but she will look after you. Her mother has taught her about herbs and healing. The men are from all around, from Orgosolo and Oliena and Fonni. The tall one who brought you here is Calogero, the chief of my village. He is a great warrior. He is feared in all Sardinia. He brought you here to be safe. Our people have always come to this cave when there is danger. Even before Roman times." Stefano stopped and grew more solemn. "I am sorry, James," he said. "I ran away and left you."

"It's all right," said James.

"No. I heard the guards coming and I was a coward. I should not have run."

"Well, if you hadn't, I wouldn't be here now," said James.

"You did a brave thing," said Stefano. "As soon as I heard that you had been captured, I started making plans to get away from the palazzo."

"I didn't tell Ugo anything," said James.

"I know," said Stefano. "I owe you my life."

"No," said James. "I think we're probably even now. But these other men, they don't owe me anything."

"They all hate Ugo," said Stefano. "Many of them worked for him, building his palazzo. They were never paid.

He was one of us, James, but no more. He kill Mauro, so now he is our enemy. Mauro had no brothers and no father, only Vendetta, so these other men will seek revenge."

"But what can they do?" said James. "They can't attack the palazzo. It's too well guarded. Ugo has a small army there."

"Vendetta wants to sneak in and cut Ugo's throat," said Stefano.

"She wouldn't get near him," said James.

"I know," said Stefano, "but that would not stop her trying. Maybe, though, we do not need to go there to fight him. Maybe Ugo will bring the fight to us. He will look for you, James, and he will look for me, and he will look for the people who helped you escape."

"I should go," said James. "I don't want to be the cause of any trouble here."

"No," said Stefano. "You did not start this. It was Ugo, when he kill Mauro. And he will surely come, whether you stay or go. He hates all the people of the Barbagia, because they know who he really is."

"I need to get back to Victor's," said James, struggling to sit up. "He'll know what to do."

"First you must rest," said Stefano, pushing him back on to the animal skins. "You have been a long time without sleep, and Vendetta's medicine will make you sick."

Stefano was right. James soon developed a killing headache and stomach cramps. This was followed by drowsiness and a burning sensation under his skin. All he could do was lie in his bed and groan, drifting in and out of sleep and muttering crazily about Victor, Amy, and Ugo.

For two days, Vendetta nursed him, bringing him food and water and applying the gray paste, and gradually the bites healed. She watched for signs of fever, but mercifully none came. It seemed he had escaped the malaria. Whether it was down to luck or to Vendetta's medicine, he would never know, but he would always be grateful to her.

At last Vendetta was able to leave him untied, and he felt strong enough to go out of the cave. It was a relief to be in the sun and fresh air and away from the attentions of the strange, silent girl and the claustrophobic shell of the cavern.

His own tattered clothes had been removed and burned and Stefano had brought him some old clothes of his own, a loose-fitting white shirt and baggy trousers. They felt cool and comfortable.

The tiredness had passed. The mountain air was clean, and at this height there were few insects to bother him. He explored the area, which was covered in mastic shrubs and sharp rocks. He could feel his battered body getting back into shape, but he was anxious and on edge. He had to get away from here.

He returned to the cave to look for Stefano and found that new people had arrived. There were some women carrying bundles of food, and more men with guns, wearing flat caps and dark heavy suits.

James was reminded of Ugo's guests at the carnival. There was a familiar air of toughness and danger about these craggy-faced men. James thought how easily, under different circumstances, they would be his enemies rather than his friends.

"They are preparing for war," Stefano explained when James found him. "They are bandits."

"I must go," said James. "I have to help Amy. First thing in the morning I need to leave for Victor's house in Capo d'Orso. Can you take me there?"

"*Sì*," said Stefano. "But it will not be easy. We have no vehicles. I could find a donkey, perhaps, but the journey will take three or four days."

As night fell, two lambs were slaughtered and set on spits to roast over the fire, and soon a rowdy celebration was in progress. There was music and singing and wrestling, and a group of bandits played an incomprehensible gambling game where they yelled numbers at each other and held up their fingers.

Much wine was drunk, and James was reminded of Ugo's comment on the wrestling at his carnival.

"*Prima bevono, poi stringono.*"

First they drink, and then they fight.

He looked around at the assembled fighters. There were some thirty of them here now, ranging from boys of Stefano's age to grizzled oldsters, whose gnarled fingers were twisted around the butts of their rifles like the ancient roots of the local trees.

Three of them brought in a log from outside and propped it up against a wall. They painted the crude figure of a man on it and daubed the letters "UGO" on the bottom. The bandits then took it in turn to throw knives into the log, seeing who could hit it most accurately. Calogero was the champion, landing his big hunting knife right in the eye of the painted figure. He laughed and waved his fists in triumph like a schoolboy scoring a goal at football.

His friends slapped him on the back and gave him

more wine to drink, and then he started to dance with a very serious expression on his face. It was a strange melancholy dance, and James was aware that he was witnessing a ritual that had been acted out here for thousands of years.

"This is the *Danza di Sangue*," said Stefano.

"The Dance of Blood?" said James.

"*Sì*."

James looked at the ring of men around Calogero, their faces red from drink and the heat of the fire. They were shouting and clapping, their voices harsh. They seemed happy, filled with a wild spark of life. Their world was a world of hardship and poverty, fighting was their only release.

Sitting in the shadows behind the ring of drunken men were the women, their faces occasionally lit by flashes of firelight. They looked blank and resigned, like age-old stone carvings that had seen everything there was to see.

Once again their men were going off to fight; which of them would return and which would die?

It was in the hands of God now.

Deep in thought, James stood up and left the party. He wondered if he would make it back to Victor's in time, and he thought of Amy trapped in her cell. If these men attacked Ugo, she would be in great danger.

Vendetta appeared at his side, staring at him with her shining black eyes.

She wouldn't leave him alone. He was reminded of Mr. Cooper-ffrench, and how he had followed him around like a dog after the incident at the tower. Both of them had been trying to look after him in their own way, but James felt as uncomfortable with this small girl as he had been with the grumpy Mr. Cooper-ffrench.

She grabbed hold of his sleeve and said something, her voice husky and quiet.

James shook his head. Her accent was so thick, her dialect so strong, and her delivery so fast that he couldn't follow a single word of it.

"I'm sorry, Vendetta," he said. "I can't understand you; I wish I could."

Again she rattled off a stream of Italian, more intently this time. James pulled his arm free and was relieved to see that Stefano had come out to join them.

"Can you help me?" James asked. "She's trying to ask me something."

"She wants to know if you have a girl back in England," said Stefano, and he laughed.

"Tell her no," said James, then quickly added, "and tell her I'm not looking for one either."

Stefano spoke to Vendetta and she snapped at him.

"What did she say?" asked James.

"She says that you are a liar. A handsome boy like you must have a girl."

"Well, I don't."

"You do now," said Stefano.

"No, no, no," said James, and he hurried back inside the cave.

He tried to settle down to sleep, but Vendetta came and sat next to his bed, watching over him.

"Good-night," he said, and closed his eyes.

Vendetta tried to copy what he had said, but her pronunciation was terrible.

James struggled to think of the Italian, and at last he remembered.

"*Buona notte*," he muttered, then added, "*grazie . . .*"

He opened one eye a crack. She was still sitting there.

"Go away and leave me alone," he said. "I can't sleep with you looking at me." He rolled onto his other side, turning his back on her, but he was still aware of her staring at him. At last he turned around and sat up.

"Go away," he said. "Scram. Vamoose. Hop it." He flapped his hands at her and tried to shoo her away, and she laughed. Then she kissed him again.

"I wish you wouldn't keep doing that," said James. "It's embarrassing."

After several more minutes of shouting and gesturing, Vendetta eventually retired a few paces and sat in the darkness of one of the Neolithic huts; but it was no good, he still couldn't sleep. The party looked like it was going to go on all night, and James wasn't really that tired. He had slept too much these last two days.

He waited, lying perfectly still, until he was sure that Vendetta was asleep, then he got up, pulled on his shirt, and went outside.

There was a chilly breeze from the north and the moon was bright, sending a wash of silver down through the scrubby trees. There were pools of intense darkness where the moonlight couldn't penetrate, so he felt his way through the woods until he came to the edge of a cliff overlooking a wide valley.

The black clumps of trees below were interspersed with white rocks that seemed to glow in the dark.

Sardinia looked very beautiful. It was hard to imagine that generations of men had fought and died in these mountains, that the soil was fed by their spilled blood. Beneath him were the bones of Carthaginians, Phoenicians, Italians, Spaniards—and the countless Sardinians who had fought to keep them away.

He sat there for a long while as the sounds of the party died down and the night became wonderfully quiet. At last he began to feel drowsy.

He yawned and stood up, and as he did so, he heard voices and the sound of men moving through the woods.

He crouched low and carefully made his way back toward the cave. It was probably just a patrol sent out by the bandits—but it was best to be sure.

As he neared the cave entrance he looked up and saw three men in purple uniforms creeping along the rocks.

James's heart started thumping against his chest.

Ugo had come after all.

James forgot about trying to be quiet, broke cover, and ran full pelt into the cave, shouting as loudly as he could. "Look out! Wake up! *Attenzione!* Wake up!"

The slumbering men stirred drunkenly and blinked at him.

It was like a nightmare. James couldn't make them understand what was happening. He didn't have the language.

"Ugo!" James screamed. "Ugo is here!"

One or two of the bandits, those who had drunk less, reached drowsily for their guns; others turned over and went back to sleep, grumbling; but in an instant James's message became clear.

There was a terrific bang and a flash. A flare had been dropped through the roof, and it lit the cave with a lurid yellow light. James heard shouts, then gunfire, and threw himself to the ground as bullets spat into the earth around him.

A group of men in uniform ran down the steps at the back of the cave, firing wildly in all directions. Some of the villagers were cut down in the confusion, some never even made it up off their beds, but a few managed to take cover and were fighting back, so that soon the air was alive with bullets. James heard them crack and fizz as they tore past him. In the confined space of the cave, the noise was appalling. The bangs of the guns were so loud they stunned him, and with each shot the air was compressed so that it punched him like a physical blow. He felt as if he were trapped inside a steel drum with someone hammering on the lid.

He crawled quickly into the shelter of one of the ruined huts, a bullet smacking into the wall just above his head and showering him with dust and shards of rock. More bullets ricocheted off the hard stones and sang away into the dirt.

An officer with a pistol led a charge in through the entrance from the woods, but a volley of shots rang out. The officer fell and his men retreated. As the villagers cheered, Calogero stood up and roared a barrage of defiant insults after the fleeing guards, but his confidence was short-lived. The attack had merely been a diversion, and another group had come in by the back entrance, including a man with a lethal Thompson submachine gun.

The gun chattered into life, spraying bullets around the cave.

Calogero fired back, standing proudly in the open, his rifle to his shoulder. He got off six rounds, one after the other, and his aim was more accurate than the machine gunner's. His last shot found its target, and as the guard went down, he dropped the tommy gun.

Another man ran to pick up the fallen weapon, but Calogero was ready for him. He aimed his rifle and pulled his trigger.

Nothing happened. He was out of ammunition. He cursed and threw the rifle aside, then pulled his knife from his belt.

He threw the knife at the exact moment that the guard took aim and fired.

A .45 caliber bullet fired by a Thompson submachine gun travels at roughly 920 feet per second.

A knife thrown by a strong man travels at roughly 80 feet per second.

Calogero didn't stand a chance.

James was horrified. A moment ago this had been a man full of spirit and laughter, and now he was a lifeless bundle on the ground and he would never laugh again.

His knife, however, was growing from the gunner's chest, and once again the Thompson was silenced.

The flare had burned itself out, and it was now difficult to see what was going on. The only light came from the guttering fire and the muzzle flashes of the guns.

James grabbed Calogero's fallen rifle. He knew that it was empty, but it felt good to hold something in his sweaty hands—at the very least it would stop them shaking. This was cold, gut-wrenching fear like he had never experienced before. He didn't know where to turn. It was chaos. Everywhere was a confusion of ear-splitting bangs, blinding bursts of light, shouting, and screaming. Whether you lived or died was largely down to luck.

A third guard now took up the machine gun, and as he pinned everyone down, the way was clear for the rest of the attackers to filter into the cave through the front entrance. Luckily, the machine gunner was no expert and the gun leaped about unsteadily in his hands, scattering shots inaccurately. His friends were almost as scared of him as were the cowering bandits.

The man with the Thompson slowly advanced into the center of the cave, only firing sporadic bursts now, as no one dared expose himself to the gun's deadly gaze.

James spotted Vendetta crouching in the remains of another hut nearby. She had her *resolza* knife in her hand, the blade drawn, and as he watched, she darted out toward the machine gunner.

James jumped up from his hiding place and threw himself at her, knocking her to the ground in a clumsy rugby tackle, as a storm of bullets screamed past inches above their heads.

They rolled behind a wall, and James lay on top of her to keep her out of harm. Vendetta's eyes were wide and frightened. She clung on to James, and he had the horrible feeling that they were both going to die here.

He felt a hand on his back and realized that they were not the only ones hiding here. Stefano was also cowering behind the wall with the squat, bowlegged shepherd who had been with Calogero when he rescued James. The shepherd smiled crazily, despite the fact that it was not going well for the villagers. He was evidently still drunk.

The shepherd suddenly sprang to his feet and ran out of hiding, firing his rifle. One, two, three of Ugo's men went down. The stocky shepherd bellowed in triumph, but someone calmly stepped up behind him and pointed a Luger at his back.

It was Smiler.

The Luger spoke once and the battle was over.

There weren't enough villagers left to put up any resistance. The few who had survived threw down their guns and crept out of hiding with their hands up.

Smiler, who seemed to be in charge of the attackers, barked a command, and the purple-clad guards regrouped in the center of the cave.

Smiler walked over to where James and the others were sheltering and beckoned them out with his pistol.

With heads bowed, they stood up and shuffled over to where Ugo's men were waiting by the fire.

Smiler saw James and grinned, a real grin, showing his yellow teeth, his eyes happy.

"James Bond!" he said. "We meet again. Ugo will be very happy when I bring him your ears." He swiveled his gaze to Stefano and tutted, as if telling off a naughty child. "Stefano," he said, "you've been a very silly boy. What were you thinking of?"

Stefano said nothing.

Smiler raised his Luger at the small group. "Do you think you'll be going to heaven or to hell?" he said, and chuckled. "I'd give you a wee blessing, but"—he shrugged—"I never did finish my training to be a priest. Now. Who wants to be first? Huh? I know who'll be last. . . . James Bond. Always save the best till last. So, Stefano, it's time to say good-bye, my son."

He raised his Luger and aimed it at Stefano's heart. James heard the boy quietly muttering a prayer.

"Save your breath," said Smiler. "He doesn't listen." He laughed again and steadied his pistol.

He never fired it, however.

Before Smiler could pull the trigger, he grunted and coughed, then dropped to his knees. A large, ugly whaling harpoon was sticking out of his chest.

His men were caught off guard and looked around in

panic. Standing at the top of the steps was the giant figure of Tree-Trunk, Zoltan's Samoan lieutenant.

A second later there was a burst of gunfire, and men shimmied down from the opening in the roof, unfurling ropes like great black spiders.

Another hail of bullets from the front entrance convinced Smiler's men that the game was up. They threw down their weapons and put their hands in the air.

A man appeared through the fog of gunpowder smoke, clutching a Beretta.

It was Zoltan the Magyar. He looked down at the lifeless body of the Scotsman.

"Ah, well," he said, "at least he died with a smile on his face."

He saluted James.

"You are always getting into trouble, James," he said. "What are we going to do with you?"

The following morning, James was sitting outside the cave on a tree stump, feeling empty and numb. The battle had been a brief, insane explosion of terror that had drained him of all emotion.

He had had to sleep out in the open. It was impossible to stay in the cave. The smell of blood was too strong.

"Here, James, I brought you this." James looked up to see Zoltan carrying his battered suitcase. He slung it at James's feet.

"I thought you might need some clothes," said Zoltan.

"Thank you," said James flatly.

"You left it in the changing room at the stadium after

the fight," said Zoltan. "I've been looking after it for you."

"How did you know where I was?" said James.

"We followed Ugo's men. Word went around that you had escaped. I hoped to get to you before they did, but Smiler surprised us. He attacked you at night while we were sleeping. The sound of the gunfire told us what was happening. We were a little late in arriving or we would have stopped the bloodshed sooner. Your friends lost many men. I am sorry. It's lucky they only brought one of these."

James saw that Zoltan was carrying the Thompson sub-machine gun.

"Ugo is such a miser," said the pirate. "I gave him a crate of these things and he sends his men out with only one, in case they lose them." He sat down and ran his fingers over the black metal and polished brown wood. "She is beautiful, isn't she?" he said. "Beautiful but evil. A machine for killing. And so simple. The gas released by the blast of the bullet being fired shunts the bolt back, releasing the spent cartridge and loading another one. The whole thing is powered by gunpowder. So simple and so deadly."

He fired a burst into a nearby tree and watched as a shower of shredded leaves and twigs rained down.

"It was invented by John T. Thompson of America, during the war. You know how he described it? He called it a trench broom. For clearing men out of trenches. It is a disgusting thing. I prefer my Beretta. She is small and has no great stopping power, but I like her. She suits me; she is fast and reliable, and I can hide her easily."

"What happened with Ugo?" said James, who had had enough of guns and killing.

"You were right," said Zoltan. "I cannot trust him. After you escaped, he came to me. He was very angry, and said I must have helped you. We argued. I accused him of being a fool, and he accused me of being a traitor. He said he would never pay me what I was owed. It was like the past all over again. He is a thief. Now I have nothing. If I had not had my men with me, I think he would have tried to kill me."

James felt shifty. His lie to Ugo had turned the two men against each other, but without that lie he would probably be dead.

Besides, he had to keep reminding himself, Zoltan was a murderer and not his friend.

The Magyar lit a cigarette. He looked tired and his whole body was shaking.

"Don't let my men see me like this," he said, looking at his good hand and trying to stop it trembling. "They will think I am scared. I cannot stop it, and every movement tires me out."

"What will you do now?" said James blankly.

"These people know about revenge. And I will have my revenge on Ugo. I will destroy him."

"You're going back there?" said James. "But there aren't enough of you."

"The odds are leveled after last night," said Zoltan. "His army is smaller. I have all my crew and the surviving bandits."

"You still won't stand a chance," said James.

"I have a plan," said Zoltan. "Your cousin gave me the idea. We took some mining equipment from one of Ugo's tunnels. I will bring his house down on his head."

"And what about Amy?"

"Ah, Amy . . ." Zoltan looked up at the sky and sighed. "She is the cause of all this. I will try to get her out before the end, but if I can't have her, then neither will Ugo."

"That's what this is all about, isn't it?" said James. "You and Ugo competing to see who has the bigger gun. You're fighting over the prize like two dogs with a rabbit. But Amy's not some sort of trophy. She's a girl, a frightened fourteen-year-old girl. You'd let her die, wouldn't you? Just to spite Ugo."

"No," said Zoltan. "I don't want her to die. Which is why I need your help, James. You are the only one who knows where she is. That palazzo is a rabbit warren. I would never find her in time."

James rubbed his temples with his fingers. He couldn't deliver Amy back into the hands of this pirate.

"I can't help you," he said.

"It seems there are three of us who want her," said Zoltan. "And as you say—when men fight over something, it usually gets broken." He stood up and stamped on his cigarette with his heel. "Think about it, James. I am the only hope of getting Amy out. If you don't tell me, then Stefano will."

Zoltan walked away, leaving James alone with his thoughts. Everything had changed now. He didn't have time to get to Victor's. He needed a new plan. He opened the suitcase and looked inside.

There was the jumble of things he'd grabbed and thrown in without thinking as he'd hurriedly left Casa Polipo after the robbery. His wash bag, a clean shirt, his underwear; and there, tucked in one end, were the schnorkel, goggles, and fins that Victor had given him. With a pang he remembered the time he'd spent with Mauro on the beach.

Mauro, who he would never see again.

He was suddenly overcome with a terrible sadness. All the emotions he had held back since hearing of Mauro's death bubbled to the surface, and he wept silently.

A few minutes later he heard a footfall and saw Stefano bringing him something to eat. He quickly dried his face, wiped his eyes, and kept his head down, pretending to sort the items in his suitcase.

"I have been talking to Zoltan," said Stefano, giving James some bread and cheese. "He wants me to take him back and show him where Amy is. If I don't tell him, I don't know what he will do. This is bad, James. I think you must forget about the girl."

"No," said James. "I promised her. I can't leave her there."

"There is not time to go to your cousin's now," said Stefano.

"I know," said James. "I need to go back to the palazzo instead, and try and get her out myself."

"You cannot," said Stefano. "It is too dangerous."

"Not necessarily. One person can sometimes do more than a whole army. I know where she is—"

"But there is no way inside the palazzo," said Stefano. "Unless you come down from the dam, up from the valley in the railway, or through the mining tunnels. But all those routes are heavily guarded."

"What about the aqueduct?" said James. "I could go across there."

"They would see you."

"Not if it was dark and I was swimming."

"Even then—"

"No. I know a way," said James. "Now listen. Zoltan is planning some sort of attack. If I can get there before him, free Amy, and be ready, we might be able get out while everyone else is distracted by the fighting."

Stefano thought about this in silence for a while, but at last he seemed to make up his mind. "Zoltan does not know the way back," he said. "It is easy to get lost in the mountains. I will take him, but I will go a long way round. Someone else will take you to the aqueduct by a quicker path."

James smiled at his friend. "Thank you, Stefano," he said.

Stefano clasped him and gave him a hug. "You are a brave boy, James," he said. "It will be an honor to die at your side!"

"I hope it won't come to that," said James.

That evening, as James fixed a mosquito net up under a tree, he listened to the dull murmur of voices from the cave as the men prepared for the attack in the morning.

Zoltan's plan was to hit the palazzo at first light. If James wanted to get there before him, he would have to leave in a couple of hours, so he needed to rest now if he could.

He doubted that he would sleep. He had been too close to death lately, and tomorrow there would likely be more killing.

He was sick of it. He wanted it to be over.

But he couldn't leave Amy there.

He had made her a promise.

With a knot of tension in his stomach, he watched as the

bright blue of the sky dulled to violet, then to purple, and finally to black. The racket of insects filled the night. Since his experience in Ugo's swamp, James was all too aware of insects. They were everywhere, countless millions of them.

Men thought they were so much more advanced, so superior, but it was the insects that ruled the world. They were here before man and they would be here long after he disappeared from the face of the earth.

James wondered how the battle yesterday would have appeared to a giant. The mass of angry men, fighting and dying, would have looked like nothing more than two rival swarms of ants.

Staring up at a patch of stars visible through the branches of the trees, he slowly drifted into a troubled sleep and dreamed of gunshots and bright blood hanging in the air like a red mist.

Some time later he felt himself being shaken, and awoke to find the familiar face of Vendetta staring down at him. She was all in black, with a short blouse over trousers and a scarf tied around her head.

She smiled, then kissed him before he had a chance to dodge it. She beckoned him with a slim bony finger and he got up stiffly.

He felt dog-tired and longed for more sleep, but he knew that wasn't possible. Stefano had given him a knapsack, which he'd packed with the few things he would need. James picked it up, slung it over his shoulder, and followed Vendetta into the cave, where he looked around for the man who was going to take him back to the palazzo.

There was nobody here. Zoltan's men and the handful of bandits who were going with him had already left.

"Who's taking me?" James whispered. Vendetta said nothing and ran off up the steps in a crouch, more catlike than ever. James noticed that she was carrying a canteen and a small leather bag, and he suddenly realized who his guide was going to be.

"No," he called out. "Not you. You can't."

CHAPTER 26—IT'S ALWAYS DARKEST JUST BEFORE THE DAWN

Vendetta was pointing down the hillside, but try as he might, James couldn't see anything. He gave her a questioning look and she pointed again, more insistently this time.

"Zoltan," she whispered, and James at last made out the dark shapes of several men hurrying through the trees below and some way behind.

So the plan was working. They were ahead of Zoltan.

Vendetta gave a triumphant smile and led James on.

James reckoned that they had been traveling for over two hours, and Vendetta's pace had never faltered. They must have been following a track of sorts; she knew exactly where she was going, but an outsider would never have found any signs of a path. And she was barefoot. James couldn't begin to imagine how tough the soles of her feet were. James's heel still throbbed occasionally when he was tired. If this girl trod on a sea urchin she probably wouldn't even notice.

James was exhausted; he longed to sit down and rest, but having seen Zoltan he was reminded of their need to keep moving.

He had tried to argue with the girl before they'd left. He put a hand on her shoulder, but she pushed it away with a contemptuous look, and carried on up the steps.

"Please," James had called after her, "it's too dangerous. . . ."

But his words faded on his lips. Too dangerous? Who was he kidding? This was the girl who had rescued him. Who had killed the guard. Who knew these mountains better than anyone. He was the one in danger, not her. She could perfectly well look after herself.

So he shrugged and followed her.

The journey had been tedious and largely uneventful. The only thing that had broken the monotony was when a moufflon leaped across their path, and James flung himself to the ground in fright. Vendetta laughed at him, but he didn't care. He was glad that he was still alert. His nerves were wound so tightly that his reactions were incredibly quick and sharp. It was better to be cautious and alive than foolhardy and dead.

At last they stopped for water, and Vendetta produced a half-eaten loaf.

James wasn't sure what time it was; the fat moon still sat up in the sky and there was no glimmer of light from the east, but he knew that dawn came up fast here.

As he squatted in the dark to eat, she watched him, like a mother watching her child, and he found himself endlessly chewing a dry lump of bread, unable to swallow under her curious gaze.

They heard a rustle in the undergrowth, and the next thing they knew they were surrounded by wild pigs. They approached, making tiny grunts and squeaks, quite unafraid, their inquisitive wet noses sniffing the air.

James wondered what string of events, what cast of the dice, had brought him here to the side of this Sardinian mountain in the middle of the night, sharing his breakfast with this strange, dangerous girl and a herd of wild pigs.

And he wondered how the game would end.

Well, he'd know the answer to that before the day was through.

Without warning, Vendetta was off again. James threw the crust of his bread to the pigs, sighed, and stood up, his joints complaining. The girl was already way ahead. He tried to catch up with her, but she was too fast for him and was apparently able to see in the dark. He was constantly tripping and stumbling.

Hour after hour they hurried on, and James was just beginning to think he couldn't go any farther, when he noticed a familiar peak and realized that they were near to Ugo's stronghold. Vendetta slowed down now and they went more cautiously. At last James saw the wide curve of the dam; they stopped. They were on a steep cliff slightly below the dam and on the opposite side of the ravine to the palazzo. Vendetta hid herself behind a rock and nodded toward the aqueduct about sixty feet below.

Guards patrolled the dam, and James knew that several more were stationed in the winch house, but he could see no sign of anyone guarding the aqueduct.

The only problem was how to get down there.

Vendetta answered that question. She slipped over the edge of the cliff and started to climb down. James had no choice but to follow. He felt dreadfully exposed on the rock face. If one of the guards were to look over the parapet of the dam, he would easily spot them, so they descended as swiftly as they dared.

Thankfully, they made it safely down the cliff and got

among the cover of some bushes. They rested for a while, then crawled through the undergrowth until they came to the edge of a dirt track. James saw a brick building set into the side of the hill, where a sleepy guard dozed in a concrete sentry post.

What had Ugo said, all those days ago at dinner? That the water came down this side of the mountain through the turbines and into the aqueduct, which crossed over to the palazzo. The brick building must be the entrance to the turbine rooms where the electricity was generated.

Vendetta nodded toward the guard. James wondered if she meant for them to enter here and reach the aqueduct from the inside. That seemed hugely risky; they had no way of knowing what they would find inside, and there was the problem of how to get past the guard.

James was looking around for another route when he saw that Vendetta had her knife between her teeth and was edging out of the bushes toward the guard.

He grabbed her and hauled her back, then shook his head. There would be no more killing if he could help it, and besides, he had seen something. Leading down the mountain toward the aqueduct was a thick iron pipe made of riveted sections.

He pointed to it and set off, skirting around the edge of the track then darting across it once he was out of sight of the sentry post.

Vendetta reluctantly went after him. This was not her plan, but when James showed her how easy it was to slither down the pipe using the joints between each section for footholds, she smiled and followed him.

At the bottom water frothed and gurgled out of a large opening and into the canal in the top of the aqueduct.

The two of them peered across to the other side. The aqueduct was exposed for its whole length, but James was confident that he could get over without being seen.

He put down his knapsack and opened it. Vendetta was watching him with her gleaming, dark eyes. They went very wide when she saw what he had brought with him, and was even more amazed when he slipped on the goggles and put the schnorkel between his teeth. She shrank back, scared for a moment. James laughed and pulled the goggles up onto his forehead.

"I'm going now," he said. "You wait for me here." He pointed to the ground with both his hands. "*Aspetta*—"

"No," she said walking toward the aqueduct. "*Vengo con voi.*"

"You can't come with me," said James angrily. "I can't be responsible for you, and I need you here, to help us get away."

"*Vengo con voi*," she repeated, and James pushed her roughly backward.

"Stay," he said, as if to a dog, and he wished that he could speak her language properly. He put the goggles back on, grabbed the fins and moved toward the canal, but he sensed movement behind him and turned to see that she was following him.

"Please," he said desperately. "You can't come. This is my problem, not yours." He pushed her back again, more gently this time, and turned away from her; but she suddenly leaped at him, knocking him over. Restricted by the goggles, he couldn't see what was happening clearly and fell awkwardly, hitting his head on the hard ground. He twisted onto his back and tried to wrestle her off, but he was winded and she was lithe and muscular. It was like trying to fight with a wild animal. He didn't want to hurt her, and had to put his hands up to defend his face as she landed a rain of vicious slaps down on his head.

Then there was a flash of steel as she whipped out her knife and held it to his throat.

They waited like that for some time before James realized that she was crying. A salty tear fell and landed on his lips. He took off the goggles and put up his hand to dry her cheeks.

"Amy," she said quietly, then rolled off him and turned away in a sulk.

"Yes, Amy," said James harshly. "Is that what this is about? Look. I'm going to get her, all right? Not because she's my girlfriend, or any nonsense like that, but because I promised I would. I don't love her. I don't love you. But I need you, and I need you alive. So stay here." He stood up. "Look, I know you can't understand what I'm saying," he said more gently. "But I'll be grateful to you for as long as I live. It's just that, if you come with me it'll make my job twice as hard."

He picked up the fins and touched her on the back. "I will come back," he said. "Wait for me."

He took four steps, then ran back and kissed her hard on the mouth. He left her there—frozen in surprise, her jaw hanging open and her eyes wide—and ran down to the aqueduct before she knew what to do.

He ripped off his shoes and slung them in his knapsack,

which he strapped over his belly so that it wouldn't stick up, then he put on the fins and goggles and lowered himself into the canal.

The water was cold, but James was too excited to really notice. He slid underwater and started to swim with the current. He could see just enough by the light of the moon to stop himself from bumping into the sides, and he moved quickly along, paddling hard with the fins.

Anyone looking this way would see nothing; all that was visible was the narrow top of his schnorkel moving smoothly along the top of the water.

He didn't dare risk putting his face up to see how far he'd come, but it was taking much longer than he had expected. He seemed to have been swimming for ages. He was just considering taking a quick look above water, when he heard a rushing, roaring sound and a deep rumbling that grew steadily louder. And now he saw the water boiling up ahead and a mass of seething white bubbles. The current suddenly got very strong and he found himself being pulled ahead too fast, out of control. He tried to brace himself against the sides, but before he could get a grip, he was smashed into a metal grille. He was stuck there, held in place by the force of the water, and his schnorkel was swamped. He fought back the panic, took hold of the grille, and hauled himself sideways across it until he reached the edge.

He had to put his head up to a take a breath and found to his relief that he was underneath a ledge of some sort. He heaved himself out of the churning water and rested on the uneven concrete surface.

He slipped off his sodden knapsack, took out his shoes

and two coils of rope, and replaced them with the fins, goggles, and schnorkel. Then he hid the knapsack in a dark corner, put on the shoes, and looped the rope over his shoulder.

Cautiously he crept out from below the shelter of the ledge and looked around. Above him was the funicular railway car, waiting by the piazza. There was no sign of any guards. Presumably they were in their hut, playing cards.

He crawled over until he was behind the car and made doubly sure that there was no one around.

So far, so good.

He looked down the railway. The moon was bright and it was a long way to the tunnel and the big outcrop of rock; luckily, though, the palazzo walls were throwing a wide shadow across the tracks.

He would have to risk it.

He dashed across the tracks into the shadows and started down.

He remembered from the other night how slow and awkward it was negotiating the steep slope, and he began to worry that he would be too late. He looked up at the sky. There was still no sign of dawn, but he knew that it wouldn't be long in coming.

By the time he got to the tunnel, the heat of his body and the warm night air had dried his clothing, but he was tired. More tired than he had ever been.

There was nothing he could do about it. He had to keep moving, to keep pushing his exhausted body onward. He had to get to Amy before it was too late.

He climbed around the rock and up to the base of the palazzo wall, where he scaled the wooden scaffolding on to the roof of the unfinished building. It was little different from before: most of the tools were still here, but as he had expected, the rope had been taken away.

No matter. He had his own. He uncoiled one length and tied a pickaxe to the end of it. He secured the second rope to the same column as Stefano had done, then tied both ropes around his waist, took a deep breath, and lowered himself over the edge, the pickaxe dangling beneath him and clinking against the wall. He stopped at the first window, untied the pickaxe, and lowered it gently to the floor of the empty room.

A minute later he was perched on the window ledge outside Amy's cell. He softly called out her name.

"James?" It was Amy. And there was her pale face at the window.

"I told you I'd come back for you," said James.

"Thank God," she said, her voice catching. "Who's with you?"

James hesitated before replying. "No one—it's just me."

"Oh . . ." Amy tried to hide her disappointment.

"Don't worry," James said quickly. "I have a plan. Listen to me. Any minute now, all hell's going to break loose. As soon as it does, keep to the edge of your cell and wait for me. If anyone comes to your door, yell."

"Okay."

"Trust me," said James. He climbed up to the window above, crawled inside, and undid the rope.

He grabbed the pickaxe.

He was ready. Now all he could do was wait for dawn.

He sat by the window and watched the sky, looking for the first glimmerings of light.

He felt a long way from home.

He wished he were back in England. He had had enough of feeling scared. But beneath his fear there was an electric current of thrill running through his veins. So close to death, he felt fully alive.

He was a member of the Danger Society, after all.

He wondered what Pritpal and Tommy Chong might be up to now and smiled when he thought of them. But then he thought of Mark Goodenough. He remembered how he had looked in the car, sent mad by his pain and grief.

James was reminded of who had done that to him—Ugo and Zoltan and Peter Haight.

He had told Mark that he would do anything he could to put things right.

Well, now he had the chance.

Stefano, too, was watching the sky, trying to hold back the daylight to give James as much time as possible to get into the palazzo. He hoped that James was already in place; there was nothing more he could do to delay Zoltan's men.

They had come down the mountain by an old goat track and waded across the shallow river. Now they were waiting under some trees near the entrance to the mines. The men were talking quietly, checking their guns and preparing the fuses in the grenades.

An hour ago they had left Zoltan up at the dam with Tree-Trunk, and he had run through his plan of attack.

As soon as the sun cleared the top of the mountains, the *Charon*'s first mate, Davey Day, was to lead the attack on the mines. Using the grenades and the tommy gun, they were to take out the sentry post then fight their way up to the palazzo through the tunnels.

They had to cause as much noise and confusion as they could.

"You know what to do when you reach the palazzo, don't you, Davey?" Zoltan had said.

"I go with two men and get the girl. When we find her, we bring her out the way we go in."

"Good man. When this is over, you can all take home as much loot as you can carry."

Stefano shivered. He dreaded going back inside the palazzo. His chances of getting out alive were less than slim.

He jumped as someone put a hand on his shoulder. But it was only Davey Day, his pale face gray in the moonlight.

"Your job's done," he said. "We've got your map. We know where we're going. You needn't come any farther. It's going to get pretty hairy in there."

"Thank you," said Stefano, and tears of relief sprang into his eyes. He felt like hugging the man.

"Good luck," he said.

"We're going to need it," said Davey.

Stefano left them and ran back across the river toward the goat track.

He would go back up the mountain and look for Vendetta.

He was not going to die after all.

He hoped it would be as easy for James.

He stopped and look back at the palazzo, way up on the mountainside. Then he closed his eyes and mouthed a silent prayer for James's safe return.

It was a beautiful sunrise. A pale glow lifted the darkness to the east, and soon the whole sky became a hazy screen of gold and blue. Watching from the window, James saw the shape of the mountains form in shadow on the floor of the valley as the countryside changed from gray to faded green. Finally the edge of the sun showed itself and birds began singing in the trees.

The day had begun.

There was a feeling of peace and calm. The air smelled clean. On a day like this, only good things could happen.

Then there was a deep boom, and a flock of white doves flew up into the sky like a spray of litter.

The boom was followed by distant bangs and the sound of panicked shouting.

It had started.

James moved quickly. He lifted the pickaxe and swung it as hard as he could at the center of the floor. He paused, listening for Amy's warning yell, but all he could hear was the growing sound of confusion and gunfire in the palazzo. He swung again, and a crack appeared. Again he swung, and again, until a chunk of concrete gave way and dropped into the room below. Two more swings and he'd opened up a sizable hole. He saw Amy looking up at him, with dust in her hair.

"Are you all right?" he said.

"I think so."

"Any sign of your guards?"

"No."

"Good. Stand back, and keep as close to the wall as you can."

James lifted the pickaxe and carried on swinging.

In a few minutes he had a hole wide enough to fit into. Then suddenly there was a great crash as half the floor collapsed. He lowered the rope to Amy.

"Grab hold of this," he shouted, and braced himself. Amy climbed, and he pulled, and eventually she slithered up through the hole into the room. She was covered in chalky powder, and her eyes were glassy with fear.

She gave James a big hug, and he was glad of the human contact.

"We've got to get out of here," he said. "Can you swim?"

"Yes."

"Come on then, let's go."

James was about to go to the window when he heard a key rattling in the lock. Thinking quickly, he gave one end of the rope to Amy and pointed to the other side of the door. Luckily she seemed to understand what he meant, and they took up their positions, flattened against the wall.

The door flew open and a guard rushed in. They yanked the rope and he tripped, falling face forward into the hole, smacking his head on the edge as he went down.

"Let's get out of here," said James, and Amy didn't argue.

They ran through the door that the guard had unlocked

and found themselves in a dark, twisting corridor that eventually led outside into a sunny square.

There was panic and confusion everywhere. People were running in all directions, yelling. The servants were trying to get away and the guards were trying to get to the fighting, although they didn't seem too sure of which direction they were being attacked from. James and Amy passed unnoticed through the chaos, working their way up through the palazzo toward the aqueduct.

After a couple of dead ends, James spotted the equestrian statue.

"This way," he said, running along a walkway.

The sound of gunshots grew louder.

"We've got to try not to get mixed up in the fighting," he shouted. "Or we won't stand a chance."

Amy's face was set in a grim mask, her lips white. She nodded quickly, too scared to speak. James grabbed her hand and pulled her up a flight of steps. At the top they nearly ran straight into Jana Carnifex, who was going the other way with a small entourage.

She looked so surprised to see the two of them that she didn't have time to react, and before she could do or say anything, James and Amy had run off. James could smell her perfume wafting on the still air.

It was a smell he didn't think he'd ever be able to forget.

The terrace in front of the temple was deserted apart from one of Ugo's men, who was stretched out on the ground. He appeared to be just lying there, resting, and there was nothing to show how he had died. He was a young man with a simple, open face, and he wore a slightly puzzled look.

James felt desperately sorry for him. This fight was nothing to do with him. He thought of all the other soldiers who had died in countless wars without ever really knowing why.

As he was standing there, looking at the dead man, he felt something tug at his sleeve a split second before he heard the bang of a gun. The bullet tore his shirt, but only grazed his skin, not causing any damage. He had no idea what direction it had come from, or who had fired it, and he didn't wait for an answer. He grabbed Amy and ran for cover before another shot found its mark.

They hurried in silence through the network of alleyways, steps, and courtyards that led up to the main piazza. When they got there they found that between them and the aqueduct on the opposite side were Zoltan's men, who were involved in a fierce firefight with the palazzo guards.

James saw in an instant that the pirates were badly outnumbered and it would soon be over for them.

"Come with me," said James. "And keep your head down."

Not giving Amy a chance to object, James pulled her into the piazza.

They pounded over the paving stones and dived into the fountain, where they shuffled backward until they were up against the central support, hidden behind a curtain of water.

"We'll wait until it's safe to go over to the aqueduct," said James.

"Please," said Amy. "You have to tell me what's going on."

"Zoltan's attacking Ugo."

"But why?" said Amy. "It's hopeless. What's he trying to achieve?"

"He told me he had a plan to destroy the palazzo. He said my cousin Victor had given him the idea."

"What plan?" said Amy. "What did your cousin say?"

"I don't know," said James. "I've been trying to think. We all rode down from the dam together in one of the railway cars."

"And what did you talk about?"

"The dam," said James, and an awful realization struck him. "He's going to try and breach the dam."

"He wouldn't," said Amy. "All these people . . ."

"What would he care about that?" said James.

"He wouldn't," Amy repeated quietly.

"We have to stop him," said James.

One of Zoltan's men ran past. There was a crack, and he toppled over into the fountain. His blood quickly stained the pool, and in a few moments the curtain of cascading water had been turned pink. James and Amy cringed back against the central support. They both wanted to get out of there as fast as they could now.

"What are we going to do?" said Amy.

"We could try and go up to the dam on the railway," said James.

"Shall we risk it?" said Amy, who had evidently got her courage back.

The firefight had moved on. The last of Zoltan's men had fled inside the palazzo, with Ugo's guards following.

"Well, we can't stay here all day," said James. "Come on!"

They darted out of the safety of the fountain and sprinted across the piazza, their wet feet slipping on the polished marble. As James ran, his whole body was tensed, waiting for a bullet to hit him; but they made it unhurt, and he glanced quickly back. There was nobody around.

They climbed aboard the railway car and pulled the doors shut behind them. For a while they lay exhausted on the floor in a slowly spreading pool of water. Then James sat up and saw a terrified guard crouching in the shadows at the other end. He had a tommy gun in his hands but it was shaking all over the place, and he obviously had no desire to use it.

James yelled at him. "Get out! Just go."

The guard didn't think twice. He jumped up and bolted away like a startled rabbit, leaving his gun behind.

James studied the car's controls but could make no sense of them.

"How does it work?" said Amy.

"It's a counterweight system," said James. "The two cars are connected by a cable that winds around a big drum up at the dam. The car at the top is filled with water until it's heavier than the one at the bottom. Then it rolls down the slope and pulls the other car up. Once it reaches the bottom it empties the tank and the process is reversed."

"How do you empty the water out, then?"

"It's one of these levers," said James, and he started to yank and twist everything he could find. Amy joined him, and at last they heard a flushing sound as the tank below was emptied into the drain.

There was one big lever that must surely be the brake. James pulled it, but nothing happened.

"Hell," he said.

"What is it?" said Amy. "Why aren't we moving?"

"Obviously somebody needs to operate the car at the top," said James. "They need to fill it with water and release the brake. We're stuck here, I'm afraid."

But then, with no warning, the car moved forward with a jerk and they were traveling up the cliff.

Amy laughed with relief.

"How did you do that?" she said.

"I don't know," said James. "It's a miracle."

Halfway up, the "miracle" was explained as they passed the other car coming down.

It was packed with a group of confused and frightened guards from the dam, reluctantly trying to join the fight. The surprised look on their faces as they saw the two children serenely clanking up the hill past them was almost comical, and it was a few moments before they realized what was going on and started to shoot at them.

There was a sudden deafening racket as bullets slammed into the car. James and Amy threw themselves to the floor, and they were soon lying in a thick carpet of shattered wood and broken glass. The cars quickly moved too far apart, though, for the men to fire accurately, and neither of them was hurt. Once it was safe, they got gingerly to their feet and brushed the debris from their clothing.

The rest of the journey up passed without incident, but they forgot all about applying the brake when they reached the winch house, and the car slammed into the buffers, knocking them to the floor again. James was covered in tiny cuts, but felt nothing. His body was flooded with adrenalin. No pain signals were getting through to his brain.

They dragged themselves back on to their feet and looked out. The place was deserted. James picked up the tommy gun. It was heavy and smelled of oil.

They jumped down and James went over to the cable that supported the car.

He aimed the machine gun and pulled the trigger, fully expecting that nothing would happen. But the gun came alive in his hands and jumped crazily, pushing him backward. The din was terrific. He managed to hold it reasonably steady, though; and in a few moments the shredded cable gave way with a loud twang, and the car rolled back down the cliff, picking up speed as it went.

"There's no way of anyone following us up here now," said James.

"Yes," said Amy, "but how do we get down?"

"We'll worry about that later."

The noise of the shooting below was tinny and distant; it sounded like nothing worse than a fireworks display. Here by the lake it was calm and peaceful. The sun sparkled on the water. The mountain peaks were honey-colored against the perfect clear blue of the sky. But James knew that somewhere up here was a killer, intent on turning this idyllic postcard scene into a vision of hell.

"Is he here?" said Amy.

"I don't know," said James. "Maybe I was wrong."

He scanned the lake. Along the left-hand side was a small run of low buildings. There was no reason why Zoltan would have gone there, but where was he?

"What did your cousin say, exactly?" said Amy.

"He thought that that long overhanging rock over there was unstable," he said.

"So he'd have headed for that, then," said Amy.

"I suppose so," said James. "Let's go and look."

Ugo's motor launch was moored next to the big, ungainly seaplane at the jetty. James ran out and jumped into it.

"Do you know how to work one of these things?" he said.

"Yes," said Amy excitedly as she climbed aboard and cast off the rope. "I've spent half my life on boats."

She busied herself with the motor, glad to be doing something to take her mind off the danger they were in and the terrible violence they had witnessed.

Soon the motor launch was speeding out across the water, churning up its glassy surface and disturbing the fragile peace. Amy was steering and James pointed her toward the right-hand side of the lake. Once they were near the overhanging shelf of rock, they slowed down and cruised slowly along, keeping their eyes fixed on the coast, looking for anything that might give them some idea of where Zoltan was.

And then James saw the black mouth of a cave.

"Over there," he said, and Amy moved the boat closer. They saw that the entrance had been enlarged and was shored up around the edges to make it safe to enter.

Amy maneuvered the launch into the cave, and they found themselves in a short tunnel lit by a string of bulbs in the ceiling. They followed the lights around a corner into a small, gloomy cavern. It was cold in here and the air felt damp. Water ran down the walls and dripped from the roof, and everything was coated in green slime.

James quickly took in the details. There was a small dock for mooring boats and a rotting wooden platform built on concrete piles with an iron staircase leading up from it through a fissure in the rock. There was a stack of moldering barrels on the platform, and as James tied up the boat, Zoltan stepped out from behind it. His face was covered with a film of sweat and his eyes were mad with fever and burning red.

"James," he whispered hoarsely. "You are a clever boy. You found me. Well done. You have brought me Amy. Thank you."

Amy turned on James, suddenly angry. Had he betrayed her? Had he tricked her into coming here?

James took hold of her hand and squeezed it reassuringly, praying that she would trust him.

He looked down at the machine gun lying in the bottom of the boat. Zoltan saw it too. "If you try to use that, I'm afraid I will have to kill you," he said, drawing his Beretta from his tunic. He jerked the gun sideways, indicating that the two of them should come out of the boat and join him.

Maybe that would convince Amy that he was on her side.

As they crossed the platform James noticed a tangle of wires disappearing into a hole in the rocks. Tree-Trunk was crouching down in the shadows, uncoiling more wire from a big spool of cable.

"What are you doing?" said James, his voice echoing in the cave.

"Please. Don't try to stop me," said Zoltan. "I have to do this."

"You're going to blow up the rock?"

"I will wipe out Carnifex and his whole pathetic empire," said Zoltan.

"You mustn't," said James. "You can't. Think of the people who will die. Innocent people."

"Innocent? Who? They are all dogs and pigs. They are scum. I will be doing the world a favor."

"But what about your own men down there?"

"They are all probably dead already," said Zoltan with a shrug. "They were outnumbered. They were merely a diversion. I can find more men."

James tried to protest, but the big Samoan swept him up in one strong arm. He swept Amy up with his other arm and held them both as fast as if they were shackled in iron.

"Bring them with us," said Zoltan.

"No!" James shouted. "Please don't do this."

"It is too late," said Zoltan quietly. "It is done."

Zoltan took up the cable spool and unwound it behind him as the three of them clanged up the steps. James struggled in Tree-Trunk's effortless grip, but it was no use.

They emerged into sunshine above the lake and climbed farther up the mountainside until they came to a concrete viewing platform where a detonator had already been set up.

Zoltan sat down heavily. He was worn out from this small exertion and was breathing painfully. He fastened the ends of the wires to two brass connectors on the top of the detonator with trembling hands, cursing his clumsiness. He was evidently very sick now and had to stop to wipe away the sweat that was dripping down his face and blinding him.

James and Amy watched in horrified fascination as he turned the crank on the side of the box to charge the battery, then put a hand to the switch.

"Carnifex should never have crossed me," he said. "Now we will see if Victor Delacroix was right." He waved toward the dam and saluted. "Good-bye, my emperor."

He shunted the switch across, and James was sickened to hear a muffled boom from below. He felt like weeping. This shouldn't be happening. He had failed.

A few stones and smaller rocks dropped from the ledge into the lake with feeble splashes, and then nothing.

Silence hung over the mountains.

James's spirits lifted. He looked at Amy. There was a glimmer of hope in her eyes.

Zoltan laughed crazily. "He was wrong," he cried. "Victor was wrong. Carnifex is the better engineer after all. It seems that his dream will stand." He laughed again and cursed the lake in Hungarian.

It was then that James felt the ground shift beneath his feet, as if he were standing on the back of some huge beast waking from a deep sleep. There was a crack, a sound like ice breaking, deep within the mountain, and the air seemed to split around them as a shock wave passed through it. It hit James in the chest, and he could feel the effects of it through his whole body.

There came another long crack, then another and another, like rolling thunder. It was awesome, a tearing and ripping sound on a massive, unimaginable scale. The ground gave another giddy lurch, and James actually saw ripples pass through it.

Then there was silence again.

Time seemed to have stopped. The world was waiting. The whole area had gone completely quiet. No insect or bird made a sound.

James realized he was holding his breath.

Down below, at the palazzo, Ugo had heard the sound and felt the mountain quake. He looked up at the dam, towering tall and white in the sun. His great pale brow creased.

"*Ita fua cussu?*" he said. What was that?

The question was aimed at no one in particular, and no one replied.

He frowned and sniffed. It was probably nothing.

There was work to be done. His guards had rounded up the last of Zoltan's men and herded them onto the piazza by the ruined funicular railway.

He turned to the captain in charge of the execution squad. "When you are done," he said, "you will get rid of the bodies and wash the stones. Clean the whole palazzo. I cannot stand this filth." He stepped forward and raised one arm. "Now, prepare your guns," he said. "When my hand drops, open fire."

Stefano and Vendetta had heard the explosion, too, and some instinct told them to run.

"*Aio caida,*" Stefano yelled. He dragged the girl up the mountainside as fast as he could, away from the ravine.

Perry Mandeville and the other Eton boys had been playing

football when they heard the bang. They were out in the fields next to Ugo's stadium and they stood now, shielding their eyes from the glare and straining to see what was happening.

Peter Haight and Mr. Cooper-ffrench had disappeared, and Quintino, their Italian guide, had been supervising them. Left to their own devices, they had done what boys everywhere will do, and started kicking a ball around. All morning they had heard the strange noises from up at the palazzo and assumed it was part of the carnival, but this latest mighty thump had sounded different.

"I wonder what's going on up there?" said Tony Fitzpaine, his heavily bandaged nose making him sound stuffy and nasal.

"Oh, they're m-mad, the Italians," said Perry. "Quite m-mad . . ."

James was still holding his breath. He felt an unbearable tension. Zoltan was standing staring at the lake, his right fist clenched.

"Come on," he whispered. "Come on, damn you."

Then James saw the gentlest puff of dust rise from the ground; next to it a second puff danced into the air, and then a third plume that zipped along the rock, like the dust thrown up behind a speeding animal, as a long black fissure opened in the top of the ledge.

"Oh, my God," whispered Zoltan. "She is going."

He was right. The whole ledge began to topple over, slowly at first, then in a great rush, as half the mountainside came away.

It was a terrifying sight: a hundred thousand tons of rock crashing downward in one great, crumbling, roaring mass.

As it slammed into the lake there was a deafening crash and water was sent steaming up into the sky, so high it blotted out the sun for a moment. One minute it had been a calm, sunny day, and the next James was in the center of a torrential downpour of stinging water so thick he couldn't see his hand in front of his face. When the air cleared he saw something he could hardly believe: a vast, twenty-foot high wave was traveling along the length of the lake.

The surging water scraped the edges of the basin, tearing up trees by their roots and wiping out the little run of buildings on the other side. Then it picked up the big white seaplane like a child's toy and tossed it over the side of the dam.

James watched as the plane glided a little way out across the valley before tipping and plummeting downward.

Ugo was standing on the piazza, transfixed, one arm raised to give the signal to his men, looking up, unable to comprehend what was happening, as his beloved Sikorsky flew over the dam and dropped toward him.

Behind the plane a solid block of water filled the sky.

"No!" he said and stretched his hand out still farther as if to hold it back. "No!"

But he could do nothing to hold it back. The plane swatted him like a fly, and an instant later the water smashed into the palazzo, washing the other men off the piazza.

The wave had completely swamped the dam, cracking the stonework; but as the flow diminished, James saw that it was still standing.

It wasn't over yet, though.

When the ledge had hit the water it had sent out massive underwater shock waves unseen by James and the others, and the stonework was fatally damaged. It would take next to nothing now to push the dam out and release the tremendous pressure of water behind it.

And there was something coming, something big.

A second wave had gone the opposite way up the lake, hitting the rocks at the far end and, like water splashing about in a bathtub with nowhere to go, it was coming back.

It was smaller than the first wave but it was still powerful, and as it crashed into the dam, the wall finally collapsed.

The massive force of twenty million gallons of water pushed the broken concrete out of its way in a mindless rush to escape. The plug had been pulled from the bathtub. The lake was draining and nothing could stop it now.

The aqueduct was obliterated, wiped out in an instant, sending stonework and masonry tumbling down into the valley. The palazzo didn't stand a chance either: an unimaginable torrent of water and concrete and rock was sent hurtling into it. Columns and pillars were washed away like twigs. Whole buildings were ripped from their foundations and tossed down the mountainside. The parapets and walkways, the courtyards, and all the fine squares and fountains were scrubbed into oblivion.

The people who were left inside had no chance. There was nowhere to run, even if they had had time or warning. The merciless water found its way into every hole and hiding place; nothing was spared. The few remaining roofs collapsed and the last of the walls buckled and broke apart. The tapestries and paintings, the statues and fine furniture, the silver ornaments, and chandeliers were all utterly smashed to pieces and swept away.

After the water came the mud—an avalanche of sludge from the bottom of the lake and earth from the mountainside—an evil flow of dark, stinking slime. It forced its way through what was left of the windows and filled the rooms, so that soon there was nothing to see of Ugo's palazzo, and it was as if there had never been anything there.

"What have you done?" said James to Zoltan, who was staring at the lake that had quickly become a fast-flowing river.

"I have drowned him," said Zoltan. "He was always worried about filth in his precious palazzo; now it will take a thousand years to clean."

Countess Jana Carnifex stood in the valley, looking up at the ugly smear of black mud that was crawling down the mountain like a flow of cold lava. She knew that everything had gone. Her home, her beautiful clothes, her gold and silver jewelery, everything.

She had been born with nothing, and now she had nothing again. Nothing except a cold, dark lust for revenge. She was from the Barbagia. She had grown up being taught all about the code of vendetta. She didn't care whether she lived or died now, as long as she destroyed everyone who was responsible for this thing happening.

When the shooting had started she had been in the palazzo infirmary. Every week she visited the doctor for a checkup. She had a weak heart, and he gave her pills and injections for it. But just as he was holding the syringe up and tapping it to free any bubbles, they had heard gunshots and shouting.

The doctor had glanced out the window, then turned back to Jana with a concerned frown. Jana had pushed him out of the way and looked for herself.

There had been confusion in the palazzo, men running and shooting, servants screaming. There was an explosion nearby, shockingly loud, and the doctor had said that they should leave. They had made their way outside and run toward the mines.

And then she had seen the English boy, James Bond, with the girl, Amy.

She had thought about him all the way down as she joined the stream of servants fleeing from the fighting through the mining tunnels.

As she had emerged into the light at the bottom, she heard explosions above and stared up just in time to see the dam collapse, bringing down half the mountain with it.

Most of the people in the valley had had time to get to higher ground and avoid the roaring flood as it charged into Sant' Ugo. They were already joining with the survivors from the mining tunnels to organize rescue parties. Jana recognized the schoolboys from Eton, from James Bond's school, and again her cold heart beat faster.

She would not sleep until she had her revenge, and she knew where she would start.

With James Bond, and all his family.

All the dogs in the valley were barking. They had sensed that something terrible had happened. Stefano and Vendetta could hear them even from here, perched on a rock looking down at where the water had carved out a great crescent in the ground below.

Vendetta looked over toward the ruins of Ugo's palazzo.

"James Bond," she said.

"*Mortu est*," said Stefano. He is dead. "You will never see him again."

Vendetta didn't cry. There were no tears inside her. She had had her revenge for Mauro. Ugo was gone and his palazzo destroyed. She would return now to her life in the mountains. She had always had a hard heart; now it would be even harder.

She turned away from the scene of carnage.

She could not have James. She knew now that that was not to be. God had chosen another fate for him, but there was always Stefano. . . .

James, Zoltan, Tree-Trunk, and Amy had made their way around the top of the mountain and were riding down the other side toward the Gulf of Orosei on horseback. They had found the horses in a stable set some way back from the edge of the dam. With no vehicles up here, this had been the only way for Ugo's men to get around.

James was sitting behind the massive bulk of the tattooed Samoan, and Amy was clinging on to Zoltan, as much to stop him from falling off as herself.

Zoltan looked very weak and sick, as if he had done all he needed and was giving up. He swayed in the saddle, his head lolling.

James didn't know if he and Amy were prisoners or if they were all escaping together. The only thing he knew for sure was that he had to get off this cursed mountain and back down to safety and civilization.

He felt empty and numb and couldn't look at Amy, whose eyes were red from crying.

As they were leaving the ruined dam, a group of Ugo's men had shot at them halfheartedly from a distance. Zoltan had fired back to scare them off, emptying his Beretta, and they had disappeared.

After that they had seen no one.

It was very hot, and James had nothing to shade his head. He sat there, staring at the complex tattoos on Tree-Trunk's back and listening to the incessant *clop-clop-clop* of the horses' hooves on the rocky ground. He found the sound intensely irritating, and even when the horses stopped the sound carried on inside his head, *Clop-clop-clop* . . .

After an hour or so they came to a small stream and dismounted. Amy wandered over to get a drink and stretch her aching legs. James approached Zoltan, who was sitting in the shade of a tree, fiddling with his Beretta.

"What are you going to do?" he said.

"I am going back to my boat, where I belong," said Zoltan.

"And what about us?" James asked.

Zoltan looked up at him with filmy eyes. "Everything that happened is because of that girl," he said quietly.

"Then let us go," said James.

"I cannot. She is all I have now."

"Then damn you to hell!" shouted James.

A look of fury came into Zoltan's eyes, but it soon faded. He sighed and put his gun away.

"I am already damned," he said. "I hoped that Amy would save me. She was something good in my life."

"Well, you weren't anything very good in hers," said James.

"You are right," said Zoltan. "As usual." He paused and stared down at his useless left hand. Finally he spat, and James saw that his saliva was thick and yellow.

"Do you believe in forgiveness?" said Zoltan quietly.

"I don't know," said James.

"I have done many bad things," said Zoltan. "For once I will do something good." He struggled feebly to his feet and went over to his horse. "I know now that I must get away from her, or she will be my death. Here, take this." He tossed a bag of coins to James. "Head always eastward, until you hit the coast, then hire a boat and go home. Look after Amy for me."

"What? Wait . . . No . . ."

But Zoltan couldn't be stopped. He muttered something to Tree-Trunk in Hungarian, and the two of them climbed into their saddles and galloped off.

Amy ran over to James.

"Where are they going?" she said.

"We're on our own now," said James.

"We're free?"

"It looks like it. Free to die out here in the sun like dogs."

They suddenly felt very small and lost and alone.

"What do we do?" said Amy.

"We walk."

After half an hour of stumbling through the scented maquis, the tough plants tearing at their already tattered clothing, James and Amy came out on a dirt road and followed it down the hill toward the coast.

They plodded along in silence, too weary to speak, staring at their feet as they slapped into the dust.

Now and then James imagined he could still hear the horses *clop-clop-clopping* along. He thought he might be starting to get delirious from sunstroke.

The sun was pitiless, burning into the back of James's neck. Amy was suffering as well, the sweat dripping off her nose and chin. In the end, she tore some strips of material off her hated yellow dress, and they tied them around their heads. It was better than nothing and offered them some relief from the scorching rays.

They passed through a narrow gorge and came out on to a wide, dry, stony plain. There was a stand of cork oaks on one side of it and high cliffs on the other.

James could imagine nowhere more bleak and exposed.

"This is stupid," he said to Amy. "We should take shelter and wait until it cools down. We'll be roasted alive out here."

Amy nodded, and they left the road and set off toward the trees.

The forest was farther than it had looked, and the plain seemed to go on forever. They walked and walked, but the dark shimmering line of the trees didn't seem to be getting any nearer.

Amy sat down.

"I can't go on," she said. "Can't we just wait here?"

"No," said James. "We need shelter."

"Can you hear that?" said Amy.

"What?"

"It sounded like horse's hooves. Maybe Zoltan's coming back."

James strained to listen. He hadn't imagined the sound after all. He looked around to try and see where it was coming from.

Then Amy stood up and grabbed his arm.

"James, look," she said.

Through the heat haze he could see the dancing shape of a horse and rider walking slowly toward them.

He squinted. Now he knew he had sunstroke. The rider appeared to have on the ceremonial outfit from the carnival, with the deathly white woman's mask.

And he held a silver sword at his side.

The horse broke into a trot, then it started to canter, then it was galloping at full speed, and James realized that it was headed straight for them.

The rider raised his sword, the point aimed at James's heart. James backed away. There was nowhere to run out here in the open, nowhere to hide.

He stood his ground, eyes fixed on the sword. The rider's eyes were hidden behind the mask. The horse's hooves pounded on the hard ground. The air was hot and still. James waited until the horse was almost upon him and then threw himself to the side. The point of the blade swished harmlessly by, and James was aware of a blur of flashing hooves.

He rolled onto his feet and saw that the horse was wheeling round for a return attack; but it hadn't gone far enough to pick up much speed, and as it came back, James dodged across in front of it so that he was on the opposite side to the rider's sword arm.

But then the rider turned and switched his attack to Amy. She stood there not sure what to do as the horse bore down on her. However, at the last moment, she scooped up a pile of powdery dirt and threw it into the air, startling the horse, which shied away.

James knew they couldn't keep this up for much longer.

The rider galloped away and calmed his horse, then began to circle them, planning his next move.

"Split up," said James. "I'll try and get him to come after me. You see if you can get to the woods."

"No," said Amy. "We're in this together."

James saw movement off to the side and looked over, amazed, as two more horses burst out of the trees.

It was Zoltan and Tree-Trunk, the big Samoan in the lead, his harpoon held up like a spear, a fat cigar clamped between his teeth.

The rider in the mask dug his heels into his horse and charged at them.

Tree-Trunk was well ahead of Zoltan, heading straight for the other horseman.

Closer and closer they approached, until, at the very last moment, the Samoan let fly with his harpoon.

The masked rider ducked, the harpoon sailed harmlessly over him, and he came up with his sword and thrust it at Tree-Trunk in a quick, deft movement. The next moment their horses collided, and Tree-Trunk went down, his mount rolling on top of him.

The horse got up, but Tree-Trunk didn't.

The masked rider stayed in his saddle, but had to fight to control his horse, which was prancing and rearing nervously.

Zoltan arrived and galloped past James and Amy.

James caught a glimpse of his face. He was grimacing in pain.

"No," James shouted. "Go back."

Zoltan's pistol was useless. He had used up all his bullets shooting at the guards near the dam. While the masked rider was distracted, he galloped past him, leaned over in the saddle, and plucked Tree-Trunk's harpoon out of the ground, then pulled up and turned his horse.

The man in the mask glanced briefly at James then back at Zoltan, deciding on his next move.

Zoltan decided it for him.

He put the harpoon in the crook of his right arm, yelled, spurred his horse forward, and charged like a medieval knight with a lance.

The masked man straightened his arm and pointed his sword at Zoltan. Then, with a shout, he was galloping at the Magyar.

James clutched Amy as the two men thundered toward each other, dust flying up behind them, their horses foaming with sweat. As they got nearer it became clear that neither of them was prepared to give way. It was going to be sword against harpoon, and James hated to think who might be the winner. Zoltan had the longer reach with the harpoon, but he was sick and weak, and the point wobbled in front of him. The masked man held his sword arm perfectly straight and firm, and the light flashed off his cruel, thin blade.

"I can't watch," said Amy, and she covered her face with her hands.

At last they met.

There was a grating clash and both men were knocked from their saddles. They fell heavily to the ground and their horses slowed to a walk, then wandered off to crop the grass as if nothing had happened.

The masked rider had been impaled on the harpoon and sat, resting forward on the haft, the fingers of one hand clawing at the dirt, the other hand still clutching the sword, whose tip was broken off.

He stiffened and grew still.

James went over to him and removed the mask.

It was Peter Haight, his handsome face as blank as the mask he had been wearing.

He was already dead.

"James, help!"

Amy was crouched over Zoltan, holding her hand to a wound in his chest. "He's hurt," she said.

James peeled back his shirt.

The broken end of Haight's sword was deeply embedded between his ribs. Blood bubbled out from around it as he breathed.

"Should we pull it out?" said Amy.

"No." Zoltan opened his eyes, the whites as scarlet as the blood that trickled from his chest. "Leave it."

He looked at James.

"Always getting into trouble, James . . ."

"Don't try to speak," said James, ripping the sleeve off his shirt to make a bandage. Zoltan clutched at his arm.

"Please," he said, "I don't want to die here. Get me back to my boat. Please, let me die at sea. . . ."

The sun beat down onto the tiny boat as it skimmed over the turquoise waters of the Mediterranean. James had his hand on the tiller and his eyes fixed on the horizon as it see-sawed up and down. His throat was dry and his lips were cracked and burned. Amy was worse, her pale skin, softened by days spent locked in her dark cell, was red and peeling. The wind was with them, but the boat made slow progress.

Zoltan was lying in the bottom, shivering. A thin line of blood ran from his lips down his chin and his eyes were cloudy. The noise of the blood bubbling in his lungs was horrible. He mumbled something in Hungarian. Amy bent down close to listen.

"What did you say?"

Zoltan blinked. "I thought you were my *anyám*," he said. "My mother."

"No," said Amy. "I'm not."

"I thought I was at home," said Zoltan, his voice very faint as if it were coming from far away. "The sea . . . It was a sea of grass. You would like my home, Amy. The Great Plain goes on forever. In the winter it is frozen, and in the summer it bakes. We had a farm, in the middle of nothing. There were long-horned cattle in the fields, geese in the yard, and around the house some mulberry trees. And that was all. Wherever you looked there was nothing else to see, just cattle and grass. That was my world. That was the whole world. I should have stayed at home."

"You can go home again," said Amy.

"No. I cannot. I am drowning," said Zoltan, with some effort. "I am drowning in my own blood." He gripped Amy's shirt with his good hand. "I always knew that you would drown me," he said. "I should have left you where I found you."

"You'll be all right," said Amy, and Zoltan laughed, then choked and spat a mouthful of clotted blood on to the deck.

"I will not be all right," he said, and sobbed. "I wish I was home. I wish I was in my mother's arms. . . ." He stopped. James saw that he was crying.

Amy took hold of him. "You'll be all right," she said again, and James wondered which one of them was hugging the other.

"At least I am at sea," said Zoltan. "Even if I am not on my own boat. . . ."

After they had covered the bodies of Tree-Trunk and Peter Haight with stones, they had struggled to the coast, Zoltan tied to the saddle of his horse.

They had eventually found a tiny fishing village. None of the villagers owned a vehicle, but an ancient fisherman had sold them an equally ancient sailing boat for much more money than it was worth. They put out to sea and steered northward. The farther they got, however, the worse Zoltan's condition had become.

"I am not going to make it," he said, staring up at the sky with unseeing eyes. "I don't want to drown in my blood."

"I won't have anyone else die," said James hotly.

"It is not in your power," said Zoltan. "You are not God. You are just a boy—an extraordinary boy—but just a boy. You have no power over life and death."

"Just hold on," said James angrily. "You mustn't die."

Zoltan spoke softly, every word causing him pain. "All your life people you love will die," he said. "And there will be nothing you can do about it. Getting angry won't help. It is the way of the world. We are born, we get hurt, and we die. But, God, I don't want to die like this. Put me in the water."

"You can't swim," said Amy.

"I don't want to swim," said Zoltan. "I want to die . . . I want to die in peace."

"I won't do it," said James. "I'll get you to your ship. We'll find someone who can help you. We can remove the blade, stitch you up . . ."

"You do not believe it," said Zoltan. "But thank you anyway. Now, put me over the side; I am hurting too much."

"No!" James clenched his teeth and looked down at his feet. There was an inch of water in the bottom of the boat, stained pink with Zoltan's blood. There was a horrible stench coming off the man, as if he were already dead and rotting. James couldn't bear to look at him any longer. He let his head drop, closed his eyes for a moment, and squeezed them with his free hand.

"*Anyám*," he heard Zoltan sigh. "*Édesanyám*. Hold me. I am scared. . . ."

There was a small splash, and when James looked up, Zoltan was gone and Amy was quietly crying.

He never asked her if she had tipped the dying Magyar

over the side or if he had found a final burst of strength and done it himself.

She never spoke about him again.

She dried her eyes.

"What do we do now?" she said.

"We go home," said James. "To my cousin's villa . . . We can sail all the way there."

Amy crawled back and put her arms around James, and they sat like that for a long time in silence.

They sailed past Terranova and continued north-westward, keeping the island always to their left. It was late afternoon when the Maddalena Islands came into view, and James pointed out the great rocky pile of Capo d'Orso and the wind-carved rock in the shape of a crouching bear.

How comforting and familiar this part of the island seemed to him. The prickly pears and the low umbrella pines, the little secluded inlets, the pink rocks, and above it all, the bear, which had watched over this stretch of coast for countless thousands of years, ignoring the insignificant comings and goings of the people below.

They steered around the headland, and there was the beach with its clean, white sand. The beach where James had swum with Mauro.

How long ago that all seemed now, and how peaceful this place remained. They had escaped the madness and were safe at last.

They maneuvered the boat into the shelter of a big rock and took down the sail. All day they had been aware of the wind flapping in the canvas, but now there was just the sound of the water gently lapping against the hull.

James's hair was matted with salt, and his skin felt as if it had been rubbed with sandpaper; his lips were gritty and swollen; all he wanted to do was get into the cool water.

"Come along," he said, and tore off his ragged clothes and dived in. Amy followed him, neither of them caring about their nakedness.

The water felt like a soothing caress on James's skin, washing away all the pain and heat. He luxuriated in it, twisting and turning, swimming to the bottom, then drifting up and floating on the surface. Finally he swam slowly to the shore and crawled on to the sand, where he lay half in the water and half out.

He felt as if he could just lie there and sleep for a thousand years.

Amy lay next to him, and they stayed there face-to-face, looking into each other's eyes, wordlessly sharing something, a knowledge of all they had been through.

At last James summoned the energy to raise his head.

"We should secure the boat and get up to the villa," he croaked.

"Can't we stay a moment longer, James?" said Amy. "This is so heavenly."

"Five more minutes, then."

When they felt strong enough, they swam back out to the boat and climbed in. James realized just how exhausted he was when he could barely lift himself over the side. At last they dressed and grabbed the two small paddles from under the seats.

Wearily, they rowed round to the little natural harbor to

moor the boat. Everything looked exactly as it had done when James had left.

Victor's dinghy sat there, ready for an outing.

Victor?

Would he be here?

Would he be all right?

What was waiting for them up at the villa?

James remembered about the robbery. Would the place seem empty and bare without all the paintings?

He had tried not to think about that until now. He had simply pictured an idyllic scene of Victor sitting sipping wine with Poliponi on the terrace, jazz music playing on the gramophone.

Amy jumped off the boat and James tossed her the rope. She tied it to an iron ring and James clambered out to join her.

Too tired even to speak to each other, they tramped up the steps cut into the rock. James just wanted to be in his bed, asleep and recovering.

The thought of bed had never been so delicious. Another picture came into his mind. A picture of crisp white sheets, and a mosquito net gently moving in the breeze from an open window.

He smiled.

He was nearly there.

Soon it would all be over.

Victor appeared at the top of the steps wearing one of his Moroccan robes, and James smiled.

But then he noticed that Victor looked worried, and there was a nasty bruise on his forehead.

"Victor," said James, "are you all right?"

Before Victor could say anything, he gasped and dropped to one side.

Someone had hit him from behind.

Jana Carnifex stepped forward, her high heels clicking on the stones like the claws of a dog. Her makeup was smeared. Her wig was at a mad angle, and straggly gray hair was falling from under it in a messy tangle about her face. Her gold dress was filthy and dusty. In her brown, silver-ringed hand she held a pistol, her long fingernails curled around the handle. She must have been holding it in Victor's back and then struck him with it.

James looked at Victor. His hands were tied behind him and he appeared to be unconscious.

"James Bond," said Jana. "I have been waiting for you." She had a crazy, wild-eyed look about her, and James knew that she would not hesitate to use the gun. But what could he do? He and Amy were trapped on the steps. If they rushed her, it was possible that one of them would be able to reach her unharmed, but it was too big a risk.

Whatever happened, though, he had to try and shield Amy.

Perhaps they could jump into the sea? James knew that water bent light so that it was hard to aim at something beneath the surface. How good a shot could Jana be?

It was a slim hope, but it was all he had.

He glanced down. They weren't as high up as the ledge he'd dived off that day with Mauro, but he'd have to be careful of the sea urchins that lay everywhere on the rocks like a black blanket.

How could he explain it to Amy, though? There wouldn't be time.

He edged up closer to her. He could see drops of sweat sitting on the skin of her neck. She was trembling slightly.

"Leave Amy out of this," James shouted, trying to buy some time. "This is nothing to do with her."

"Isn't it? Well, I don't care," sneered Jana. "I am going to kill you both anyway. You have ruined my life, killed my brother, and buried my home under filthy mud. I am going to shoot you, and you will be food for the crabs. They will eat your pretty faces. Then I am going to shoot your cousin and the other prisoners in the villa."

At that moment, Victor stirred and tried to sit up.

Jana turned on him. "Lie still," she hissed, "or I will shoot you now."

It was all James needed. Jana was distracted long enough for him to grab hold of Amy around the waist and brace his legs against the rock.

"Jump," he hissed into her ear and pushed off hard.

Amy had just long enough to flex her legs and spring backward, so that they flew out over the water, narrowly clearing the rocks below.

They landed with a splash and sank to the bottom.

Jana howled in frustration and fired off two wild shots that punched harmlessly into the water, well wide of their mark.

She swore and ran down the first couple of steps to get a clearer aim, but her high-heeled shoes weren't designed for these conditions, and they slipped on the rocks. One ankle turned over and she fell onto her knees, grazing all the skin off them. She flung out a hand, trying to grab hold of the slippery polished stone, but her long fingernails prevented her from getting a grip, and she tumbled down a few more steps and over the side, where she went slithering and scraping down the rock face into the water, the gun dropped and forgotten, her fingernails snapping off as she tried to cling on.

She landed among the sea urchins, piercing herself all down one side. She bellowed in pain and tried to climb out of the water, but wherever she put her hands there were more urchins. Her palms and fingers were soon studded all over with broken spines, so that it looked like she was wearing hairy black gloves.

She couldn't stand in her heels, and her long sodden dress was caught on a rock. In her panic to scramble free, she slipped and fell face-first into another bed of poisonous spines.

James forced himself to turn away as she clutched at her cheeks, trying to pull the spikes out, but only driving them deeper. She was wailing like a trapped animal, and she sank under the water for a few seconds before coming up, spitting and retching.

James swam over to try and help her, but she thrashed about, screaming like a maniac, and wouldn't let him near. He caught a brief glimpse of her ruined face. One eye was pinned shut.

He couldn't begin to imagine how much pain she was in. He had only trodden on one urchin, and it had been agony.

At last she gave a horrible, strangled snarl and clutched her chest. Then she curled up into a ball, and as she flopped back in the water, her head struck a rock and finally she lay still.

James tried not to look at her as he helped Amy out of the water onto the steps.

"Thank you," she said, and hugged him. Then she winced and gasped.

"What is it?" James asked.

"I've got spikes in my foot; I must have stepped on one."

James looked into her face and smiled, pushing her short hair back off her forehead.

"Don't worry," he said. "I know exactly what to do. . . ."

back in there... Her head nodded back, essentially she lay
still.

Jesse tried not to look at her for a [?] Sleep. She carried
the water onto the table.

"Thank you," she said, and hugged him. Then she
sat... and said...

Whatever Jesse should...

"I suppose, or a kiss, I mean, never mind anyway,"
By James to disable time and stand it up in her back
hand seat of the recliner.

"Don't worry," Eli said. "I know exactly what to...